DARKNESS UNDONE

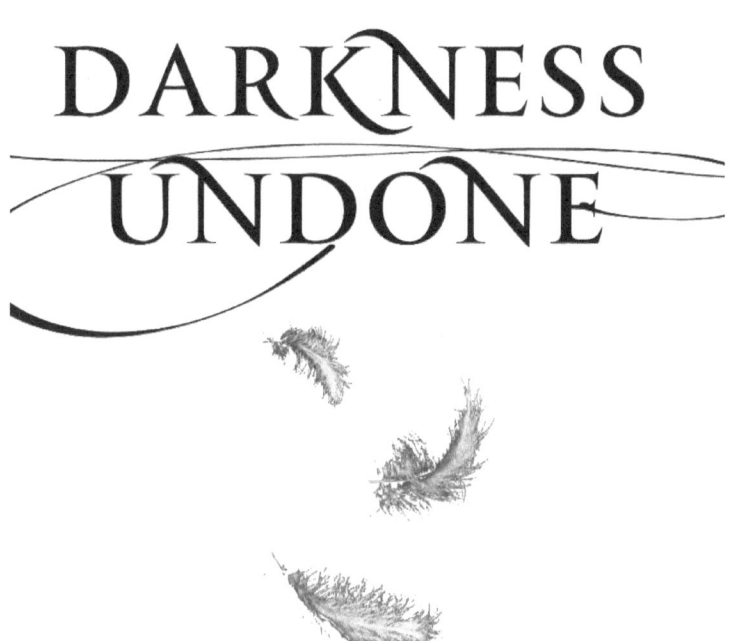

A WARLORD OF EMPYREA NOVEL

GEORGIA LYN HUNTER

GENRE: PARANORMAL ROMANCE

This book is a work of fiction. Names, places, characters and incidents are either the product of the author's imagination or are used fictitiously. Any resemblance to actual people, living or dead, businesses, organizations, events or locales is entirely coincidental.

DARKNESS UNDONE
Copyright © 2016 by Georgia Lyn Hunter
First Edition: February 2016
Editor: Chelle Olsen
All cover art copyright © 2016 by Georgia Lyn Hunter
Cover artist: Montana Jade
Images: ©123rf.com, Obsidian Dawn
All Rights Reserved

All rights reserved under the International and Pan-American Copyright Conventions. No part of this book may be reproduced or transmitted in any form or by any means, electronic or mechanical, including photocopying, recording, or by any information storage and retrieval system, without permission in writing from the author.

For my readers who love my broken heroes.

DARKNESS UNDONE

Chapter 1

The sudden hush in the busy little café should have been his first clue shit was about to fly.

Wrapped in his thoughts, Reynner savored his dark roasted coffee hot enough to scrape a layer off his throat, when he became aware of the unnatural quiet. Looking up, he got an eyeful of a tall female sashaying toward him, not in the least surprised she'd found him. Again.

Lustrous black hair framed a face of sheer perfection, one that made gods and men whimper for her favor. A long, fitted white dress with a slit up to her thigh hugged her body and fell to her ankles.

Oh, he understood the awed silence all too well since he'd once succumbed to that same sensual spell. Easing his grip on the mug, he set it aside, wishing he'd taken his coffee to go. A chair scraped on the linoleum opposite him. A moment later, her stiletto heel rode up his leather-clad leg to caress his inner thigh beneath the tablecloth.

He shoved her foot off him. In a measured move, he

picked up a coin from the change on the table and spun it so he wouldn't be tempted to reach across and strangle her.

"Get lost, Inanna. I'm busy."

"Reynner..." She held out a hand in appeal, her topaz eyes luminescent with tears. "Don't do this..."

Ignoring the Sumerian Goddess of Love and War hadn't worked in the past, and certainly not now.

He cut her an implacable stare. "Don't do what? Ignore you? Or prefer other females?"

Her face darkened at his mention of the women. "Why would you want these weak, pathetic creatures?" Her tears vanished as fast as they appeared. "I'm powerful. I'll make it wonderful between us again."

Reynner leaned back in the wooden chair and ran a cool, dismissive gaze over her stunning face and lush body. More flighty promises, but no hint of an apology for what she'd done to him. The thought would never have entered her narcissistic mind.

"I enjoy *other* women."

"You lie."

Reynner shrugged. Picking up the fallen coin, he worked it between his fingers. He just wanted coffee and a few minutes of quiet before he went back on the streets. Instead, he got her.

It should have felt good torturing Inanna, but he got no enjoyment, just a prolonged headache that had started over two millennia ago.

How could he have known then that stopping at the Sumerian pantheon would so irrevocably change his life?

"You've become cold and unfeeling. One little mistake and you're still making me pay." Her sulky voice drew him back.

"One little mistake?" His tone made glaciers seem warm.

"It was just a teeny-tiny year—"

"A year?" His hands crashed on the table. The coin flew and disappeared beneath a chair. "It was a fucking century in Hell!"

Inanna jerked back and blinked. Several humans turned their way in curiosity.

"Your deception caught me unaware, never forget what I am," he said, his warning clear.

Her eyes flickered. Not from fear, Inanna didn't believe there was anyone more powerful than her, but with a gleam of sexual promise. She knew all too well what he was, and why she hounded him.

Empyreans were a race of beings as old as the celestial angels and just as powerful, but far more carnal.

She leaned forward and rested her arms on the table, her low neckline displaying an eyeful of cleavage. "I'll make it up to you…" Her voice lowered to a smoky promise. "I'll make you my consort."

He'd rather be imprisoned in Hell again.

"You have a mate."

"I am a goddess. I can do whatever I want. Come on, lover," she wheedled. "It will be good between us again…then I'll help you find what you seek."

Reynner stilled, his instincts on alert. Did she know where the missing Stone was? But meeting her watchful gaze, he dismissed the thought. No immortal would know for sure. The damn thing hid from them all. Even if she could aid him, he would never accept her help. It always came with a price.

Reining in his irritation, he ignored her baiting and turned to take in the busy café.

The brunette waitress at the table farther down watched him from beneath her lashes while she served a customer. She'd been sending him all sorts of signals from the moment she'd set his coffee down. Ones he didn't encourage since he had no interest in females as a whole. Besides, he knew what a jealous bitch Inanna could be.

A virulent hiss erupted from opposite him when she spotted the waitress. As if to prove his point, with a flick of her hand, the waitress flew backward, crashing into a table. Chaos erupted, drowning the female's frightened cry. Two human males rushed to help her.

A cat-like smile curved Inanna's mouth. But her eyes flared with ire as she played with the deep blue lapis lazuli stone set in intricate silver filigree around her neck. "Look at another human tart again, and I will hurt her."

Of that, he had little doubt. With his mind, Reynner froze every customer in the café and rose to his feet. Fists planted on the table, he leaned forward, his anger leashed by a thin thread. Her scent of myrrh and exotic crap hit him square in the face, bringing back memories he far preferred locked away in permanent amnesia.

"Reynner..." Her breath came out in a tiny puff, her expression brightening with lust. She raised a hand to stroke his face. He jerked away. "You were a one-night-fuck gone wrong. Go find some other fool to dupe."

"Arghhhh," she shrieked and flashed out from the café.

Unfortunately, she'd be back with lust or vengeance on her mind. He far preferred the latter—*fuck!* He clenched down on his teeth at the sudden spike of pain in his left pec at her retaliation—one he could never escape. Breathing hard through his nose, it took several moments before it eased to bearable levels.

No, it never did to tell one of Inanna's stature it was over. He'd learned that the hard way when she'd tossed his drugged hide into Hell in a fit of temper. And a worse nightmare had begun.

Reynner clamped down on the destructive memories that would take over and released the humans from his psychic hold. As the din resumed, he walked out of the café. The dissonance and sweltering heat of the Lower East Side welcomed him.

Itching for a no-holds-barred fight to haul him back from anger that rode him, he headed down the street, hoping to come across a horde of demoniis. Those soul-suckers made perfect punching bags, and he got to kill them.

More, it frustrated the hell out of him that he still couldn't get a bead on the foretold mortal female he'd been searching for. Only her blood could awaken the mystical scroll and lead him to the missing artifact needed to power the waning Stones of Light his world desperately needed.

Lucan, their mage, had foisted the job of finding the girl onto Reynner and pointed him to New York, the one place he'd spent the least amount of time over the centuries. But whomever Lucan had sensed was no longer here. Several weeks of tramping around this city had proven that.

Slipping his hand in his coat pocket, he snagged the last piece of cherry candy, unwrapped it, and popped the thing into his mouth. Perhaps it was time to move on—

His cell went off. Balling up the wrapper, he scored

it into a nearby Dumpster before answering. "Yeah?"

"I'm at Club Anarchy, see you in five," the male on the other end said. Reynner's cell went dead. He scowled. When the archangel called, it meant more crap was about to fall. Usually on him.

***

Eve Leighton climbed out of the taxi and into a blast of humid air, half tempted to jump back into the cool, protective barrier the interior of the cab offered. The Lower East Side in late August, nope, not a fun place to be right now. Shutting the door, she turned and stepped right into the bile-inducing odor of stale beer. Christ! The stench nearly knocked her off her feet.

The human brewery grinned, displaying a mouthful of stained teeth. "Hello there, you-you gorgeousss thing."

Eve shot the drunk a withering look. She clutched her purse to her chest, dodged him, and quickened her pace. Her own fault for being late, she'd gotten lost in her work. Again. It took Eric's irate call to get her rushing from her studio to her apartment, and like a berserker, she'd changed and called a cab. But she'd forgotten a fundamental rule for Friday nights: always leave early. Traffic had been a nightmare.

Nine thirty-seven wasn't too late, she decided. Her friends couldn't get mad at her on her birthday. Then she wrinkled her nose wryly. Her bag vibrated, startling her. *Like A Virgin* belted out.

"Dammit!" Eve snatched her cell phone and shut off the song. Her new ringtone had Kataya's big footprints stamped all over it. She knew precisely why Kat had downloaded that stupid track.

"Eve, tell me you're on your way." Eric's annoyed voice grated in her ear.

"I'm here, just around the corner—"

"Good. I'll meet you outside."

"No-no, you don't have to—"

The line went dead. Darn it! She glared at her cell. She didn't need a bodyguard. Shooting a wary glance behind her, Eve grimaced when she found the greasy-haired drunk stumbling after her.

She hastened her steps and cut through the busy traffic. As she approached Club Anarchy, she blew out a wry breath. Why had she bothered wasting five precious minutes deciding what to wear when leather and skin seemed to be all the rage? Still, she straightened her strappy black top and smoothed her short skirt.

Two brawny bouncers guarded the club entrance, keeping order in the long line of noisy party revelers snaking down the alley.

Eric wasn't out front, but Kataya was, dressed in sleek, dark pants and a sleeveless top. She stood away from the crush at the entrance, smoking. Her corkscrew red hair was scraped into a French braid but a few curly strands escaped to frame her pale face. She waved when she saw Eve, her engagement ring glinting in the light from the streetlamp.

"You know Jake will have a fit if he finds out you're smoking again," Eve said as she neared her.

Kataya shrugged and killed the stub on the wall, then she hugged Eve. "He won't. He's in the Middle East. Happy birthday."

"Thanks…" Eve frowned at her tense tone. "What's wrong? You seem to be wound up tighter than my copper wire sculptures."

Kataya snorted, but her whiskey-colored eyes appeared troubled. "I haven't spoken to Jake in months… I miss him."

A tiny stab of envy pierced Eve's heart. Hastily, she blocked the unkind emotion. If anyone deserved happiness, Kataya did. Disowned by her parents when she became pregnant at sixteen, then losing her baby, Kat's personal life had been a mess until she met Jake.

Kataya popped a breath mint in her mouth. Her gaze fastened on the Band-Aids Eve used to cover up the scrapes and cuts on her hands. "What happened?"

"It's nothing." In a protective gesture, Eve balled her fingers, the old scars from her childhood accident pulling tautly over the new injuries. She shrugged. "I got a little too enthusiastic with my sculptures—I'm okay."

"Hmmn…" Kat murmured. "If you say so. Gloves, Eve."

At the reminder, she pulled out a dark red pair from her purse and drew them on. Kat didn't bat an eyelid, used to Eve's colorful handwear. Since she had to spend her lifetime wearing them, she might as well make a fashion statement. "So, who's here?"

"Eric, Brenna…and David," she mumbled the last name.

At her friend's innocent expression, Eve glared. "What did you do, Kat?"

"Nothing. I thought you liked him. Didn't you say he's the only one you can tolerate touching?"

"Yes. So?"

"So, I invited him." Kat glared right back. "You're twenty-five today, and you're going to get laid. Get rid of the damn V. Tonight. Tomorrow. But it's going to happen." With a huff, she turned away. "Whoa. Look at him."

"What? You've changed your mind about David and

picked out a one-night stand for me now?" Eve taunted.

"Oh, shut up and just look, would you?"

Curious, since Kataya rarely paid heed to any guy except Jake, Eve glanced to where Kat nodded. Her attention instantly captured by a tall, pale-haired man heading for the club entrance. He moved with a lazy, sensual saunter, reminding her of a predator stalking prey...for something far darker. Erotic. Her tummy dipped.

"Have you ever seen anything sexier? Bet he's totally scrumptious from the front. He's got the whole"—Kataya waved a finger in an attempt to draw what she meant—"dangerous, X-factor thing going for him."

Eve didn't speak, didn't breathe, her focus riveted. His long burgundy leather coat flared out behind him as he disappeared into the dark, gaping maw of the club. He had to be a movie star or something because the bouncers didn't even stop him.

"Oh, no, get your eyes off him, Eve." Kat grabbed her arm, dragging her attention away from the entrance and stepping in line to enter the club. "He's great to drool over, but the badass will probably fry your brains the moment you touch him. That would make your first time a little too *spectacular*."

"Sheesh, you're a total buzz-kill, Kat," Eve grumbled.

She snorted. "So, yes, David."

Her cover charge settled, they headed in. Rock music threatened to rupture Eve's eardrums. Overhead, strobe lights worked the crowd on the dance floor, turning their movements to frenzied jerks and shakes. The sharp odor of alcohol and heavy perfume crowded her nose as they cut through the masses. Kat's slinky strides took on a bump and grind movement as she headed for a table near the dance floor which their friends occupied.

Eve grinned and gave them a quick wave.

Eric, lanky and dusky skinned, shot to his feet and hauled her into a hug that made the air swoosh out of her lungs. His hazel eyes darkened with concern. "Next time, no excuses. I'm picking you up. I know you're busy but I see you way too little these days."

Yep, growing up with someone gave them rights to play big brother. But then he was…in a way. After all, his parents were her guardians.

Thankfully, Brenna saved her from near asphyxiation and slung her arm around Eve's waist in a quick hug. Her crystal-blue eyes sparkled, a startling contrast against her caramel skin and silky black hair. She brushed Eve's cheek in a quick kiss and said in her ear, "I'm so sorry, I couldn't stop Kataya from her nefarious plans for your induction into womanhood."

With a deep sigh, she couldn't suppress, Eve slid a glance to David—the guy who would make her a woman, if her friend had her way. As if having boobs and PMS didn't already mark her as one, she thought with wry amusement.

David waited patiently to greet her. An artist like her, his collection of paintings would debut tomorrow at Eric's gallery. A few inches taller than Eve's own five-foot-six, he was slender with overgrown sandy-brown hair that had a tendency to flop into his eyes. Colorful dabs of paint marred his navy tee. Eve hid her smile, knowing he'd probably forgotten to change. But then David's philosophy ran along the lines "as long as I'm not naked." She doubted even that would bother him.

"Hello, David."

"Happy, happy day, Eve." Pleasure lit his narrow, attractive face as his gaze skimmed over her in appreciation.

"Thank you," she murmured. Yep, he made no bones about the fact he liked her. But the gleam in his light blue eyes and the empty wine glass showed that he'd already made headway into starting the party. He took her gloved hand and kissed her knuckles, making her smile.

She sat in the chair he held out and accepted the flute of sparkling wine Eric handed her.

"A toast." He raised his glass. "To our girl, Eve."

The music made speeches impossible, but emotion crowded her, and she basked in her friends' love. They accepted her despite the fact that she could never touch them without a barrier of protection. Not since the accident.

The car crash that had killed her parents didn't just leave her with scarred hands, but also a far bleaker legacy. She couldn't touch another without being drawn into their minds, seeing their thoughts, and feeling their emotions. And it wasn't without repercussions.

A sudden influx of strong, emotional energy from another, and unbearable pain followed, so much so that she sometimes lost consciousness.

Eve pushed the painful thoughts aside as Kataya had set a small bakery box on the table.

"Okay," she yelled above the music, tucking a few spirally red strands behind her ear. "Before we all get rip-roaring drunk, here…" She flipped open the cover to reveal a red velvet cupcake. The creamy icing on top simply read, 'Happy Birthday.'

Brenna stuck a pink candle in the center, lit it, and slid the box to Eve. She smiled, flashing twin dimples. "Because we love you and know you hate the fuss. So, make a wish, make thousands, and may they all come true!"

Overwhelmed, Eve tugged at the small, gold, half-hoop earring she wore. She didn't have any family, but this little group was hers.

Eve glanced at her friends' happy faces. Ten long years without physical contact and emptiness crowded her heart. Just once she yearned to hold them—to hold someone she loved.

Inhaling roughly, because she might as well wish for the moon, Eve blew out the candle.

They handed her a card and a small flat box covered in red foil and tied with a silver bow. They'd covered the card with well wishes and xoxo's. Then she ripped open the package and found a gold bracelet with four charms nestled in white tissue.

At a guess she knew exactly which charm came from whom. The daisy from Brenna, because Eve loved them, the ladder from Eric—probably for her success in her new venture, the clover leaf from Kat, for luck—she hoped, and the double heart? David.

She really, really wished he hadn't given her that.

"Thank you." She slipped on the bracelet then drank her wine to ease the tightness in her throat.

David nudged her arm, picked up the wine bottle. "Top up?"

"No, not yet."

She'd met David several months ago through Eric. Even though she could touch David without a painful influx of thoughts and feelings flooding her, it wasn't all smooth sailing. Instead, his creatively charged mind usually pulled her into a maelstrom of colors that left her with a low-grade headache.

If she decided to date David like he wanted, she'd have to tell him of her affliction. She could only hope he wouldn't run off in the opposite direction.

"Ready for your show?" she asked him.

David blew out a heavy breath, picked up his wine and took a deep swallow. "Ask me after."

Eve laughed. She understood his qualms since her own debut loomed in front of her just over a week away. Her stomach knotted at the thought. If her sculptures didn't take off, she may as well find her own cardboard box and call it home.

Eve pushed the gloomy thought aside. She wanted to enjoy this evening and not think of *what if.* Sipping her drink, she took in the crowded nightclub. Her attention wandered to the VIP section on the second level, corded off from the common folks for the rich and famous and their wild partying.

The hunk with the pale hair would be up there, she mused. Bet he wouldn't be alone for long. Women must be drawn to him like bees to pollen.

Ugh, when had she become this petty? And over a man? A stranger, for goodness sake!

"Dance?" David yelled in her ear. His smile took on a fiendish appearance in the eerie purple strobe light. He crossed his eyes, exaggerating his odd look and nodded to the dance floor. Eve laughed, putting the stranger out of her mind.

Perhaps Kat was right, maybe she should take a chance with David.

***

Heavy rock music blasted off the walls and settled in

Reynner's head. Flashing lights almost blinded his sensitive eyes. He wished Michael had rethought their meeting place. The club thronged with people. And he didn't like crowds.

Reynner leaned against the steel balustrade running the length of the gallery that overlooked the dance floor. He ignored the skimpily dressed women trying to make eye contact, his attention on the approaching male.

Dressed all in black, the leader of the Guardians fit in with most of the club's clientele, but for his exceptional height of six foot nine. Strands of night-dark hair escaped their tie and framed a face that appeared carved from granite. Shades covered eyes Michael didn't reveal to the human populace.

The females tracked him with covetous looks, drawn by the angelic allure, but something about him made them keep their distance. Had to be the hands-off, hard-ass look the archangel wore like a mantle.

Michael had been the one to find him eons ago, killing demoniis like some demented being after he'd escaped Hell. The archangel had hauled Reynner off to Exilum, a sanctuary for immortals and a place he now called home. Yeah, he owed Michael big time, and it was why he continued to hunt supernatural evil wherever he was while searching for the foretold one.

Michael handed him a squat glass before taking a swallow of his coke.

Reynner cocked a brow. "What's up?"

"Aethan's back in New York."

Hearing that name, Reynner's stomach churned. Nothing would ever ease his guilt. He'd accepted long ago that *he* should have been banished for Ariana's death, not Aethan. Not the male who'd once been his best friend.

"Anything else?"

Michael gave him a long, hard stare. "Why don't you meet him? Get this shit out of the way. You were friends once."

"Friendships fall apart all the time. Besides, it's too late for that." Three millennia too late. Aethan probably hated his guts.

"You're one stubborn bastard," Michael muttered.

Whatever. He needed to focus on finding the female tied to the scroll. Two damn months in this city, and still no sign of her. It was time to move on, to scry for another possible location. He had no desire to bump into his old friend and revisit a past they could never shake. Or put right.

"Thanks for the heads up." Reynner handed his untouched liquor to a passing waitress and headed out. As he cleared the stairs, a visceral hunger slammed him square in the chest. He skidded to a halt.

What the hell?

Inhaling harshly, he rubbed his sternum and scanned the place. Beneath the layers of liquor, sweat, and heavy perfume, a delicate fragrance with a tantalizing hint of peach seeped into him and stroked his senses. His body went into slow burn. Blood heated. His groin hardened. A strange, urgent need took hold of him. Compelled, he tracked the scent down the corridor. But the trail disappeared into the restroom where a pack of females took their own sweet time entering their shrine. Did women do nothing solo?

Irritated and forced to cool his heels, Reynner waited. His cell vibrated. He checked the text then ignored it. Damn interfering angel. Michael never gave up trying to fix a broken past.

Reynner leaned against the wall several feet from the bathroom door and willed off the light above him. With his height and hair, the attention he drew was a bloody nuisance. Throw in his cursed angelic allure—yeah, the shit was a guaranteed trouble magnet. He clamped down on his psychic shields, his attention fixed on the restroom, cell phone tapping against his thigh.

Whoever the female was that had worked her mojo on him would wish to the high heavens she hadn't. He'd made that mistake once with Inanna and had paid the price for his stupidity. He wasn't about to let it happen again.

***

Eve stared at her reflection in the restroom mirror, tucked her long bangs behind her ear, and inhaled a deep breath. Everything about this evening was heading in the direction she wanted. So why was she having second thoughts?

Deep down, she understood her hesitation. She wanted to fall in love—have what her parents had had before their deaths—but with her affliction, it was but a dream.

She raked back her hair and sighed. Earlier, she'd casually touched David's hand minus gloves, just to be sure, and colors had roared to life in her head. Thankfully, without the painful invasion of thoughts and feelings she normally got from others. But the impulsive brush had left her with a slight throb in her temples.

So what did she do?

Surrender to dating a man she liked despite the headaches or live a lonely life?

A noisy group of women entered and broke through her depressing thoughts. Her cell beeped. She grabbed her gloves off the basin, retrieved the phone from her bag, and read the text. A belated wish from one of her old coworkers.

Smiling at the exploding birthday cake gif, Eve left the bathroom and crashed face-first into a brick wall of muscles.

Aw, crap! Her open purse flew to the floor, scattering its contents. She stumbled back but her half-hoop earring caught on the soft fabric of his shirt, jerking her forward. Pain blinded her. Gasping, Eve blinked back tears as she pulled free. Calloused hands steadied her. At the strong grip, goosebumps flooded her skin and the fine hairs on her arms rose.

Her gaze snapped up. And up. The air rushed out of her lungs. Apology and throbbing ear forgotten, Eve gaped at the man holding her.

So beautiful...

But there was nothing feminine about him. A beautiful warrior. A towering wall of unyielding muscles, the only thing missing was a sword. Power stamped his tough body and etched the hard lines of his incredible face. His pale, moonlit hair was tied back to reveal the sculptured lines of his jaw. Eyes like midnight skies, stroked with a slash of indigo, remained cold. Flat.

Eve faltered at the complete lack of emotion on such a handsome face. She snatched her hands back from the soft leather of his burgundy coat, heat streaking her face at gawking like an idiot and lowered to her knees to gather her strewn things. Lipstick, brush, tissues...

She started in surprise when he hunkered before her in a rustle of leather, and in fluid moves, collected the rest of her things. The man smelled incredible. Wild and crisp like the forest after the rain. Without a word, he dropped her stuff into her bag, handed it to her, then picked up his cell and slipped it into his coat pocket.

It took her a moment to collect her scattered wits, aware of his cold, dark eyes studying her. Uneasy, she pushed to her feet and closed her bag. "Er, thank you."

Still silent, he rose, too. And startling all heck out of her, he reached out and touched her ear. Eve jerked away and winced, pain simmering to life once more, then she saw the blood smeared on his fingertips.

Oh, wonderful, she was bleeding. Before it dripped down her neck and her friends called 911, she hustled for the restroom again. She tore some paper towels from the dispenser and examined the wound in the mirror when another image joined hers. Her breath strangled her throat.

Him.

She swung around, wariness overriding her attraction when she looked into that cold, unforgettable face. "You can't come in here?"

"I just did."

Chapter 2

Her voice—just the sound of her voice—and it eased his edginess, soothing the nightmares and constant pain riding him. It shook the solid foundations of the walls he'd built around him after he'd escaped from Hell so long ago.

"What are you doing—this is the ladies?"

Her horrified voice hauled Reynner back to the dank bathroom and feminine whispers. He issued a silent command for the gaggle of females eyeing him like some damn prize to leave.

"And so it is," he said as the door closed behind the women, turning the loud music from the club into a muted thumping.

She blinked her thickly fringed forest-green eyes. With skin a dusky gold, she appeared as if she'd wandered out from one of the desert climes. Nervous, scarred fingers brushed back hair the color of black coffee. The silky strands fell in a seductive sweep around her face to settle on her shoulders. Blood dripped down her neck from her injured ear.

"You're hurt."

"I know that, but you can't be in here."

In response, he reached out and tugged free the paper towel she clutched to her chest like armor. "I hurt you, I'll aid you."

"It was an accident."

Yeah, one he'd instigated. He cupped her delicate face, angled her jaw to examine the wound, and found her lobe had torn a little. Gently, he dabbed the blood.

She gasped, recoiling in pain. He didn't let go. Her pulse beat rapidly beneath his thumb as he wiped away the blood on her neck and scanned her psyche for that unexplained pull.

Nothing. So what the hell was it that drew him to her?

Except for his body's reaction to her, he could pick up no false reading from her emotional grid. If anything, she seemed wary of him.

He met her suspicious eyes. "This is hardly a come-on. If I want a female, this is the last place I'd take one to for a tryst."

Color rushed across her cheeks at his blunt words and her gaze lowered. A spark of remorse pricked his conscious. He didn't care for this feeling of guilt—didn't like being enclosed in this claustrophobic place with its overflowing trashcans. But her essence enfolded him in sunshine. Light. All he'd need to survive. It made him uneasy.

Why would a human affect him this way?

Empyreans didn't do well when trapped in darkness for prolonged periods. They lost control and became raging beasts...

Reynner shut off those dark thoughts and concentrated on his task. The pale blue light of his healing powers streamed from his fingers and coalesced on the injury. This wasn't his strongest ability, but he'd do what he could and be on his way.

Her smooth brow puckered. She probably sensed the slight heat from his healing. Her slender fingers grabbed his wrist, barely circling it.

"Look, I'm sure it's stopped bleeding." She tugged at his hand. "Thanks for your help."

The abrasions on her palms scraped across his skin, yanking him back to another place, another time...

His wrists bled, rubbed raw from the manacles. Unimaginable pain shimmered through him, rendering him breathless. His old wounds opened and new ones formed.

"I should thank the bitch-goddess for drugging you first before tossing you my way," the demoness, Kalinin, said with an avaricious smile. "So rare to have one of your kind in my care."

"Fuck...you." His snarl sounded more like a drunken slur.

She laughed, flicking back hair the color of coagulated blood from her pale, frighteningly exquisite face. "That beautiful power, that light, is all mine. Imagine, I can take your blood and revel in the brightness without becoming demonii." Her laughter spilled out and flayed his flogged skin like broken glass.

And he, the most powerful of his kind, lay there like a fucking statue, unable to move, to fight. While the succubus bitch he'd been trapped with relished in his torture.

Urias, he had to find a way out of this hellhole—had to—

Kalinin smirked, as if she knew his thoughts. "None can escape me, Empyrean...you'll see." A taunting gleam lit her malevolent black eyes. "I always get what I want."

Never! Unmitigated hatred burned his soul and lanced his skull—

"Hey? You okay?"

His grip tightened around the slender throat. The fragile bones beneath his inhuman strength made little impact on him.

The sound of harsh coughing slammed his ears. Frantic fingers clawed at his hands. "Stop—*stop it!*"

Fear hit him hard, bringing him back fast. Reynner stared into panicked green eyes and tried to shake off the red haze stealing his mind.

Kalinin was dead—*dead*!

Hastily, he let her go and she stumbled back, hitting the basin. She rubbed her throat, fear and anger welling in her eyes.

He had to get out of here before he totally lost his fucking mind and did the female irreparable harm. The bitch was dead! And still his past continued to haunt him.

Willing her pain into him, Reynner tore out of the restroom like the gateway to Hell had reopened and would haul him back.

A short distance from the club, he stopped and fought to calm down. He'd never lost control like this before. Too many unpleasant memories surfaced. It had to be because of the green-eyed female. Her soft peach-like fragrance saturated his senses and messed with his mind.

He rubbed a shaky hand over his face. A coppery odor drifted to him. Beneath the silvery moonlight, he stared at the traces of her blood on his fingertips. Compelled by some unseen force, he licked the smear…a faint melodious note hummed through his body.

Magic? In *her?*

His heart thundered in his ears. Was she the one?

If she could awaken the scroll and locate the Stone—he had to go back. Speak to her. And ask her for more blood. He needed to get a proper reading.

Yeah, right.

After terrifying her, she'd probably knee him in the balls and call the cops. But determination rode him. Despite the unexpected complication of his reaction to her, he would let nothing stand in his way. Saving his fading realm was all that mattered.

***

Eve rejoined her friends, her mind reeling, grateful they wanted to call it a night.

In the cab, she closed her eyes and stroked her neck which strangely didn't hurt. Her thoughts returned to the bizarre episode in the restroom.

The only time she'd ever been more terrified than tonight was when she desperately tried to drag her parents from the burning car wreck so many years ago. Absently, she peeled off the Band-Aid from her fingers. She honestly had no idea what had set the man off. It wasn't as if she'd seen his thoughts or felt his emotions, for which she was grateful…

Eve froze. Her heart banged against her ribs. She'd touched him—*touched* him with her bare hands—and all she'd felt was blessed silence. Not a jolt of an image, a whisper of a thought, not even color. Nothing. Except for his pain that had constricted her chest like a rubber band, before vanishing like it'd never been.

Eve frowned and touched her injured lobe. Even that didn't hurt anymore. How odd. But darn, she'd lost her favorite earring. She undid the remaining hoop and dropped it in her bag.

No, Kataya was wrong. He didn't fry her brains. But he sure left her with a trembling need for something more. Ugh, maybe she was insane, but the man fascinated her. Dangerously sexy and utterly gorgeous, he looked like he could tear down walls with his bare hands, and yet those big hands had been gentle when he tended to her ear. A shiver raced through her.

Well, that was before he'd wrapped his fingers around her neck in a deathly grip.

Yep. She was definitely certifiable.

***

Reynner scanned the chaotic club for the female with the green eyes, but it was a waste of time. He picked up nothing except a shitload of intoxicated emotions from the humans partying there.

A hand drifted down his back where he stood on the landing. A sweet scent combined with liquor crowded his nostrils. He cut the busty, dark-haired female an impatient look and stepped away. He had to find green eyes, had to know for sure she was the one he sought.

How the hell was he going to do that when she seemed to have vanished right off his radar?

No matter, he would locate her. Besides, she was mortal. How much trouble could she be compared to the wily prince currently living with him, one who had a penchant for roaming mortal nightclubs?

With Aerén's trigger temper and his immense power, wiping out the city was a sure thing. Michael would definitely kick Reynner's ass into oblivion. Or worse, make him a Guardian of the human race.

Damn. He wasn't cut out to be anyone's protector.

Reynner left the club and headed down the alley,

rubbing his chest where she'd knocked into him. Warm, feminine, she was—*no*, he couldn't think about how perfect she felt against him. Something scraped his palm. Frowning, he freed the piece of metal caught on his shirt and stared at the small, gold, half-circle.

Her earring. He ran a thumb around the misshapen loop, lowered his psychic shields, and tried to read her magic on the piece of jewelry. A slight tingle teased his senses. Dark green eyes flashed in his mind and his body hardened again.

Shit, not the effect he wanted. Reynner dropped the earring into his coat pocket when a wavering shape took form beside him, snagging his attention.

"Sire, we have a problem," the ghostly figure of his houseman said. Izzeri's face appeared paler than usual, his copper hair disheveled, his apparition flickering in the dark alley.

The fact that the male would contact him in this manner meant only one thing. Aerén had taken off again. Dammit!

***

Eve shivered, desire coursing through her blood, her entire attention focused on the glitter of the cool blade trailing down her bare abdomen. Her stomach clenched when he *glanced up at her from his hunkered position, the dim lights turning his pale hair into a shimmering halo.*

At the predatory look in his night-sky eyes, she sucked in a shuddering breath at the raw need he elicited from her. She tugged at her hands, but he'd shackled her wrists above her head to the wall.

"Tell me what you want, Eve." The husky taunt of her name on his lips stretched her taut nerves further. Arousal burned higher. He was playing with her. He

knew what she wanted. For him to touch her, finish this off instead of tormenting her—

"How much longer, Evie?"

Brenna's voice threw ice water on images that wouldn't leave her alone. *Christ.* Unfulfilled sex dreams had kept her awake last night, and now they seemed equally determined to take over her day. Eve forced her mind back to her work and off a stranger she had no business dreaming about in the first place.

"Another ten and I'm done," she told Brenna.

Afternoon sunlight streamed into the warehouse, flashing off the assortment of metal sheets, wire, and narrow steel pipes. She'd rented this place a block from her apartment since it provided the right amount of space. The huge windows made it perfect when she worked, without the need for extra lighting.

"This isn't like painting, I don't have to stay abso-still, right?" Brenna flexed her foot where she lay in her underwear on the makeshift daybed near the window. "It's almost three P.M., Evie. I still have to get home and get ready for tonight. David's opening, remember?"

"Hmmn, yes," Eve murmured. She warmed the copper strip she held between her palms then bent the metal and attached it to her sculpture to shape the outline of Brenna's supposedly relaxed foot, now tapping to the soft strains of Debussy drifting from the CD player.

Of all of Eve's friends, Brenna was the only one who seemed to sail through life with her ready smile and charm paving the way. Despite the fact that her family had gone back to Scotland a few years ago, Brenna was content. She dated, but never got seriously involved with anyone.

"Are you excited about your showing?" Brenna asked. "The big day draws closer."

Eve struggled to contain the sudden flutter of butterflies in her stomach. "I try not to think about it. But I sure don't regret giving up painting yellow ducks on nursery walls," she said with a wry grimace, thinking of her unsatisfying job as a mural artist and the menial tasks her ex-boss usually dumped on her.

"Well, Eric raves about your pieces he's seen." Brenna sat up on the bed. "He's the owner of a successful gallery and only his opinion counts, right?"

"Absolutely." Eve smiled at her friend's loyalty as she ran her fingers over the sculpture. The hum of the metal made up for her lack of human contact, almost like it sang to her. She'd never explained this phenomenon to anyone. They would think her nuts. But it helped her put the parts together. Almost like a musical opus as they formed the fluid shapes she wanted.

The intertwining of copper sheets and wire worked well with this piece. Backing up, Eve studied the fusion of metal that made up the reclining life-size sculpture.

"Being a nude, it looks female—for which I'm grateful—but I don't see the resemblance," Brenna said, coming to stand beside her.

"It's an allusion, not meant to be realistic."

Her friend knew as little about art as Eve knew about...sex. She rolled her eyes at the thought. Then blew out an anxious breath. "This has to work, or else I'll be living on the street come month end."

Brenna slipped her arm around Eve's waist and hugged her, careful not to touch her hands. "The sculpture's beautiful, hun. And you can come live with me anytime. Maybe I get to see you a little more then.

You work far too much, you know."

"Soon, Bren, after the show, we can all get together. Since I have another home to go to, you're released from captivity," Eve teased, returning Brenna's brief embrace. "I'll see you at the gallery."

A rustle of feathers and cooing sounds came from her worktable, alerting them that they weren't alone. Brenna pulled on her clothes then made a detour to the dove Eve had rescued outside her apartment several days ago. "Hey there, little guy. You ready to leave the roost, or do you like your new home too much?"

"Like he understands you." Eve snorted. She reached out and stroked the bird's gray, pearlescent feathers. A light, almost incandescent joy seeped into her. Animals were far safer to touch, no painful emotions at all. "I tried to get him to fly. He does everything but that. I'm hoping for a miracle. I don't mind, though, I like his company."

"You're in good hands, then," Brenna told the dove and picked up her bag from the table. "See you later, Evie." She wiggled her fingers in goodbye and left the studio.

Eve went back to her sculpture, and when she thought of what was at stake, she pressed her hand to her knotting stomach.

Several months ago, she had quit her dead-end job, used up her small savings, and put everything she had into this. She'd been both terrified and exhilarated about taking charge of her life, leaving behind her safe job as a mural artist. But her show was fast approaching.

Unable to concentrate, she rubbed her hand down her sweats, her troubled mind drifting to *him* once again.

Last night hadn't been a good one. The most erotic

dream had drawn her into a place where she'd been manacled to a wall while *he*, just in his leathers, taunted her with a dagger. Helpless and under his absolute control, it hadn't been fear coursing through her but unbearable desire. Her limbs had turned to molasses when his tongue followed the trail he made with the blade down her stomach... leaving her hot and needy.

Christ! She had to stop this. Submission and domination games weren't her thing. Jesus, she was still a virgin for crying out aloud. Eve rubbed her eyes with the back of her hands as if she could erase the images.

Last night, she'd totally lost her common sense. The man, it seemed, was a hazard not only to her life but also to all things that made her a woman.

Thank God she'd never have to see him again.

Chapter 3

Reynner took form on the terrace of his home, built on a high ledge carved deep into the rock face of the Exilum mountains. It was a place beyond the veils of the human realm, accessible only through a portal, and a sanctuary for exiled immortals.

Railless balconies ran around the perimeter of all three levels. Reynner could see for miles on end. Not another soul in sight—just him, the cliffs, and the gigantic waterfalls. He liked it this way, preferred the isolation. Unfortunately, solitude was not an option with a moody prince in residence.

Sliding the doors open with his mind, he walked into the sparsely equipped gym with its smooth granite floors, rough walls, and recessed orbs in the ceiling. He inhaled deeply, trying to ease the unexplained restlessness prowling through him since he'd left New York.

It had nothing to do with *her*, he told himself, but with Aerén taking off.

Usually, he didn't care where Aerén disappeared to, so long as he wasn't trawling clubs on the human realm. But, dammit, he should have left a bloody note!

At the thought, Reynner's mouth tightened. He'd wasted the night in the city, then an entire morning here searching for the prince, only to find Aerén on the mountaintop, near the waterfalls. Brooding.

He really wasn't cut out for this babysitting chore, but he did it because of a friendship long lost. Besides, one didn't say no to the high ruler of Empyrea.

A figure materialized on the balcony moments later. Aerén walked inside, having followed him. He stopped near the doorway, his features drawn tight. His damp trews and tunic clung to his body, and his pale blue hair hung limply around his shoulders.

Two millennia had passed since Reynner had left Empyrea. The young, playful boy Aerén had once been had disappeared. In his place, a tall, muscular man stood, his lean face and tormented eyes bearing the tragedy that had ravaged his family.

Aerén's oldest brother had been banished for the tragic death of their little sister, and with the recent disappearance of his parents…yeah, Aerén didn't have much to smile about. His only kin left was Daén, the middle-born son and now ruler of Empyrea.

"Are you training?" Reynner asked him.

"For Urias' sake, Reyn!" Aerén glared at him, his silver eyes burning with unleashed emotions. "Strife plagues our dominions, our magic grows weaker, and life declines. I can't be left here doing nothing!"

Reynner understood his concerns. Unlike other realms, the seven dominions of Empyrea resonated with arcane energy, siphoned from the seven mystical Stones of Light.

Two thousand years ago, one of the Stones had vanished and the link was broken. Their realm would eventually fade and die unless the missing artifact was found and brought back.

The green-eyed female had better be the one they sought. Heavens help them all if he was wrong.

First, Reynner had to get his hotheaded prince to calm down before he could go after her.

His body still far too tense, Reynner willed the door to open farther. He hoped the breeze would cool his ardor, but that thought got shot to Hades when his dick seemed hell-bent on reminding him of how he'd responded to her.

"Do you know who you ambushed and almost killed before Daén sent you to me?" Reynner asked, trying to shut off desires that had no place in his life.

"Rebels, who else?" Aerén's lips curled in disgust. "Those insipid degenerates deserve nothing less than a slow, torturous death."

"No. Those were Darkrean males returning home after a stint of hunting. Had you killed them, the Darkreans would have retaliated, and you would have started another civil war."

"And you see a difference? Rebels, Darkreans, they are just leeches who will bleed Empyrea into oblivion."

Reynner nailed him an annoyed look. "They are still Empyreans, and as such, it is Daén's job as ruler to deal with this situation. You need to stand beside your brother and help him. Not be a bloody hindrance." He hoped his words landed with the impact of a boulder on Aerén's hard head.

He glared. Apparently not.

"You're high-lord of Ademéras. What are *you* doing to protect your domain?" Aerén demanded.

"Ademéras doesn't need me, it has a ruler," Reynner stated, his tone flat. "My mother can take care of her territory."

Aerén stared at him in disbelief. "Lucan's right. You have become cold and heartless."

"It's good you know that."

"Hell sure killed you," Aerén shot back.

"Be thankful you never have to live that shit. Now, get yourself in gear and train with me, or go vent your frustrations elsewhere." Reynner stalked off to the other end and the small, roughly excavated space he used as a changing room, Aerén's words following him.

Cold. Heartless.

They pounded in his head as he grabbed a pair of sweats and a tee from the wooden shelf. Pain, he could live with since it was his constant companion. But guilt ate at his soul, knowing he was responsible for Ariana's death and for much of Aerén's anguish.

Scrubbing a hand over his face, he changed and headed back to the gym.

Aerén turned from the window, regret crossing his face. "Reyn, my pardon. I should not have said that."

"It's all true. I'm not what I once was."

Eons ago, he'd lived for the fights, fun, and females—in any order.

"I guess none of us are. But I cannot be closed off here. I have to do something." Aerén shoved an impatient hand through his damp hair. "Let me fight with you in the mortal realm."

Reynner understood Aerén's frustration and helplessness all too well, but it was far too dangerous. "I kill demoniis, Aerén. They're vicious, and they feed on the blood and souls of humans who cannot protect themselves."

Except it wasn't really about protecting humans. It

was the one thing that gave him purpose after his escape from Hell, to end every one of the soulless fuckers.

"And for that you have to learn control, especially with the kind of powers we possess. Your shield slips even for a second, and you'd destroy more than just the city—you'd leave no survivors. You'd bring down the wrath of the archangel.

"Trust me, you don't want Michael on your ass. Or worse, Gaia, the ancient goddess who watches over that world. You're pissed at everything right now. Learn to control your temper, and then we'll talk."

Aerén's mouth thinned.

Good. For a hothead like him, it must have been difficult to lock down his jaw.

Reynner pulled off his tee and tossed it on a bench. Aerén's gaze honed in on the scar on Reynner's left pec. He said nothing, but compassion flickered in his light eyes.

Irritation surged. He should have kept the damn shirt on. He didn't want anyone to see his branding of shame, a moment of weakness that had changed his life and left him with an eight-point star on his chest, proof of a randy goddess's ownership.

He'd been forced to reveal the truth when Aerén had come across him several months ago where he'd chained himself to the dungeon wall, out of his mind in pain. The only way he wouldn't break free and give into Inanna when she summoned him by way of the mark on his chest. The pain she inflicted was the price he paid for ignoring her calls.

"Don't waste your pity on me. I deserve what I got."

"To be owned by a whore goddess?"

"A lesson well learned—never trust a female, never

promise anything. Now, are you joining me?"

Exhaling roughly, Aerén nodded and flashed out from the gym.

Reynner rolled his shoulders. Loosening the tight muscles of his back, he released his wings. A grunt of relief escaped him. The rustle of feathers caused a light breeze to sweep across the gym. His image in the windowpane reflected the cream-tipped and bronze color of his extremities. Keeping them hidden while in the mortal realm was a pain in the ass, but immortals could never call attention to themselves. Besides, he didn't care to have his wings on display. And even more, he hated them being touched.

Glancing away, he set the treadmill for an uphill run. Not an easy thing, running with a six-foot wingspan behind him, but he needed the work out, to exhaust his mind and dull his endless pain.

"Why do you think I cannot protect myself?" Aerén asked, reappearing in a shimmer near the free weights, wearing gray sweats and a t-shirt. "I can so easily overcome any adversity."

As if to prove his point, his body started to glow. The hairs on Reynner's arms rose at the staticity—as if all the fiery energy in the realm had condensed inside Aerén and was minutes from releasing a deadly electrical storm.

Shit! A miss, and he could bring down this mountainside. With a flick of his hand, Reynner obstructed the flare with a psychic block. "Rein in that godsdamn power. I happen to like my house where it is," he growled. "Dammit, Aerén, you're a bloody prince, one I've sworn to protect. Just stay here—you'll be safe."

"*Safe?*" Anger darkened Aerén's face. "You mean

keep the spare heir safe, ready to take Daén's place if anything happens to him. Is that what you think I want?"

"It's not a matter of want, it's a must. You are the carrier of all that is light. It's in your blood. You know this. Empyrea will be restored to what it once was, and you *will* go back."

In response, Aerén stormed out to the balcony and dematerialized.

That went well.

Inhaling an annoyed breath, Reynner tried to empty his mind of his problems while he ran, the power of each footfall adding to the burn in his thighs.

He focused his attention on the frothy white waters of the roaring falls, but it did little to ease him. He dashed the sweat off his brow with the back of his hand. Still, his edginess didn't ease as thoughts of *her* persisted. His mind couldn't let go, couldn't rid itself of the damn peach scent that seemed to have settled inside him. Or forget how her warm, feminine form felt against his. His body heated, his groin hardened.

Shit! He scaled over the handlebars of the treadmill and sprinted out onto the edge of the balcony. Retracting his wings, Reynner dove in a free fall into the churning, icy waters of the plunge pool far below.

***

A while later, Reynner left his room, coat in one hand and his cell phone in the other. If the female from the club was really the one they all were looking for, he had to find her fast, before the Darkreans did. They wanted rule of Empyrea, and they would do anything to get their hands on her. At the thought of those emotionless bastards taking her, his stomach knotted.

No! She meant nothing to him except as a device to

be used in his search.

Scowling, he headed for the stairs leading to a well-lit circular foyer. His phone beeped. He glanced at the display and frowned at the reminder.

David's opening. Artist Inc. Gallery. DON'T BE LATE!

What the hell—this wasn't his phone.

Reynner backtracked to the last time he'd used his cell...the previous evening in the club. His heart kicked up a notch.

This was *her* cell. Their phones must have gotten switched when they crashed into each other, a meeting he'd orchestrated. He checked her voice messages.

An annoyed female snapped, *"Eve, where the hell are you? I called you several times today!"*

"Eve," he breathed her name.

Finally, something worked in his favor. He scrolled through her messages, a clear invasion of her privacy—like that'd stop him—and opened an unread text from David.

Okay, not mad you haven't answered my calls. Guess you're working, eh? See you at the gallery. Is later tonight still on?

What the hell was going on *later tonight?*

His gut twitched, jaw clamped—dammit. He had no business worrying about *that* aspect of her life. His first priority was to make sure she was the one he sought, and to keep her safe until she completed the task of awakening the scroll to find the Stone.

Too bad for little green eyes, saving his world trumped her tryst.

Reynner slipped the cell into his pocket, walked outside, and found Aerén there. He stood precariously on the edge of the balcony, hands shoved in his sweats pockets. He glanced back, his gaze sweeping over Reynner's leathers and the coat he'd hooked with a finger over his shoulder. The bleakness in his eyes scored a layer off Reynner's closed-door attitude.

"I may have found someone who can awaken the scroll," he said. He had no clue if this Eve could rouse the ancient parchment. Just because her magic blood did strange things to his dick meant nothing. But the question of *why* settled in his head, gnawed a hole and refused to leave. Brutally, he shut it off.

"The mortal's been found?"

At the flicker of excitement in Aerén's expression, Reynner wished he hadn't opened his yap so soon. "Don't get your hopes up just yet. The scroll responds only to the touch of one whose blood will awaken it. I'd have to make sure she is the right female first, then find a way to convince her to help us."

Aerén cut him a dry look. "That shouldn't be a problem. I recall the females haunting your halls in Ademéras, and your many assignations with them."

Seduce her to help their cause?

"Yeah, should be a piece of cake," he muttered, aware of his lack of enthusiasm.

Why the hell was he hesitating over this one? He'd used females before. If Eve had magic in her, then he'd do what needed to be done. All that mattered was saving his world. His fingers curled around the delicate earring in his pocket.

Once it was over, he'd just clear her memories and send her on her way...

***

Eve wobbled in her vivid blue icepick heels, attempting her usual quick stride. Unless she wanted to fall flat on her face, she'd better slow down. She was already late, hurrying now made little difference.

The stifling heat rose off the asphalt and moistened her skin as she fished for her cell phone in her evening bag to check her messages, surprised Brenna or Kataya hadn't called to rant.

Only to find it locked. And her password didn't work. Ugh, she'd just sort it out later.

Dropping her phone back in her purse, Eve rubbed her damp palms over the hips of her blue-green strappy cocktail dress. Its flared hemline fluttered around her thighs as she pushed open the glass door into the snazzy foyer of the brick building where Artist Inc. Gallery was located. She sighed in pleasure at the blast of coolness against her skin. Thank God for air conditioners.

While the ancient elevator chugged her up to the sixth floor, Eve drew on her black gloves. With this kind of crowd, she didn't dare risk going in with bare hands.

Soft voices and tinkling glass greeted her in the gallery, along with the nose-tingling scents of expensive perfumes and oil paints. Eve stopped, stunned, and stared at the canvases on display. David's absentmindedness definitely hid a brilliant artist.

"Hi," she greeted the couple next to her. "His work is amazing, isn't it?"

The brunette threw her a cold look and turned away. Her male companion, on the other hand, smiled appreciatively at her.

Odd. Eve shook her head and concentrated on the canvas titled *"Life,"* done in the Impressionist style. The enormous conglomeration of brushstrokes coalesced into a group of homeless people sheltering around a garbage can of fire. David had captured the very mood and nuances of his subjects while they enjoyed a simple pleasure. The sheer brilliance of his work boggled her mind.

She spied Eric and David with a group of people on the other end and gave them a little wave before she wandered to another canvas. A jasmine perfumed cloud enveloped her seconds later.

"There you are, you slacker," Kataya growled into her ear. "You don't answer your cell anymore?"

"I'm so sorry, I was working." She accepted a champagne flute from a passing waiter who gave her a thorough once over.

Eve frowned. What was it with the lust-filled stares since she'd entered the gallery? Heck, Kataya was the looker with her pale skin and slant-shaped eyes. Tonight she was decked in sleek black evening pants and matching bustier top. Her dark red hair flowed in a sexy cascade of corkscrew curls down her back.

"I don't know much about Impressionism," Kataya said, her whiskey-colored eyes taking in all the paintings. "But everything sure looks good. So, are you and David heating up the sheets tonight?"

Eve sputtered. Champagne sprayed, wetting her gloves.

"Jesus, Kat!" She glared at her friend, found a tissue in her bag and cleaned off her damp gloves. "We're merely having drinks later, nothing else."

"Hey." Brenna glided over in a figure-hugging red dress. She looked at them both and raised an eyebrow. "What happened?"

"Kat needs a distraction. Badly." Eve snorted, squashing the used tissue into a ball. "Her mind's in the gutters."

"Aah…" Brenna smiled, then her quizzical blue eyes

pinned Eve. "You didn't say you and David were an item."

"We aren't, Bren. I haven't made up my mind yet."

How could she, when *his* face haunted her now? Their first encounter had been disturbing enough. Then her dreams had taken over. No way she could ever forget those sensual lips set in that stunning face, taunting her as he trailed the dagger down her stomach—

"You go on with that mindset and the worms will be the only ones enjoying your virginity," Kataya muttered. "I'm going for a smoke."

Brenna took her arm. "Come. I want you to see something.

Eve frowned at Kataya's cranky attitude. "What's with her?" she asked, letting Brenna lead her. "Her editors giving her crap again?"

"Either that, or she's missing Jake." Brenna brushed her inky bangs from her eyes. "And she's smoking like a junkie, too—ta-daaa!" She flashed her arms open as they stopped in front of a painting. "So, what do you think?"

Eve didn't answer. How could she when her jaw had dropped to the floor?

There she was on canvas. Larger than life. The narrow strap of her top had dropped off one shoulder to expose the curve of her right breast. Thank God at least her nipple was covered! Dreamy green eyes stared back at her. Her mouth looked like she'd lip-locked a bee. At the seductive expression on her face, heat fused her cheeks. "I never posed for *that*!"

The painting was done in a multitude of delicate brush strokes that made her look...sexy?

Sheesh, she had to be the least sexy person ever,

when she practically lived in her sweats or threadbare jeans. Well, they were her work clothes. But, sexy? Her gaze veered to the title on the right. Eternity. Just as well he didn't call it Seduction. Eve shuddered at the thought.

"Like my surprise? Must say, I've received several offers for you," David said from behind her.

Eve whirled to him. "Why would you do this to me? Oh, Lord, now I understand the reason for the looks I've been getting," she moaned, dropping her head into her palms. "And don't say that! It sounds like you're my pimp or something."

David rubbed her back. "It's beautiful. And that's how you look."

Her head snapped up to meet his grin. "No, it's not. I know what I look like when I wake up. And when did you see me—" The memory surfaced in pixel clear clarity.

She'd been sick one evening several weeks ago, and had taken flu meds before attending a get-together with the gang at David's loft. She had dozed off.

"When you awoke, you looked so…" David's ears turned red. "Alluring. I had to capture you on canvas."

So being sick made her sexy? Oh, God! Eve snagged another flute of bubbly. "I need to drink and forget I saw that. Or that all the women here probably hate me."

"I wouldn't worry. They're just jealous that they can't look as hot as you do, even when sick," he teased, then turned when someone hailed him. He gave her another pat on the back and strolled off.

***

It was close to midnight, people showed no sign of leaving, and Eve was still sober. Her feet threw a tantrum in her torturous shoes. She wished she could sit down and pull off the stilettos. With work and now this party, heck, even the floor looked inviting after sixteen hours on her feet. Stifling a groan, she took another sip of her champagne.

Kataya joined her after another little excursion outside. A fresh wave of jasmine and mint came off her.

"You okay?" Eve asked, studying her friend's pale face.

"Yeah, I'm good. Trying to give up ciggies is a damn pain-in-the-ass. I'm gonna call it a night. You want a ride home?"

Ah, now she understood Kat's crankiness. "Please."

"So, you dislike the painting, huh? Not happening with David, then?" Kat asked her as Brenna joined them.

Eve wrinkled her nose. "The painting's okay, I suppose. It's not like I'm naked or anything. I'm too tired for drinks or to think about *that* tonight, so home it is. Anyway, we have a date for Wednesday… What?" she asked when her friends didn't respond but stared behind her.

The sudden silence was broken by startled gasps.

"Would you look at him!" Fine lines creased Kataya's brow. "Now, why do I feel like I've said this before? But Jesus, the man *is* beautiful."

Eve whipped around, her heart racing. Déjà vu hit her hard.

So tall, he stood heads above everyone there. Black leathers covered his muscled legs and were teamed with a dark dress shirt and a long, black coat. His pale hair was tied back, revealing the stark lines of a face she never thought she'd see again.

In the bright lights of the gallery, he was even more stunning.

"He could just stand there and pretend to be a statue of a Greek god or something equally divine," Brenna said on a dreamy sigh, checking him out. "Definitely mandelicious."

"Oh, yeah," Kataya agreed. Then she scowled. "That's not even a word."

"But got you to agree with me," Brenna snickered. "Bet he has gorgeous sapphire eyes to match the rest of him."

Midnight blue, Eve mentally corrected, even as her mind struggled to accept him being here, in the gallery of all places. Memories of her dreams, of the cool metal blade he'd trailed down her belly, swamped her. Arousal flared to life. Shit!

"I need the, er, bathroom," she told her friends. She didn't wait to hear their response. Shaken by her strong feelings, Eve slipped out into the passage, but with women going into the restroom, she headed for Eric's empty office at the back instead. The single light from the passage cast a soft glow into the darkened room.

Eve set her glass down, pulled off her sticky gloves and dropped them on the desk, then rubbed a shaky hand over her fluttering stomach. *I'm fine—I'm fine.* She inhaled deeply, picking up the small sample sculpture of a vase she'd done for Eric, and let the humming of the metal soothe her...

Her neck prickled. Eve stilled, a dart of wariness creeping up her spine.

She wasn't alone.

Swinging around, she almost pitched on her heels. Her heart crashed against her ribs as her gaze fastened on the tall, shadowy figure filling the doorway, blocking her only way of escape.

Chapter 4

The lights flickered on in the office, Eve blinked at the sudden brightness. And fear took on a different heartbeat when she looked into unforgettable, midnight blue eyes.

He'd followed her from the gallery?

She eyed him warily. But he remained at the entrance, as if not to scare her.

The sudden sharp pain in her finger had Eve hastily easing her death-grip on the metal sculpture. Her defense mechanism kicked in. "Are you lost? Or are you here to finish off what you started last night?"

He went motionless at her words.

Oh, yes. She'd obviously lost her ever-loving mind, reminding him of *that*.

"You want the gallery, can't miss it—" And she couldn't seem to stop. "Go back through the short corridor on the left—double glass doors leading into this enormous room with paintings. That easy."

Something dark and dangerous sparked in his narrowed eyes. He prowled closer, crowding her in the small office. Eve had to dig her toes in not to run, mostly because she had nowhere to escape.

He stopped a foot from her, his gaze skimming over her as if searching for something. A tiny crease marred his brow. "You hurt yourself again."

Eve glanced at her stinging finger and saw the red stain. Ugh, she seemed to make a habit of hurting herself around this man. He reached for her hand. Panicked, she shoved the sculpture at him and backed away in horror.

It was one thing for her friends to see her scars, but for him to see the shattered tissues and burn marks? Nope. Not happening. She balled her fingers into fists. People, she'd found out in painful clarity, didn't like anything ugly. They either gawked in pity or tried to avoid touching her hands, like her ex-boss had. As if her scars were contagious.

"Eve, let me see."

His low, accented voice almost melted her resolve to stay detached from that tangible pull of him. Disturbed at the near lapse, she put the desk between them. "It's nothing—a scratch. How do you know my name?"

Cool, night-sky eyes flickered to the wooden barrier separating them. She doubted it would be much of a defense. He looked quite capable of tossing the desk away.

"It doesn't take a genius to find out your name with the painting of you on display." His unexpected curt tone held a cold bite.

Heat crept into her face at the thought that he'd seen her portrait. It was obvious he didn't like it. She scowled. "What do you want?"

"Are you always this difficult when someone tries to talk to you?"

"Only to those with a hand around my throat."

His gaze shifted away from hers for a second then came back, unreadable as ever. "I wasn't myself last night."

That was an apology? Her eyebrow arched, but on an inherent level, the knowledge trickled into her that it was the best she'd get from a hard man like him. She let it drop.

Eve knew it wasn't fear that had her reacting to him in such a defiant manner, but something else she didn't want to name.

He studied the sculpture she'd dumped on him. "What is this?"

"A sample I did for Eric."

His gaze flickered back to her. "You're an artist."

"A sculptor. I'll have my own show soon." Eve cringed at what must sound like a weak attempt to issue an invitation. As if he'd want to come. She stuck her sore finger in her mouth—or at least she had attempted to when he grabbed her hand.

Her heart tripped. She hadn't even seen him move around the desk. "It's just—"

"A scratch. So you said. Let me."

Before she could figure out what he meant, his mouth closed around her finger. Her breath tangled in her throat, her gaze trapped by his. A blue flame flickered in those dark depths. She forgot about her scars as his warm tongue lapped at the tiny wound, caught in a whirlpool of sensations.

Oh, dear God! Need roared to life, lighting a fuse that led directly to the most feminine part of her.

Struggling to tamp down the wayward desires, Eve tugged her hand free and clutched the desk to support her shaky limbs. She didn't even know his name, and she'd already been more intimate with him than any man.

"Why–why did you do that?" she croaked.

He shook his head. His fists bunched, then he shoved them into his pants pockets. "My name's Reynner. We need to talk."

"About what?"

Amusement tugged his lips. "Why so suspicious?"

Dear Lord—that smile! Before she did something mortifying like grab him and take a bite of his sexy mouth, she said, "Talk fast."

His brow climbed up. "I can't 'talk fast' about this."

Snorting, Eve brushed past him and walked out from the office. She needed her friends. Maybe Kataya and Brenna would slap some common sense back into her head.

As she made her way down the short corridor, Eve struggled to remain composed—a darn difficult thing to do when his quiet presence behind her tugged at her like a magnet.

Relief flooded her as she entered the gallery and spied Brenna and Kataya heading her way.

"There you are. We've been looking for you—" Kataya broke off, glancing behind Eve in shock.

"I...umm, I got detained."

"Eve?"

No touching, just her name in his lightly accented voice, and it put the brakes on her flight response. Her friends did a perfect impression of two landed guppies.

"It's important." His low tone stroked her senses like a warm caress.

Oh, heck, she was in so much trouble. She flicked a quick look at him over her shoulder and met his dark blue stare. Yes, the man was a stranger, but one who called to her on an intrinsic level. It left her with little choice but a burning need to find out what it was about him that affected her in this way. And he said he wanted to talk. "Okay."

Eve turned to her dumbstruck friends, and introduced them. "These are my friends, Kataya and Brenna," she told him. "Kat, Bren, this is Reynner."

He gave them a polite nod.

Their hellos were a croaky effort at best, for which she couldn't blame them. With that face, Reynner would probably leave many breathless.

"I won't be long. Five minutes and we can leave, okay?"

Eve took her purse from a still gaping Brenna, then slipped past the guests and walked out into the busy foyer. She turned to Reynner and tried to ignore the attention he drew from the women there. They didn't bother with her after the first dismissive look. With her hands on display, she wasn't even a contender in their eyes.

Eve tightened her fingers on her purse, yearning to dig out her spare pair of gloves, but she refused to let them win.

A leggy blonde in a figure-hugging black cocktail dress glided up to them. The front V of her bodice dipped low, revealing her gym-sculpted body. Her gray eyes bright with carnal interest.

"Hello," she murmured to Reynner in a throaty voice that annoyed Eve.

His gaze flickered to her.

"I'm Selene. Did you enjoy the exhibit?"

"I'm not here for the art. I came for Eve." Cool. Dismissive.

A tingle of delight burst through Eve at his statement.

"Well, then…" Selene gave Eve a disdainful glance. "I'm sure you'll feel differently tomorrow. Give me a call." She slipped a small card in his pocket and sashayed away.

Yes, better to get this over with, or her self-worth would never stand the onslaught. But the insult stung.

"What do you want to talk about?" Eve kept her tone level, aware of the small card residing in his coat pocket like a poisonous asp.

"Not here. It's too crowded. Let's walk." He summoned the elevator.

Walk. Her feet rebelled at the word. "My stilettos are going to kill me."

He glanced at her killer heels. "We won't go far."

"Matters little when you're wearing torture devices," she muttered.

He didn't say anything. Discreetly, she studied him while they waited for the elevator. He stood with his feet slightly apart, arms crossed over his chest. His hands-off vibe all but smacked her in the face. Maybe it was just with her…but no, he'd brushed off the other woman, too.

The door to the elevator clanged open. Moments later, they were descending to the ground floor at a snail's pace.

Eve leaned against the metal wall. Enclosed in this small cage, she fought to keep her breathing shallow. God, but the man smelled really, really good. It was almost as if she stood in the middle of a forest after the rain.

However, now that he'd gotten her agreement to talk, he didn't seem ready to do so. He stared at the receding numbers of each floor as if it were a far more interesting sight.

Just her luck.

Eve flexed an aching foot and sighed. It kept her from obsessing about why a man who looked like him would suck her finger. He turned then and eyed her foot, only to ask a different question.

"The ear's healed?"

"What?"

He nodded to her ear.

"Oh. Yes, it's fine." She touched her unadorned lobe. The fast healing had surprised her, but the hole had closed, which meant getting it re-pierced. Not a visit she cared to think about. She'd suffered through enough pain in her lifetime. Her scars hurt more when she worked long hours, like today. She curled and uncurled her fingers to ease the stiffness.

"What happened to your hands?"

Eve struggled to breathe at his question. Flames of the past leaped up and consumed her. "An accident, ten years ago..."

"Fire?" Something in his dark stare told her this went past polite interest, like he was truly concerned. And maybe that's why she told him about the car crash.

"I couldn't save them," she whispered. "My parents were trapped…the fire…."

"I'm sorry."

She swallowed the tightness in her throat and nodded, rubbing the old scar on her chest.

He reached out and gently stroked her face. Startled, her gaze flew to his. He looked like someone had taken a sledgehammer to his head. His jaw rigid, his hands disappeared behind his back. He remained silent, but she caught the brief flicker in his haunted gaze, like he understood tragedy. She couldn't be sure because he pivoted as the doors opened.

Still, something had moved in his shadowy gaze and touched a deep visceral part of her. Almost like a connection was made between them in that single moment.

Eve stepped out of the elevator and discarded her fanciful imagination. A *connection* with this self-contained fortress? Right. The only connection she had was one of arousal that left her damp and edgy. And dammit, she'd had it with her shoes.

Resting her hand on the wall, Eve pulled off her stiletto. A moan of relief escaped her, one she cut off when she found him watching her. "It's been a long and *tiring* day. So what did you want to talk about?"

She slipped off the other shoe, hooked her finger through both straps, and felt like a midget next to him. Her head must barely touch his shoulders because she certainly couldn't see over them.

He held out a black iPhone. As if on cue it rang. *Like a Virgin* belted out loud in the quiet night. Eve dove for her cell, heat rushing to her face. How the heck did he get her phone?

"Sorry," she mumbled in embarrassment and pushed open the lobby door into the sweltering night. He followed her. Within seconds, she felt like a wilting rag while he, even in leathers, appeared cool, gorgeous. And untouchable.

Reynner exuded that inaccessible air like a thick cloud...*but clouds can dissipate,* she thought with a little smile and answered her call.

***

Reynner shoved his hands into his pants pockets, inhaling sharply to clear the smell of her from his lungs, and failed.

Urias, this wasn't turning out as he'd planned.

Locked in the elevator with her, her subtle peach fragrance combined with the scent of her arousal taunted him. The latter he'd caused by sucking on her finger. He was only supposed to taste her blood, not behave like a bloody leech. Everything about her drew him in. She was too compelling, even with those strange blue-painted toenails. It'd taken every bit of willpower he possessed not to haul her to him and devour her mouth instead.

She sent him a quick look as she spoke on her cell. Her gaze, like an erotic caress, tightened his skin, and his cock hardened uncomfortably against his zipper.

How the hell could one tiny human unravel his mind—his defenses—so easily?

The taste of her blood hummed through him like a symphony. Any more, and he'd have the whole bloody orchestra playing in him. Yes, she had magic in her. He doubted she was even aware of it. His heart quickened at the enormity of what this meant for his realm.

Would she agree to aid him in his search for the artifact?

It mattered little. He needed her help, and he would get it.

Reynner brought his attention back to his job and realized to whom she was speaking. The artist. His eyes narrowing, he strolled closer.

"It's been a long day, I'm sorry about tonight, David…yes, Wednesday… Bye." She ended her call. "Sorry about that. And thank you for my cell. I didn't realize I'd lost it—oh, that means I have yours." She dug through her purse, found his iPhone, and handed it to him.

He slipped the cell into his pocket. "That painting of you?"

"What about it?" A defensive note entered her voice.

"You're dating the artist?" It surprised him he hadn't snarled the question, considering his territorial thoughts.

"What?" She blinked those darkly lashed forest green eyes at him. "No. Why?"

At her answer, perverse pleasure surged through him. The artist wanted her. It all but screamed from each brush stroke. Too bad for the human, Eve was going to be under his protection while they searched for the artifact. But it didn't stop him from wanting to rip off the male's head for daring to imagine her so—like she'd been made love to.

"I'll give you a ride to your home. We can talk on the way."

She hesitated, probably picking up on his anger. "It's not necessary. We can talk here."

Hell, he needed to lighten up before she bailed. Deliberately he glanced at her feet. "It'll take a while, and you can save your friends a trip. Or you could put on those torture devices, go back inside, and tell them to wait."

Her pained expression at the thought of wearing her shoes again told him he'd knocked down the first obstacle.

"Let me call—"

"No need. The cavalry's here." Reynner nodded toward the gallery entrance as her friends hurried out. Cold amusement seeped through that they would protect Eve from him. He'd allow no harm to come to her, ever.

"I won't be long." Barefoot, she ran over to them, the short hem of her bright aquamarine dress fluttering around her golden brown thighs. Reynner forced his gaze away and tamped down the sudden image of what they'd look like wrapped around his waist. Thanks to his heightened senses, he easily picked up on most of their conversation.

The redheaded grabbed her arm. "Eve, did you go find him yesterday?" she hissed. "That's asking for trouble."

Find him?

"No, Kat, I didn't. He helped me out last night at the club. I'm sorry I didn't tell you. I didn't think I'd ever see him again... Jeez, no, nothing happened! I crashed into him, and our phones sort of ended up with each other. He came to give it back. That's all."

"And now?"

"And now...he offered me a ride home. I'll be fine."

Her friend snorted. "You're hoping to get rid of the dreaded V with the badass, right?"

"Christ, Kat, hush! He'll hear you..." She leaned in closer, and he missed some of her words. "...nothing. I feel nothing at all with him," she said. "You don't know how wonderful that is. For the first time, I don't have to worry about anything."

The redhead sighed. "Okay. But be careful. Have fun, and we want deets. I'll call you."

She felt nothing for him? Reynner frowned. She wanted him, he knew that, so why—

Urias, what was he doing? It was better this way, less complication. He had a job to do, no matter what his dick wanted.

Eve stifled an embarrassed laugh and hugged her friends. Her fingers fisted as she did so.

Was her wound worse than he thought? The sculpture had made a small cut, but his saliva should have healed it. And what the hell was this dreaded V?

Reynner stiffened, his nostrils flared. A trace of sulfur drifted to him.

Demoniis.

Since his escape from Hell, his one true enjoyment had been destroying the bastards. He glanced around and hoped none crossed his path right now. He should have let Eve go with her friends, instead of giving into temptation and offering her a ride. Hell, he could have had this conversation with her later, but her haunting scent and the painting in the gallery with her incredible sensuality splashed all over it messed with his rational mind.

No, he didn't like that the artist had captured the very essence of her, or the fact that she'd posed for the damn thing.

Pulling his cell from his coat pocket, Reynner frowned at the two cards he drew out with it. Tossing the scented one into a nearby dumpster and using the other, he made his call.

***

Eve watched her friends walk away and wondered if she'd lost her mind leaving with a complete stranger.

She didn't know Reynner, she only understood that from the moment she saw him, he drew her like a magnetic field. That haunted expression she'd glimpsed earlier made her want to ease him, to soothe the hurt in him.

She walked back to the man who scrambled her good sense. Only he wasn't watching her, but the street. At her approach, he turned the full force of that stunning face on her. She had to clench her fingers not to reach out and touch him.

He ushered her into a dark gray Porsche parked at the curb. Eve sank into the luxurious seat, inhaling the smell of expensive leather and a faint hint of wild forest. She dropped her stilettoes on the floorboard, leaned back, and exhaled in gratitude as she stretched out her aching feet.

Reynner circled the hood, opened the door, and slid in beside her. Then the soft purr of the engine filled the interior.

"Where to?" he asked, voice clipped. Eve cut him a sharp look, unable to pinpoint what had set her inner alarm cranking its rusty bells. Okay, the man had that dangerous persona thing going for him, but something was seriously off.

"East Village." She reeled off her address. "What's wrong?"

"Fasten your seatbelt."

Her tummy dipped at his flat tone. Hastily, she strapped herself in. He stepped on the gas and sent the car flying down the empty street.

And the past came flashing back—her parents' car swerving and colliding into another, the ripping of metal, the shattering of glass. Flames leaping—flesh burning—

"Slow down!" she yelled, her heart crashing against her ribs. He glanced at her, his jaw tight. But he eased up on the gas and detoured through a quiet thoroughfare.

By the time Eve snapped out of her panic attack, Reynner had pulled into a deserted alley in a really rundown part of town and switched off the engine. Night enfolded them. There were no streetlights, just the looming buildings, and slashes of moonlight. Her uneasiness grew. "Why—"

"Stay in the car," he cut her short. "Don't leave, no matter what you see." He opened the door. The interior light came on to reveal his profile hewn in granite. She grabbed his sleeve. "Wait—wait. You can't go out there. This place is dangerous."

Reynner turned. His face, his sensual lips mere inches from hers. But the utter coldness of his expression worried her.

"Stay here," he repeated. The door slammed shut and he headed into the alley. Several figures emerged from the shadows and circled him. Fear took hold, anxiety clawing her stomach. Was this some kind of gang fight?

Then Reynner moved, unbelievably fast, right into a sea of black figures. She could barely keep track of him, glimpsing just flashes of his pale hair. A flare of fiery-red light zapping out from one of the thugs startled her.

Oh, God. They had weapons—laser guns? Reynner was unarmed, alone.

She scrambled for her phone in her bag to call 911.

A thunder-like roar resonated throughout the alley. Her mouth dropped open, her call forgotten, her gaze pinned to the dark figures crashing to the ground like falling dominoes.

Reynner grabbed one of the fallen by the hair. Steel gleamed. He slit the pale, exposed throat. Blood sprayed. Then he plunged his dagger into the man's chest.

Chapter 5

Oh, God—oh, God! He...he... Reynner killed a man!

Run. Get out of here! But Eve's legs refused to obey.

Terror turned to dread when she saw clear in the moonlight that it wasn't blood that flowed from the man's neck, but something like...thick, black goo?

Reynner dropped the man—thing, whatever it was—to the ground. He catapulted into the air and tackled another racing for the car. They crashed on the Porsche's hood like a boulder dropped from the sky. Eve clutched her seat, fingers digging into the leather.

The man-thing pushed up, his eerie red eyes glowing like neon moons in the dark. Reynner seized him by the hair, ruthlessly ran the blade through his heart, and tossed him aside. The fallen man convulsed on the pitted asphalt. Within seconds, he deflated like a balloon and disappeared from sight.

A sickening realization dawned. No, they couldn't be. Things like this only happened in horror movies.

Jesus, what did she walk into?

Another red streak of light hissed through the air, slamming into Reynner and sending him staggering back. The remaining monsters attacked.

Oh, no! They were going to kill him! Eve grabbed her pepper spray from her bag, opened the car door, and stepped out, her heart clocking like a racehorse.

Breathe, Eve, breathe. You can do this.

"Eve, get inside the godsdamn car!" Reynner's roar reverberated through the alley.

She swallowed but didn't back down. She didn't think he'd been keeping an eye on her. One of those things turned, grinned, and in the next instant appeared in front of her.

Her heart pounding, adrenaline spiking, she sprayed him good in the face. The fiend yelled and cursed in a terrifying, raucous voice, rubbing his eyes. Reynner suddenly appeared like some avenging angel in front of her. A faint glow appeared in his hand and a six-foot-long sword took shape.

Where the hell did that come from?

Then she forgot her question as he swung that sword. Her jaw dropped.

She'd known Reynner was dangerous. His stone-cold features and tough body told her so. Kat had called him a badass, but Eve had never seen anyone cause so much carnage like he did. His sword arched, a deadly gleam of silver decapitating heads. The bodies fell to the ground and disintegrated, not even the clothes remained.

Now she was alone with this ruthless man who wielded an enormous blade like it was an extension of his arm. His eyes glowed a fiery blue in the night. Strands of his pale hair escaped their tie and streamed to his shoulders. Beautiful, menacing, he strode to her.

"What the hell were you thinking? I told you to stay in the damn car!"

Clutching her can of pepper spray like a protective shield, Eve stood face-to-face with a man who'd single-handedly taken down a small army of those creatures. They didn't scare her as much as he did right then, with the cold fury emitting off him.

Slowly, she backed away.

"*Now* you're afraid of me?" Like a whiplash, his voice stung her.

She stiffened her spine. "No, I wanted to help. It seemed unfair so many were attacking you—"

He growled, his glare morphing into disbelief. Then in a move that made her head spin, he hauled her to him just as a blinding red flash came hurtling toward them. The blast sent him forward, and he fell against her. Her breath exploded out of her lungs. Eve struggled to hold onto him, his powerful body a sensual blow to her senses. She fought to keep him on his feet and not topple them both to the ground.

With a snarl, he pushed off her, his enormous sword still in his hand. Eyes blazing, he scanned the alley. She hurried to him. "Reynner—"

Cursing, he grabbed her wrist and hurried her toward the car. "I have to get you out of here."

"What were those men—things?"

"Hell on Earth—dammit!" He stumbled and let her go, bracing a hand against the grimy, graffitied wall.

"Let me help you." She tried to prop him up.

"No." He flung out a hand, stopping her. Then dug into his coat pocket, his movements jerky as he searched.

"But you're hurt."

"No."

What the hell was the matter with him? She wanted to help, not cop a feel. Teeth snapping together, Eve waited for Mr. He-Man's orders.

Leaning against the filthy wall, Reynner brought out his cell phone and attempted to make a call. The device fell from his unsteady hand and landed on the ground with a dull thud. Curses in English, mixed with some strange language she'd never heard before flooded her ears.

Eve picked up the fallen phone and held it out. His fingers clenched. She waited, didn't say a word. His pained, furious gaze pinned hers, almost like he hated asking for help.

"Star one. Michael. Call him." The words were wrenched from him as he slid to the dirt-encrusted asphalt. Worried now, Eve pushed aside her hurt feelings and pressed star one. A man answered. His voice was low. Compelling. "Reynner?"

And scary.

She cleared her throat. The chilling air from the man had her speaking quickly. "Reynner's hurt. He asked me to call you, I'm not sure where we are..." she glanced around the creepy place with its dingy buildings.

"I'll find you." He rang off.

Reynner rested his head against the wall, eyes closed, his hand still gripping his sword. The reek of decaying garbage from Dumpsters nearby blindsided her. Breathing through her mouth, Eve crouched beside him and pushed his cell phone into his pocket.

She hoped this Michael would come quickly. Her skin itched, she rubbed her arm. Something wet and sticky clung to her fingers. A coppery smell wafted to her. *Blood?*

Eve remembered that red bolt hitting him. Quickly, she pushed her hand behind his back, but he was too heavy to move. When he didn't protest, her anxiety grew. She tried again, harder this time. Her knuckles scraped against the walls. Ignoring the burn, she ran her fingers over his body. There. Across the solid width of his back, she found the gashes in his coat and the wetness surrounding them. She pulled her hand away and stared at the bloody mess on her fingers.

"You're hurt."

"I know..."

Her heart slamming against her sternum, she jerked to her feet.

"No, don't...leave..."

"I'm not." Eve sprinted to the car and snatched the cell she'd dropped to the floorboard then hurried back to him. About to call 911 again, she saw a dark figure striding up the alley.

Please...please don't let it be one of those things. Her can of pepper spray wouldn't help them because there was no way she could haul Reynner to safety. Eve pushed her cell into the seam pocket of her dress, rushed to his side and picked up his sword now lying on the ground, and grunted.

Crap! The darn thing was too heavy. Heaving it, she stepped protectively in front of Reynner and struggled to appear calm—and hopefully dangerous—wielding his weapon.

The man closed in on them. The moonlight revealed dark hair falling in careless layers over wide shoulders. Shades covered his eyes, despite it being night.

Eve pointed the blade at him, her hands shaking like a leaf in a squall. She prayed she didn't drop the weapon. Heat seeped into her palm, connecting with the metal she held. *No, no dammit! Not now.*

"Stop right there."

He did. His gaze dropped to the sword she clutched and then came back to her face.

"Who are you?" she demanded.

"Michael."

She recognized the dark cadence of his voice from their brief conversation on the phone minutes ago, and relief flowed through her. He must have been close by to get here this quickly.

"You have to let me tend to him, before he worsens."

"Yes-yes, of course." Eve stepped back and gratefully lowered the heavy weapon. The enormous man hunkered beside Reynner, pulled him forward, and examined his back. "Helluva place you chose to nap."

"Ritz...not available."

Michael snorted, then he glanced at her. "I have to take him with me."

"She comes, too."

"Why?" A cool note entered the man's voice.

"Fuck—" A pained groan left Reynner. "Gonna keep me in this roach-infested dump 'til I answer your damn questions?"

"You know the rules, Empyrean—free will."

Empyrean? Free will? What the heck were they going on about? Reynner needed help.

"Eve..." Reynner's voice slurred. His dark gaze lifted to hers. "Come...with...me?"

"Of course, I'll go with you," she reassured him. He'd saved her, taking the hit that surely would have killed her.

"There, Michael...happy?" Reynner's indistinct words held a mocking edge.

"I'd kick your sorry ass if you weren't already down, but we need to get out of here."

At his statement, Eve's fear increased. "You can't

move him—he's hurt. I'm calling 911."

"Your doctors can't heal him. We have to go now. Come here."

Warily, she eyed him. "What do you mean *my* doctors?"

"Explanations later. Do you want his death on your conscience?"

When he put it like that—darn it. Eve hurried over and prayed this Michael knew what he was doing. "What do you want me to do?"

"Hold on and don't let go."

She frowned. "I don't understand."

The big man shook his head. He picked up Reynner's sword then touched him on the shoulder. "You will soon enough."

He held out his hand. Eve eyed it as if it contained a nest full of vipers. "I can't..."

He studied her for a second. Then like a rattler, he struck and hauled her to him.

"Hey! I'm willing to *hhhhhelp*—" Her last word ended in a yelp. The alley disappeared as they were sucked into a mist of swirling darkness.

***

Sebrasius, leader of the Darkreans' militia, stared out through the window at the dark silhouettes of the trees and shrubs in the distance, highlighted by the full moon. The incredible views here were the only thing from the mortal realm that appealed to him.

It didn't compare to the deadly beauty of Dregarus. The ice-bound seventh dominion of Empyrea where his kind dwelled. A place he called home, a place where monstrous ice bluffs reigned.

He cared little for this elegant mansion overlooking the Hudson River they'd procured in upstate New York as a base. But the lush forest surrounding the estate had a soft spot, making opening portals into their realm easy and private.

Sebris's gaze settled on his reflection in the windowpane. Nickel bronze hair fell past his shoulders. His eyes appeared almost black, his mouth a slash in his tight features. He was pushing it, remaining in this place when he should have left days ago to equate and recharge his waning powers. But the job came first.

Pushing his balled hands into the pockets of his trousers, Sebris turned as two of his warriors walked in, their expressions detached. Their dark gazes empty.

"Anything of import I should know about?"

Xever, his second-in-command squatted near the empty fireplace beside a huge white wolf, his hand burrowing through the beast's long fur as if seeking succor. "No... No trace of the artifact or the female."

Taegér shook his head. He prowled the enormous room as if measuring it for new carpets, his tight jaw revealing his discomfort.

Damn, not what he wanted to hear.

"It's been months, Seb." Xever rose, and a forlorn whine left the wolf. Xever's narrow face wore a granite edge. Strains of black had taken over his gray irises. It was one of the main reasons they were known as Darkreans. "We've remained here for far too long. We grow weaker. We must go back to Dregarus and equate."

That was a bit of a bother. As Darkreans, they needed to equate by connecting with their realm's magic so they could function once again. Away from their realm for any length of time and they had to bury their emotions. An overload of feelings and pain became constant, eating away at their powers.

But nothing would keep Sebris trapped in Dregarus when their quest for freedom was all that mattered. They would take back what was rightfully theirs.

"We fought far too long to slow down now," he stated. "The moment we have the missing Stone of Light, all will be as it should."

"Yes…" Taegér stopped pacing. Anger flickered in his gaze. "Wipe out what's left of the ruling family, and Empyrea is ours."

"We didn't come this far to screw up now." Sebris cut him a cold look. "We still have the six high lords to contend with. Our chances at success lie in finding the foretold mortal first, then the lost artifact."

Shuffling footsteps sounded, and Paxyn stumbled into the study. The warrior had taken far too long to return from canvasing the city. His ebony wings dragged on the floor, unable to use his depleting powers to conceal them.

He could no longer remain on this realm with those extremities in view.

"Anything on the artifact?" Sebris demanded.

"No," Paxyn responded, tone flat, eyes a dull ebony. "We've searched homes, museums, galleries, even the labyrinth beneath the city for the Stone, and nothing."

Sebris remained silent as he deliberated. Using the Empyrean to do the work held far more appeal, and it would mean a slower depletion of their abilities.

"There's something else," Paxyn said. He leaned against the doorjamb as if to keep upright. "Could be nothing. Reynner had a female with him last night when he tackled a horde of demoniis."

A spark of anticipation jolted through Sebris at the information, a fresh rush of pain spreading beneath his skin at the elation. Finally, news he'd waited eons for.

He glanced at Taegér. The warrior's darkening irises still held remnants of their blue-gold color. Good. He could hold out for a while longer.

"Shadow the Empyrean," Sebris instructed him. "Xever, you and Paxyn have two days to equate, then I want you back."

Once the two warriors had left, he turned to Taegér. His tone cold as the ice-laden seas of their dominion, he said, "I want that female."

Chapter 6

Eve found herself on a couch when she came to, the dizziness fading from her mind. Sunlight streamed into the semi-circular room from enormous windows with scenic views. Transparent white curtains fluttered in the soft breeze flowing in from outside. She frowned at the rough, dark granite walls surrounding her. The place appeared as if someone had excavated deep into a mountainside to form this space. It held a raw, rustic appeal.

Movement in her peripheral vision caught her attention. Turning, she saw the huge man toss a smoky gray comforter to the foot of the bed then pull a matching sheet to cover the naked form lying on the bed.

Reynner!

Eve lurched to her feet and stumbled across the room to the giant-sized bed.

Reynner's discarded clothes were in a heap on the dull, granite floor. He lay on his front, his face turned away. A gasp of horror escaped her when she saw the wounds across his back, like someone had used a blowtorch. Black, charred skin surrounded the open lesions, and they oozed bright red over darkened, drying blood.

"That looks awful... He won't, he won't—" She found she couldn't say the word *die*.

Michael glanced up.

Eve gaped. Finally, she understood why he wore shades. His deep blue eyes appeared like splintered glass. An eerie silvery glow escaped from the cracks...

Otherworldly, the thought seeped into her mind.

Uneasiness stirred at his piercing stare, like he could see into her soul or something.

"Don't worry, he won't die," he muttered, straightening the sheets over Reynner. "He's too damn stubborn for that. How long have you known him?"

"Not long—yesterday...actually, I'm not sure." Eve looked out the window and at the bright afternoon sun. It had to be the following day, she decided, unable to make sense of time. "I met him on Friday night..." She explained about the mixed-up cell phones. "He offered me a ride home before those, er, things with red eyes attacked."

Michael looked at her for a long second, probably making sure she wasn't some nutcase spurting garbage then nodded. He crossed to a door at the far end of the room and disappeared inside, only to reappear a few minutes later with a container of water, a small glass jar, and towels.

"What where those things that hurt him?" Eve asked, her gaze on Reynner's ruined back.

"Demoniis." Michael set the items on the bedside table.

"*Demon eyes*?"

"Yes. They are what demons turn into when they

first steal a human soul."

Shocked, Eve pressed a hand to her roiling stomach. "Why?"

"To experience the light of a mortal soul." He picked up a thick towel and tore it in half. "Once they steal a soul, the demon's own dark spirit dies. To survive, they constantly need new ones because human souls were never meant for them. It fades, and the cycle starts all over again. That's why we—Reynner and I and others like us—exist. We hunt and destroy them."

God. Eve dragged both hands through her hair. This all sounded so unreal, like she'd wandered into an alternate world. But if she'd suddenly developed abilities after the accident, like being drawn into people's thoughts when she touched them, then demons existing shouldn't have surprised her.

I'm such an idiot. As if I could protect Reynner from those things.

"You need to be careful," Michael said, folding the ripped terrycloth into an even smaller square. "Not only humans walk this realm. Others do, as well. And evil is one of them. In the future, don't put yourself in dangerous situations."

At least he didn't yell at her like Reynner had. "What Others?"

"I'm sure Reynner will fill you in."

Nodding, she watched as Michael laid a hand over the gaping wound on Reynner's back. A silvery glow pulsed out from his palm. Fascinated, Eve leaned in closer. "What are you doing?"

"Aiding his recovery."

"You're like a healer?" She saw the slight smile tugging at his lips. It rearranged his hard features into a stunning visage.

"I've been called many things, but never a healer." Michael dampened the square and started to clean the messy wound.

"Let me." She hurried around the bed and joined him.

"No—" Reynner turned to them. Michael's healing had awakened him. Sweat poured down his face and pain darkened his eyes to dull blue stones. Worry took over when she met his feverish gaze. "No, not her. Get Izzeri," he rasped.

"Don't be silly, I'm right here."

His shoulder muscles bunched, causing a fresh spurt of blood to leak out. "No."

"But—"

"Get. Izzeri," he cut her off.

Eve stared at him, dumbfounded. He disliked her touching him that much?

"The Guardians are stubborn sons-of-bitches." Michael's tone matched the walls of the granite room. "Them, I *have* to deal with, but you—"

"Not interested."

"—are an ass. Izzeri isn't here. Either let her tend to you or wait until tomorrow. Your choice. It means you're off rotation longer. You may not be a Guardian, but you will follow the rules. I don't want you on Ear—in New York until you're healed."

He slapped a small bottle on the bedside table and said to Eve, "If he gives you any trouble, pour the damn thing down his throat—should knock him out and give his thick hide time to heal."

Michael strode out of the room. Eve turned to Reynner and was seared with a stay-the-hell-away glare. The only reason she'd offered to help was because he got hurt trying to protect her.

"If you don't want me tending to you," she told him in a determined voice, "you're going to have to get out of that bed and throw me out."

She ignored his narrowing eyes, picked up the terrycloth Michael had discarded, and dampened it with warm water. Her hands shook as she reached for him. Despite her brave words, she expected him to jump up and physically toss her out of there.

When he didn't, she hid her relief and carefully wiped away the blood smeared on his back. Awareness flowed through her at the warmth of his skin beneath her hand, the rock-hard muscles. She wanted to stroke every inch of his tan, sexy body—

Ugh! Eve forced her mind back on her task. Not wanting to hurt him, she kept her touch light as she cleaned off the mess. She dared a glance at him and her heart lurched painfully when she found his dark, intense gaze fixed on her.

Idiot. It means nothing. He's just making sure you're treating his injuries and not copping a feel of his gorgeous bod.

But ignoring him became a test of endurance when his burning gaze tracked her every move. She dropped the soiled towel, picked up the jar, and uncapped the ointment. A musty, mossy scent permeated the air.

"What is this?" she asked, needing a moment to calm her fluster.

"A potion. Helps heal the wounds from the hellfire bolts those dead bastards deal out."

Her gaze flickered to him. Did he expect her to run screaming from the room now that she knew demoniis existed? At times, he frightened her more than those demoniis did!

Ugh, who was she kidding? Her attraction to him

terrified her the most.

Taking a deep breath, Eve scooped up the green paste with two fingers and applied it gently to the wounds. "Will this help you? It looks really bad."

"I'll heal to fight another day."

She stopped her ministrations, studied his closed off expression.

His detached response troubled her. Did he not care what happened to him? "Why do you hunt demoniis if you dislike it?"

"You misunderstand me. Destroying the bastards gives me one of life's few pleasures." The intense hatred in his voice appalled her. "Shocked you, did I?"

Yes, she was shocked. She was only trying to help. Did he think she was responsible for his current situation? Then she winced. Okay, maybe she was. So she remained silent.

***

Reynner gritted his teeth, pain and fever razing through him. He needed, *wanted* her touch... It soothed him. *No—no*, he tried to clear his hazy thoughts. *Females—they're all the same...*

He didn't want *her* touching him. *Too aware of her...not good...not good.* Then icy dampness settled over the scorching fire of his wound, blessed relief hissed through him. Cool fingers stroked down the edges of the gauze and he shuddered under her gentle care.

There was something he needed to say, but whatever the hell Michael had pushed down his throat was fogging his mind, and her touch wiped out the rest of his lucid thoughts.

"What is this place?" Eve's soft voice drifted over him like a tormenting caress.

"Exilum," he snapped.

She stiffened at his harsh tone. A jagged breath barreled out of him. "It's a retreat."

Her hands came back, and another stroke of her cool fingers on his burning flesh. Soothing. Calming.

"Is this like a healing center? I hear water."

"No. My home."

"It's er...nice."

"It's not *nice*. It's a damn fortress, impenetrable and all that matters. Go wash your hands, don't let that crap stay on you any longer." Good. That's what he'd wanted to tell her.

"Crap?"

Must she question every godsdamn thing?

"Blood, dammit. Now go." He turned his head away, muttered, "I don't want that shit tainting you."

***

Eve entered the bathroom and stopped. She glanced around in appreciation at the grotto-like place with its huge windows overlooking a stunning view of the mountains.

Dropping the stained towels on the counter, she emptied the bloodied water in the white bowl-like basin. Then she stared at her hands as she held them under the open faucet, traces of Reynner's blood washing away from her puckered skin.

His words had chilled her. Why would he say that? His blood appeared red like hers.

Filled with unease, she closed the tap and looked up. Faced with her reflection in the mirror, she cringed. Dear Lord, it's a wonder Reynner didn't mistake her for a ghoul. Her eyes appeared like dark holes in a face gone pale, in spite of her tanned skin.

Exhaling in annoyance, she rubbed her hands over

her cheeks, hoping to get some color back, and went back to the bedroom. She stopped at the bedside to find that Reynner had finally fallen asleep. A relieved breath left her. At least he'd get some rest.

She re-checked the gauze over the wound and noticed the tie on his ponytail had slipped to the ends of his hair. Pulling it off, she sat beside him on the bed and combed the shiny strands away from his shoulder. They appeared like moonbeams sliding through her fingers.

"I'm sorry you got hurt because of me," she whispered, her guilt expanding. "I should have stayed in the car—"

A knock sounded. Eve snatched her hand away, heat riding her face as the door opened. Her jaw hit the floor at the man striding toward her.

Where the heck was she? All the men here seemed to have walked right out of a fantasy world. He appeared to be younger than her, closer to Reynner's height but leaner. He wore some kind of soft black pants. They molded to his muscled thighs and disappeared into well-worn, knee-high black boots. A white tunic with suede lacing in the front emphasized his muscular shoulders.

The guy's silver eyes flickered to the bed then he turned that extraordinarily handsome face to her. "I came for a visit. But I see he is still out."

Eve pushed to her feet. "Yes, he is."

"I am Aerén."

"Eve—Eve Leighton." She hid her hands in the folds of her dress, hoping he wouldn't expect a handshake. He didn't. Instead, he lowered his head in a sort of half-bow, an *olde worlde* kind of gentility.

"It is a pleasure to meet you, to know he finally

found you," Aerén said. "You don't know what a relief this is."

Eve frowned at his solemn expression. Oh, he must mean about the cell phone mix-up. "Yes, he did. Don't worry, it's all sorted out."

"I'm glad. Eve Leighton, you have my undying gratitude. If you are ever in need of anything, you can call on me."

For returning Reynner's cell phone?

"Er, thank you." Her gaze went to his hair. How could she miss that? Pale blue, like a faded summer sky, it flowed to his shoulders.

"Perhaps you would join me for a meal?" he asked her, pulling her attention back to him.

Despite hunger gnawing a hole in her belly, she desperately wanted a bath, needed to get the grime from the alley off her before she ate. "I'd like a shower first, but I don't have any—"

"Clothes?" His gaze glided over her again, but in male appreciation now. Eve wanted to roll her eyes.

"Not a problem. I'm sure Izzeri will find you something."

Her tummy growled and she cringed in embarrassment.

Aerén merely said, "You should eat first. Come."

Okay, then. She might as well go eat and satisfy her stomach and her curiosity about Reynner's home. Eve glanced back at him, but he was still asleep. So, she followed Aerén out of the room and down a short barren corridor.

She stopped at the landing and simply stared around in wonder while Aerén waited patiently beside her. A wooden balustrade and stairs joined the top floor to the ground one. In front of her was a picturesque glass wall. She could see far off into the horizon. The forest far down below took on the appearance of paint smudges in various shades of green. The dark gray mountain range loomed around the house and meandered into the distance.

Did Reynner build his house into a mountain?

Eve glanced around at the granite walls and floors…had to be. Holy crap! "It must have taken a miracle to do this."

"It did take some time, from what I understand," Aerén said. "When Reynner sets his mind on something, he gets it done."

Eager to see more, Eve ran down the staircase to the lower level. The sounds of rushing water drew her. She opened the first door and entered a room with soot-colored leather couches and armchairs. Her gaze flew to the window, and she came to a halt.

"Oh. How lovely." The power of the cascading waterfalls took her breath away. So close, if the glass wall weren't in her way, she could almost feel the cool sprays on her face. Beyond the window, a railless balcony ran the perimeter of the place.

Did Reynner not understand how dangerous a balcony with no protective railings was? Guess not. The man did kill demoniis, after all.

"It has a compelling beauty," Aerén agreed from beside her.

"Where is this place? Reynner said it was a retreat?"

"That it is. Come." Aerén led her down a short passage toward the kitchen.

The tantalizing smell of fresh bread and something savory teased her nose as Aerén opened the door. And she almost whimpered with hunger.

However it wasn't the kitchen, which had the same

scenic windows as the rest of the place that snagged her attention, but the wiry man working at one of the counters. Attired in a navy tunic and pants, he was of indiscernible age. He'd fastened his long, copper hair into a loose braid, revealing his sharp, pale features.

At her entrance into the room, he looked up and his gold eyes widened in astonishment. He stared at her like he'd seen a miracle or something.

And she stared—because dammit, how could she not? His ears—the tops were tapered into points!

"Hey, Izzy. You're back?" Aerén said from behind her.

"Indeed." The man winced, probably at the nickname, but his gaze remained on her.

"Forget it, fae." Aerén snorted. "Eve, this is Izzeri, Reynner's houseman."

"Mistress." He bowed his head at the introduction. "A rare pleasure, indeed. The meal is almost ready. You must be hungry."

"I'm fine," she lied, aware of the mewling grumble of her dying tummy. "I'm sorry you had to delay going home."

"I don't mind at all." He smiled. "Excuse me, mistress."

Eve glanced away, taking in the small kitchen. The thick, massive glass panes muted the roar of the falls, but allowed the waning sunlight into the kitchen. Bronzed wood cupboards with gray granite countertops took up one part of the room. On the other side, near the window, a wooden dining table overlooked a stunning view of the mountains and was set for a meal for one.

Izzeri quickly and efficiently added another place setting, while Aerén held out a chair for her and then took the one opposite her. The setting sun cast a fiery shimmer over his pale blue hair.

"Is that real, the color of your hair?"

Aerén's expression turned stark. He pulled a swathe to the front and stared at the strands. Remorse filled her at the grief in his eyes. Hurriedly, Eve backtracked. "I'm sorry. I didn't mean to pry. It's just so unusual."

"It's all right. We—I mean my brothers and I inherited this hair from our sire... Ah, here is our food."

His entire mood changed when Izzeri approached, a smile chasing away the grimness. The houseman gave her another appraising look as he laid the dishes on the table then uncovered their contents; fresh rolls, curls of soft, golden butter, and a tureen of steaming broth.

"Why does Izzeri look at me like that?" she lowered her voice to ask as she split open a fresh roll and lathered it with butter.

Amusement lifted the corner of Aerén's lips. He shook his head. "Let us eat first. Questions later."

***

Night settled like a blanket around them. Orb-like lights from the ceiling cast a golden glow over the house when Eve headed back to Reynner's room.

She had gotten an answer of sorts from Aerén. *Izzeri had never seen someone like you.* She didn't know how to take that remark. But mostly, dinner conversation had included Aerén firing question after question at her about her life. You'd think he'd never heard of a woman living alone and working. Sheesh. Men!

Eve closed the door softly behind her. As she crossed the room, she saw the black tunic Izzeri had draped over the armchair. She checked on Reynner, but he remained in the same position she'd left him, his eyes shut and his mouth in a tight line.

Fighting against the impulse to stroke his face and ease his discomfort, she grabbed the tunic and headed for the bathroom. In relief, Eve shed her rumpled clothes and stepped into the glass shower, only to discover that there were no faucets. She stared at the gentle flow streaming down from the high ledge in the granite wall. Her hopes of a bath dashed.

Now what? How the heck was she to flatten herself against the rough stone surface to shower?

A sudden gush of warm water hit her square in the face.

Argh—Eve sputtered. Wiping away the wetness, she scowled. Sensor operated. She should have known.

Glancing around, Eve found a bar of soap and a jar of gel in a small niche in the wall. She stuck her finger in the goo. Like the forest after the rains, the fresh, familiar scent teased her nose. The pang in her grew. He called to her like an irresistible, seductive flame. God, she didn't want to start feeling this way about someone, whom instinct warned her to steer clear of.

Eve pushed aside those feelings and hurried through her shower. After toweling off, she hung her washed undies on the towel rail then pulled on the tunic. The shirt swamped her, dropping to mid-thigh. At least it was black and would not reveal her lack of underwear.

She fastened the suede ties, rolled back the too long sleeves, and stilled as an eerie sensation slid over her. The hairs on her arms rose.

Eve hurried into the softly lit bedroom, rubbed the goosebumps on her skin, and glanced around. Movement on the bed diverted her. Reynner strained and grunted, his fingers digging into the mattress like he fought some nightmare that held him in its grips. He rolled over as she sprinted to his side.

"It's okay, it's okay." She soothed, sweeping the sweat-dampened hair away from his face. And prayed his agitated movements wouldn't cause his wounds to bleed again. Keeping her tone gentle, she sat on the bed and stroked his arm as she spoke, hoping to ease him.

A sudden slash of pain slammed through her, she jerked back, unable to breathe. Darkness surrounded her, seeping into her mind. It hauled her into its carnivorous jaw, pulling her into his dreams. Panting hard, she blinked and struggled to see through the hazy gloom.

A wet, coppery odor drifted to her. Bile rose to her throat at the stench. Raucous breathing grated her ear.

And there against the shadowy walls of an obscure cell, she saw him.

His gaze wild as an animal's, he crouched in the shadows, naked. Waiting…

Chapter 7

Reynner remained motionless in the dark dungeon as sludge squelched between his toes.

His wings trailed behind him in the muck, an added weight, unable to conceal them. There wasn't a smidgen of light to aid his sight. He had no idea how much time, how many years—decades—had passed in this shithole.

The metallic scent of blood layered his nostrils and coated his tongue like he'd sucked on pennies. His breathing labored. Two obscure shapes slithered across the slimy floors.

The bastards were back for their games. He didn't need light to know that. Their putrid stench of decay took over the sulfur that had become a normal part of his existence.

A flash of cunning obsidian eyes, and the huge, seven-foot-tall, lizard-like creatures attacked, claws ripping at his wounds that had no time to heal. His powers were so muted, all he managed was a weak flare that flickered and died. Only his will spurred on by adrenaline unleashed the beast raging inside and drove him for the kill. He grabbed one scaly fucker around the throat as its talons pierced into his flesh, and twisted the thing's neck.

A shriek ricocheted off the walls. A lash of razor-sharp nails in his chest forced Reynner to his knees. Pain saturated his being. Slimy saliva dripped over his hair as the wyvern opened its jaw, revealing a mouthful of pointy teeth.

Maybe he'd finally find oblivion. Prayed for it.

Death. So close...so close.

"Enough!" a bell-like voice ordered.

No matter what kind of demonic monsters Kalinin sent to torture him, they weren't allowed to kill him. None dared go against his captor, the succubus bitch.

A flicker of candlelight cast a dim glow in the dungeon. Kalinin stood behind the metal bars. Her dark red gown matched her hair. A lust-filled expression on her pale face.

Urias, *if only she stepped foot into his cell, even an inch—he'd rip her fucking head off. Then he'd go after Inanna for putting him in this hell.*

Reynner lowered his head and kept his gaze glued to the thick gleaming puddle he knelt in as blood dripped down his body to pool on the floor beneath him.

"Well done, Empyrean. Now..." She drew out the moment, like it was some fucking game. "Time for your treat."

His stomach churned at her words. Through the bars, someone flung water over him, washing away the blood and filth. A hissing erupted as splashes made contact with the heated black walls.

His prison gates rattled and clanged open. Hands grabbed him and tossed him onto a raised stone slab. His wings bent under him, unbearable pain shimmering through his entire being. He bit down on his molars. Manacles cuffed him to a base covered with a thin pallet. It wasn't for his comfort.

She strolled over, avaricious black eyes skimming over his naked body. Reynner kept his gaze fixed to the roof, dripping with some shit that fell in a resonating plink to the ground.

"Who knew lack of light would be your weakness, my Empyrean. Submit to me—say the words, and this torture will end."

"Fuck...you." His profanity came out in a garbled rasp from a throat gone rusty with lack of use. Her nails dug into his open wound. Reynner gritted down against the agony spearing him.

She smirked and trailed her pointy talons over him. Then she leaned in and licked across a deep gash on his chest.

"Do you like that, warrior? Hmm, the power of your blood, there is nothing like it," she murmured, face flushed in excitement. "Do not fear, I'll give you mine soon. I know how you love that."

Hatred filled him. His fists balled. He could do nothing but lie there while she sucked on his wounds...then she backed away, circling around him. Stopping by his shoulder, she ran her fingers along the inner arch of his left wing. He jerked but was held back by his restraints. She laughed and caressed him some more. His sex rose like a fucking rod. He knew right then if he could, he'd rip off his wings.

Humming a little, Kalinin slid out of her gown and tossed it aside. He kept his gaze locked on the leaking ceiling. Bile rose up his throat when she dipped her hand into some shit she had in a jar and wrapped her fingers around his shaft. His mind switched off.

A smile lit Kalinin's sly features. "Hello, big guy," she crooned and straddled him, tossing back her red mane—

"Reynner—no! Oh, God, no!" A distraught, familiar voice cut into his nightmare.

He stiffened. *Eve?* Urias, *for all that's merciful, don't let her see me this way.*

Something warm and wet dripped on his chest. His lids snapped open and a cloud of dark hair, not red, filled his vision. Green eyes shimmered with tears.

She'd seen him. Saw his memories. Saw the scum he was. The filth—the whore he'd become.

She fucking saw him!

Unmitigated fury exploded, crashing through Reynner in a poisonous haze.

***

The metallic scent of blood and unadulterated hatred flooded Eve. In a violent move, Reynner flung her away from him. She landed on the other end of the bed, doused from his pain. His eyes glowed like the very demons she'd seen in his nightmares. Darkness's greedy fingers clawed at her, blurring her thoughts. The pain, the shock, too much for her fragile mind to process.

God, no! Don't let me black out now.

"What the hell did you do?" Reynner's snarl vibrated off the walls and yanked at her fading thoughts. Her breath escaped in tiny gasps as she lay across the huge bed. Eve struggled to get her mouth working, to form coherent words and push through the thick fog seeping deeper, attempting to haul her into a void.

"I'm so s-sorry." Her voice broke, unable to see past the horror.

"You were in my mind—*you were in my fucking*

mind!"

"No!"

"Don't lie. I felt you!"

Terrified, Eve broke through the haze and managed to roll off the bed before he grabbed her. She fell to the floor and landed on her bottom. Bones jarred and pain spiked through her spine at the impact, dissipating the edges of darkness. "I didn't mean to. It was an accident."

Naked, he leaped over the bed.

She scooted back.

Reynner crouched in front of her, like some wild animal with death in his eyes. Tears crowded hers. Eve tried to find the man she knew, but nothing of him remained in his tortured gaze.

"You came into my mind, took what was not yours."

"I didn't mean to. I'm so sorry. I only touched you to—"

"Touched me?" He mocked her. "So you want to *touch* me? Well, then, go ahead, touch." Reynner rocked back on his heels and held out his arms.

Eve pushed to her feet, fear swirling through her. His eyes, glowing an eerie black, tracked her. A feral smile rode his face as he, too, rose.

More beautiful than any Greek statue she'd seen, his hair was a wild tangle of silver around his wide shoulders. He had some kind of star on his left pec. Ripped abs, muscled legs. Then her gaze locked on his heavy erection, hard and thick, it reached his navel. Eve took a hurried step back but hit the craggy wall, scraping her skin and leaving her nowhere to run.

He slammed his palms on either side of her head. "Maybe that's not what you want." The smile turned sly. A knowing look settled on his face, one feral with carnality. "Maybe you want me to fuck you—it's what they all want, to own one like me. Is that what you want too, little Eve?"

Slowly, he leaned forward, his body trapping hers against the wall. His thigh slid between hers and shoved her legs apart. Her tunic rose higher. Eve's heart crashed against her ribs, aware she was naked beneath the thin fabric.

"Please...don't." She pushed at the solid wall of his heated chest with balled fists, too scared to touch him again. His body pressed into hers, his arousal a hot pulsing length branding her thigh.

He growled at her clenched hands, uncurled her fingers, and planted them on his chest. Eve breathed in harshly and waited for the onslaught—nothing. He'd already locked down his shields again, she realized.

He lowered his head to hers and sniffed her like some wild animal. She turned her face away.

"No, you don't." His hand wrapped around her throat, holding her in place. His thumb stroked the rapidly beating pulse. Eve stared into the eyes of a stranger.

"Afraid of me, are you, little Eve?" he taunted. "This is what happens when you cross the line. Don't fear, when I'm done with you, all will be forgotten...no, maybe I'll leave you with memories of me. Would you like that?"

"Stop, please—" She pushed at his chest. He grabbed her hands and held them above her head. Her heart tripped and then pounded so hard, Eve was sure it would burst out of her ribcage.

"I can hear your heart beat." His husky whisper sent a shiver down her spine. A warm tongue licked her neck, right over her pulse. Her breath came faster. His teeth grazed the throbbing muscle. Pushing his thigh farther up ever so slowly, he brushed her core. She stiffened as desire surged, heating her blood, chasing away her fear. Dampness flooded her.

A roguish smile lit his face. "You're wet—do you want me, little Eve?"

Like wildfire, heat streaked across her cheekbones in humiliation that he had evidence of her arousal.

"I can do chained to the wall, chained on my back...or maybe I'll just go down and eat you." His words had her feminine muscles tightening. "I know you'll taste exquisite—tell me you want me."

Helplessly, she stared at him.

"Say it." A demand.

She did, but not like this.

"Reynner, please—" She struggled to break free, but his ruthless hold kept her pinned against the wall.

"Very well, let's see if I can change your mind." Releasing her hands, he removed his thigh from between hers and lowered into a crouch. Inch by excruciating inch he raised her tunic, his gaze pinning hers.

The words dried up in her throat as she watched him. She should move away, say no, but her tongue refused to work. He ran his palm up her inner thigh. Then he slipped his hand into her damp curls and she froze. He ran a finger up her wet center and she shuddered.

Eve squeezed her eyes tight as wanton need engulfed her. Her heart threatened to explode. She tried to yank free, unable to handle the sensory overload buzzing through her body, but his grip on her hip tightened.

"Look. At. Me." At the low order, her lids flew open. His eyes, dark and fierce, held hers. Something intense flickered in those midnight depths.

Need. Hunger?

Then it vanished like it'd never been there. He leaned in and licked her.

Eve's mind splintered. Desire erupted, a feeling so alien that she jolted and lost her footing, falling over him. With a hand on her stomach, he braced her against the wall, picked up her leg and put it over his shoulder, opening her to his gaze and his mouth. He ran his tongue up her cleft and circled her clit. Lost in the unbelievable sensation he tore from her, she grabbed his hair and held on as he tormented her, pushing her to the edge. His eyes on hers, he grasped her clit with his lips and teeth, gave a little tug—her inner muscles started to contract—

"Eve?"

At the intrusion, a low growl left Reynner, the sound reverberating against her clit. She moaned, moved against his mouth, wanting more, but his hand held her in place, not allowing her the relief she craved.

"Eve?" Aerén called out again. The handle of the locked door rattled. Sanity cracked through her sensual haze, bringing her back with a hard thump.

"No—" She pushed at Reynner. This wasn't about her. It was payback because she'd seen his horrific past.

"What, little Eve? Am I not good enough for you, now that you know where I've been?"

Behind the mocking words, she glimpsed his anger. He pushed her leg off his shoulder and rose to his feet, his lips gleaming wet from her.

Eve tugged down her tunic with shaky hands.

Deliberately, he wiped his mouth. "Go. Get out of here."

Her chest constricted, her stomach hurt. Her body

hummed with unfulfilled desire as she stared into his hard, mind-numbingly handsome face. The ropy muscles of his naked body vibrated with his harsh breathing. Then she noticed the rigidity of his jaw, and eyes that were no longer black but burned with a neon blue flame. His fists clenched so tight, the bones showed white through his skin.

"Leave. Or I won't be responsible for what happens next."

His words were a whiplash to her heart, his voice cold, devoid of emotion. A click, and the door unlocked. Eve fled, crashing into Aerén, who stood in the doorway.

"Eve?" He grabbed her by her upper arms. She shook her head. Tears clogging her throat, she broke away and ran for the stairs, unsure if she cried for herself, or for Reynner.

***

His breathing harsh, Reynner stormed into his dressing room. He snatched his sweats and yanked them on, his movements jerky.

She shouldn't have touched him.

He shouldn't have touched her!

The moment he realized who he'd woken up to, he'd been caught in an alien time warp. One so strange, it stroked his senses. As furious as he'd been, all he knew was that he had to touch her, to taste her. It was as if his life depended on it.

Gods, he rubbed a hand over his face. All Eve had shown him was kindness, but he couldn't seem to stop the moment he touched her. Didn't want to, and when he saw the flare of desire in her eyes, it was the nudge he needed. And taste her he did.

Big. Fucking. Mistake!

Now he wanted more. Wanted something he could never have.

Anger raging through him, he stalked out from the dressing room and found his way blocked.

Aerén stood there, hands fisted, looking like he wanted to clock him. Hard. Reynner didn't have to guess what had gotten the prince's dick in a twist.

"Get out of my way."

"You touched her—I can smell her on you. What the hell is wrong with you?"

Reynner clenched his fingers so he wouldn't be tempted to punch Aerén. "She is none of your business—"

Aerén lashed out.

Reynner reeled back several feet at the force of the blow, the pain in his jaw vibrating to his head. He'd asked for it. Hoped it would reroute his horny cock to limp oblivion.

The shit didn't work.

"Eve is not your damn plaything," Aerén snapped, chest heaving in anger. "She is here for one purpose only—to help our realm!"

"You've said your piece, now get the fuck outta my way." Reynner waited for him to take another shot, welcomed the all-out fight this would be.

"I am going," Aerén growled. "And to think, I always looked up to you."

Didn't that just suck? A big friggin' blow to his pride. Not.

But nothing, absolutely nothing, could stop the bile working its way up Reynner's throat at what he'd done. The taste of Eve still on his tongue, the scent of her arousal wafting in the room coated his senses, and a yearning took hold. He squeezed his eyes tight.

Females, they could never be trusted!

She's different.

No! He had to get the hell away. She was here for one purpose only, like his prince so helpfully pointed out. She was here to save their realm.

***

Eve sat in an armchair near the window and looked out into a sky studded with sparkling stars. The huge moon hung low, flooding the room with silvery light. Her skin took on a pearlescent sheen, like a marble statue. She rubbed her arm and wondered dully, if she stayed motionless, would she become one?

But nothing could take away the powerful emotions rioting within her. She scrubbed her burning eyes and let her gaze drift around the smaller room with its wraparound windows. Aerén had given her his room after he'd found her curled up in the living room. There wasn't another bedroom, he explained.

Eve shifted on her seat, her fingers tightening on the comforter Aerén had draped around her shoulders. Her emotions were frayed raw, and she struggled to calm down. She didn't know which was worse—the unfulfilled desire that hummed through her, or the images that now haunted her.

She drew her knees up, locked her hands around them, and buried her face in her arms as the vicious visions clamored back. The pain. The suffering...

Oh, God in Heaven! How did anyone bear that kind of torture? He'd been so viciously brutalized—violated. Why?

Who would do something so cruel to another person?

"I'm so sorry," she whispered again. He'd been furious that she'd seen his memories, and in anger, he'd touched her. Except, she'd never experienced anything like it. He hadn't been brutal, just determined to get a response from her. Her fleeting fear had vanished, giving way to raw need at the look in his burning blue eyes when he hunkered between her legs.

The mind-numbing pleasure he'd drawn out of her overwhelmed her and left her wanting more. Made her wonder at her own state of mind. Reynner had only reacted in anger. She wasn't stupid, she understood that on an inherent level.

Resting her head against the backrest of the armchair, she stared into the night, trying to forget the bleakness in his torturous gaze.

A knock on the door hauled her back. The light from the passage silhouetted Aerén's tall figure in the doorway.

"May I come in?"

She nodded, then realized he couldn't see her actions in the darkened room.

"Yes." The word hurt her throat gone numb from tears she fought not to shed. "You can switch on the lights."

Seconds later, a soft yellow glow flooded the room. Aerén crossed to her, his eyes dark with concern. "You okay?"

"I'm fine." She forced a smile. No use worrying him because she'd misjudged the effects—the consequences—when she touched Reynner.

"I brought you a drink. It will help relax you." Only then did she notice the tall glass he carried, filled with a pale amber liquid.

"Thank you." Eve took the frosty crystal from him and sipped some of the juice.

Tart with a hint of sweetness, it slid down her throat

and eased the tension of her body and her throbbing head.

She glanced at the liquid. It had the appearance of apple juice, but it tasted like no fruit she'd ever had. She couldn't quite pin down the flavor. "What is this?"

"The nectar of the angels," he said, his smile back.

"Right. But thank you. This helped, a lot." She left the juice on the small table opposite the chair.

"Eve…" He set the glass on the floor and sat on the table. "Look, Reyn is a hardhead, and I'm sorry for what—"

"No-no." She cut him off and prayed he wouldn't notice her heightened color. "It's my fault, I shouldn't have touched him. He had a nightmare. And I-I only wanted to offer comfort, but I got pulled into his dreams instead…"

Eve stared at her ruined hands. *Why me?* The bitter question flared in her mind, but it wasn't like she'd get an answer now.

"What do you mean?"

She looked up as Aerén's brow puckered in confusion. He glanced at her fisted fingers and understanding lit his gaze. "When you touch another you can see their thoughts?"

"Yes."

"How?"

She clasped her knees again, tried desperately to find some measure of control.

"A car crash, a long time ago…" She told him about the accident and the ability it had left her with.

"Would it not be an advantage to know?" he teased.

A harsh laugh escaped her. "No. Fate is not that kind. When I touch another, I'm drawn into their mind, I see and feel their thoughts, and it hurts. The darker it is, the worse it gets for me. I sometimes pass out."

"I'm sorry. I really am," he said quietly. "What happens if *I* touch you?"

"Nothing. Just me. I couldn't *see* Reynner's thoughts either, until now. His shields must have fallen...." While he was asleep, and she'd tried to comfort him, thinking him safe.

Oh, God. Eve buried her face in her knees as the awful memories swamped her again.

Warm, calloused hands took hold of hers.

"What are you doing?" Her head snapped up. Terror choked her, pain squeezing her chest.

"Easy," Aerén soothed her. "I am safe. Listen..." he said, his thumb rubbing her scarred palms. She tried to pull back, then stilled when she realized the only ache she felt came from her compressed lungs. Eve inhaled a shuddering breath. "How?"

"It's the way we are. We learn to shield at a young age."

About to ask what he meant by that odd comment, Aerén placed her splayed fingers on his face, distracting her. "Feel..."

Eve closed her eyes and let the sensation lost for so many years steal over her, allowing herself a moment to savor finally being able to touch another. And became aware of warm masculine skin with a rasp of beard beneath her palm.

"See? You can touch me. There is no need to be afraid," Aerén murmured, continuing to caress her hands.

Eve opened her eyes and met his warm sterling ones, so close to hers. His gaze drifted down to her mouth.

Oh, no. She tugged her hands, but he didn't let go. "Aerén, don't."

"Why?"

Because I want another.

A wry smile curved her lips. "Besides the fact that I just met you several hours ago—you're what, twenty—twenty-one? I'm twenty-five, a quarter of a century."

Amusement twinkled in his light eyes. He let her go. "If it makes you happy to think so, by all means."

Eve understood Aerén's flirting was to take her mind off what had happened earlier. But the questions prowling in her head refused to remain silent any longer. "Aerén, do you know what happened to Reynner? When I touched him, I saw his dreams—his nightmares. Why was he locked in a cell?"

Aerén pushed to his feet, looking uneasy. "You will have to ask him. My advice, don't. He doesn't ever speak about his captivity."

His words landed with the impact of a punch to her stomach.

Reynner had been...*captured?*

Chapter 8

After a grueling run through the forest, which did little to ease the remorse prowling through him, Reynner flashed back to his aerie. And barely stopped himself from scanning for Eve as he headed for the shower.

The water sluicing over his body only served to remind him of her hands on him...in his hair.

Heavens, he squeezed his eyes tight, fists braced against the rough surface of the walls. He had to stop thinking about her.

He hadn't seen her since she'd fled from him, after he'd scared the hell out of her. At the thought, his stomach hollowed out, but the exquisite taste of her lingered in his mind.

With unsteady hands, he shoved back his wet hair and left the shower, heading for his closet. He dried off then grabbed a pair of loose, white cotton pants, pulled them on, and walked out of the bedroom.

Barefoot, he ran down the wooden stairs to the lower levels and came to a dead halt in the kitchen.

Aerén slouched in a chair, staring out the windows. Instead of Eve, Lucan was there. The pain-in-the-ass mage looked up from his coffee, his pale greenish-blue eyes narrowing.

He really didn't need Lucan's shit right now.

Reynner opened the fridge and took out a decanter of ice water. Pouring some in a glass, he leaned against the counter and took a deep swallow.

The prince's cold stare warned he still hadn't forgotten what happened with Eve. Reynner definitely wasn't interested in revisiting *that* incident. He picked up an apple from the fruit bowl behind him and took a bite.

"You look like…shit." Lucan's gaze skimmed over him and settled on the tattoo on his left pectoral.

Reynner fixed him with a cool stare while he chewed his fruit. "Why are you here?"

Like he didn't know. Through the centuries, Lucan would pop into Exilum for an update on the search for the foretold one. And here he was again, just when Reynner had found Eve. He took another bite of his apple.

"What's the plan to take the scroll now that you've located the mortal?" Lucan leaned back in his seat, taking a sip of his coffee.

No beating around the bush with the annoying bastard.

"We have bigger problems," Reynner informed him. "A few nights ago in New York, I took down a small horde of *demoniis,* but I sensed another in the alley. One of our kind."

Aerén shot up from his chair. His silver eyes flared in anger, his animosity toward Reynner forgotten. "Darkreans?"

"Yes. The thing is, he would have seen Eve—she took it into her head to help me fight the demoniis." He wanted to curse again at how she'd put herself in danger.

Aerén's jaw dropped, then his guffaw resounded through the kitchen.

"*She* wanted to aid *you*?" he spluttered.

At the cold look Reynner pinned him, hastily he sobered, cleared his throat. "But females don't do that. We are supposed to be their protectors."

"Not in her world." Reynner's gut knotted, the apple a solid lump in his belly. He'd never forget his fear when the demonii had flashed to her. "I had to bring her here. We can't take chances leaving her unprotected with those damn Darkreans lurking about."

"Did you speak to her? Explain what's going on?" Lucan asked him.

Reynner shook his head. "No. Not yet."

Hell, he still had to mend fences with Eve. If she told him to take a flying leap off the mountains sans wings, yeah, he couldn't blame her. Except it wasn't an option until she awakened the scroll and found the missing Stone. Maybe then he'd oblige her.

***

Eve smoothed her palms down her freshly laundered dress, grateful that Izzeri had seen to her things. At least she had on underwear again.

She raked her shaky fingers through hair still damp from her shower, drew in a deep breath, and tried to calm her frayed nerves.

Now, she had to face reality. Face Reynner.

Unable to linger any longer, she left the room and made her way toward the kitchen farther down the corridor, concentrating on what she had to do. First, she'd apologize to him. She owed him that. And he had asked to speak to her, so she'd hear him out. Then she'd leave.

The aroma of coffee, baked biscuits, and something savory wafting in the air did little to tempt her appetite with her stomach in a tangle. But raised voices stopped her in her tracks.

"What do you mean you've done nothing yet?" Aerén demanded.

She couldn't hear Reynner's words, but his low tone resonated with impatience.

"I figured that out last night," Aerén retorted. "Why didn't you ask her?"

"Because I was too damn busy evading shitheads from Hell and trying to keep her alive!"

They were arguing over her. Eve pushed open the kitchen door, wanting to put an end to this disagreement. The air there was so thick with tension, she paused in the doorway, sure if she took another step she'd suffocate with the rising levels of testosterone in the room.

The heated discussion stopped, all eyes turning to her.

She was barely aware of Aerén and another man there. Reynner drew her gaze like a magnet. Shirtless and impossibly beautiful, he leaned against the counter, his expression grim. Loose, white drawstring pants sat low on his lean hips. One hand rested on the counter beside him, the other held a half-eaten apple.

His pale hair hung unbound, falling to his shoulders, a startling contrast to his tanned face. But when she met his gaze, the flatness there had her swallowing. He wasn't going to make it easy to apologize. Well, she'd have to get him alone and do it then.

Taking a deep breath, Eve looked away and clashed gazes with eyes like turquoise glaciers.

The tall man leaning against the edge of the table wore pants and a tunic similar to Aerén's. Swathes of sable hair were drawn away from his cold, striking face and tied at the back of his head. His gaze drifted from the top of her damp hair to the tips of her toes.

Uneasy at the intensity of his perusal, she took a step back in sheer self-preservation. "I'll come back—"

"No," Reynner's low voice stopped her. "It's midday, and you've missed breakfast."

Before she could open her mouth to tell him she wasn't hungry, Aerén leaped up and pulled out a chair. "Come, Eve. You didn't eat much last night either."

The warm smile on his face stopped her retreat, melting the ice forming in her veins. He loped over, put a hand on her back and ushered her to the table.

Eve ignored Reynner's stony stare. Whether it was because Aerén had taken the seat beside her and was so attentive, she had no idea. But she appreciated Aerén's attempt to put her at ease.

However, the tension emitting from him enclosed her in its force field, as if he were about to explode. He shifted on his seat, knees bouncing—it surprised her he hadn't toppled off his chair yet.

Something had happened. They were all on edge. And like a virus, it took root in her, too. She ran nervous fingers down her dress. A mug of coffee appeared by her elbow. Grateful for the distraction, she gave Izzeri a quick smile. "Thank you."

As she reached for the cream, the prickling sensation swarming over her grew. Eve looked up and found herself being studied by the cold stranger. There was nothing sexual about his scrutiny, but she understood exactly how a bug under a microscope must feel.

"Eve, this is Lucan." Reynner introduced her. "Luc,

Eve Leighton."

Lucan merely stared in response to her croaked "hello." But there was a note in Reynner's voice that had her glancing at him. Was he irritated? Did he not like the man?

Her questions vanished when she met Reynner's dark, brooding stare. Instantly, memories pulled her back to his room where he'd trapped her against the wall. Her stomach dipped in painful remembrance. But when his gaze blanked out, became unreadable, a pang of regret settled in her.

To give herself something to do, Eve drew the sugar bowl closer. She needed to get her head screwed on right. The only feelings Reynner had for her were ones of revulsion. He must despise her for what she'd unintentionally seen. But the images of the horrid creatures hurting him, and then what that awful woman had done...

Unable to completely shut off those thoughts, she loaded her coffee with several servings of sugar then gulped down half the syrupy brew hoping it would steady her.

The question she'd overheard Aerén ask lingered in her mind. Eve wondered if it was the same reason Reynner wanted to talk to her. Might as well get this over with, then.

She set her coffee down. "What is it you wanted to ask me?"

Reynner focused those night-sky eyes on her. A spark of blue flickered in them. "When you've finished with your meal, meet me in the living room."

He waited until she nodded, then left his half-eaten apple on the countertop and strode from the kitchen, his bare feet soundless on the floor. Eve watched him go, and her brows knitted in confusion at the rough scabs already forming over his wounds.

Yesterday, the wounds had appeared as if they would take weeks—months to mend, and now they were almost healed. How was that possible?

"Reyn, wait." Aerén pushed off his chair and went after him, his boots thudding on the granite floor.

Lucan gave her a long, considering look as if he couldn't believe she was...what? Too lacking? Too simple? Before he too followed the others.

Why couldn't they just ask their darn questions, instead of leaving her to stew in curiosity? For all she knew, Lucan wanted her gone. And Reynner would probably be all too happy to concur.

***

Reynner paced along the balcony. The heavy winds snapped at his unbound hair. He stopped at the ledge and stared at the craggy rock face of the mountains. More than anything, he wanted to fly, to feel the winds gliding over his skin while he cut through the heavy drafts and away from what was to come.

Anger, laden with guilt, twisted his gut. Anger that Eve had seen the very things he despised about himself—his helplessness in the hands of that demoness, his humiliation. And guilt that Eve's scent had him losing control.

Dammit, she shouldn't have been able to see his thoughts. How the hell was that possible? Why had she touched him?

You were thrashing around like an insane bat, dumbass. She was trying to comfort you.

Reynner tried to work through it logically. She'd touched him and saw his nightmares...

If Eve had magic in her blood, then she would have

some kind of psychic ability. *Oh, shit!* Self-recrimination tore through him as understanding sparked. What the hell had he done?

Breathing hard through his nose, he scrubbed his face. Aerén was right, he was a bastard, and he couldn't sink any lower than he did right then. And he'd accused her of deliberately invading his mind.

Lucan came to stand beside him, flanked by Aerén on his other side.

"She's so frail," Lucan said. "I cannot believe our future lies in her hands." He pinched the bridge of his nose. "Tell her, Reyn. If you don't, then I will. We're talking about saving a realm, and you want to wait—for what?"

Reynner's gut churned at the reality. If—no, *when* Eve agreed, he'd take her down a path from which there was no return. He'd bring her into his world, his life, and all the dangers and usual damn shit that went with it.

Demoniis. A goddess determined to get her claws in him. And Darkreans, who'd be only too happy to capture Eve for the chance to awaken the scroll so *they* could locate the missing Stone for whatever the hell they planned.

And the latter could not happen. Ever.

Inhaling the crisp air, he concentrated on the task ahead. He'd ask Eve for her help, if she didn't decide to use his dagger on him. No, *first* he had to apologize for scaring the crap out of her with what he'd done. He knew all too well how to awaken arousal in someone who didn't want it. A pit opened in his belly, but he refused to consider why he felt that way at the thought that she didn't want him.

He had forced her—he'd fucking forced her. He was

no better than the demon bitch, who had done the same to him.

"Eve is mortal. She doesn't even know our kind exists. Her life," he gritted out, "consists of hanging with her friends and visiting art galleries. So unless you want to send her screaming back to her world and lessen our chances of getting her help, you'll have to let me handle this my way."

Lucan glared at him. "No. Now."

Reynner thrust his fists into his pants pockets so he wouldn't cork Lucan in the face. The gusty winds carried the cool sprays from the waterfall and drenched his heated skin but did little to ease his temper.

Then the truth hit him, his blood blazed. "You always knew I'd find her, didn't you?"

That was why Lucan had demanded he go to New York two months ago. So he'd be at the right place, at the right time, and in the right fucking century.

"Did you know?" Aerén asked, coming round to the mage's side. "Why did you not say anything?"

Lucan shrugged. "Nothing about the future is certain. The Stone has been missing for centuries. An intimation of success means nothing if it's not achieved." He cut Reynner a calm stare. "I had to make sure you didn't mess this up. We've waited eons. Sleep with her if you have to, but get her agreement."

Sleep with her? Lucan's words hit too close to the truth of what had nearly happened, even if it was for a different reason.

"You're still the talk of Empyrea. No one can touch your repute when it comes to the females."

Why the fuck was that all anyone remembered about him?

"Shut the hell up, Luc," Reynner snapped. Like he

needed a reminder of his other life. "You have no fucking clue what you're talking about. You live in your damn tower like a closeted virgin, communicating to who the fuck knows for what."

The mage's eyes slitted dangerously. Power surged to swirl around him. "I live in that *tower* because it's the only way I can keep our realm safe and preserve what's left of it. Do your job, Reynner of Ademéras. She wants you. I don't have to be a mage to see that. Your scent already marks her."

Reynner moved like lightning. He grabbed Luc by the throat as the truth hit him. Marking. Like she belonged to him. No-no! "I brought her here for one reason only. I know my fucking obligations—I don't need you to ram it down my throat!"

"It's just your scent, not a bloody bonding," Lucan retorted. "As long as her eyes stay clear—"

"Oh, hell."

At Aerén's soft curse, they both turned. Reynner swore viciously.

Eve stood by the door, staring at them. The winds tugged at her hair and flirted with the hemline of her bright blue-green dress, revealing golden brown thighs Reynner was intimately acquainted with. His heart felt like it would kick through his sternum.

She had to have heard him. Reynner shoved Lucan away.

Fuck! He swore again. He glowered at Lucan, whose only concern was restoring Empyrea back to its formidable state. He didn't care who got trampled along the way. As if their realm would disintegrate within minutes if Eve didn't find the Stone straight off.

"Relax," Lucan said, straightening his shirt. "Unless you've taught her our language, I doubt she understood a word of our conversation. Now go do what you must."

For some reason, he didn't feel relief knowing she didn't understand them. He felt worse, like he'd betrayed her. Dammit, he wasn't deceiving her. He had a job to do. But when he met her wary gaze, everything inside him protested. And Reynner knew he could never do that to her.

Yeah, he'd enlist her help, but he would never seduce her and taint her with the darkness prowling through him.

Chapter 9

Eve struggled to breathe air into flattened lungs, unable to get over her scare. Reynner had almost fallen over the ledge, fighting Lucan. Why the hell didn't he have railings if he chose to live this high up?

She hastily stepped aside as Lucan strode past her, looking like a pissed off panther, short a snarl. He didn't even look at her. Her worry deepened when Aerén merely nodded as he followed, his easy smile missing.

What's going on?

She glanced across to Reynner and found him still at the edge of the balcony, his back to her. The winds lashed at his hair and snapped at his pants, his stance rigid. Whatever they'd been arguing about hadn't left him in a good mood.

"Reynner?"

He turned, raking back the gleaming strands whipping into his face.

For a second, Eve simply stared. Oh, yes, he'd make the perfect subject for her next sculpture, to capture all that wild, raw power harnessed in a solitary figure.

Come on, Eve, get this over with!

Pulling her mind off her work, she stepped out onto the balcony. Her stomach twisted into knots at his grim expression. She had to haul her apology past a throat gone bone-dry, and coughed it out, "I know you're angry at me for what happened last night—"

He stiffened at her words.

Right. Eve straightened her spine. If he didn't care for her apology then she wouldn't waste her time giving it. She grabbed at her flying hemline with impatient hands. "Look, I think I should just leave."

"Last night was…regrettable," he said, his voice flat like his eyes. "But you can't leave. Not yet."

Her chin kicked up. She didn't want his apology or whatever the heck that pitiful excuse was. "I thought it's what you wanted, me gone?"

"You have no idea what the hell I want." A nerve ticked hard in his jaw. "But I do need your help."

"With what?"

"To locate something."

That stumped her for a second. Most times she couldn't even find her own apartment keys, so how in the world would she be any help in locating anything? "I'm not the best person for finding things. I'm more prone to losing them."

"You are the one," he insisted. "The only one who can find the artifact I need. I've searched a long time for you, Eve."

"You have?" Eve shook her head, trying to clear the buzzing sensation in there. If she fell down a rabbit's hole and saw a grinning cat—well, she wouldn't be surprised. Since she'd met Reynner, her life seemed to have gone off-kilter. But his words intrigued her. "What artifact?"

"It's a mystical Stone of Light, one of the seven which disappeared millennia ago."

Mystical stone? This had to be some kind of weird dream. "How can you be sure I'm the person you want?"

"Your blood tells me so."

"M-my blood?"

"Yes. When you hurt your ear, your blood called to me. Then I tasted—"

"Tasted? My *blood*?" Eve backed away in horror, felt as if the ground had shifted beneath her feet. "What-what are you?"

"I'm an Empyrean." He prowled closer. "And yes, I tasted your blood. The second time when you cut your finger, I knew for sure."

Hastily, she took another step back. Her stomach coiled tightly as the truth hit her. "That's why—" she struggled to breathe "—that's why you came after me."

"Yes."

Despite all the confusion and the chaos in her mind, that single word smashed her fragile hope like glass. How could she be so stupid? *That* was the only reason he'd insisted she accompany him when he got hurt. And she thought…

God, she was such a fool.

"Eve—"

She shook her head and took a step back, unable to look at him, mortification burning clear through her brittle emotions. *I guess that's all someone like me can expect.*

Biting her lip, she struggled to lock down the sudden ache in her chest. Hell, she'd just have to get over this, too. She was a survivor, wasn't she?

Dusting her bruised pride, she met his gaze to

decline. Instead, she found herself agreeing. "Fine, I'll help you find your artifact."

Obviously, she was an idiot, too.

His eyes narrowed. "What do you mean '*someone like you?*'"

Christ! She'd said *that* out loud? Was there no end to her embarrassment?

"It's not important. Now, if you don't mind, I'd like to go home." Eve spun for the door.

But Reynner caught her by the arm, hauling her back. She stumbled into his chest and breathed in his warm, heady scent. And the slumbering demon of desire surged again. She really didn't want to be reminded of what she could never have. The brief taste of what could have been would haunt her for the rest of her life.

His hard, dark gaze trapped hers. "I asked you a question."

"I chose not to answer." Eve yanked at her arm in a desperate bid to be free and tripped backwards. She lost her footing and fell...into nothingness. There was no more ground to catch her. The mountains around her went spinning. A strangled cry of sheer terror rushed out of her, the sound swept away by the winds as she plummeted straight down to the gorge below.

"Eve!" Reynner's horrified yell came from far away—too far. He couldn't help her now.

No one could.

Caught in a vortex of spiraling air and roiling terror, she hurtled headlong for the rocks. Eve squeezed her eyes tight as death approached at a chilling speed.

Oh, God—oh, God, let it be quick.

The next moment, hands grabbed her. Her body slammed into something hard, and the familiar scent of cool forest flooded her nose. It couldn't be Reynner. He wasn't going to jump off a ledge and follow her into death.

"Eve, dammit! Talk to me—look at me."

"What did you do?" she cried, flinging her arms around his neck, and tightened them in a deathlock. "Why did you come after me? Now we'll both die."

"No one's dying. For heavens sakes, Eve, open your eyes."

"No. Can't look. I just can't." She buried her face in his neck.

"Eve, look at me, please. I promise we're not going to die...look at me," he coaxed. "Come on, baby," a whisper.

Then, a hair-roughened cheek rubbed against hers, jolting her from her mind-numbing horror. She dragged in a harsh breath and opened her eyes. And blinked. She wasn't hurtling to her death. Instead, they appeared to be hovering in the brisk air. *What the...*

"Thank the heavens." He hugged her tightly. The air she'd managed to inhale whooshed out again.

"Reynner," she whimpered. "Can't breathe."

He eased his hold, and for a moment, she thought she felt as if his lips brush her head. Then she looked over his shoulder. Her thoughts scattered, her mouth dropped open. Wings?

Reynner had *wings*?

Enormous and gleaming bronze, they flared out behind him. Fear gave way to wonder. "You—you have wings."

"What?" His brow furrowed.

Eve didn't answer. Drawn by the beautiful, shimmery tones, she released her chokehold on him and reached over his shoulder to run her palm over the warm arches of the smooth, glossy filaments.

His body jerked, as did his wings, causing them to falter midair. His mouth tightened. His erection stirred against her hips.

Heat flooding her face, Eve yanked her hand back. Her mumbled words of apology whisked away by the winds.

He shook his head. Tone flat, he said, "The inner arches of our wings are sensitive, like certain parts of our body would be to touch."

How stupid of her. Of course, he'd react differently. He wasn't a bird like the dove she cared for and could just touch whenever she felt like. Then reality sank in.

He's not human. Immortal, the thought whipped around her mind. Now it all made sense.

Angels and demons.

"You're staring. Did I grow another head?" he asked as she searched his face, his tempting mouth a whisper away.

"What are you?"

He cut her a sharp look. "What difference does it make? I'm still the same person I was a few minutes ago."

"No. You're not—you're not who I thought you were."

"Gods, Eve, just shut up," he growled, burying his face in her hair. And he held her like she mattered. His wings flapped, and a draft of sheer unadulterated sensuality, wild and masculine, one that was all him, wafted to her.

Eve closed her eyes, absorbing the feel of him—of his hard male body flush against hers.

Not *human*. An *immortal*, her mind repeated, but she didn't care. Sliding her open palm over his shoulder, she let the seductive pull of his warm skin seep through her.

However, the moment didn't last. Reynner set her down on a sun-warmed bedrock, some distance from the waterfalls. He didn't immediately let go of her, though. His dark eyes roamed her face. He tucked a strand of hair behind her ear. "Are you all right?"

She nodded, emotions crowding her, unable to say a single word. Then his arms fell away and he stepped back. Blowing out a rough breath, he prowled along the riverbank as if trying to get himself under control, his stunning wings just about sweeping the ground. The primary flight feathers were a creamy silver, the same color as his hair, and a stunning contrast to the bronze.

Then he swung back to her, eyes blazing now, and still, he looked utterly magnificent. "Don't you ever scare me like that again. Understand? While we're here, you will stay indoors—dammit, Eve, are you listening to me?"

"Yes," she said, her gaze skimming over his dark wings in awe. And realized why she hadn't seen them in his dreams. They'd been concealed by the thick gloom in the cave. "No going onto the balcony—You're an angel."

"Not according to the Empyrean lexicon." Mouth tight, he snapped his wings closed and drew them to his body. With a final shimmer, they disappeared from sight.

Her gaze widened. "Where did they go?"

"They are there, just invisible."

"I don't understand."

"It's an ability we have. It makes it easier when I'm in the mortal world. We are nothing like the humans' concept of angels, Eve. At least not like those in

Heaven. *We*, supposedly, were shaped to resemble the impossible perfection your God created." A mocking note entered his voice. "*We* were meant to be all things perfect. Or, so our creator intended, but flaws will find a way."

"Flaws?" But he was perfect. "I thought God created all angels."

"Your God did. Like Michael."

"Michael is an ang—*the* archangel?"

"Yes."

It all fit, Michael's otherworldly appearance, his glowing eyes.

"Then who er- made you—the Empyreans?"

"Urias." Reynner shoved back his wind-mussed hair and glared at the flowing river. "Spawned off Chaos, he wanted nothing but the perfect race. Seems he forgot everything is about balance. You cannot have yin without the yang. Perfection doesn't come without a price." His bitter words flayed her.

"I'm sorry…"

"It's not your fault." His laugh was harsh, his expression dark as he continued to stare at the river. "Now we must find a way out of this damn mess he created—a way to survive."

"How?"

"Find the Stone first and hope like hell it all works out," he said flatly.

"The artifact you want me to locate—that's what your world needs?" she asked a little stunned.

He nodded. The crashing falls, the only sound between them. Eve wanted to tell him it would be all right, but what the heck did she know about anything. About Reynner's world? She rubbed her arms at the sudden spread of goosebumps and waited. Hoped he'd talk more.

After a long moment, he turned to her. "About last night...I'm sorry."

That took her by surprise. Obviously, it was on his mind, considering how upset he'd been moments ago. Then a blush heated her face, recalling exactly what had occurred in his room. She remained silent.

"You offered comfort while I—" He pinched the bridge of his nose, then lowered his hand. "You didn't have to be subjected to that horror. How bad was it?"

"What?" she asked, wariness creeping back.

"You took in all that shit from me, there had to be repercussions. How bad was it?"

Right, he meant what she'd seen in his memories, not what had happened between them. "I'm okay." Now.

His eyes became blue steel. "Tell me."

A shiver racing over her, Eve wrapped her arms around her waist. "I can feel and see a person's thoughts through touch..."

"And?"

"I saw those monsters hurting you." She didn't want to talk about the terror, the pain she'd felt. She especially didn't want to discuss what she'd seen next, and prayed he wouldn't make her. That horrid woman digging into his wounds and what she'd done to him after... It had only been a brief flash before he'd awakened and shoved her away, but Eve knew...she saw. A lump lodged in her throat.

A harsh expletive left him. "I could have done you lasting damage."

She swallowed, tried to brush it off. "No-no, I'm fine."

"Don't lie, Eve. Don't you lie to me. I saw your

face—the pain! You experienced *every*thing you saw, didn't you?"

She bit her lip and stared silently at him.

Furious, he pivoted and paced the banks again, the muscles of his back vibrating with each breath he took.

Determined to put an end to his self-recriminations, Eve hurried over and stepped in his path. He glared at her. "Stop pacing for a minute and listen to me. *I* am fine. You can see I'm all right. It's you who still suffers."

"I could have hurt you badly," he bit out. "Don't ever touch me again. Understand?"

She searched his tight features. Did he mean don't touch him, period? Or only when he had nightmares? But she had a feeling she knew which. "Yes. I understand." Then she said softly, "If there was a way I could help ease those nightmares, I would. Who was she, the one who did that to you?"

He went motionless for a second before his expression contorted into a mocking one. "I don't need *that* kind of help. With females it always comes with a price. Don't expect anything more from me, Eve."

Her temper flared. Is that what he thought? Okay, maybe she did want him, but that didn't mean she'd chase after any man.

"Did I ask you for anything?" she snapped, "I don't have to be an empath to get your 'keep off' message loud and clear, Reynner. You wear it like a damn shroud."

Annoyed, Eve spun away, but he grasped her arm and hauled her back. His taut features a scant inch from hers. "The one who did that to me? Who trapped me in that godforsaken hole? She's dead. A demoness whom I took great pleasure in beheading before incinerating her. She will never rise again."

Eve swallowed. The brutality of his words just about stopped her heart. Just about, but it did little to tone down her irritation. "Is that supposed to frighten me?"

"It'd better. I'm not human."

Yes, she knew that...now. Knew how lethal he could be, too. She shrugged. "I'm not scared of you. Not scared of dying either. I am mortal, I cannot escape that, so your threats hold no substance."

His gaze darkened at her words. "Don't push me, Eve. Don't."

Unable to bear his touch, she pulled free. "Why are you so angry with me? You've painted a clear picture of what you want. So, yes, I got it—you need my help, nothing else. So why?"

His lips compressed. A tick beat hard in his jaw. She wasn't surprised by his silence, it wasn't like he'd open up now and spill all to her.

A movement in her peripheral view hauled her out of her frustration, and she found Aerén heading for them.

"Eve—" His gaze skimmed over her in concern. "You gave me one helluva scare falling off the balcony like that. When Reynner did not come back—" He shook his head as if he expected the worst.

Eve forced a smile when it was the last thing she felt like doing. "I'm fine, Aerén."

"Take her back," Reynner instructed Aerén.

He was sending her off with Aerén?

Eve's heart dipped at how easily he'd dismissed her. She straightened her spine, but couldn't stop her irritation from spewing out. "Don't you dare think to shove me off to someone else because you have no answer for me. I'm not some chew-toy for you to toss aside because you don't like what I say—"

"You sure you want to take me on, little Eve?"

She hated when he called her that in that taunting manner, more that she'd lost her temper. Eve stomped off.

Stopping several feet from the crystal clear water of the plunge pool, she wrapped her arms around her shaky body.

Aerén came up beside her. "You okay?"

She glanced over her shoulder, but Reynner had disappeared. She blew out a ragged breath. "I'm fine."

"That bad, huh?" Aerén teased.

"I'm sorry. I don't usually get this mad, but Reynner…"

"No apologies necessary. I've been living with him for a few months. This is the most emotion he's shown, which, trust me, is good."

And just like that, her remaining anger fizzled out. A pang opened up inside her. If those nightmares were what drove him, no wonder he'd shut down his emotions—shut her out.

Shut her out?

When had he let her in? The distance Reynner put between them stretched as vast as the universe. It was an expanse he'd never willingly cross, she realized, not after what had been done to him.

"It's good to have you here, Eve," Aerén said, pulling her out of an impossible longing, a sudden twinkle in his light eyes.

"Oh, really?"

"Absolutely. Had I attempted what you just did, he'd have drawn his sword on me. To see him faced off by a female made my day. Come, my lady, let's get you back to the aerie."

Aerén made her want to smile. It occurred to her then that he was immortal, too.

"How did you get here? I didn't hear you fly down—where are your wings?"

He grinned. "I don't possess any. Don't worry, my mode of travel is far safer. You can't fall."

Can't fall? "What do you—"

Aerén grasped her hand. The next instant, everything around her swirled, spun, and she was sucked into a world of swirling opaqueness, her shriek echoing in her ears.

Chapter 10

They took form on the balcony moments later. Eve lurched forward on unsteady feet. Aerén grabbed her before she fell flat on her face.

"Whoa, easy there. Eve, are you all right?"

"Don't know...when I find my head...maybe."

"Hold onto me." He helped her into the living room. She collapsed on the couch, lowered her head between her legs, and moaned as bile fought for freedom.

"Be right back." Aerén disappeared. Then reappeared a few seconds later. "Here."

She lifted her head. "What did you do to me?"

"I don't possess wings, so I had to dematerialize with you. Drink this, it will help."

A little shaky, Eve took the glass he offered. She sipped the light golden liquid. The sharp sweet taste of ginger tea slid down her throat, making her eyes water. She wrinkled her nose. Ack, she far preferred ginger ale to this horrid mixture.

The queasiness easing, she eyed Aerén. "So you're an Empyrean, too?"

"I am." He sank on the couch opposite her and

propped a booted foot on the pretty, dark wood coffee table, which someone had created from slicing a large tree-trunk in half. "But not all of us acquire wings. Unless one parent is a Fallen from the Celestial Realm. But even that is no guarantee."

Slowly, Eve set her glass on the table. "What do you mean?"

"When a divine angel and an Empyrean mate, their offspring can be born with wings."

"Like Reynner?"

"Yes. His father is a divine and consort to his mother, who rules over Ademéras—" Aerén broke off as Lucan walked into the lounge. The air around him shimmered with power.

He stopped a few feet from Eve. "Reynner has spoken to you about the Stone?"

Ugh, she'd far prefer hearing more about Reynner's life than face this man. "He did, but are you sure I can find this object for you?"

"Yes. It will only respond to a mortal whose blood sings."

She gave him a dubious look. "Sings? What are you talking about?" She couldn't even carry a tune without sounding like a dying frog.

"Not literally," Lucan said, impatient now. "Your lifeblood resonates with the supernatural. It's a quiet hum that flows in your blood but will vibrate within our psyche if one of us tastes it. Our world fades. We need to find the Stone to restore the balance of magic."

"I see…" No, she didn't. She really didn't. Why couldn't her blood be like everyone else's and just carry oxygen to her heart? Eve inhaled deeply, not ready for any of this. She pushed to her feet, needing to keep moving, then stopped. "Wait, does this have anything to do with 'the mess' Reynner spoke about? About finding a way to exist in your world? Is your world truly dying?"

Lucan's turquoise eyes sparked with quiet anger. "It is. The white cliffs of Empyrea have started to fade since the Stone disappeared over a millennium ago—"

"What he means is that life ebbs from us," Aerén explained, pulling her gaze back to him. "Children haven't been born in thousands of years. Being who we are, we don't have many offspring, which only bonded pairs are blessed with. We need to find the missing Stone to strengthen the realm, or our race will disappear."

"A Stone," Eve repeated, overwhelmed by all they were telling her.

"Yes," Aerén said, rising to his feet. "All realms contain magic, even the mortal one. Except it's not vital to human survival. We require both, magic and light. Our magic stems from the seven mystical Stones of Light, which reside in the white cliffs of Empyrea. With one lost, the link is broken. It's why we desperately need your aid."

She stared blankly at him, her mind in a whirl. "How…how can something that important just disappear?"

Aerén's jaw tightened. "With the ongoing war with the Darkreans' fight for power, the Stones cannot exist in negative energy."

"Wouldn't it be better to just have a truce with your enemy, then?"

"Does it work that easily in your realm?" Lucan's tone dropped to a lovely degree of sub-zero.

Okay, the iceberg had a point. Eve began to pace again, unable to breathe at the sheer enormity of what they were asking of her. "You can't—you can't just drop the burden of your dying world on me."

"So you won't help us?" Lucan's expression chilled further.

"Eve." Aerén touched her arm and stopped her marching. "We've searched a long time for you. You are our only hope."

"I already told Reynner I would help..." She rubbed her cold, damp palms down her dress. "If I don't find this Stone, if anything happens to your world, I'm not taking the blame for it," she warned and moved away to stare out the window. God, when Reynner asked for her assistance, she had no idea it would be this immense. Scary. What if she failed?

Then something else clicked in her mind, and she spun back. "You said children haven't been born in thousands of years...how old are you?"

A twinkle lightened Aerén's somber gaze. "In mortal years, it's difficult to determine. Time moves differently for us."

"Centuries?"

He smiled.

"Millennia?"

A chuckle left him. "So curious. We are a lot older than you are."

At Aerén's teasing, Lucan snapped, "If you feel it's that important to know, we are thousands of years old."

Eve stopped breathing. These men—agh, immortals, were so old it made her feel insignificant with her few measly decades. Lucan and Reynner appeared to be in their late twenties. But who was counting a few thousand years?

At Aerén's hint of a smirk, she scrunched her nose. No wonder he'd been amused when she'd so righteously told him that she was older. She must seem a child to him.

"We had no idea which century you'd be born in," Lucan said, his irritation replaced once more by his glacial demeanor. "So we had to keep searching because the Stone will only respond to you."

"Yeah, I don't get that. If something this important belongs to your world, wouldn't it call to your own kind to find it?"

"No," Reynner said, striding into the room. "It won't."

Eve turned, and her heart missed a beat. Dressed in unrelieved black, he took her breath away with that stunning face and shoulder-length sweep of pale hair. Tossing his biker jacket on the couch, his cool gaze met hers.

"It will respond only to the magic in your blood. A safety precaution against it being found by an immortal who would wield it for a purpose other than its original one."

Bad—evil things, that's what he meant. Eve rubbed her buzzing temples, surprised she didn't have a raging headache.

Okay, focus, Eve. She resumed her stressed walk around the room.

How difficult could this be, finding a Stone?

Eve dropped her hand from her head and discovered all eyes on her. Didn't that just make her want to run?

"Fine, tell me where it is. I'll go get it."

Reynner shook his head. "Searching for the artifact isn't that simple."

Artifact? Wait, that meant it was probably priceless and well protected. *Oh, no, this can't be good.* "For the love of God, tell me I don't have to break into someone's home, or worse a...a museum?"

At the heightened silence, her belly rebelled. Of course. Why would it be that easy?

She swung around and stared at the mountains, and just as fast she spun back. "Where am I? Yes, I know you said Exilum. Wait"—she gulped—"are we even on Earth?"

"No," Reynner answered. "You're just beyond the veils of the mortal realm, accessible only through a portal."

The air rushed out of her lungs. "You-you took me away from my world without even telling me?"

"Right, almost unconscious, and in an alley crawling with demoniis is the perfect place for explanations."

She scowled. "Don't you dare throw your sarcasm at me. You could have just asked."

"I *asked*—" A tic worked his jaw. He looked more than pissed. "*You* agreed."

Aerén stepped between them. "Eve, I promise, it will be okay. I'll be your protector during the quest if needs be."

"She's min—my responsibly," Reynner's voice turned cold. Deadly. No hint of the heated fury she'd witness moments ago. "Stay the hell out of this, Aerén."

"You're upsetting her," he retorted. "I won't have that." Aerén turned back to her. "Eve—"

"I'm all right." Her frustration seeped out, leaving her drained and weary.

When Reynner had asked her in the alley, she had no idea what he truly meant. She realized then even if she had known the facts, she still would have come. He'd been hurt and *that* she couldn't stomach.

God, what a mess! Rubbing a shaky hand over her

face, she turned away, and much to her misfortune met Lucan's cool, watchful gaze.

"How you came to be here is irrelevant," he said. "What matters are the scroll and the Stone. Since the artifacts have a symbiotic link, to locate the latter, you must first retrieve the former."

Eve blinked. "*Scroll?*" Her gaze rushed right back to Reynner. "What is he talking about? What scroll?"

"You did not tell her?" Lucan demanded.

Reynner ignored him. "We know where the damn thing is—"

"Then why didn't you tell me?" she countered.

"Where was the time, Eve?" A growl. "We were attacked by demoniis. I was knocked out, healing. You fell off the balcony—you nearly died!"

When he put it like that. "Fine. Where is this scroll?"

Aerén glanced at Reynner, as did Lucan. No one spoke.

Ack, men! "Please, don't all answer at once."

Reynner pushed his hands into his pockets, probably to stop himself from wringing her neck. She folded her arms across her chest, held his stare, and waited.

"The Museum of Natural History," he finally said.

Her mouth dropped open. "Are you crazy? How am I supposed to steal the scroll from the most popular museum in New York, with a crapload of security, and come out of this without being thrown behind bars for the rest of my mortal life?"

"Stop being so melodramatic. You won't get caught," Reynner muttered. "I'll be with you. Now, we're leaving." He snatched his jacket and stalked from the room.

Eve glowered at the empty doorway. The man was maddening, impossible and…and still he drew her like a helpless moth.

She stifled a massive sigh. No matter how mad she was with Reynner, she would get them what they needed... Yeah, break into a museum.

Ugh, she pushed that stomach-turning thought aside.

"Come, Eve, I'll see you to the front," Aerén said.

Rubbing a weary palm over her face, she followed him.

***

Reynner stopped at the edge of the balcony and scowled at the forest below him. Eve had to be the most argumentative female he'd ever met. Instead of yelling accusations at him and questioning everything he said, all she had to do was trust him to get her into the museum to take the scroll.

And just how long did it take for her to say goodbye to Aerén?

It sure as hell couldn't be Lucan who held her attention. His lips thinned at the thought of her being in his prince's too eager arms. About to go haul her, the sounds of footsteps reached his ears.

"Reynner?"

His gut tightened at the sound of her voice. He turned to find Aerén walking away, and Eve hesitating near the door. He motioned for her to join him with a nod. "Come."

She bit her lip, her gaze dipping to the ledge.

It hit him then. She was afraid. What the hell was he thinking? She'd fallen off this damn balcony. If he hadn't been here... *Shit.* Good thing she wouldn't have to come back here again. Having wings, he needed the balcony railless to take flight and make landing easier.

He crossed to her. "I won't let you fall, I promise. Take my hand."

Her chest rose as she inhaled, then barefoot, she stepped out. Ignoring his hand, she clenched the fabric of her dress, instead. "I'm fine."

Despite her usual "*I'm fine*" answer, he saw the edges of fear in her deep green eyes. The fact she could walk onto the balcony again after this morning awed him.

Well, he wasn't letting her do this alone.

Reynner untangled her fingers from her dress, grasped her hand, and pulled her close. The bumpy skin from her childhood injuries slid roughly against his palm... Darker memories of manacles restraining him took over—pain slicing through his wrists. The muscles in his shoulders tensed, he forced himself to focus and not push her away. He breathed in her scent, and a calm descended. With his mind, he gathered the light energies of the realm around him. The air shimmered, parted, and the portal opened.

He glanced at her. "Ready?"

Despite her uneasy expression, she nodded, her gaze fastened on the wavering gateway. "Where will this take us?"

"Central Park. From there, I'll dematerialize us straight to your apartment." At her strangled breath, he said, "Or I can send you to sleep and do this."

"No." Her fingers tightened on his. "Let's get it over with."

***

As twilight stole into the city, Reynner followed Eve into her fourth-floor apartment. And felt like he'd stepped into an orchard.

A hint of her peach scent drifted through the place and stroked his senses. His body wired hard since last night, he'd found it difficult to clamp down on needs that refused to settle, and now, alone in her home, it was damn near impossible.

She's here for one purpose only—to help our realm. Aerén's words chimed like an unwanted omen in his head. With centuries of practice locking down his emotions, he managed to get his mind back on track.

Eve disappeared into her room.

Reynner turned and took in the open space. Brightly painted sketches, mounted in black, lined one wall. Colorful Navajo throws in shades of blue, orange, and gray cheered up the ancient brown couch and armchairs. A circular glass-top dining table situated opposite the counter separated the galley kitchen from the rest of the place.

Supernatural beings couldn't come into a human home uninvited, but still. He went back to the front door, and with an intricate movement of his hands, he weaved the wards, whispering the enchanted words as he put up a protection shield. Invisible to the human eye, he could feel its magic flow over the apartment.

Eve would be safe as long as she didn't invite the fuckers inside.

Satisfied, he made his way across the room to the few pieces of metal sculpture Eve had displayed on a small bookcase crammed with paperback novels. But a photo in a copper frame caught his attention. Picking it up, he studied the couple posing in front of the souks of…Morocco. He'd been there and knew the place well.

"That's my parents. I dangle between both worlds," Eve said, coming back into the room.

He could see that. Her mixed-race heritage was visible in her skin that was a lighter shade of her mother's aged gold, but she'd inherited her dark green eyes from her father. However, instead of the tall, robust build of her father, or her mother's curviness, Eve appeared fragile, delicate.

Reynner looked up. His heart tripped. Eve had reached across the counter and was plugging in her cell to recharge. Her top shifted, revealing a hand-span of gorgeous tan skin.

He wanted to walk over, slide his palms on her bare skin while he ran his lips down every inch of her...

"My dad was an archaeologist," she said, oblivious to just how close to the edge he was. "He met Mom while on a dig in Morocco, fell in love, and married her."

Hell, he never should have tasted her, now it was all he could think of—

His jaw hardening, he forced his mind off dangerous needs. Setting the frame aside, he picked up the metal sculpture of a horse rearing up on its hind legs. The untamed wildness, the energy of the animal captured in the metal molding was exquisite...and full of life, just like the artist.

His gaze drifted back to her. "Where do you craft these?"

She'd opened a plastic container and was scooping up something in her hand. "I have a studio in a warehouse down the street next to this building."

"You have a rare gift."

She cast him a surprised look as if praise were the last thing she'd expected. "Thanks. That's just something I did for myself. You can have it if you'd like."

He stared at the sculpture. Her generosity touched something deep inside of him. It took Reynner a moment to collect himself. Usually, gifts always came with a price tag—namely him.

"Eve?" He waited until she looked at him. "Don't ever invite anyone you don't know into your home. No immortal can enter without an invitation. But I put up a protection ward, too. An added precaution."

She blinked, then nodded. "Oh… Okay. The only ones who come here anyway are my friends." She shut the container and disappeared from sight.

Following the sound of her voice, the horse gripped tightly in his hand, he found her kneeling on the kitchen floor. A shoebox with one side cut out was layered with…straw? Fresh breadcrumbs were scattered in a corner.

"Hey there, little guy. I'm sorry I wasn't here," she said softly, caressing the bird's wing with a gentle finger dusted with crumbs.

And his cock hardened again, the same way it had this morning when Eve had stroked his wing. She'd had no idea what she'd done. He'd been moments from taking her right there in the air. Her tender touch had diminished the nightmares that usually sprung up when anyone touched his wings. But Eve, with her innocence and gentleness, had made him forget, even if it was for a brief moment.

He set the horse on the counter and crouched beside her, his leathers creaking.

"He won't fly," she told him, "and he doesn't seem to be hurt—" She broke off when he reached for the bird and eyed him with concern.

Did she think he'd hurt her pet or tackle her to the floor with the bird as witness?

Reynner picked up the dove and scanned it, then zoomed in on the injury. He let his power flow out of him to heal the hairline fracture he found in the fragile skeleton of its wing. The silvery blue light coalesced into the wound, and, moments later, the bird flew out of his palm, a flutter of wings filling the apartment.

A startled laugh escaped Eve. "What did you do?"

"He had a small crack in his humerus bone. It affects the flight muscle, it's why he became grounded."

"I didn't know. I thought he liked staying with me. Thank you."

He saw the guilt on her face. She'd grown attached to the avian. "No one could have known," he reassured her, then added softly, "You have to let him go, Eve."

Her mouth opened as if to protest, then closed. She nodded. Rising to her feet, she walked over to where the bird settled on the low wooden beam of the ceiling and tried to coax him down.

Reynner followed her. "Eve, it's safer if you step away." She wouldn't like what would happen standing under a perched bird.

"Why?" She frowned at him, looked back at the creature and enchanting color surged across her face. Hastily, she backed away, a wry curve to her lips. "Right."

Her smile beckoned him like a flame. He could feel his control cracking. Shit, too risky, he had to get out of here. He lifted his hand and willed the bird to him. It swooped down to grasp his finger with its tiny talons. Reynner headed for the door. "I'll see you later."

"Wait." He heard her light footsteps hurrying after him. "What about the scroll? Aren't we supposed to stake out the museum or something?"

He turned, bird cupped in his hands. "You're not staking out anything. I'll do the legwork, get you in, you take the scroll, and that's it."

Her eyes narrowed thoughtfully. "You tried to take it

before, didn't you?"

"Yes, we attempted to, but when one like us touches it, it disappears. We let it be, but kept track of it over the centuries."

"And if it doesn't respond to me?"

"So easy you forget why it will: your blood."

At his brusque tone, her mouth tightened. She lowered her gaze to the bird. "I'll take him."

Gently, she scooped the bird from him, her fingers brushing his. He jerked back—felt like a thousand volts had hit him hard in the chest. Her gaze flickered to his, hurt crossing her face. If she only knew the sad bloody truth—it had nothing to do with her damn scars—he could barely be close to her, without wanting to touch her.

"I'll see you later. I have to pick up my car." He strode out, the door banging shut behind him.

Outside the apartment, Reynner dematerialized to the backstreet where the car he'd acquired on the day he went to the gallery was parked—still safe with the protection spell he'd cast on it, which had been more for Eve's safety.

He dragged in a deep breath and tried to get his aroused body to calm down. He leaned against the grimy building and hoped a couple of demoniis would troll his way.

He needed a godsdamn fight, needed to work off his frustration.

Shoving his hands into his pocket, his fingers brushed against a piece of metal. He drew it out and ran his thumb around Eve's earring. The essence of her imprinted on the gold loop seeped into him... The taste of her branded in his memory...her hands clamped in his hair while he had his mouth on her...

Hunger, raw and wild took hold. His fingers tightened around the earring—his jaw clenched so hard, it was a miracle his molars didn't crack.

He dropped the earring back in his pocket. *She's off limits.*

His was a soul trapped in endless darkness, not something any sane person would want to take on. Besides, he'd never trust a female enough to even try. He'd rather cut off his balls first.

A sudden spike of familiar pain spread from his chest and he gnashed down on his teeth. Godsdamn Inanna, she was back to her fucking stunts.

Pulling in a harsh breath, Reynner tried to ride out the shitstorm just as an odd vibe brushed his psyche. He scanned his surroundings. No sulfur, definitely not demoniis or humans, so who the fuck was following him?

Lowering his shields, Reynner tracked on the psychic plane. That strange sensation swept through him again, one he couldn't quite place. He pushed off from the wall and headed out of the alley. In a flash, Reynner disappeared into a recessed doorway and dematerialized. And took form in front of his stalker with the white-tipped mohawk.

"Dark— *shit*!" Reynner's voice dried off. His gut churned. Only those emotionless bastards would dare to look him in the eyes and not care that he could kill them. And he was so in the mood for an all-out fight.

"Guess that makes you *light*…shit?" the male drawled.

"Why the fuck are you on my ass," Reynner snapped.

"I don't roll that way. But if you're willing—" He struck, head-butting Reynner. Stars exploded behind his eyelids.

Reynner lashed out and landed a solid blow to the Darkrean's belly. He crashed into the building with a hollow thud, cursing. Not so emotionless, after all. Grabbing him by the scruff of his collar, Reynner drew out his dagger. He flipped the blade in the air, caught the hilt, and pressed the edge against the Darkrean's throat. It meant little to him to end this asshole's life, but for the fact the Darkreans would be on his ass for killing one of their own. And he wanted answers. He scanned the icicle in his grip for information. But their damn shields were just as strong as an Empyrean's.

"What are you doing here, on this realm?" Like he didn't know.

His expression guileless, Mohawk panted, "Mortal females are way too tempting—"

"You don't want to fuck with me, Darkrean."

A sly smirk rode the male's face. "Let me make this real easy for you, since you seem to have lost your rational mind being away from Empyrea so long. What you have, we want. The foretold one."

"Not happening." Icy, thread-like fingers slithered into Reynner's head. At the psychic intrusion, he snarled.

Mohawk laughed. "I know her face."

Fury pouring off Reynner, he smashed Mohawk in the face with a power-driven fist. The Darkrean's head hit the wall behind him with a resounding crack, and he slid to the ground, lights out.

Reynner stepped back, breathing hard, his fingers clenched.

Did the bastard really think he'd just hand Eve over? He'd kill the emotionless fucker first. No one touched what was his.

And she sure as hell was, even if he couldn't claim her!

Chapter 11

Once healed, the bird wouldn't settle, it flew all over her apartment, causing a ruckus.

Reynner was right, she had to set the dove free. The moment she opened the window, sensing freedom, it flew off.

A little despondent and unable to relax, Eve headed for her studio in the short, dead-end alley next to her building. The heavy heat almost suffocated her. Fitting for the mood she was in. Three hours had passed, and Reynner hadn't come back.

He doesn't need a keeper, Eve.

How could she forget? Her fingers tightened around her can of Fanta. He'd made it clear he wanted nothing from her. He didn't need anyone, it seemed, only her help in committing a felony. She had to stop thinking about him. His time here, with her, was momentary.

Eve turned into the narrow street and stopped farther down at a worn, brick building. The shrubs in the ceramic pots she'd arranged near the entrance to her studio detracted from the dinginess. She unlocked the door and disarmed the security system. A flick of the switch and bright lights flooded the interior of her workplace, revealing the madness—or her "artistic creativeness," as she called it.

An eclectic mix of everything metallic inhabited her studio. Shelves set against rough brick walls held her inventory of metals and sheets.

Several of her finished works stood on the far side. The familiar acrid odor of soldered metal combined with the earthy smell of timber drifted to her. She headed for her worktable, skirting an enormous skein of fine copper wire lying on the floor, and left her Fanta, keys, and cell phone on the wooden surface.

Crossing to the life-size sculpture she was almost done with, she studied the figure. Ribbons of metal in various shades interwove with each other, emphasizing the man's muscular physique, caught in the middle of swinging a sword. The guy, it seemed, loved swords. It was a commissioned piece for Brenna's friend, who wanted to gift her husband with something unusual for their ten-month anniversary.

It made Eve realize just how empty her life was. Why did she have to meet the one man she wanted, who was so far out of her reach in every possible way?

She pulled back her hair and bunched it into a haphazard ponytail. Her cell went off. *Like a Virgin* erupted in the quiet like a bad omen.

God, she really hated the tune. She snatched her cell, answered. "Hel—"

"Dammit, Eve, next time answer your darn phone," Kataya's annoyed voice blasted her ear. "At least let us know you're alive."

Guilt flooded Eve. Of course, her friends would be concerned and want to hear how it all went. She'd seen their missed calls, but couldn't bear to talk about what had happened. She'd rather eat a tub of slimy snails.

"I'm sorry, Kat. I meant to call, but I got stuck in my work and time just got away from me."

"You're telling me you left with the hunk and nothing happened? Yeah, right," she said, disbelief rampant in her tone. "Now spill. Gimme the deets. What happened during the weekend?"

The weekend? It seemed like a lifetime ago.

"Nothing much," Eve evaded. "We spoke, and he dropped me off at home—"

"Are you freakin' kidding me?" Kataya exploded, making her wince.

"No. Or I would have called you earlier," Eve fibbed. But her mind flashed to him pinning her against the wall in his bedroom and heat licked through her veins—she struggled to shut off the thought. "I was busy, Kat. You know I have a show coming up."

"Oh…" A defeated sigh. "Just as well, then. David's probably a better bet anyway."

"Look, I have to go. So much to do. Talk to you soon." Eve hung up, tossed her cell back on the table, and scrubbed her face with her hands.

God, David—she had a date with him. After Reynner, she couldn't think of anyone else.

Work. She needed to work. It was the one area of her life she could actually lose herself in and forget for a while.

She switched on the CD player that stayed on a shelf. And as heavy rock music took over the silence, Eve pulled out the materials she needed to finish the final piece for her show; the reclining nude Brenna had posed for. She gathered the rusty, scrapyard chains she required and set them nearby then started to screw on several lengths of rusty links, depicting Brenna's bobbed hair.

A while later, she stepped back and surveyed the sculpture. Strips of metal and skeins of wire intertwining made up the body. Grueling work, but she liked the eye-catching results.

Finally. All her pieces were ready for her show. She'd so much invested in this. Before she started panicking at just *how* much, she dragged out a wooden pedestal and started on a new project.

But thoughts of him took hold once more, possessed her, like she was under some spell. Memories haunted her of being trapped by his warm body, his mouth...

The sudden silence jolted her back to her surroundings.

"Eve?"

At the sound of his voice, she squeezed her eyes tight because she'd been locked in thoughts best forgotten. Spine stiff, she glanced over her shoulder.

"Where's your cell?" Reynner asked, his voice even, but his features appeared molded in stone as he moved away from the CD player he'd switched off.

"Table."

He picked up her phone, and his fingers flew across the display as he entered something into it.

"How did you find me?"

"You said you had a place here. When you didn't answer at your apartment, I was concerned. Next time, Eve, don't leave without me. You have my number now. Use it." He set the phone back on the table.

He'd been worried about her?

Only because you have to find the artifact for him.

She yanked a twisted piece of metal free from the sculpture and tossed it aside. "I had work to do. Besides, I'm not used to anyone keeping track of my whereabouts."

"That was before. Now, I expect to know."

At the undercurrent of steel in his tone, Eve opened her mouth to inform him just what she thought of that idea, and bumped into his unyielding gaze. She swallowed her irritation. "Well, I can't oblige you, I'm an artist, inspiration strikes at any time."

"Dammit, Eve—"

"How did you get in?" she cut him off.

"I don't need a key to do so," he muttered. Picking up her soda, he drank some.

While sugar would probably sweeten his mood, Eve had to force her gaze away from his lips, aware of what that mouth of his could do.

"What are you working on?"

She studied her new project. The pieces of metal fused together depicted nothing but a clutter of snaking strips at the moment. "A sculpture."

She rose from the bench she'd been seated on. With her foot, she pushed the loose metal aside.

"I can see that. What is it going to be? Bird, tree—"

"A man," she said abruptly.

Silence. "Who?"

"A…friend."

"I see…"

Her gaze flashed to him. But those dark eyes had settled on the nude sculpture of Brenna. "Do your subjects pose for you?"

Why was he pushing this? "Yes. What's with the twenty questions, Reynner?"

He sauntered over. Stopping an inch from her, his cool gaze met hers. "He only comes when I am here."

She scowled. "Let's get one thing straight. You're here for one reason only, and that's to find your artifact. When it comes to *my* life—*my* work, it's off limits!"

She spun away in frustration. God, he made her so mad. All his little rules, one would think he was jealous. But she knew better. He just didn't want her distracted until she found his precious Stone!

"You're angry."

"You think?" She swung back, snatched her soda from him. "Shouldn't you go home? You'll want to be well rested before the big B&E."

He shrugged off her snarky comment about breaking and entering to say, "I'm staying here with you."

Eve choked on her drink she just sipped. Coughing, she swiped at her mouth with the back of her hand and glared at him. "No, you're not. Exilum is just a portal away from this world. You don't even have clothes here."

He cut her a bland look. "That's covered. Izzeri will bring my things over later. Until this is over, I will remain with you. For your own safety."

"My safety? Who'd want to harm me?" The only hazardous thing in this entire venture, besides ruining her untarnished reputation, was getting her heart broken. And she had a feeling she was already on the path leading to heartache.

"We have enemies, Eve. Dangerous ones."

"Who?"

"Darkreans. I came across one of them following me this evening. Bastard got your image from my mind. I won't leave you unprotected."

"So *you* put me in danger?"

His expression darkened. "You are the foretold one. If I hadn't found you first, they would have."

Eve pressed a hand to her tummy, a thread of fear

slithering through her.

Reynner slid a warm, calloused palm on her nape and gently kneaded the tension there with his fingers. His gaze held hers in promise. "I will keep you safe."

The sheer magnetism of him constricted her chest. With Reynner living in her apartment, how was she to pretend he was just another person—when he was all she wanted?

Breaking away from his hold, Eve picked up her keys, pushed her cell into her sweats pocket and headed for the door. Right now, distance was safer. "I'm done for the night."

After she'd locked up her studio, they walked up the alley. Reynner said, "And just so you know, we're *taking* the scroll. Not stealing it."

"Not where the museum is concerned," she retorted. "In their minds, it belongs to them. And what are the plans for this heist? All thieves have something concocted. If I'm to become one, I demand to know the details. I won't walk in blindly."

"Why are you being difficult?" His voice held a note of impatience. "We're not stealing the damn thing. It did once belong to us. When the Stone vanished, the scroll disappeared from the mage's tower only to resurface several centuries ago in this world."

She cut him a curious glance…then understanding dawned. "And you've been keeping track of it all this time."

A terse nod, even though it wasn't a question. "It remained in the Louvre. Except for the odd times it's been on loan to other institutes. Now, it's on exhibit here as part of the Ancient Artifact collection. Tomorrow night, we'll get it."

"I remember reading about the exhibition. No—"

She halted beneath a streetlight. "Tell me you're not planning to steal the thing while it's still on exhibit?"

***

"No. The exhibition ended today." Reynner dragged in a deep breath, then another, and concentrated on Eve.

The flare of pain on his left pec felt like he was being doused in acid. It had been growing steadily ever since he'd fought the Darkrean. Damn Inanna!

When he could speak again, he said, "The scroll will go into storage, ready for shipping. It's safer to get into the storerooms than the main museum."

"Good."

At the sudden chagrined expression on her face when she realized what she'd just said, amusement tugged at his lips. She glowered like a riled kitten. "My life's truly screwed now. I have just agreed to your insane idea." She stomped off.

By the heavens, pissed off or not, everything about her drew him in like a magnet. One he had little resistance against. He pushed his hands into his pockets and caught up with her.

As they turned up the street toward her apartment, he asked the question that had been on his mind since the demonii attack. "The night after we left the gallery, you told your friends you felt nothing for me?"

Her embarrassment enclosed him like a thick cloud. "You heard me?"

"Eve, I'm immortal. Heightened senses are a given. What did you mean by that, *not feeling anything*?"

She cut him a wary look. "Just that when I touched you that first time, I wasn't drawn into your mind and thoughts. I sensed nothing. No emotions, no pain, for the first time ever."

"So you've never touched anyone since you received

that power?"

"It's a curse," she said, her expression dimming. "I can't touch the people I love. Dating is a disaster, so I rarely did, until Da—" She broke off. Delicate color rushed across her face. He could see her blush clearly, even with just the moonlight.

"Until the artist," he finished.

"Yes, until David," she agreed.

Reynner reined in the urge to go after the male and shake him 'til his teeth rattled. He'd told Eve in Exilum not to look at him for more, so he had no right to interfere. No cause to be angry. But that didn't mean he had to like it.

The pain on his pec intensified, and he welcomed it this time. It was damn good incentive to get his mind off Eve.

Once back in the apartment, Eve dropped her things on the dining table and headed for the kitchen. She hadn't said much to him, except to ask him if he was hungry. He wasn't, but sheer perverseness made him say yes. And forced her to remain with him.

"Fanta or Pepsi," she asked, opening the fridge.

She gave him the Pepsi he asked for and started on whatever she was preparing for him. Setting the soda on the countertop, he braced his palms on the granite surface. The sizzling aroma of mushrooms and onions soon teased his nostrils.

To get his mind off the agony inside him, he asked, "What is the "dreaded V" your friends spoke about?"

If he hadn't been watching her, he'd have missed the slight stiffening of her spine. She picked up the egg mixture and poured it into the skillet. A snappy hiss saturated the air. "Nothing important."

The fact that she wouldn't look at him… Oh, yes, it

was. He'd bet his dominion on it.

Reynner struggled to keep his breathing even as the pain multiplied, like red-hot pokers piercing his chest. As always, it became a test of wills. He resisted her summons, and Inanna just upped his torment.

Right now, he far preferred looking at Eve. At least it took his mind off what had to be done soon.

She set down the spatula and dipped a hand into a clear jar half-filled with multicolored beans. She took a few, popped them in her mouth and turned back to the stove. Scooping up the grated cheese, she sprinkled it on the eggs. "Since you insist on staying, you can use the bedroom on the left."

At the reluctant offer, he didn't say anything. Besides, he rarely slept, not when nightmares plagued him. If he had a choice, her bed would be the only one he wanted to rest in.

The strains of the accursed binding tugged hard, winding him tighter as the burn peaked. His head lowered, his hands clenched the counter.

"What is it?"

He looked up and found her concerned gaze skimming over his face.

It floored him that she would put her own troubles aside, and worry about him.

Reynner wished he were clean and untainted, able to walk over and take her into his arms, like he'd wanted to do from the first moment he crashed into her. Because she truly was all things good. But his life was not his own, not when he was tied to a malicious goddess.

He shook his head, the damn star on his chest hurting like hell. If he didn't leave now, Inanna could very well come looking for him, and if she saw Eve—no, he would never put her in harm's way.

"I have to go. I'll be back."

Eve opened her mouth then clamped it shut. He'd seen the questions she wanted to ask, reflected in her eyes. Not like he could give her any answers.

She stared at the pan for an excruciatingly long second before nodding. Then she switched off the stove and covered the skillet with a lid. "Your meal is in here. Goodnight."

Reynner watched her go. The bedroom door closed with a soft click. Eyes squeezed tight, he blew out a rough breath and walked out of the apartment, anger raging through him.

He'd told her he wouldn't leave her alone and unprotected, but he was the biggest threat to her.

He ground his teeth against the pain slicing through him through the eight-point star burned in his flesh. A stroll through lava would be less painful than the shit incinerating him from the inside.

Since Inanna's failed attempt to get him back several days ago, she was now determined to haul him to her temple. With the mood he was in, he'd probably kill her. Tempting as that was, it would mean his own death. And that, he couldn't let happen, not while his realm needed him. Besides, the repercussions of killing a goddess meant causing a war Empyrea didn't need right now.

Memories took him back to the fateful night he stopped at the Sumerian temple.

He'd spent centuries traipsing through the Realm of the Gods—through various pantheons—searching for his friend who'd been banished, unable to live with his guilt of being party to Ariana's death. During that mind-numbing journey, he'd stopped at the Halls of the

Guards in the Sumerian pantheon. And there Inanna was.

Males surrounded her. He'd thought her just another female of pleasure who worked the halls. Sure, she was stunning, but so were the females of his world.

When she wandered over, and he found out that she was a goddess, he'd been amused that she wanted him. However, he *did* succumb to her seductive charms—a pleasant way to pass the night, he thought, and foolishly agreed not to use his powers while with her.

What the hell could she do?

He was an Empyrean, created to be all-powerful and feared.

Yes, the stupidity of his arrogance had tied him forever to his oath when he'd so foolishly agreed not to use his powers while with her.

Chapter 12

Reynner stepped through the portal mists and into the Sumerian's temple. Satisfied she had no hallucinogenic herbs burning here, he walked inside.

A lamp came flying at him, missing his face by inches. The thing hit the pillar beside him and crashed to the floor, splintering into pieces. "You dared take this long?"

Inanna sat on the rumpled bedding, her chest heaving with each furious breath she took. Inky tresses fell across her flushed face. She resembled the lions she preferred to keep as guards, who lay near her circular bed.

Their low rumbles vibrated in the room as the animals stirred, sensing her anger. Tawny eyes flickered in his direction. Reynner simply held the predators' stare. He'd faced worse than these two overgrown kittens.

Synchronous jaw-breaking yawns revealed their deadly incisors before they closed their yaps and rested their big heads on their paws.

Inanna rose from her bed and sashayed down the

three stairs to his level. As she descended, her black gown parted, revealing her nakedness. It had little effect on him. He just wanted this over.

Her lustful gaze swept over him to linger on his face. He half expected her to launch herself at him. Instead, she drifted past him to the marble columns supporting the dome-shaped ceiling in the seating area. Black cushions with silver and blue embroidery were strewn on the floor around a low table. She pushed a black bowl aside, then picked up a pewter carafe and poured a ruby-red liquid into a matching goblet then glided toward him.

She held out the wine, but he continued to stare at her.

"It's not drugged." She pouted. Then, to prove a point, she sipped the liquor. Seconds later, she flung the goblet. It flew through the air, hit the opposite pillar, and fell to the floor with a dull clunk.

Yeah, he'd learned his lesson never to eat or drink anything in this place the hard way. But the unfamiliar musky, aromatic smell in the air grew stronger, and a light haze blanketed his mind.

Inanna drew closer, a smile curving her lips.

Reynner shook his head, trying to clear the haze...*have to get back to...to...*

The fragrance drifting through the room seeped into his pores and infiltrated his thoughts. His body started to relax. Hands caressing his back, slid to his front. The name he wanted vanished from his thoughts. A ripping sound echoed the chamber. Cool air brushed his skin, and his shirt disappeared. Heated hands stroked his chest.

His usual abhorrence of anyone touching him faded.

This was *her*.

Needs he'd suppressed for eons resurfaced. He had to have her…had to have—gods, he'd waited so long—

In the lust-induced miasma surrounding him, he grabbed her arms, pushed her against the pillar, and met gleaming, topaz eyes.

Something wasn't right…the eyes…

Reynner shook his fuzzy head, tried to clear the haze. As she reached up and tried to kiss him, he grasped her face and peered into her eyes.

No—no, not green—topaz. His gut twisted in pain at the truth. Revulsion tearing through him, he shoved away. Next time, he'd fucking chain himself in his dungeon like he usually did to avoid her calls.

Desperate for clean air, he flung open the windows with his mind, then grabbed the black bowl with smoke rising from it—and hurled it outside. He should have known she'd try her shit again.

"Say what the fuck you have to. You have five seconds," he forced out through clenched teeth.

"Reynner…" Low. Sultry. "Let me make it up to you. I know I can. Give me a day, it's all I want."

"Once was a mistake that will never be repeated," he told her, his voice flat as the desert beyond the temple.

Her face darkened with frustrated desire. "Don't push me aside, Reynner. You won't like what I will do."

In response, he turned away and looked for his shirt, then remembered she'd torn it off him.

"Whoever keeps you from me will regret it. Do you honestly think I don't know where you spend most of your time?" she spat at him.

His gaze hardened. "Once again, you waste my time. I have work to do."

At his dismissal, her shriek reverberated through the

chambers. A blast of her power sent him slamming into the wall. She leaped at him and slapped her hand over his heart. The searing pressure of her touch had him grunting in pain. Her power pulsed through the mark she'd branded him with when he'd first tried to leave her eons ago.

Breathing hard, he shoved her off him. She stumbled and landed on the couch.

"Do not threaten me."

Rage sparked off her. She tossed her hair away from her flushed face, her expression lethal. "I will never let you go."

Of that, he had little doubt. Two millennia had already proven that. Reynner walked out of her boudoir, weary of her games. He desperately wanted the god-awful stench of this place—and her—off him.

***

The truck arrived on time the next morning. Eve had made the arrangements with Eric several days ago for her sculptures to be transported to his gallery. He liked things in early so he could prep the place and lay out each piece to its best advantage.

Eve cast a quick look down the short passage and bit her lip as she slipped her cell into the pocket of her jeans, after answering the driver's call.

Reynner was still in the shower, and she had to leave for the studio. But she refused to bang on the door like some demented woman, one she was close to becoming if last night were an indicator of her emotions.

It was humiliating enough to know she'd lain awake in her bed, listening for his return. He'd come back in the early hours of the morning and had made no sound, but instinct had alerted her to his presence. She heard the soft click when the door opposite her room closed.

But a faint whiff of an exotic scent drifted to her as if to let her know where he'd been.

Another woman.

A hollow pit opened in her stomach.

Christ, she wasn't doing this to herself. Reynner's life was his own, as he'd made it known.

She grabbed a pen, jotted a short note, and set it on the kitchen counter before leaving her apartment.

At her studio, Eve dismantled the larger art pieces first, then tried to keep out of the men's way. She watched anxiously as they bubble-wrapped and crated each sculpture, making sure her precious cargo wouldn't bounce around. She trusted Eric to take care of her future.

"Hey, girl, you coming to the gallery today?"

Eve glanced at the enormous man who'd been humming some kind of jazzy tune. A flirty grin rode his wide, dark face. He'd tied the sleeves of his overalls around his waist to reveal a navy tee with ripped-off sleeves and thick, tattooed arms.

Eric used Joe Livingstone whenever he wanted work carted around the city.

"No, Joe. I know you'll take care of my babies. I have some work to complete. I'll pop in tomorrow."

"Don't you worry, I'll make real sure it's all safe." Joe called out instructions for the crates to be carried out to the truck.

Eve followed the men. She stood to the side and watched while they loaded the vehicle with the smaller crates, when Joe abruptly stopped singing and looked past her.

A tingle snaking up her spine, Eve didn't have to turn to know why. But she did.

Reynner strode down the alley like a black tornado

ready to destroy anything in his way. He stopped an inch from her, his clean, warm scent enveloping her.

"Why the hell didn't you warn me you had this happening?"

She tilted her chin, not caring that he was rocking mad.

Damn him. How could he just waltz back like everything was all right? As if he hadn't been with someone else last night? The hated fragrance may be washed off him now, but she'd smelled the truth. Her chest tightened, her heart sliding into that black hole in her stomach.

She would never show him how much he'd hurt her.

Calm and collected, she said, "You weren't around last night when I remembered."

"And this morning?"

She lifted a shoulder in a shrug. "I left you a note."

His eyes blazed. Oh, good, she'd finally rattled him enough to break through the cool mask he wore so well. Crossing her arms beneath her breasts, she stepped away.

His fingers closed around her nape and he hauled her close. At the unexpectedness of his action, she stumbled. Her hands fluttered against his chest.

"Don't Eve, don't push me."

"Or you'll what?" she shot back.

His gaze skimmed over her up-turned face and settled on her mouth for a tormenting second. A bright blue flame sparked in his dark eyes, and that low, treacherous buzz that took up residence whenever he was near started in her belly again.

Her blood heated in anger. She didn't want to want him. Christ help her, she really didn't.

"This is *my* life, Reynner." She shoved at his chest,

but that was like trying to move a wall. "I don't have to report every step I take to you. So back off, I'm not your damn prisoner."

Brave words, but her tears weren't far off.

"Prisoner?" he bit out, looking as if he were moments from shaking her. She didn't care.

"You forget the threat—"

"I forget nothing. My work is important, too."

"Gods, Eve—"

A distant yell cut off what he'd been about to say, broke the moment fraught with tension, anger, and something deeper...something so tangible that her heart jumped straight back into her chest. And pounded against her ribs. Whether it was from what just happened or the shout, Eve had no idea. Reynner vanished. She spun around and froze.

Noooo—God, no—!

But Reynner was already there. He seized a sliding crate seconds before it met with the asphalt, nearly destroying one of her major pieces.

It took several long seconds before she could breathe again. She pressed a trembling hand on her chest. Her legs felt like they would never manage another step again.

Reynner leaped into the truck and helped secure the sculpture. As he worked, he cut her a sharp look then said to Joe, "Let me give you a hand with the rest."

"Good save, man." Joe wiped his sweaty face on the hanging sleeve of his overalls. "Wouldn't want this pretty little girl upset." His smile didn't replace the panic in his eyes.

"Thank you," Eve told Reynner when he walked past.

He stopped, those night-sky eyes searching her face.

"I would never let what you worked so hard for be destroyed."

He pulled off his shirt. A slight sheen bathed his golden skin. He was probably feeling the heat, but the sight of all those rippling muscles had her transfixed, yanking her mind out of her terror of nearly losing one of her sculptures.

Reynner grasped her arm, drew her to the side as the men came out carrying more of her work.

"Hold this for me." He handed her his shirt, then headed inside.

Eve crushed the t-shirt against her chest, struggling not to press the soft fabric against her face, like some schoolgirl with a first crush. She turned and met Joe's dark gaze. He nodded and resumed his low-key singing of the jazzy tune.

As Reynner helped load the truck, Eve realized he could have single-handedly picked up the crates and done the job in a shorter time. Yet he didn't let his immense strength show as he assisted the moving crew.

His body gleamed with a light layer of sweat. The muscles trapped beneath his skin rippled with his movements, the scars on his back just a fading red patch now.

Reynner paused when Joe started singing another song. "Satchmo?"

A wide grin flashed across Joe's dusky face. "Hey, you like Louis Armstrong?"

"I saw him—his videos," Reynner corrected. "Incredible musician."

Eve realized then that Reynner had probably seen the man play live.

They finished in record time. Joe pulled out his kerchief from his overall pocket and mopped his face, his tee plastered to his skin. The heat rose off the asphalt, saturating them like a shimmering sauna. "We're playing jazz down at Scorpions on Saturday. You want to come over and hang with us?"

The night of her show.

Reynner shook his head. "Thanks, but I have to be elsewhere that evening. Rain check?"

"Anytime, man."

Eve watched the truck trundle off and inhaled an anxious breath. Wrapping her arms around her waist, she walked back into her studio and stared at the looming empty space. Her babies were gone.

Had she done the right thing?

***

Reynner followed Eve into the studio, his fear and ire at finding her gone from the apartment finally easing.

He took the t-shirt she'd left on the table and pulled it on. The place looked bare with all the sculptures gone, save for the tall one covered with a white sheet and the messy one she'd started last night.

A male, she'd told him. One who'd have to pose for her, judging from the tangled mess she made. He hated the bastard's guts. Yes, small of him, but he didn't care.

However, the sight of her tensed body pushed aside his irritation. He stopped beside her, and the desire to ease her fears, to soothe, took over. He stroked her back. "You have a good eye," he murmured. "And an extraordinary gift with crafting metals."

"Thank you." Then she said in a quieter tone, "I've put everything I have into this. If it fails…"

"Eve—"

"Ignore me." She raked a restless hand through her hair and leaned into his touch. "It's just nerves. Once the show's over, I'll be all right."

Hell, it would be so easy to pull her into his arms and offer comfort. But if he did, it would lead to the one place from which there was no return. She removed the tormenting decision by heading for her worktable and stopping to survey the mess there.

Reynner had no clue what she was looking for. Piles of sketches and a handful of colored pens and pencils cluttered the surface. Files were stashed haphazardly in a tray against the wall, along with her jar of colorful jellybeans.

His gaze caressed her face as she hunted through the things on her table. *Urias*, she was so damn beautiful. She seemed to glow from within. A brightness he realized he needed in his life with growing desperation.

She picked up the sketches then dropped them. "I can't deal with filing now. I have work to do."

He joined her at the table. "I thought you were done?"

"One more." She nodded at the tall sculpture covered with a dustsheet. "I need to finish that... Chinese for lunch?" She scratched through the papers, looking for the menu.

Reynner watched her for a moment. She seemed distracted, jumpy, her thoughts all over the place. "I'll get it. What do you want?"

She turned confused eyes to him, the menu in her hand. "Huh?"

"Food, Eve."

Her gaze drifted back to her sculpture. "Anything."

He grasped her upper arm when she walked past him and removed the menu. "You need to calm down. Tonight we get the scroll. We cannot afford any mistakes."

Like mist, the confusion in her eyes dissipated. She glowered. "And you wonder why I'm nervous."

"It will be okay, I promise." He let her go and studied the menu. "I have a replacement scroll, so that should settle your sense of righteousness."

"How is that possible? There's only one."

He looked up, gave her a bland stare.

"Jesus, ask a stupid question," she huffed. "You probably just conjured one up—it doesn't matter anyway. The scroll belongs to your world. It's more important to save your realm than us keeping it locked in a glass box."

She headed for the covered sculpture and tugged the sheet from the massive form.

Females! After giving him a hard time about *stealing* the parchment, now she did a complete turnaround and gave him the big, A-Okay.

Watching her, Reynner made his call and ordered their food, but she seemed to have already forgotten him, her attention on the giant male sculpture. She ran her hand down its metal thigh and fiddled with a strip there.

His entire body tensed. Dammit, it's just a freaking statue!

He took a deep breath and shut down his increasing possessiveness. Him and her couldn't happen. To keep his thoughts off her, he parked his ass down on her only decent stool and perused her sketches.

She drew with a delicate hand, but the hard, massive, metal sculptures themselves held an alluring appeal. A lot like her. Fragile, but wired with a steely, determined core.

He picked up the working diagram of the horse she'd given him. The ribbons of interweaving metal and the solid core layer all worked out in the illustration. Then he studied the one of her friend, the dark-haired female, Brenna.

Reynner knew it was her because of the face Eve had added in for the nude sculpture. She'd included crossed eyes and a gap-toothed grin, instead of leaving it blank like the others. The caricature of her friend made him smile.

The doorbell buzzed.

"I'll get it," he said. A quick psychic scan confirmed it was their meal.

Reynner paid the delivery boy then set the bags on the worktable, cleared a space, and laid out cartons of food. The savory aroma of soy and peppers with hints of ginger drenched the studio as he strolled over to her. "Take a break."

"In a sec. I want to finish this," she said absently, attaching a metal strip to the sculpture's midriff and slowly sliding her palm over the piece almost in a caress.

His irritation gave way to fascination when the thing just bent in her hand and she molded it into the shape she wanted. Intrigued, he ran a finger over the strip and found it hot, but not uncomfortable to touch.

Frowning, Reynner studied her expression while she worked. No, no indication the high temperature hurt her. Still, she was human...it should be painful.

"Eve, what exactly did you do to this metal?"

Her startled gaze flew to him. A light flush swept over her cheekbones.

When he saw how his question bothered her, he softened his tone. "Eve?"

Her hands tensed on the metal she held. "I guess it was only a matter of time before you found out. The accident also left me with an ability to heat things like metal."

Reynner stared at her, stunned. It wasn't what he'd expected. "What intensity—I mean, what heat level are we talking here?"

"I don't know, just hot enough to soften and bend metal. Usually, I solder or melt heavier pieces in the kiln." She pointed to the small oven-like structure in the corner of the room. "That just takes too much out of me."

He seized her hands and examined her palms.

"Jeez, Reynner." She tried to yank them back, her fingers fisting. "My hands are fine."

"I don't care about your scars. I want to see if you've burned yourself."

"I haven't."

He didn't relent, just held her gaze with determined ones.

Scowling, she uncurled her fists. He traced the bumpy scars and calluses with a finger. Satisfied she hadn't hurt herself, he let her go.

She cut him an I-told-you-so-look, then turned back to study her life-size sculpture. "A little more work and it should be ready."

To him, the sculpture looked done with all the weaves and gaping slits. But what did he know?

"Do you mind handing me that sketch on my table? The one with a photo attached," she asked him.

Playing errand boy, Reynner went back and flipped through her stack of sketches. His gaze landed on the photo and he froze.

"Eve—" He broke off, unable to speak—to breathe, like someone had used a vise on his chest. "Eve, where did you get this?"

She glanced over her shoulder and saw the photo he held. "Oh, that's for Brenna's friend. It's a present for her husband. She gave me the pic and specifications."

His attention back on the photo, Reynner felt the precarious foundation he lived on shudder beneath his feet.

"You okay?" Eve's voice came to him from a distance.

He nodded, wondering why Eve hadn't made the familial connections. Sure, Aerén's hair was far lighter, and Aethan's looked much darker than normal in this picture.

"You—" He had to clear the rust from his throat to ask. "You do commissioned work?"

"This is my first one. Echo seemed to like the unusual. Said my style appealed to her."

Liked the unusual? Naturally, she would. She was mated to his friend.

"Did you meet them?" he asked, waiting for an answer and dreading what he'd hear.

Eve gave him an enquiring look. "Just the wife—she's pretty nice. She's coming to see the final product today before I send it off. Why?"

The vise eased. He could breathe again. At least he was spared that meeting. "Just curious."

Eve finally left the sculpture and came to the table. She took the photo from him and studied it. Seeming satisfied, she set it aside. Then she hopped on the high, swivel stool, picked up a carton, took one of the plastic forks, and started to make inroads in her chicken noodles.

Reynner ignored the other stool—a really rickety one that guaranteed to have him falling on his ass the moment he sat his weight on it.

"Why aren't you eating?" Eve lifted her gaze from his untouched food and frowned. "Is something wrong?"

Yeah, he could very well face his past. Something he wasn't prepared for and would never be. Not now, not after so many millennia.

Unable to answer that question, he shook his head. He picked up his fork and forced down food he didn't taste—and was spared a second bite when he felt a brush against his psychic senses.

He stilled. Waited. The same sensation he'd experienced in the alley last night crept over him. Sticking his fork in the carton of noodles, he was out the door in seconds.

Moments later, a light peachy scent drifted to him.

Shit, of course, Eve would follow. His inner alarm continued to sound.

"Reynner, what is it? You're scaring me." She glanced about her where they stood on the dirt-encrusted asphalt, the clammy noon heat enclosing them.

He searched the lane, farther up where the alley met the main street. A man leaned against the wall, smoking and conversing to another. Cars droned by. But the alley itself remained quiet.

The back entrance to the furniture warehouse opposite her studio was shut. However, the trails of boot prints in the wood dust leading to the next building caught his attention.

He scanned the boarded up place and his anger went into slow burn.

Chapter 13

"Eve, go back to the studio, lock the door and stay there 'til I come for you," Reynner said, his attention on the barred warehouse decorated with grimy graffiti.

"What is it?" She looked around the alley. He didn't want to alarm her about the danger he sensed. With a hand on her lower back, he gave her a nudge to get her moving.

Once he was sure she was safe and locked in her studio, with inhuman speed, he dashed across the street to the boarded entrance. He shoved hard with his mind. Timber exploded. Debris flooded the air and clattered to the dusty floors. Then utter silence ensued.

Reynner paused at the entrance and probed the interior with several darkened corners. Dust motes jostled in the slants of light pouring in from the windows. With preternatural swiftness, he lunged for the shadows in the right corner and seized a body. He slammed the male against the wall. A grunt echoed in the quiet interior.

Shit! It was the same Darkrean fucker who'd followed him last night. Anger tore through Reynner.

His danger radar vibrated in alarm—he ducked. And a dagger whisked inches past his face to embed in the wall behind him. Mohawk tore free and joined his taller pal with the metallic colored hair and cold eyes.

Sebris. The Darkreans' deadly combat leader. Only he possessed that distinct multihued nickel bronze mane.

The bastard didn't move to strike. He simply stared with all the arrogance of their kind. As if he knew Reynner's every dark secret. But that crap meant little to him, he just wanted their heads for daring to come after Eve. Preferably separated from their bodies.

"Darkrean," Reynner drawled.

"Empyrean," the leader countered. It surprised Reynner that he'd gotten a response.

"We fight for the same cause."

"Oh? You have something to share, then? By all means, go ahead," Reynner invited. Did they think him that gullible—that he'd believe they fought for the survival of Empyrea? The bastards wanted the power to rule. This was just a stall tactic while they waited for the chance to grab Eve and run.

"Give us the female—"

"Yeah, right." Anger prowled through Reynner like a deadly beast ready to destroy anything in its path. No way in hell would they get their hands on Eve. He summoned his sword as theirs flashed into their hands. They charged him. Reynner deflected. Steel met steel, the sound resonating through the empty warehouse.

A red haze taking over his mind, Reynner spun around, his blade coming down in a brutal arc, slicing viciously through flesh and connecting with bone.

A growl erupted, the first sign of emotion from Mohawk.

"Hurt, does it?" Reynner snarled.

A winging hiss resonated in the dank air. Reynner jumped back and barely avoided the sword that nearly skewered him. But the damn thing sliced him across the chest anyway. Pain spread. Not a sound left his mouth as warm blood drenched his shirt. Rage erupting like wildfire, he leaped at the cold bastard, struck hard.

The leader grunted.

Blood spilled. More damage. Good. Reynner prowled around them, ready to hack them into fucking pieces for coming after his female.

***

Eve paced in front of the huge industrial windows, her gaze pinned on the dark doorway of the adjacent building. The only thing keeping her here was the knowledge that the last time she'd tried to help Reynner, he'd gotten hurt instead. Her stomach heaved at the thought.

Please, please let him be all right.

Her fear fled the moment he strode out from the broken doorway. Sun glinted off his pale hair, but his face was drawn tight in anger... pain?

She flew out of the studio like a gust of wind, as he crossed the narrow road. And stumbled to a halt. The blood drained from her head when she saw the slash on his tee and the sticky wetness saturating the material.

Oh, God. Not again.

She must have swayed. Reynner grabbed her arm, steadying her. "It's nothing. I'll heal."

That brought her back fast. "Who was it—tell me you killed them!"

She didn't care that she sounded ferocious and bloodthirsty. She wanted them dead for hurting him.

"Eve," he murmured, gently touching her face. "I'm

fine. And no, they aren't dead. I don't want them on us right now, and that's guaranteed if I kill one. Let's go inside. They've disappeared, but they could send reinforcements."

Eve's anger deflated when she thought of what was at risk. Not only could Reynner die in this fight but his entire realm was under threat, too. From what Aerén had said, the Darkreans would do anything to rule Empyrea.

"Do they think we have the Stone? Are they looking to steal it?"

Ice flowed into his eyes. "Right now, it's you they want."

That stumped her…for a second. "Well, I'm not that easy to get to, not with you here."

A wry smile chasing away his grimness, he ushered her back into the studio. "Glad to know you trust me."

With her safety? Absolutely. But with her heart? Eve didn't dare.

She fetched the first-aid kit from the sink cupboard in the corner of the studio. Turning, she found Reynner had his t-shirt bunched up in one hand, revealing his tanned abs while he examined the wound on his chest. The urge to run her fingers over those sculpted muscles had her tightening her hold on the box. She crossed the room and set the kit on the table.

He tugged his tee down. "Eve, I don't need tending to, I'll be fine."

"Well, I'm not. So remove the shirt, or…" She eyed him. He was far too tall, and since she couldn't very well climb up him to yank it off, she threatened, "Or I'll cut it off."

He arched a brow, amusement lighting his gaze. But he did as she wanted and lowered himself onto the stool. She took out gauze and disinfectant from the box and paused. Darn, she hadn't thought this through. She'd have to stand between his parted thighs, be close to him.

Fix him up and step back, Eve, she told herself. *This can't go anywhere.*

Right. Concentrating on cleaning the long gash across his right pec helped. As she worked, the bleeding eased. Eve didn't comment since he probably had quick-healing abilities, too. She tossed the soiled gauze on the table, far too aware of the jittery sensation spiraling through her. And touching his warm, naked skin didn't help matters.

His hands settled on her hips. "You always seem to be patching me up."

She gave him a quick look. Her breath caught at the intensity of his dark stare. She forgot her question. Need unfurled low in her belly.

"You're hurt...I want to help."

Focus, Eve, or you'll only land in a hard place from where there's no turning back. Except with a broken heart.

Focusing back on her task as if her very life depended on it, she reached for the antiseptic ointment, squirted some on her finger, and applied it to the wound. But the burn-like tattoo on his left pec drew her gaze. She counted eight points to the star. On impulse, she traced the edges with a finger—

He grabbed her wrist. His expression violent, grip painful. "Don't."

Shocked. Eve wrenched her hand free and stumbled back. He pushed to his feet. "I don't like you touching it."

It? He meant *him.* "Yes, you made that very clear."

Her movements jerky, she scooped the things back into the first-aid box.

"It's not what you think—"

"There's no need for explanations."

Cursing, Reynner thumped the table with open palms, making everything on it jolt.

Mouth tight, Eve snapped the lid shut and stopped, a memory seeped into her of him chained in that hellhole dungeon, and that demoness clawing his wounds, doing those horrific things to him...

It's why he didn't like being touched.

Her stomach dipped, her hurt and anger fading. She wanted to go to and wrap her arms around him, take away those ugly memories.

"Your client's here," Reynner muttered, the lines of his face rigid.

She'd almost forgotten about her appointment.

A car door slammed.

That got her moving. She cleared up the bloodied cotton pads and stored the kit in the cupboard then washed her hands. As she hurried back, she sensed the tension in Reynner, even if she couldn't read much from his expression. And wondered if he was in pain.

"Why don't you sit down while I deal with this?" Then she headed for the door.

***

Sit down? Reynner couldn't move to save his life.

His body vibrated with need at being so close to her. She had to go and touch the filthy brand on his chest. He didn't want her tainted with that shit. And she thought he didn't want her touching him. Yeah, he usually loathed when anyone got too close or touched him—but not Eve.

The sound of feminine voices drew him back.

Reynner got his first glimpse of Aethan's mate. She wore a sleeveless, flowing white top that skimmed the waist of her jeans. The color offset her light honey-gold skin. A shallow dimple dented her chin. A little taller than Eve, her black hair was cut in a spiky style.

She smiled at something Eve said and came to an abrupt halt when she saw him.

Her gaze widened, the mismatched eyes unexpected, one a light gray and the other amber. The otherworldly light glowing in them while she studied him made him uneasy. Then her entire manner changed as if awareness filled her.

Oh, shit, she sensed him. Knew what he was. How was that even possible? Hell, he should have left—no, he couldn't leave Eve unprotected—especially not with those emotionless fuckers sniffing about.

"I didn't know you had company, Eve," Aethan's female said, her voice held a hint of a rasp.

Eve came over to him and introduced her. "Reynner, this is Echo. Echo, Reynner."

Reynner nodded. If this female mentioned his name or her suspicions to Aethan—fuck. Too late now.

"I'm so pleased to meet you." A smile lit her attractive, angular features. Then her gaze lowered to his chest and her brow furrowed. "What happened? Was there a fight?"

Shit. Shirt. He needed his damn shirt!

Where was the bloody thing? A quick search, and he found it on the floor near the foot of the stool. He picked it up and yanked it on, ignoring the sticky blood plastered on his skin once more.

"It's nothing. All sorted out now," Eve said, surprising him at her discretion. "Come. Let me show you the sculpture. It's almost completed. Another week or so and it should be done."

Echo's gaze settled on the metal figure that Reynner never in a thousand years would have guessed was a depiction of his friend. She stared at it for so long, Eve gave him a nervous glance. Reynner nearly asked the female to say something.

"It's amazing!" She grasped Eve's arm. Eve flinched. The female didn't notice the way Eve immediately stuck her hands into her jeans pockets.

Echo let Eve go and circled the sculpture then ran a reverent hand over the metal.

The thought that Eve had done the same, hell, it was stupid, but he didn't like it—didn't like her touching his friend, even if it was just a damn sculpture.

"I love it. You've captured exactly what he is. All that wildness, that power," Echo said in delight. "He's going to be so—"

"So what?" An amused voice asked from the doorway.

Reynner froze as three thousand years melted away. He stared at his old friend.

Aethan had changed. He appeared older, harder, tougher than the male he'd once been. All the shit he'd suffered through for so many millennia would do that to a person. Hell, Reynner knew more than anyone how life could change you. But that teasing tone remained the same.

The urge to walk over and say hello grew so strong, it took all of Reynner's willpower to plant his feet and remain where he was.

"Oh, there you are." Echo hurried over to him. "I want you to see this. It's supposed to be a surprise, but I was too excited and couldn't wait."

"You called me, *me'morae*." Aethan smiled at his

mate and brushed her cheek with his knuckles. "It's not like I'd ignore your summons."

Called him? Reynner frowned. How? She didn't use her cell—dammit! How could he forget? If theirs was a soul bonding, she must have mind-linked with him.

"Summons?" Echo snorted. "You follow no one's rules but your own."

A smile ghosted his mouth. Playfully, he tugged a lock of her hair, and she laughed.

The tender moment had Reynner looking away. His chest hollowed out. There was no redemption for one such as him. No mate.

Yet, he was aware Eve had moved closer to him. He wanted to hold onto her. Instead, he clenched the table edge he leaned against.

"What do you want me to see—" Aethan turned. Shock and utter disbelief crossed his old friend's face. As if in a time warp, Reynner was hurtled through the millennia to the last time he'd seen Aethan in Empyrea. His expression held a similar look, except it had been shock at the atrocity that had occurred, one Reynner had caused.

The phantom of his careless words rang out in his head.

"Is that all you have?" he taunted Aethan. "You fight like a female."

Aethan growled, looking pissed. His sword flashed, his deadly ability powering his weapon to a lethal white glow. He flew at Reynner, his blade swinging in a dangerous arc.

Laughing, Reynner evaded the attack. Whatever was troubling Aethan, a good fight would soon take care of that since neither one of them would accept defeat.

It was always about outdoing the other.

"A'than!" A childish voice swept through the arena. "Here, for you."

No, no, no! Reynner's heart slammed against his ribs in horror.

Aethan spun around, his sword slipping from his sweaty hand, went hurtling across the field in a blaze of his deadly power light. "Ariana, no! No! Get back!"

Reynner tried frantically to shield her. Too late.

The sword struck the little girl, the power of the sword dragging her several meters before she fell.

Blood flowed profusely out of her small body to pool where she lay still on the ground.

"No!" Aethan's anguished roar reverberated the arena.

Reynner stood there, unable to move, frozen in shock as they fought to save Ariana...

Breathing hard, Reynner struggled for calm. He waited for Aethan to grab his mate and storm out from the studio instead of looking into the face of the person responsible for his little sister's death.

If he hadn't taunted Aethan into a stupid fight, Ariana would still be alive.

The next minute, Aethan strode over. He grabbed Reynner in a hug he'd never expected. "*Urias*, I never thought I'd see you again!"

Reynner stood still, unable to move. He had no words.

Aethan pulled back. His expression held no recrimination, which made things worse. How could Aethan look so happy to see him?

"What are you doing here?" he asked, seizing Reynner's biceps in a painful grip. Pleasure lit his gunmetal gray eyes. "When did you get here?"

It was then that Reynner realized Aethan had no idea

of how bad things had gotten in their realm. Or the farce his life had turned out to be.

"I've been searching for the missing Stone of Light." Yeah, that was safe to talk about since Aethan wouldn't know that the scroll and Stone had disappeared.

Aethan froze. "What—*how*?"

Reynner shrugged. "War, strife—the usual political crap. It vanished two thousand years ago."

Aethan lowered his gaze to the floor as if assimilating what he'd just heard. Then he glanced at Reynner and nodded. "You need my help, let me know. Look, come over to the castle, we can talk. There is so much to catch up on."

He had to be joking. Go to Aethan's home, when he could barely live with himself? Reynner shook his head. "I can't. There's much to do. Time's essential."

Finally, his cool, unresponsive attitude pierced through Aethan's pleasure. He stared at Reynner for a long moment. "We were best friends once. I understand why you can't see past the unforgivable sin I committed."

When Reynner said nothing, Aethan nodded and stepped back. His jaw tight, he strode back to his mate. "Echo, I'll wait for you in the car."

The pain on his friend's face was exactly like the one he'd seen eons ago when Ariana lay bleeding on the fields. It cracked through Reynner's walls.

"You did nothing!" The words tore free. Rage, guilt, and self-loathing ate at Reynner like acid.

Eve stepped closer. But he couldn't look at her. She'd seen enough of his hideous past, now she'd know more. Yet he couldn't stop. "Did you not think if I hadn't taunted you into a damn useless fight, that tragedy wouldn't have occurred?"

Aethan dismissed his verbal deluge with a shake of his head. "How could you have known that I'd had an argument with my sire when I met you on the training fields? I needed an outlet, it's why I accepted the challenge."

Urias, his friend was still so fucking honorable and godsdamn blind. "I started that fight, *I* should have been the one banished."

"Why? Ariana died by my sword—"

"Because of me—*me!*" Reynner swallowed hard. Unable to look at Eve and see the condemnation in her eyes for being responsible for the death of a child, he said in a voice gone numb, "Eve, call me when you're ready to leave."

Then he stalked past his friend and left the studio.

***

Eve had no idea what had happened. It was obvious Reynner and Echo's husband knew each other. But the pain from both men, their emotions, overwhelmed her.

She had to go find Reynner, see if he was all right. How much more could one person take? Being captured by a vicious demoness and tortured. Then meeting a friend after so many millennia, who, by all she'd seen, mattered very much to Reynner. And she'd seen, too, the gut-churning anguish beneath the guilt. He'd looked as if his heart were being ripped apart.

"I'm so sorry," she told Echo. "Can we do this another day?"

The younger woman nodded, her bicolored eyes clouded with anxiety. "I think it's best. Aethan, let's go."

When he didn't respond, she stroked his arm and said softly, "He'll come around. He just needs time after seeing you again."

The tall man pulled his gaze from the empty doorway through which Reynner had vanished. He reached out, brushed a hand in a tender gesture over Echo's hair. "He blames himself," he said. "I didn't expect that. I know better than anyone what self-hatred can do to one's soul."

Echo stroked his chest as if easing old pains then she hugged him.

A pang of envy struck Eve, a longing for what the couple had. She pushed her yearning aside and walked out into the stifling heat. Stopping on the sidewalk near the sleek, black Lamborghini parked there, she searched for Reynner. Up the street, few people were about. She glanced down, and there in the shadows of a narrow thoroughfare she saw him standing, head lowered.

She sprinted across. "Reynner?"

His looked up, his hunted expression shutting off. "Not now, Eve. Go back inside."

As if she'd let that stop her. She was coming to understand this complicated man. He was hurting, he could hide it all he wanted, but she knew. He needed her.

"No. You shouldn't be alone."

"You shouldn't worry about me. I'm not worth it."

She didn't agree. He'd walled up his emotions—retreated again, showing the world the cold, hard man she'd first met.

Well, she refused to stand by and watch him further destroy himself.

"You may be all big and strong, terrify demoniis and Darkreans, but you need someone right now. Let me be there for you."

Reynner shut his eyes at her words, then with unerring accuracy, he reached out and hauled her to him and held on tight, as if afraid she'd disappear. He buried his face in her hair. "You know what I am—what I'm responsible for. Why aren't you running?"

"How could I when you're hurting?" she whispered. "Besides, from what I've heard, it was an accident." Eve pressed her face into his neck and hugged him back, breathing in his intoxicating scent and soaking in the sheer wonder of being in his arms.

After a short blissful moment, she asked, "Who is he?"

His hands stroked her back. "Can you not see the similarity?"

Eve stilled. Her heart nearly kicked out of her chest at the truth. She thought the man had tinted his hair in that varied blue. She pulled back, eyes wide. "Is he related to Aerén?"

"His brother." Exhaling roughly, he let her go. "Aethan was banished eons ago for the death of their little sister. It would have never happened had I not dared him into a useless fight. Ariana died. He was exiled. And I…"

"You did what? Did your family disown you?"

Derisive laughter left him, haunted blue eyes met hers. "No. The blame wasn't mine, or so my sire insisted. I was to carry on like nothing happened…"

"But you couldn't," she said in understanding.

"No. I couldn't live with that. I left." He glanced at the studio. The pain in his eyes was like a clamp around her heart. The man in there meant a lot to Reynner.

"You left Empyrea to search for him, didn't you?"

His lack of response told her what she wanted to

know. And right then, Eve decided she would do what she could to help him.

"Reynner, you can tell me it's not my business, but give him a chance—"

"Eve, stop."

She pinned him with a firm look, determined to knock some sense into his rock-hard male skull. "No, you listen. Not often in life do we get second chances. Some people are afraid of what they might find if they delve too deep into themselves, so they build walls. But Reynner, you have to open old wounds to discover the truth. Once the bleeding stops, the healing begins."

For a length of a breath, he simply stared at her. "Not for me, Eve. There can never be absolution for me."

"I don't believe that. But, you have to forgive yourself first. And I know you're not a coward," she said softly, accepting his scowl. "You will do the right thing. Or else you'll leave another scar on your friend. He's lived with the memory of killing his sister, but he's made peace with himself. You've blamed yourself for something no one could have foreseen."

"You have blood on your shirt."

She glanced at the smears on her blue top, then back at him, refusing to let him distract her. "Reynner, to have a friend like him is rare. I have few, and I treasure them since…" She blew out a breath and pushed on, "Since not many like me because of my abilities."

"Then it's their loss—" He stopped when he realized what he'd said. "How is it that I've lived so long filled with self-hatred, and you make it all sound so simple?"

"Because you've been hurting for far too long. It's time to let go and heal. Besides," she added drily, "I'm sure most are far too scared to try and talk to you with that aloofness you wear like armor."

He snorted, a rare smile tugging his mouth.

A low purr of an engine resounded in the alley. Reynner looked past her.

Eve turned to find the Lamborghini heading up the road. She shot a quick look at him to find the mask of remoteness back in place. She sighed.

Chapter 14

Sebris eased off his shirt. Blood seeped from his wound and dripped down his abs. The lesion scored deep in his stomach ran parallel with the pain eating at him. His hands shook as he rested them on the countertop. He glanced at the enormous mirror above the porcelain sink in his bathroom and took in his injuries. If he hadn't used the last bit of his ability to dematerialize, the Empyrean would have had his head as a trophy.

He hadn't lived this long to die because of carelessness. Displeasure resurged when he thought about why he was in this state.

Taegér. Observe and report had been his orders. Not draw attention to them. But the warrior couldn't resist getting closer when a female was involved, and the Empyrean had sniffed him out. If it weren't for the fact that the warrior was one of his most trusted men, Taeg would meet Urias face-to-face sooner instead of later.

Sebris snagged a fresh towel and held it against his wound. It didn't heal quickly like it would have if he were on Empyrea. Nor could he use his powers since his had all but flatlined. He wouldn't die from his injuries, but it just hiked his pain levels. And ignoring the damages wouldn't make them go away.

He dampened another towel in water and washed the blood seeping from the gash, but the thing just wouldn't quit. He gushed like a slaughtered animal.

Sebris glared in annoyance at the disaster of his wound.

He yanked open more cupboards, found several rolls of bandages, a small skein of silk thread, and a stitching device. He threaded the needle, pinched the wound closed, and pushed it through his flesh. The sticky mess of plasma made the needle slippery. Teeth clamped, he sutured. Sweat beaded on his skin. Pain rose, adding more to the rioting deep within his bones.

One, two, three, he continued sewing, his molars crushing down on the agony saturating him until the last stitch was in place. He knotted and snipped the ends.

Cotton pads, gauze, and three Band-Aids later, he covered the wound. He sucked in a deep breath and braced his hands on the counter.

Damn, too much pain—too much! He needed to heal faster.

Sebris glanced up and encountered his reflection in the mirror. More black bled into his eyes, he could barely see their pale color anymore. Harsh lines creased his face, while his mouth held a cruel twist.

Well, he *was* in a shitload of agony.

One good thing had come out of this, though. Satisfaction spread through him. Reynner had sent the female away before he confronted them. That alone told him everything he needed to know. She was the foretold one.

A knock on the bathroom door distracted him. Xever walked inside, looking alert, his eyes back to their usual storm-gray. Good. His warriors were back and had powered up.

Xever glanced at Sebris's wound. "What happened?"

"Had an encounter with the Empyrean. Call the others."

Nodding, Xever left the bathroom.

Sebris headed for his dressing room, found a clean white shirt, and pulled it on. He snagged the vodka from the dresser, poured a shot, and took a draft of the drink, relishing in the fiery buzz the liquor gave him. Then he walked into the bedroom, straightening his shirt as Xever, Taegér, and Paxyn entered.

"I've seen the foretold one. Taegér will fill you in on her description. If you get a chance, bring her here. I'll be back in a day."

His powers needed to recharge.

***

The woody scent of trees and moist earth drifted toward Eve, along with a heat that just wouldn't quit. She rubbed nervous hands down the sides of her black yoga pants. Her short-sleeve black tee kept her cool, but she wondered if she was dressed right for this. Wearing black was so clichéd, but right now, standing in the fringes of the park opposite the museum, she blended into the shadows and that was good.

Reynner stood beside her, his body motionless. His expression bore the same stillness. She wondered if anything ever ruffled his cool composure because her heart thumped violently in her chest. Surely he could hear its terrified rhythm?

He glanced at her then slid his hand around the back of her neck, his warm, callused touch steadying her.

Oh, yeah, the man was no fool. He knew how uneasy she was about this. He didn't say anything, but his thumb stroked the rapid beat of her pulse before sliding to her chin and tilting her face to his. "Trust me."

She inhaled a deep breath. "Let's get this over with so I can breathe again."

Amusement tugging his mouth, he slid his arm around her waist then bent his head and pressed his lips to hers. Eve gasped. The air swished out of her lungs, and the world around her swirled and disappeared into a vortex.

Oh, crap, they were dematerializing. She clung to him despite her body having the consistency of air. His arms tightened around her. Before she could get her racing mind to understand that he'd actually kissed her, they took form again in a dimly lit corridor.

"Don't ever do that again!" She shoved away from him and stumbled, the floor rushing to meet her. He steadied her and raised an eyebrow. "Did you think we'd knock on the front door?"

She scowled. "Very funny."

Her lips still tingled from his too brief kiss, aware he'd only done that to distract her. Taking a deep breath, she glanced around. They were in a part of the museum never seen by visitors. Reynner must have done a thorough investigation if he knew this maze of passages so well.

"This way." He led her down the eerily quiet corridor to a door at the end. A second later, a soft click sounded and it opened.

"Know your way around, do you?" she snipped.

"Made it a point to know. Always. On the off chance I found you."

Eve scrunched her face at his words. But she'd never

tell him how glad she was that he could cover their tracks. She dreaded what could happen if they got caught. Ugh! What a lame-head. They wouldn't get caught, he'd probably just dematerialize them out of the place.

Reynner stepped into the darkened room, grabbed her arm, and held her back when she would have walked past him. The musty odor of ancient objects and wood remained suspended in the air. A shiver ran through her. "What is it?"

"We don't want to set off any alarms."

Edgy, Eve shifted on her feet and waited at his side while he scanned the place before letting her go. "We're good."

"What did you do?"

"I cast a haze around this room. It won't interfere with the surveillance monitors as long as no one comes looking.

At the appearance of a glowing white light, Eve spun around, her heart in her throat, and saw the small orb leaving Reynner's palm to hover above them. The ball immersed them in a circle of light. As they headed for the crates, the thing followed.

Of course, he'd be able to do things like this. First the sword he'd summoned in that alley, now this light. She still had to wrap her mind around the fact that he was an angel, one who was hell-bent on getting her in trouble.

She glanced about, taking in the enormous storeroom. Towers of crates of different sizes loomed above them. "Are you going to open everyone?"

Jeez, they'd be here the entire night—if not the week.

He passed several open crates, avoided the bubble

wraps and polystyrene bags, and stopped to look around him. "No. It will take too long. Go—just touch the boxes."

He had to have lost his ever-loving, ancient mind. "My abilities only work on living things."

"Eve, there are dozens of crates here. *I* will have to open each one, but you just need to touch the lids. Even if I do find the scroll, I can't touch the damn thing, it will disappear again and we don't have the luxury of waiting centuries for it to reappear."

When he put it like that... She touched the wooden box closest to her. Waited. Nothing. She tried another.

"Why did it disappear in the first place?" she asked him.

"It's linked to the Stones. Seems it has to co-exist for harmony."

"What if the scroll tears or burns?"

He cut her a terse look. "It's mystical. It will disappear when it senses treachery or danger."

Okay, then.

"You need to concentrate," he said, hovering like a menacing shadow next to her, his attention on her hands while she stroked a lid. The brightness from the orb made all the flaws of her puckered skin visible. The urge to hide them grew. Instead, she headed for another crate and laid her palm on the covering.

Reynner followed.

She spun to him, her fingers curling into fists, and snapped, "I can't do this with you hovering over me."

He narrowed his eyes at her tight expression. "Very well. I will wait here."

A half-hour later, she let out a rough breath. This entire venture had failure stamped on it. She felt nothing but rough wood, literally. Reynner would see soon enough that they were wasting time. Heck, he could have just opened the boxes with his mind, but no—

He startled all holy hell out of her, hauling her into a dark corner, her front plastered to his.

"What is it—" His palm shot over her mouth. The orb vanished. The room plunged into darkness. He held her tightly against him. Eve was too terrified to enjoy the contact. She could see nothing, then she heard the voices. Footsteps came closer.

Her grip tightened on his shirt, her heart thumping wildly while his continued its steady beat.

Flashlight zipped around the room and right across where they stood. Eve froze.

"All's good here. Was so sure I heard a noise," one of the security guards said.

"Nuh. Probably a rat or something." Their steps receded, and the door closed behind them.

Christ! Eve collapsed against Reynner.

His arms tightened around her. "You okay?" he murmured against her ear.

Eve pulled in a deep, shuddering breath, nodded, and pushed away from him for the sake of her sanity. A little unsteady from the shock of near discovery but more from being crushed against Reynner's body.

He summoned the orb once more. She started on the boxes again.

Eve worked her way through several more crates. Except for adding to her collection of splinters, she sensed nothing. And she really, really wanted to get out of here.

"Anything?"

His voice, so close, startled her. How he walked in those heavy boots without a sound, she had no idea.

"Nothing. Not even a hum," she said. "I'm sorry."

"Dammit, Eve, it's here." His tone held a harsh bite. "You've made up your mind it doesn't exist, so it doesn't. Do you think I don't exist, too?"

"Oh, I know you exist, or else I wouldn't be in here, committing a felony and nearly getting caught."

"Don't. My world being in peril is not something to take lightly."

At his rebuke, she fell silent and bit her lip.

She was ashamed because a part of her didn't want to believe in this scroll. Finding the Stone would make everything right in his world. Aerén had said it was the only way Empyrean couples could soul-join and have children again. And Reynner would find someone, too.

Her stomach hollowed at the thought. Not wanting to think about that, Eve forced herself to concentrate on her task. Slowly, she worked her way through the boxes, stroking them, once, twice—

"Dammit!" She snatched her hand back.

Reynner appeared at her side. "What is it?"

"Splinter—shh." Ignoring his raised brow, she rested her palm on the lid again. A tingle darted through her hand, like a low-voltage electrical current. A sliver embedded in her finger wouldn't do that. She ignored the sharp sting and ran her hand over the wooden surface of the small chest. The hum whizzed through her once more. "Something's in here, if the buzzing in my hand is what you meant."

Reynner stared at her, almost in disbelief. Then he moved and she hurriedly stepped aside, she didn't want to be railroaded by a huge Empyrean. He made quick work of unsealing the box. And nodded. "Take it."

Eve picked up the old lead cylinder nestled inside the bubble wrap. She uncapped the tube and carefully eased out a yellowed, aged, parchment before dropping the tube back in the crate. The paper crackled between her fingers, and the humming whirred through her. Like flames, it spread through her blood and pooled between her thighs.

Whoa—what the heck?

Eve grabbed onto the nearest crate to steady herself, squirmed, and shifted on her feet. Unexplained arousal took her hard. No slow build-up. She sucked in air, tried to steady the rampant pounding of her heart. Clenching her aroused feminine parts just made it worse.

Nothing worked. Her gaze fell on Reynner as he substituted the replacement scroll and resealed the box. The man was dressed in leathers again and so damn hot. She wanted him. Heck, she had from the moment she'd first crashed into him. The scroll slipped from her limp fingers and fluttered to the floor.

Reynner turned and frowned. "Eve?"

She didn't respond. She simply walked over, grabbed him by his shirt, and yanked him down, kissing him right there in the musty smelling room.

He went motionless.

A heartbeat.

Two.

Then he hauled her into his arms and took over, his tongue sweeping into her mouth. The taste of him was a punch to her gut. White-hot desire tore through her. She rubbed her sensitized body against his, her fingers tangling in his hair.

He picked her up, spun around and pressed her up against a stack of crates covered with sack, his groin grinding into her core as his mouth devoured hers. Her legs tightened around his hips.

Desire burned higher. She wanted his hands on her bare skin.

"More, I need more," she whimpered against his mouth. Lost in her need, she pulled his t-shirt free to slide her hands under the cotton fabric to caress his warm, muscled back. "I need you."

"Eve—"

"Stop talking—" She wrapped his hair around her fists, keeping him there. She kissed him harder.

His hands dropped to her hips, holding her still. Lips lingered. Hands stroked her back, once, twice, and then he broke the kiss and held her in a tight embrace.

"Gods, Eve—" A half groan tore free from him, his erection a hard, tempting length against her throbbing center. "Eve, stop." He lowered her down to her feet. Easing away, he searched her face.

"Why?" she growled. "I know you want me."

He rubbed his jaw; a streak of red slashed his cheekbones. "I can't take advantage of your vulnerable state."

"Vulnerable—*vulnerable*?" she snapped, unable to think past the need roiling through her like wildfire.

"It's…the scroll. I would take it from you if I could, but I can't. Just hang onto it for a little bit longer. We'll put it in a safe place. And you'll be fine."

Panting, she glared at him. "You should have warned me," she hissed through teeth clenched so hard her jaw hurt.

"I'm sorry, Eve."

Yeah, he was sorry. Try being a twenty-five-year-old virgin, who was so horny she was seconds from ripping his clothes off. She shoved back strands from her heated face and stomped away in frustration.

After several deep breaths, which did little to ease

her, Eve went back to where she'd dropped the scroll. Keeping her gaze off him was the devil's work. But she did. She picked up the parchment and pushed it back into another lead tube he held out.

"Eve—"

"Let's just get out of here." She didn't look at him, just headed for the door with that stupid ball of light following them.

***

Eve found Lucan wearing a path outside her apartment. And was tempted not to invite him inside. Did he think she'd renege on her promise that he had to make a personal appearance?

She was well aware that he didn't like her. But right then, she cared little for his reasons because that priest—mage, whatever the hell he was, looked damn tempting, too. Being in Reynner's arms again as he dematerialized them back, did little to cool her ardor.

Lucan examined the scroll she'd removed from the tube and left on the dining table without touching it. They weren't taking any chances with the parchment disappearing again. He turned to speak to Reynner.

Whatever he said didn't register; she had no interest in their conversation.

Good thing Lucan was easy on the eyes. Far better to gaze at him than to long for what was so far out of her reach. Hell, it would probably be easier to get Lucan into bed than Reynner. She certainly didn't want Lucan, but with needs so rampant, she felt like someone else possessed her body.

She rubbed trembling palms down her yoga pants. God, she needed some damn relief…

***

The musky scent of Eve's arousal tormented Reynner

as she paced near the window. His entire body wired hard in response to her needs, his sex rigid and uncomfortable behind his fly.

He shoved clenched hands into his pockets. She didn't understand. If he touched her the way she—hell, *he* wanted, he'd taint her with the filth roiling inside him—the darkness—and *that* he refused to let happen.

"Eve," Lucan called out. "Let's get started."

She paused in her restless walking. Desire stroked a flush across her cheekbones. Reynner doubted she actually saw Lucan, but while she was still trapped in the grips of the scroll's spell, if anyone touched her right now, she wouldn't care, all she'd seek was relief—

"No." Reynner intercepted, putting himself between them. "Keep that away from her."

"Reyn," Lucan said impatiently. "This is hardly the time to get—" He stilled, nostrils flaring, irritating the shit out of Reynner. Yeah, the bastard could smell Eve's arousal, too.

His cool eyes shifted to her for a second, then without a word, Lucan set a lead box on the dining table. And waited.

"Eve, come." Reynner motioned for her to join him.

She wrapped her arms around her waist and shook her head. "I'm not coming near th-that thing again."

"Eve." He hardened his gaze so she'd get moving. "Put the scroll back inside the cylinder. We'll do the scrying later." When she didn't, he snapped, "*Now*."

Scowling, she shot him another heated look, one laced with anger and edged with desire.

But to be the focus of her passion—gods, if that didn't make his bloody cock stir in anticipation.

She marched over, snatched the scroll off the table,

and dropped it into the tube, capping it.

Her cell rang. She dropped the cylinder like yesterday's trash in the lead box, grabbed her phone off the table, and answered. "David." A breathy sigh left her as if all were right in her world. Her tone dipped, became throaty. "No, of course, it's not too late..."

Not too late? At fucking three in the morning?

Reynner walked over. Just because he couldn't touch her didn't mean she could saunter on to the next available male.

"Yes...tomorrow's still on... why would I cancel? All right, see you then." She wiped her palm down her black pants again. "Er, David, would you—"

No. Fucking. Way. Before he did something they'd both regret, Reynner snatched the cell from her and disconnected the call. "Speak to the artist when you're less susceptible to the scroll."

Her eyes narrowed dangerously. "I didn't ask for your advice. And it's none of your business if David comes over."

He stepped closer, lowered his voice. "Oh, yes it is, Eve. If you think him to be my replacement—"

Rage flashed in her green eyes, stopping him dead in his tracks, and breathless in anticipation.

"You bastard," she hissed and shoved him hard in the chest. He barely felt the hit, but he let the momentum take him back. Her hurt and anger lashed at him, pounding him with regret.

She stormed off. Seconds later, her room door banged shut, the sound resonating down the short passage and into the pit in his chest.

A crack ricocheted through the air.

Reynner glanced at her cell he held; the glass sported a spidery crack. Breathing harshly, anger bleeding through his pores, he tossed the phone onto the counter.

"Put that thing someplace it can't cause any more problems," he snapped, nodding at the scroll.

Lucan locked the lead box. The tight set of his mouth slapped Reynner with the truth. Lucan was just as aroused.

He didn't give a fuck. He wanted him gone.

Lucan, however, made no move to leave.

"What the hell are you waiting for?"

"The morning. So we can try again."

"You think that shit flies with me? Get out, Luc, and take the damn box with you. I'll bring her to Exilum in the morning." Reynner stalked to the front door and yanked it open.

His brow climbing up, silently, Lucan picked up the lead box and strode from the apartment.

Chapter 15

Eve's eyelids cracked open. The bright sunlight streaming in between parted curtains made her wince. Groaning, she squeezed her eyes tight feeling as if she'd crawled out of a fog...

Then reality smacked her in the face and last night's debacle came back in all its ghastly detail.

Ack, now she'd have to face Reynner.

So not the way she wanted to start the day. A pity hiding in bed couldn't be a constitutional right for gut-churning embarrassment.

Forcing her lethargic limbs to move, she rolled off the bed and stumbled from her room, down the short hallway, and to the bathroom. Eyes half closed, she turned on the faucet, undressed, and stepped into the shower. The rush of cool water beating down on her slapped her back into normalcy.

No, hiding wasn't the way she rolled anymore. She'd just have to chalk this up to another of life's little lessons. Eve took stock of herself. No buzzing or sexual hum or whatever the heck spell the scroll had had her under. All was as it should be with just blood flowing through her veins. She heaved a sigh of relief.

After a quick shower, she toweled off and pulled on underwear, followed by khaki-green capris and a white cap-sleeves top. She fastened her damp hair in a high ponytail, slipped her feet into flip-flops and headed for the kitchen, the scent of coffee drifting to her.

She found Reynner alone in the living room, dressed for the day in black jeans and a gray tee, his hair tied back with a black elastic band.

At her entrance, he turned from the window. She wondered if he ever relaxed. Everything about him was too contained, except for that time in his bedroom when he'd lost control. He may have been furious with her, but that's how she wanted him. All raw passion focused only on her.

She met his cool gaze. No, she wouldn't ever see him lose control like that again.

Swallowing her regret, she poured a mug of coffee, loaded it with sugar, and took a deep drink.

Reynner crossed to the small counter that separated the kitchen. "Are you all right?"

She nearly choked on her coffee. *Of course, he'd ask about last night.* Her gaze shifted to a bakery box on the counter and clung to it like a lifeline. "I'm fine. You got doughnuts?"

She lifted the lid off the carton and found an assortment of cakes. Selecting one powdered with sugar, she took a bite. Nope, she couldn't imagine Lucan trekking through the Village to buy doughnuts. He'd probably freeze everyone with his glacial stare. It had to be Reynner.

"Where's the mage," she asked, licking her lips free of powered sugar.

"Gone." At the abrupt response, she looked up. The

burn in that indigo stare held her breathless. He looked like he wanted to devour her. And naturally, her treacherous body melted in response.

But when his expression closed off, wiping out the moment like it had never happened, pain rose from deep within her. Her appetite disappeared. She dropped the doughnut back into the box. If he could pretend there was nothing between them, then she'd just have to try, as well.

Eve forced her mind back on the job she had to do. "What happens next?"

"Once the scroll reveals the location of the Stone, we go get it."

"That's it?"

He nodded. "I asked Lucan to hold off with the scrying since the scroll seemed to be having an adverse effect on you. It would be safer if we went back to Exilum to do the rest."

He didn't have to remind her that their enemies were lurking in the shadows, waiting for an opportunity to grab the artifact.

"We'll leave as soon as you're ready."

That's what he thought. Before she took off to another realm, her life on this one needed her attention first. She discarded her coffee and rinsed her mug in the sink. "Not today."

"Why not?"

Setting the cup aside, she shut off the faucet and faced him. "Because I have a life here, too. I don't know how long we'll be gone. And I can't have my friends wondering where I am." At his narrowed-eyed look, she couldn't resist adding, "You can come over tomorrow, I should be ready."

"So you can keep your date with the artist?" The flat

words took on a razor edge.

"That's none of your business." It wasn't jealousy that provoked his reaction, but his determination to not let anything stand in his way of finding the artifact.

Well, too damn bad. She choked back her anger, swiped her car keys and bag off the counter, and stormed to the front door. And came to a grinding halt when she found him already there. She really hated that he could move so fast.

It was pointless to say anything, especially when he had *that* look on his face. One that spelled trouble, all tight lips and hard eyes. Clamping down her frustration, she stalked out of the apartment. When she stopped beside her blue Mini Cooper, he stared at her like she'd lost her mind. Unlike normal people, she couldn't take public transport because the risks were too great. A crowd meant opening herself to a crapload of emotions. And summer was far too hot to wear gloves all the time.

Reynner strode over to his Porsche parked on the opposite side of the street. He opened the passenger door and waited. As far as the debate of wills went, she wasn't winning this one.

"Where to?" he asked once they were in the car.

"The gallery."

***

Eve thankfully stepped out of the ancient elevator when the door finally chimed open on the sixth floor. Being so close to Reynner wasn't good for her peace of mind. Now with the scroll in hand, it should only be a matter of days before the Stone was located. Then Reynner would be gone.

She pulled in a deep breath and tried to ease the compression in her chest at the thought as she entered the air-conditioned gallery. The strong odor of linseed oil and paint assailed her nose.

Eric wasn't in, but his assistant, James, was. Slender and average height, he slouched at his desk, one hand playing with his spiked brown hair as he spoke on the phone.

Whereas Reynner was beautiful in a masculine way, James was pretty with his pale skin and sharp features. He looked up.

"Eve, so good to see you, girl. David swung by earlier—" Then he did a double-take when his gaze landed on Reynner. Hastily, he cut off his call and rose to his feet, interest gleaming in his baby blues. "Eric's at the warehouse. Let me show you."

Eve snorted. As if she didn't know who had garnered James's sudden interest in playing tour guide. "Thanks, James. I'm sure I can find my way."

"Wait-wait." he stopped them, his attention still on Reynner. "I saw you at David's show."

Reynner nodded, his expression like stone. Eve was sure it wasn't because of the subtle, sexy vibes James was sending him, but rather that David had been mentioned. After last night—and Reynner's reaction this morning—she'd have to be blind not to realize he didn't like David.

James stopped and stared at them in confusion, then shook his head and went back to his desk.

"What did you do?" she asked Reynner, because she knew James. He wasn't one to walk away that easily.

"I willed him to leave." Reynner cut her a grim look. "It saves time. Where's the warehouse?"

"Fifth floor."

Not wanting to be boxed in with him again, she ignored the elevator and headed for the stairwell and took the dimly lit stairs down, Reynner behind her.

Moment's later, Eve shoved open the door to the warehouse. The drone of voices and the sounds of wooden lids clattering to the floor, welcomed her, easing the tension building inside her.

Eric, in tattered jeans and a faded blue tee, supervised several workers unpacking her sculptures. He saw her and closed the distance easily with his quick strides and a smile.

"Eve, good, you're here." He rubbed her arm in greeting then frowned at Reynner who stood beside her, looking all hard-eyed lethal with that edge of anger she still sensed in him.

"I wanted to check on the sculptures," she said quickly, pulling Eric's gaze back to her. "But they seem to have survived the journey. I better reassemble them."

"What do you need to do?" Reynner asked her.

She cut him a quick look as she pulled out the box of clamps from her bag. "It's a simple procedure putting them together. I'm good."

"Eve."

He said her name in that low, inflexible tone, which meant he expected an answer. And she really didn't want Eric drawn into whatever this thing between them was. "Okay. Let me show you."

"So, Eve, you going to introduce us?" Eric's dark brow climbed up in a manner that told her there would be questions. She stifled a sigh. That's what happened when you grew up with someone who knew everything about you—well, almost everything.

Tucking a strand of hair behind her ear, she made the introduction. "Eric, this is Reynner—Reynner, my friend, Eric Randall."

As was his habit, Reynner nodded. Eric probably took his cue from Reynner and responded in kind.

Okay, then. She could do without the tension-filled non-bonding going on.

Eve glanced at the sculpture closest to her, "Trees in a Storm." The piece was several inches taller than her, the metal branches bent over, blowing in one direction. She set the clamps on the crate. Quickly and efficiently, she reassembled several of the lower branches, showing Reynner how the clamps worked to attach them. The top was tricky, needing a specialized bracket.

The large, empty crate was still near the sculpture. She kicked off her flip-flops, shook her head when Reynner stepped up to help her, and clambered, unaided and undignified, onto the crate to attach the branch and clamp it into place.

"It's really easy," she murmured and turned to hop off the box.

Reynner grasped her around the waist. Startled, her hands fluttered to his shoulders. She met his dark, determined stare. Her heart raced around in her chest as he set her on the floor. Despite everything that had happened between them, Eve wished desperately for him to hold her just for a minute—a second. But he dropped his hands and stepped back.

Eve lowered her gaze and slipped on her flip-flops, disappointment sliding to her stomach like a ball of copper wire.

"Eve, a word," Eric said. His expression hard, he nailed Reynner a cold look. Aw, crap, Eric had to have seen that little exchange between them.

Eric led her between several large crates to the far end of the storeroom. He lowered his voice and got straight to the point. "Who is he? And what are you doing with him?"

She sighed at the brotherly grilling. When her folks died, Eric's parents became her guardians. They had been friends since she was a little girl. Several years older than her, Eric had been the one she'd leaned on while she'd grappled with her devastating loss and came to terms with the horror of not being able to touch anyone.

"He's a friend, Eric."

"Don't feed me that line. I know you met him at David's show—I'm not blind, Eve. Are you involved with him?"

She wished she could say yes. Her gaze flickered over to where Reynner was making rapid progress assembling her sculptures, then glanced away. "Not in the way you think. I'm helping him with something—and, no, I'm not telling you. Christ, Eric, give a girl some privacy."

At the concern in his hazel eyes, she relented. "I'm sorry. I like him, Eric," she whispered. "I really do."

"Does he return those feelings?"

"It's complicated." Her friend understood how difficult it was for her to form any real relationships with her disability. Whatever he saw in her face, he pulled her into a tight embrace. Her fingers balled, Eve hugged him back and blinked away the dampness in her eyes.

He glanced at Reynner, lowered his voice. "He looks...dangerous. Just be careful, okay? You're my little sister, Eve, and I don't want you to get hurt. Because then I'd have to hurt him, and he'd probably flatten me—you don't want that, do you?"

With a trembling smile, she eased back. "Thank

you."

"For what?"

"For not pushing."

He sighed. "Believe me, I want to—but I love you and trust you to know what you're doing."

Inhaling a steadying breath, she headed out of their crated forest back to Reynner. Not by a look did he reveal if he'd heard their conversation. But those indigo eyes skimmed over her face.

"Are you okay?"

"Yes."

His gaze became steel. So he did hear them.

It was foolish to hope he wouldn't. Hurriedly, Eve picked up more clamps and began reassembling the rest of the sculptures. Reynner and Eric worked alongside her.

"That should do it for now," Eric said a while later. "See you Saturday, Eve. You can check on the final display before showtime."

"All right." Eve picked up her bag from one of the crates. "See you then."

"Reynner." Eric nodded.

"Eric."

A hand on her back, Reynner ushered out, startling her at that possessive move as they headed toward the elevator. Eric followed

Stepping away from Reynner, Eve pressed the button then swung around. "Oh, Eric, I meant to ask, did that..." Darn, she didn't want to ask about this in front of Reynner, but could do little else unless she wanted to scurry back into the warehouse to ask her question. "Did *that* painting sell?"

"Yes. Same night. I can check my sales record if you'd like?"

She grimaced. "God, no, I don't want to know. Thank you."

Laughing, Eric rubbed her arm in affection. "I'll see you soon." Then to Reynner he said, "I trust you're coming to Eve's show?"

"I'll be there." A promise.

She wasn't sure if territory was marked, but she wasn't interfering in this age-old battle for dominance. Besides, she had a feeling she knew who would be the victor. Except, why would he fight when *she* was the prize?

"Good. Now, I've got to run." Eric took off for the stairs to the top floor.

Her cell phone rang. She pulled it out of her pocket and frowned at the cracked glass. But when she saw the name on the display, she bit her lip.

"Aren't you going to answer your call?"

Eve looked up and clashed with Reynner's stony gaze. He already knew.

Last night, inviting David over hadn't been one of her most brilliant ideas, but the pain of rejection had her doing stupid things.

Tired of the contradictions when it came to him, tired of hoping and longing, Eve ignored the ringing cell and asked him outright, "Is that what you want?"

A tic pulsed on his clenched jaw. Silently, he stared at her.

Well, then, guess she had her answer. Why did she even bother asking?

As they stepped into the waiting elevator, Eve firmed her chin, ignoring the painful crater opening in her stomach. No matter the attraction that existed between them, point was he refused to do anything about it. The ringing stopped, only to start up again. She answered.

"David, hi."

"Been trying to get ahold of you—are you okay?" David asked her.

"I'm fine—I'm sorry about last night." She hoped he wouldn't ask awkward questions. He didn't. But then David's mind didn't run along sex like most guys, he probably thought she wanted to talk work.

"That's all right. You're busy now?"

She rubbed her temple at the headache that had started. "A bit. I'm at the gallery."

"Aw, man. I was there earlier. I must have just missed you. Anyway, I've been thinking, about dinner. Instead of going out, would you like to... Would you like to come over to my place tonight?"

Her stomach dipped. Her grip tightened around her cell, and her gaze dropped to the scarred floor. Showed what she knew. David *was* asking. And especially after her seductive phone call in the early parts of the morning. It was the damn scroll's fault she was in this mess!

"Your place—"

Reynner moved like lightning, trapping her against the steel wall with his body, palms slapping beside her head. Her cell fell to the ground with a loud clatter.

"Don't taunt me, Eve."

"Taunt you?" A harsh breath rushed out of her. "Christ, you're a selfish jerk."

Fury tightened his face. "You think I want this? Hurting you this way?"

"I have no idea what you want." She shoved him hard, unable to bear having him so close. But he didn't budge. He grabbed her hands and pinned them to her back, reached out and jabbed the Stop button with a vicious finger. The elevator came to a jarring halt.

"Let me go!"

"No."

"Why are you doing this?" she cried. When he didn't answer, tears of despair thickened her voice. "Goddamn you, Reynner."

His eyelids squeezed tight for a brief second before they snapped open. Tortured blue eyes met hers. The pain there nearly stopped her heart. "I have been dammed, Eve. So many times over."

Then he kissed her.

Shocked, she remained still for a second. The hand shackling her wrists to her back pulled her close, every warm, tough inch of him pressing against hers. He held her like she mattered. Tears misted her eyes. She'd waited so long for this moment, for him to kiss her because it was what he wanted, too. The kiss at the museum didn't count. It was just the scroll affecting them. But here, this was all she'd dreamed of.

Reynner's lips slid over hers, nipping, tasting, and finally, demanding entry. He wrapped his other hand around her ponytail as he took possession of her mouth. Made it his own. Hot, possessive, he branded her with his lips, his touch and taste.

Eve moaned. Her head spun as unbelievable sensations tore through her. She tried to free her hands, wanted to hold him, but he wouldn't let go.

***

Reynner explored the lush mouth beneath his. Her warm, soft body wiggled against him and his sex strained against his fly. The urge to rip off her clothes and slide into her silky warmth grew. The kiss from the museum still haunted him.

She tugged again, trying to free her wrists, but he didn't dare let her touch him. Too afraid of what he'd do. His needs too dark—too twisted, and she was far too pure and innocent for one like him.

Take her. It's what you want, but don't trust her. Never trust any of them.

No! He yanked away and retreated to the other end of the elevator. Breathing hard, he fought to get himself under control.

"Reynner?"

He held out a hand to stop her approach. Shook his head. Blood pounded in his head, urging him to finish what he started, to take her here in the elevator.

No—no! She was good. Decent. She deserved better than him.

Gods, he had to save her from himself.

"Eve, I can't..." He turned away, his fists balled so tight, so he wouldn't tear a hole in their metal cage. "I can't give you what you want, Eve. I'm not whole. I'm a fucking mess—damaged. I'd just hurt you."

"Stop it!" She moved in front of him, her chest heaving. Her beautiful eyes flashed emerald fire. Passion. Anger. He tried not to look at her mouth, lush from his kisses.

"I don't know the facts, but I do know you can't help what happened to you..." She reached out to touch him but dropped her hand at the last minute. "I know there won't be a happily-ever-after for me. I made peace with that a long time ago. But I'd hoped—" She broke off, inhaled a shaky breath.

He shouldn't ask. But her answer became imperative. A lifeline. How much more twisted could he get? His mouth opened, the questions fell out. "What Eve? What did you hope for?"

Her lips trembled. She struggled with the words. "A moment—a moment of your time for me alone—to know I mean something to you."

At her soft words, a deep ache and an intense longing seeped through him. Gods, he wanted her. Wanted to be inside her, wrapped around her and the beautiful dream she offered.

But everything was too fucked up, his life so screwed. And he had no one to blame but himself.

To stop from doing something insane, like promise her all sorts of things he could never hope to fulfill—not when his life would never be his own—he stabbed the button for the ground floor. Then he picked up her cell. The glass sported even more cracks. His own gut ripping open, he said, "I'm sorry, Eve. I didn't mean for this to happen."

A long moment of silence passed before she spoke. Like the life in her had died. "Yes. I'm very sure you didn't."

And a heart he thought he no longer possessed shuddered in pain.

Chapter 16

Back at Exilum, and after speaking with Lucan, Reynner headed for the living room. As he entered, Eve glanced his way. Nothing showed on her face when she saw him. She turned back to stare through the window at the cascading waterfalls. He had to steel himself from walking over.

They'd arrived a few hours ago, and she still hadn't spoken a word to him since that moment in the elevator.

He wasn't good for her, didn't she get that?

You can't trust them. The whispers continued to torment him.

But one thing he understood about himself, if she'd gone on that date, he would have hurt the artist. He had to get her away from there, and the safest place from all the shit messing with his head was Exilum.

Footsteps sounded, and Lucan entered. Eve warily eyed the lead box he carried. Reynner couldn't blame her for her apprehension. He certainly didn't care for the way the parchment affected her.

Aerén, following Lucan, smiled at Eve and dropped

onto the couch. Reynner realized one other person had joined them.

Northaen. The change in the male took Reynner by surprise. His once striking features though gaunt were harsh, as if hewn in granite. He appeared older and was a shell of the man Reynner once knew. His dark brown hair was longer now, and pulled back in a ponytail.

Losing his mate to the wars on their realm had taken its toll. Programmed only for vengeance, he'd become one of the most lethal warlords in Empyrea.

Northaen glanced at him and nodded. His pale green eyes shifting to Eve, he stopped. Reynner saw the first sign of life enter them.

Eve looked nothing like North's mate, who'd been a statuesque blonde, but something about her had caught the warrior's attention. Uncurling his clenched fist, Reynner crossed to her and introduced them. "Eve, this is Northaen of Kalasder. North, Eve Leighton."

"Hello." She slipped her hands into her jeans pockets. Reynner could feel her uneasiness. Since a handshake wasn't their way of greeting, he shouldn't worry, but still.

North bowed. "For what you do, you have my sword and eternal gratitude."

A smidgen of relief crawled through Reynner. This had everything to do with putting Empyrea on its feet and ending the wars, not a sudden revival of sexual needs.

Then Eve smiled and pushed a loose strand of hair behind her ear. "I'm happy to help."

Reynner didn't care for the easy smile she gave North, or that the warrior was here because of her safety. But the reality was, even though Reynner could protect Eve well enough on his own, his life wasn't his.

With Inanna on his back, shit always fell when he least expected it.

"Eve."

At the sound of Lucan's voice, she inhaled sharply and her soft mouth tightened. Straightening her spine, she made her way over and knelt in front of the low table. Reynner followed and stood opposite her. Hopefully, the magic had settled and wouldn't affect Eve again now that she'd touched it.

She reached into the box and lifted the lead cylinder. Her slender, scarred fingers trembled. Like a foggy cloud, her trepidation settled over her. She slowly uncapped the tube and eased out the scroll. Setting the container aside, she unrolled and flattened the ancient parchment on the wooden table. A low whoosh of breath left her. Her fists relaxed. Loose-limbed, she sat back on her heels.

Eve lifted her head. Green eyes smoldered, slumberous in their intensity and fixed on him. The light, intoxicating musk of female arousal drifted through the room.

Reynner froze. *Oh, shit, no, no, no!*

Across the room, North stiffened. His gaze swung to Eve then dropped to study his boots. Aerén stared at her in surprise. He shifted in his seat and leaned forward, bracing his arms on his thighs. Lucan went robot still beside her.

Dammit! Naturally, they would react to Eve's tempting scent of arousal.

Reynner's teeth gnashed down, knowing he was stuck because he couldn't take her away until she revealed the Stone's location.

Fury, utter possessiveness surging through him, he grasped Eve's hand, pulled her to her feet, and headed for the open doorway. It was either that or toss all the bastards over the balcony.

He stopped just past the entrance, not prepared to risk her out on the railless terrace until he put in some damn barriers.

She slid her hands up his chest, bunching the fabric of his shirt.

"Eve," he said in a sharp voice, trying to ignore his aroused body. "Look at me."

She raised those limp green pools, and her sultry stare whacked him in the gut. A red tinge rode her tanned skin. Being this close to her, his cock hardened painfully.

"Breathe, Eve," he rasped. "Slow and deep—come on, do it, *fiyae*." He clasped both of her hands, stroked her skin with his thumbs, aware of the others watching them. The sound of someone cracking their knuckles echoed like a gunshot in the tense silence. A shudder racked Eve's body. She sucked in a deep breath, then several more. She shook her head, and he saw her panic beneath the arousal. Her fear.

"I'm sorry, I didn't realize this would happen again."

She snatched her hands back as if scalded, wrapped them around her waist, and gave him a bitter look then walked back inside.

His mouth tight, he followed her.

Why the hell would the scroll affect her this way when it never had with anyone before?

***

God, she hated Reynner right then. Her arousal hiked and tightened her body. The longer she remained near the scroll, the worse it got. And the jerk would leave her to suffer.

Eve made her way back to the table, rubbing her

arms when she wanted to tear off the clothes abrading her too sensitive skin. Her lips compressed, she kept her gaze focused on the scroll and dropped to her knees in front of the table. With shaking hands, she smoothed out the parchment again. The hum grew sharper.

Oh, God in Heaven. *Why would you do this to me?* She tried desperately to shut off the needs tormenting her.

She could never have a relationship with anyone because of her abilities, and now this artifact would torture her. As if she hadn't suffered enough.

A stronger tingle zipped through her. Desire lit like a fuse and heated her blood, gathering at her core—the throbbing there so intense. Clamping down on her sensitized, inner muscles only made her anguish worse.

Eve squeezed her eyes shut in despair.

You must fight for what you want. The light, almost musical notes floated through her mind and warmed her.

Her eyes flashed open to stare into troubled indigo ones. Reynner had taken the spot across the wide tree-trunk coffee table again.

Fight for what I want? Right. A bitter laugh strangled in her throat. She might as well scale the Himalayas. She'd have more success than breaking through the walls of the man crouched opposite her. After that devastating kiss yesterday, he'd reverted back to his cold aloof self, enclosed in his fortress.

"Hold this over the script." Lucan's voice pulled her out of her despairing thoughts. He held out a small rod-shaped crystal suspended from a fine silver chain.

Eve stared at the pendant. Her hands hummed, almost like they were plugged into a low voltage unit. She flexed her fingers to ease the tingles. "No."

"What's wrong?" Reynner asked her.

Eve shook her head, took a deep breath, and let instinct guide her. She held her palms over the ancient writings. "It responded to me this way before, maybe it will again."

She closed her eyes, tried to concentrate. But it didn't help. Her misery made her angry…her thoughts became hazy. Whispers rolled through her mind… Stone of Light… *blood*… *magic*… her heart rate accelerated as the answer came to her. Her eyes snapped open.

"I need a dagger."

Three steel blades flashed before her. Eve jerked back in alarm and almost fell on her backside, but Reynner grabbed her upper arm. Like match to tinder, his touch sent tingles straight between her legs and the throbbing started in earnest. *Oh, God!* She tried to yank free, but his grip tightened.

"Why do you need a weapon?"

Did he think she'd hold a blade to his throat and jump him? She cut him a cold look. "Let. Go. Of. Me."

"Let her do what she must," Lucan bit out.

Reynner ignored him, but whatever he saw in her eyes made him release her. She hoped it was the look of his imminent death and not desperation. His dagger took form in his hand, and he handed it to her.

Eve gripped the heavy blade and frowned. She became aware of Lucan, along with the others, shifting away from her. Even Aerén. He leaned back in his seat, looking wary. The tension in the room heightened. They were all so still, almost as if they weren't breathing.

Reynner, hunkered opposite her, looked like he wanted to kill something—or someone. She had no idea what had set him off since he'd worn that expression from the moment they arrived in Exilum.

The sooner she got this done, the sooner she could leave. Her mouth flattening, she ran the lethal edge of the blade across her finger. The sudden, painful slice stung. She winced.

Reynner snatched the dagger from her. *"What the hell are you doing?"*

"It's all about blood, isn't it?" She watched her blood seep out then she held her finger over the parchment. The sounds of booted feet drew nearer again, and the men surrounded her.

A deep red globule formed on the tip of her finger and splashed down.

Like a parched land, the scroll greedily absorbed her blood. Eve watched, waited for all this to end while her needs hiked to new levels. The urge to stroke herself, to find some release, grew. She bit down on her lip, the coppery taste of blood coated her tongue.

Oh, God, please let this be over, she begged.

And her finger burned like hell. Reynner grasped her hand, then his mouth closed over the cut. His tongue stroked the small wound. Eve stifled a gasp, her heart in her throat. Arousal burned deeper at each lap of his tongue, pushing her to the edge.

She yanked her finger free and grasped the table with both hands, breathing hard.

Seconds later, something moved—the script, written in black ink, took on a red hue. Sharp, indrawn breaths rang through the room. Then absolute and utter silence as the ancient writings stirred and whirled around the parchment in dizzying speed, like they'd been jacked with adrenaline, to rearrange themselves in a language she couldn't understand.

When no one spoke, she glanced at Reynner. "What does it say? Does it tell you where the Stone is?"

He didn't answer as he rose to his feet.

Eve bit her lip in desperation, the fresh wound there made her wince. Since no one bothered to answer her, she pushed up and glanced at Reynner, who glared at Lucan.

He didn't even seem aware of her. Why would he care now? He'd finally gotten what he wanted, the location of the Stone. She no longer mattered.

On trembling limbs, she forced herself to walk out from the room.

In the corridor, she braced a palm on the wall and drew in a harsh breath. But nothing helped. She bit back a moan. Her skin was stretched so tight over her bones, she was afraid she'd shatter at a single touch.

Was there no escape from this savage need gnawing at her? Worse, she couldn't even leave, trapped in this mountaintop aerie.

"Eve?"

No-no! She pivoted as Aerén approached. If he touched her, she dreaded to think what could happen. "Stay away from me."

"You're hurting."

"Aerén, please, just go." She sucked in another breath, but nothing would ease her humming body. Her sensitive nipples brushing against her shirt became unbearable. She wrapped her arms around her chest and pressed down. "Why–why aren't you with them? Isn't this what you waited for?"

"Yes, but they don't need me. Let me aid you." Cautiously, he approached her as if afraid she'd jump off the balcony. She saw the concern on his face and something else, too…desire? The truth hit her like a punch in the belly. *Oh, God, he knows.*

"Go away, please." Tears of humiliation blurring her vision, she hurried for the front entrance.

Cursing in his language, she heard Reynner's name mentioned, then Aerén came after her. His jaw was set, but his light gray eyes were filled with empathy, too, as he put his arms around her and drew her close. Her body shuddered uncontrollably.

"Shhh...it's okay..." He stroked her arms, her back. Then said quietly, "We'll take this slow. I'm just sorry I'm not him."

He bent his head, his lips brushed hers.

Her lungs seized in shock.

Guilt flooded her. His touch didn't repel. It felt...good.

Soothing.

No! She struggled to deny him, all she thought of— the only one she wanted was—

He doesn't want you.

Eve fisted Aerén's shirt, tried to tamp down her arousal. But it was a lost cause. She could barely swallow past the painful lump in her throat, despair and unwanted desire sweeping through her as Aerén kissed her again...

Chapter 17

"What the hell does it mean? *Go back to the start. What you seek is but a tale away?*" Reynner snarled at Lucan, jabbing his finger toward the scroll.

Everything he'd endured and put Eve through, only to end up with the scroll giving them a fucking riddle.

Lucan frowned. "It's never straightforward with scrolls and cryptic messages. *Go back to the start,* would suggest our realm, where it started, but I don't think that's it—it has to be the mortal one."

"You mean New York?" Reynner snapped, trying to hold in his impatience, wanting to take Eve and get out of there. He was aware she'd left the room. Better she was outside then with these horny bastards.

"Yes. It makes sense," Lucan agreed. "It's where the scroll was awakened. The Stone will be close. Keep Eve safe while the search is in progress."

"From what I learned before I left Empyrea, Darkreans are gathering in force on this realm," Northaen said then. "Security is paramount. It's why I'm here."

"Yeah, fine. Fill me in later." Reynner pivoted and

his heart nearly stopped. The couch opposite where Eve had sat was vacant. With her in that tenuous state of arousal—the truth slammed him like a sledgehammer.

He wouldn't fucking dare!

Anger exploded in a flare of power, couches and table crashing into the walls. The others jumped out of the way as Reynner tore out of the room, down the corridor. If Aerén touched her, then what Reynner had done to bring down Hell when he'd broken free of his prison would be child's play.

***

Eve broke away from Aerén.

Why couldn't she want him? He was sexy, gorgeous, *and* gentle. He'd be perfect to ease the savage need riding her. But the bitter truth was that Aerén couldn't ease the pain of wanting someone else.

Reynner was too filled with hatred and a darkness that sucked out every facet of emotion in him. His mind focused only on his quest and killing demoniis. Despite the sting of his rejection, she couldn't change how she felt. And she really, really wished she could.

"Eve?"

She looked up. Her breath hitched, her body too jittery to calm down. Aerén stroked her cheek, his silver eyes bright with compassion and desire. "Let's get out—"

A furious draft of wind flashed past them and snatched her away from Aerén, making her head spin. Eve stumbled and braced a hand on the wall to steady herself. A loud thud echoed in the hallway, followed by a body hitting something hard. A clay pot crashed to the floor. Soil scattered, dislodging a small, leafy plant.

Reynner stood in front of Aerén. Fists clenched,

chest heaving, his body vibrating with barely leashed violence.

Aerén pushed away from the wall and straightened his shirt. His eyes glowed white with anger. Power rolled off him, and a sizzle ran through Eve.

She gasped, her body twitching. She didn't need this added stimulant along with everything else she was going through.

"I will do what you won't. I can always invoke our laws," Aerén snapped in warning. "I will not let her suffer needlessly."

Eve had no idea what that meant, didn't care. But Reynner stiffened. The ice in his gaze turned molten. "We are not in Empyrea. Touch her again, and I will kill you. Prince or not."

Aerén stilled. Then his expression morphed to a slow, dark smirk, like he just discovered something implausible.

Not caring what that was, she darted between them and glared at Reynner. "Don't you dare! Why do you care who I'm with?" she cried, rubbing her arms to ease the tingles. "I never asked for any of this." She flung her hand in the direction of the scroll. "I didn't."

She turned to Aerén, couldn't see him with tears crowding her eyes. "I-I want to get out of here, please."

A swim in the icy lake, and maybe, just maybe, she'd be able to breathe again.

A callused hand seized her wrist and hauled her out onto the balcony. Eve stumbled behind Reynner. Fabric ripped, resonating in the morning air as he tore off his tee and flung it aside. The ruined garment landed on the floor, and his wings reappeared in all their bronzed glory. His wild forest scent surrounded her.

She backed away. She didn't want this. It hurt too

much.

His eyes a blazing blue, Reynner came at her like some avenging angel. He scooped her into his arms and soared off the balcony.

Eve's horrified scream never made it past her lips. He captured her mouth in a fierce kiss, branding her with his touch, surrounding her with his warmth.

Her heart stuttered. How could he be so cruel to torment her like this?

She tore her mouth free from his and pushed at his chest. "How could you?"

"Stop, Eve. We're mid-air." He grabbed both of her hands with one of his. His other tightened around her waist, his erection pressing against her hips.

"How could you tell them what the scroll did to me?" she cried, betrayal crashing through her.

At her accusation, he growled, "I can smell your arousal from miles away—it seeps into my skin, coats my tongue, and haunts my senses. And they damn well could, too. You think I want them catching your scent. Getting worked into a frenzy by you?"

Eve froze. They'd smelled her? *That* was why they'd gone robot-still in the lounge? They were holding their breath?

Oh, God, it was worse than she imagined. Humiliating.

The moment Reynner landed them on the flat, sun-warmed boulders, Eve spun away and walked blindly into the trees. Unable to face him.

He came after her, blocking her path, eyes vivid with anger. His spread wings slapping against the branches in fury like he wanted the pain. "Where do you think you're going?"

"Leave me alone." She tried to walk around him.

A snarl. "So you can be with Aerén?"

She didn't care. Had nothing to lose. "At least he wants me!"

Eve didn't see him move. Her back hit a tree trunk, his mouth taking hers in a bruising kiss. She fought him, pain crushing her heart. She didn't want his pity. Furious, Eve bit him.

His head snapped back, blood beading on his lower lip.

"I'd rather a one-night-stand with Aerén than a pity fuck from you—"

"He'll never have you!"

"Go to hell!"

"My life is hell, Eve..." The words seemed to be torn from him. "That's all it's ever been."

He kissed her again. Not in anger, but one filled with need. Gently, he traced the seams of her lips with his tongue, then there was only his mouth sliding against hers... She melted against his body.

He lifted his head. His skin pulled taut across the sculptured bones of his face. "You think I don't want you?"

"I don't know what to think anymore," she whispered.

He stared at her for a long, heart-shattering second. "Undress."

"Wh-what?"

"Undress, Eve. Now."

At his demand, she swallowed. She would be naked in front of a man who showed no softness. Had none to give. Still, she wanted him so badly; it hurt just to breathe. With trembling fingers, she reached for the first button on her shirt, but her hands shook too much.

The next moment, he reached out and swiftly undid

the buttons and peeled her top off. He tossed it aside. Warm, callused palms slid to her back and her bra followed. Goosebumps flooded her skin at the cool air. Her nipples hardened. At his dark, caressing stare, she covered her breasts with her arms. He shook his head. "Don't."

He moved her hands away and his gaze swept slowly down her body. His warm palms spanned her waist then slid up in a sensual glide to cup her breasts, leaving behind a trail of heat in its wake. Squeezing gently, he pressed an open-mouthed kiss on the scar on her left breast, then dragged his tongue over her nipple.

Oh, God! Eve shuddered, her body thrown into a maelstrom of sensations.

His leathers creaking, he hunkered before her and snapped open the button of her jeans, his beautiful wings sweeping the damp leaves scattered on the ground. He unzipped, then parted the fly, and dragged another heated kiss down her stomach.

Eve grabbed his shoulders as he pulled the denim down her hips. She stepped out of them, and he tossed the garment aside. He gently nipped her stomach, eliciting another shudder from her. With his teeth, he caught the edge of her panties and pulled the scrap of cotton down her thighs, yanking them off.

He was at eye level and could see her—would see everything. Instinctively, she flung one arm across her breasts and the other covered her femininity.

"Eve." He removed her hands, keeping them in a gentle but firm hold at her sides. "Look at me."

Heat washed her face. Her heart raced. Biting back the urge to cover herself again, Eve met his burning gaze. Sunlight filtered through the treetops and dappled his pale hair in shimmering gold and silver hues. He was so beautiful.

"You are beautiful, Eve."

The intensity of his stare made her tremble. And just like the time in his room, he was crouched before her once more. Except there was no fear in her now. Instead, desire and a deep yearning to be in his arms took hold.

"Reynner, please…kiss me."

He did.

Parting her legs, he put his mouth right on her core. The first lick of his tongue nearly took her over the edge. A choked moan escaped her, his gaze flashed to hers. He pulled back.

"Reynner?"

"Not here." He rose, picked her up, and carried her farther into the trees—away from the decaying smell of vegetation—and laid her down on the soft, green grass. The sweet, clean scent perfumed the air.

Eve reached for the waist of his leathers. He shook his head and removed his pants, his heated gaze not leaving hers for a second.

Like some haloed, celestial being, his wings tucked against his body, he moved over her. Warm skin and powerful muscles slid seductively over her bare skin. His hard, hot length pressed against her inner thigh.

Showered with sensations, Eve inhaled an unsteady breath. She ran her palms over his shoulders to his back, and caressed the silky arches of his wings. His cock jerked, and he stiffened. Seconds later, in a swish, his wings disappeared.

Her fingers clenched. "Reynner?"

He shook his head and covered her mouth in a scorching kiss, pulling her back into his passionate warmth. Hot, possessive, he kissed her deeper and deeper...

Panting for air, Eve broke away. He didn't stop but latched onto her breast with his mouth. Desire like a gale force took hold as he tormented her nipple—sucking and licking first one, then he moving to the other.

She moaned, shifting her hips. He let go of her nipple and slid lower. His pale hair swept over her body in a million silky strokes as he trailed more kisses down to her navel. Spreading her thighs with his hands, he lowered his head.

This time, it wasn't just for a taste. He put his mouth on her and licked down one side of her cleft and up the other side. Pleasure grew and spread like a heat wave. She grasped his hair, holding on as her mind lost all cognizance. Every inch of her focused on the sensations coursing through her body.

Reynner explored her with a deep eroticism she'd only read about, licking around her neglected bundle of nerves and teasing her opening with his tongue, driving her wild out of her mind. When he suddenly locked his mouth on her swollen clit, she near came off the ground, a rasping cry tearing from her throat.

He held her down, tormenting her with soft licks and firm pulls. God, she didn't think she could last this sensual onslaught. "Reynner, please..."

He lifted his head, his lips glistening wet from her. "Please what, Eve?"

"More," she whimpered, needing him to ease the unbearable ache inside her.

Slowly, he eased a finger into her wetness, watching her face. But at the alien intrusion, she stiffened. He pulled out. His thumb glided over her clit, once, twice, then his finger pushed in again. After another slick glide of his thumb, he added another finger. Desire sharpened.

"Better?" he asked, voice rough.

Powerless to answer with the emotions crowding her, she nodded. Release hovered...so close. Pressure built between her thighs, she arched her hips up.

He lowered his head. As his fingers worked her, he sucked her clit again, teasing it with firm pulls and soft licks, then a sharp nip.

Eve cried out as unbelievable pleasure exploded through her, yanking her up and tossing her over.

It took her a few minutes—maybe several hours to get her breath back before she became aware of him gently kissing her there, his gaze on her.

Her hands still tangled in his hair, she tugged him up. "Now."

He moved up her body, his masculine heat surrounding her. She released her grip on him and glanced down. At the sizeable length of his sex, a moment of doubt invaded her. He was huge. And she'd never been with anyone, but when she met his heated stare, her hesitation vanished.

She reached between them, wanting to touch him, but he grasped her hand. Something dark flashed in his eyes.

An ache filled Eve. Because she knew why he wouldn't let her touch him so intimately.

He squeezed his eyelids tight as if in agony, then they snapped opened. "This is about you."

Not if she could help it. This was for both of them.

He ran his palms over her inner thighs as he spread them wider, then the blunt head of his cock nudged her opening, and he slowly pushed inside her.

Eve gasped at the tightness, at the unfamiliar,

uncomfortable stretching…

***

Reynner stilled, arms straining as he hovered above Eve. Her expression and her body tense, her short nails digging into his wrists. Discomfort edged her passion-filled green eyes.

He pushed in a little more, felt the resistance. *Aaand* like an eighteen-wheeler had just rammed him, his lungs flattened at the truth.

"You're a virgin—dammit—of course, you are!"

The dreaded V!

Now he godsdamn understood what it meant. When he was half-fucking-way inside her!

He moved to pull out.

"No—" Her grip tightened on his wrists. "Don't."

"Eve, I'm hurting you." And that he couldn't bear.

She took several deep breaths. "A moment, and I'll be fine."

So brave. She would accept him into her body, knowing what he was. Where he'd been.

Before the black memories took over and ruined this beautiful moment, he shoved back his thoughts and bolted his shields. This was about her.

Reaching between their bodies, he slid his fingers over her slick flesh, thumbing the tiny nub until her discomfort dissipated and arousal darkened her eyes once more. She moved beneath him, her legs wrapping around his hips.

"Now."

Unable to resist her breathy whisper, braced on his elbows to keep most of his weight off her, he lowered his head and kissed her deeply. In a single hard thrust, he sheathed himself completely inside her. Her cry of pain echoed in his ears and squeezed his heart, her fingers digging into his forearms.

By the heavens, she was so small. He held still, waited for her to grow accustomed to him. Tears shimmered in her eyes, and something inside him shifted, softened. Tenderly, he wiped away the single drop that escaped.

She humbled him, giving him the purity of her body. Overwhelmed with all the feelings crowding him, he kissed her again, revering her with his lips. He let his healing powers—such as they were—flow into her, hoping it would ease her.

Her body tensed and she pulled her mouth free and gasped in surprise. The discomfort in her expression gave way to wonder. Reassured, he eased out of her in a long slow glide then surged right back in again. Pleasure flowed across her face.

Her legs tightened around him once more. He thrust in and out, harder, faster in a ruthless rhythm, driving her towards release. The pressure in his groin grew, pushing him to the edge. He struggled to hold on, not to spill himself inside her—his thumb rolled over her clit, her climax exploded, her body pulsing around him as she fell.

Fuck, he had to pull out before it was too late. He started to withdraw even though everything in him protested. But she grabbed his arms, as if sensing his decision. "No—" she breathed. "Don't."

"Eve, I can't do this to you."

"Don't care," she whispered, reaching up to caress his face. "I waited all my life for you."

At her tender gesture, the heartfelt words, he closed his eyes as mistiness blurred his vision.

Her fingers entangled in his hair, she pulled him to her and kissed him deeply. Like a temptress, she wiggled her hips for him to move, and naturally, his fragile resistance crumpled.

Hell, he had none when it came to her, no matter what he said…because his heart belonged to her.

She grabbed his wrists to hold on as he pounded into her. Her pants of pleasure rang in his ears. Her feminine muscles fisted him, and his entire being unraveled. As he drove faster into her, a strange, powerful force took hold of him. He could do little to stop his life force from merging with hers.

Her eyes widened, the blue mating light shimmering in her green irises as he claimed her in the elemental way of his kind. "Your eyes," she gasped. "Glowing. Pretty."

He merely shook his head.

Her body bowed up as another orgasm ripped through her. Her core squeezed his cock so tight, a strangled grunt left his throat. He followed hard, releasing himself into her as a warm light flowed through him, brightening every dark corner of his soul.

Breathing harshly, he pressed his face in the scented hollow of her neck. That claiming white light inside him, a soft glow now. There was no darkness, no crushing rage that normally consumed him after his rare sexual encounters. Ones that usually left him empty afterwards.

Peace. Warmth. Eve.

Mine.

Her arms came around him, and his heart stuttered. She held him like he mattered. He could barely swallow at the emotions swarming him. She hauled him out of the nightmarish hell he'd lived in for so long and made intimacy beautiful for him again.

She'd completely undone him.

***

Eve held onto Reynner, still in the grips of her orgasmic euphoria. She floated outside her body, had no idea what had happened to them except that this was beyond her wildest imaginings. He was hot, thick, and still hard inside of her; she loved the tight feel of him.

He raised his head to look at her. "Are you all right?"

She nodded, unable to speak.

"I'm too heavy to stay atop you," he rasped and withdrew.

Eve winced at the slight burn as the spell surrounding them broke. Concern marred his face. She glanced between their bodies and saw the red tinge coating his sex just as Reynner looked down. Heat flooded her face that he would see evidence of her virginity. She tried to sit and sucked in a breath at the discomfort. She made to slide away from him, but he caught her hips.

"Where are you going?"

His slightly husky voice sent another round of shivers sweeping through her body. "I need a swim."

He shook his head and stroked her cheek. "No, Eve. The water's freezing, and you're sore."

But that's what she wanted. The icy water would soothe her discomfort. "Reynner, please, I have to—" she broke off and gasped, shock knocking her sideways when he parted her legs and licked her.

"Wait!" She grabbed his hair, tried to tug him away. "You can't—"

"I'm not leaving, not while you're hurting. My saliva will heal you."

That she didn't know. Absolute mortification took hold as he put his mouth on her again, but her embarrassment soon gave way to pleasure. Her body shook uncontrollably while he worked her with just his tongue. She panted, her fingers tangled in his hair, as she crested and fell. Her soft moans merging with the rustle of leaves in the peaceful morning.

He waited until she'd calmed down, then pressed a gentle kiss to her tummy and rose to his feet. "Stay here, I won't be long."

Eve stared into the canopy of trees above her, unable to watch him go, her brief moment of happiness evaporating. The sun shone through the leaves, dappling her and the area around her with speckles of light. Lying in this peaceful paradise wasn't going to change the truth. The interlude, no matter how beautiful it was, was over. Besides, the grass made her skin itch.

Eve pushed to her feet and brushed the crushed flowers and bits of grass from her back and bottom. The sweet, tantalizing fragrance teased her nostrils, one she'd always remember and treasure of her time with Reynner.

She searched for her clothes and realized the tenderness between her legs was only a slight discomfort now. Finding her things a short distance away, she dressed.

Eve walked out of the trees and scanned her surrounding, but couldn't see Reynner anywhere. She sat on one of the several boulders lining the river and waited. Eyes closed, she raised her face to the sun, its warmth soothing her. The spray from the waterfalls drifted like mist over her. Licking the cool drops of the water from her lips, she tasted Reynner and relived the beautiful memories he'd given her.

But he didn't like her touching his wings. She

rubbed her temple, a memory bled through her mind—his nightmares when she'd touched him the night he got hurt. That awful demoness who'd captured him…laughing, deliberately stroking his shoulders or so she'd thought. It had been too dark to see clearly. She hadn't realized then that they were the inner arches of his wings.

Dear God, no wonder he kept them concealed. He'd said they were sensitive, now she understood why. He became aroused.

"Eve?"

At the quiet sound of his voice, she opened her eyes and forced away the painful images of his nightmares. Water droplets sparkled like diamonds on his muscular chest, which she'd kissed and stroked moments ago. She prayed this wasn't the end for them. But faced with his closed expression once again, a sharp ache settled in her heart.

It was over.

Reynner wasn't interested in any kind of relationship. Apparently, he'd taken her word when she said all she wanted from him was a moment.

Chapter 18

Reynner took in Eve's pale face and the fact that she wouldn't look at him. The darkness that had eased after they'd made love surged again like a backdraft, clawing at his mind.

You are not worthy of her. Not worthy.

And judging by her tense expression, yeah, she'd finally realized the truth, too. He was all around bad news, and he'd spilled himself into her. If he could remove that shit, he'd do so.

"What's wrong?"

Her gaze flickered to his then away. "Nothing."

At the blatant lie, his anger crawled to the surface. He yanked her off the rock and into his arms, ignoring the tiny gasp that drifted along his bare skin like a damn caress. In a furious rustle, his wings reappeared. He pushed off from the ground and flew them back to the aerie. The fragrance of peaches with a hint of musk from their lovemaking enclosed him.

He drew in a deep breath and let the scent torment him. Even though she buried her face in his neck and locked her arms around him, her tense body made

Reynner aware of the distance she'd put between them. He had to lock down his jaw so he wouldn't yell the truth at her that she could never get rid of him, she was his mate. But in reality, he had no right, could never lay claim to her verbally. That was his truth.

The moment he landed on the balcony, she let go of him and disappeared indoors. The dampness on his chest distracted him. He brushed his fingers over it and he smelled her tears. His chest constricted.

Urias. He should never have touched her, but he couldn't allow another near her, he just couldn't. She belonged to him.

No, she can't, dumbass.

Strangling back the urge to go after her, Reynner went in search of Lucan instead, and found the mage in the gym. "Why is the scroll affecting Eve in this manner?" he demanded.

Lucan set down the free weights he indulged in whenever he visited. Sweat glistened on his face and over his abdomen. He glanced at Reynner as he reached for a towel and dried off. He didn't pretend to not understand what Reynner meant.

"It's the magic in the parchment, it responds to her blood. She'll be fine once the Stone is found and taken home."

"And in the meantime?" he spat.

"I suggest you keep the affair short. Our kind was never meant to fornicate with mortals."

All the frustration and fury in him uncorking, Reynner punched him. Lucan flew across the room. A red haze blurred Reynner's view. "Don't fuck with me, Luc. *We* dragged her from her world to aid us. She didn't have to do this. You may be a mage, but by Urias, show her some respect or next time it won't be just a fist to your jaw."

Reynner stormed out of the gym. He had no idea what had changed Lucan from the easygoing male he once knew—to give it all up and become a mage—and he didn't care, but he refused to let him think of Eve as some whore.

A sharp pain flared across his pec, and the tattoo on his chest heated up, yanking at him to respond to the summons.

Fuck! Not now! He didn't have time for this shit. But ignoring Inanna wouldn't make her go away, nor could he go chain himself in the dungeon, not with Eve here. The star on his chest blazed like hell.

Anger surging, Reynner changed into jeans and a shirt then walked out onto the balcony. He opened a portal into the Sumerian pantheon and stepped through the misty veils. Only, he didn't go straight to Inanna's chambers. After he'd almost succumbed the last time when she burned that hallucinogenic crap—no, never again. She wanted to see him, then she'd meet him where he chose.

He headed toward the gardens and didn't bother to hide his presence. In this place, even invisible, they would sense him. Inanna's servants, in their flowing white gowns approached in a sedate line, dipping their heads when they passed him. But several eyed him boldly beneath their slanted, kohl-rimmed eyes. Obviously, he presented too much of a temptation to worry about their jealous goddess.

The burn on his chest made him want to tear his skin off, but he refrained from doing anything, refused to show an iota of weakness. He dropped down to the low stone wall and waited.

Eve. Thoughts of her swamped him. Her golden

limbs tangled with his, her satin-smooth body sliding beneath him. His groin hardened.

He scrubbed his face. Gods, he'd hurt her with his claiming. But the trust he'd seen in her eyes filled him with longing. Their kind never put much stock into virginity. Hell, virgins were a myth in his world. But he was fiercely glad no other had touched Eve in that elemental way but him.

The scent of myrrh and exotic spice reached him first, reminding him of his curse. It hauled his mind out of thoughts too dangerous to have in a place like this.

"Reynner?" The sexual overtones made his lips tighten. Inanna smiled and slithered closer, about as innocent as an asp. She wore a wine-colored gown, a bunch of plump red grapes in her hand. She stopped a foot away. A glitter warmed her yellowy brown eyes. Her musky perfume overwhelmed him.

He tried to remember Eve's scent. Needed her with a desperation that twisted his gut. She gave him peace, eased him.

Reynner?

He froze. *Eve?*

Another tentative touch, almost like a whisper, it swirled through his mind. *Reynner?*

She heard him? *Urias!* Shock drenched his mind.

Unable to sit still, he shot to his feet. He rubbed his chest at her warm presence in there and paced to the edge of the trees that lined the temple gardens.

Eve couldn't *see* his thoughts when she touched him because he'd bolted his psychic shields. But this? To be inside his mind? And, like a punch in his gut, the truth hit him.

He'd not only claimed her and sealed his fate when the mystical light had entered him—their bonding had opened their telepathic connection, too. For a heart-stopping, joyous moment, he reveled in her gentle presence inside him.

Then he turned and stared into the gleaming topaz eyes of his reality.

He shut down his mind-link to Eve. Grateful then, he'd taken the swim in the ice-cold lake after making love to her. It had been more to cool his ardor because his desire had barely been satiated, but if Inanna ever found out that he'd bonded and had a mate, she'd go after Eve. She would think nothing of hurting her. Or worse, killing her.

Over my dead body, he vowed. And not even then.

He would never ruin Eve's life. Once he left, the threat to her would be removed because Inanna would follow him. But he'd make damn sure not Inanna or anyone else would ever touch a hair on Eve's head.

The cool skin of a fat grape caressed his mouth, brought him out of his mind-shattering revelations.

Jaw tightening, he stepped back.

"I'm eating it, why would I drug myself?" She pouted, trailing a hand down his chest. He narrowed his eyes. She tossed aside the fruit, not deterred by his warning look. "Come, lover, give over and stop fighting me. I will continue to bring you here until you give me a day of your time, or that," she tapped the star on his chest, "will just get worse."

"This game grows tedious. I will never become one of your puppets. You knew that from the start. Release me."

She arched a brow. With a cat-like smile, she slowly circled him and whispered from behind, close to his ear. "Never."

***

Eve descended the stairs to the gym later that afternoon, listlessness making her edgy.

God, she hoped Reynner didn't know she'd cried in his arms when he brought them back. The urge to go look for him grew so strong, she stumbled to a halt and inhaled a harsh breath.

She must be going out of her mind. Since their return from the forest, she felt like he was with her, inside her mind, her heart. She even thought she heard him call her name.

Stop, Eve. He's given you what you asked for—a moment of his time. It's over.

She scrubbed a shaky hand over her face. She had to put all this behind her or she'd go crazy.

The sounds of thumping drew her. She found Aerén in the gym, pounding at a sand bag strung from the ceiling. She didn't understand his obsessive need to train so often. After the incident between him and Reynner this morning, she didn't know what to say, and Aerén didn't appear to be in a mood to talk.

Eve sat on a bench and waited. She didn't have much choice, not like she could go outside for a stroll when she was trapped in this mountain fortress.

"So, you're a prince?"

"By a misfortune of birth." He punched harder with bare fists as if to work through whatever nightmare held him in its grip. The muscles in his arms and chest bulged at the power of his strikes. She dreaded to think what those hands could do to a human.

"Are you all right?" Concern filled her at the brutality of his punches. Sweat dripped down his face and ripped torso.

Cool, silver eyes flickered to her. "I'm fine."

A brush-off. But it didn't deter her. She regarded

him as a friend, or maybe Kataya was finally rubbing off on her when it came to poking her nose into another's business. "You don't like being royalty?"

"All it's done is remind me of what I've lost. My sister. My brother. My parents. Now my middle brother, my only surviving family, sends me here to keep me safe because I took on our enemies. Can't have my royal ass hurt." Another punishing blow to the bag. Eve felt her own knuckles hurt.

She remembered Aethan and wanted to reassure Aerén that his eldest brother lived, but it wasn't her business. Lord knew what can of immortal worms she'd open then.

"I'm sorry," she gave voice to trite words. Glancing around, she searched for something else to talk about. "Aerén? Thank you for earlier…I'm sorry Reynner hit you."

Though she hadn't encouraged Aerén, she still felt a little guilty letting him kiss her.

Now a sly smile crept over his features. "Most fun I've ever had. You change your mind about him, you know where to find me."

She laughed, pleased to see the familiar, flirtatious spark in his eyes. "You're a prince, you can get anyone you want."

He grabbed the swaying bag, his expression sobering. "Perhaps. Pity you're into Reynner, but I guess it's to be expected. All the females back home were, too. As high lord of Ademéras, he was never short of female company—" He broke off and winced, remorse crossing his face. "Hell, Eve, I'm sorry. I shouldn't have said that."

"Why? It's the truth. I have no hold over him." She turned away and fixed her attention on the waterfall.

Once the Stone was found, he'd leave. But the thought of never seeing him again intensified the pain, like someone had clamped a vise around her heart. She rose and crossed to the window, wrapping her arms around her body, needing to hold herself together.

A high lord, Aerén had said. That was like nobility. She'd wondered about Reynner's life, his world. But he was about as vocal as a mute when it came to personal stuff.

"Ademéras?" she asked Aerén, who came to stand beside her.

"Yes, it's er…" He searched for a way to explain it. "It's like a country with its own ruler."

"And you?"

"I'm prince over all the dominions," he said with a slight smile. He stared at his split knuckles, a furrow marring his brow. "Eve, what I said about Reynner? That was a long time ago. He hasn't been back home in over two thousand years. After he left Empyrea, something happened, and that demoness trapped him in Hell. It changed him in a drastic way, made him hard, unapproachable…"

"I know," she whispered. She doubted she'd ever forget the horror of the images she'd seen. "I saw when I touched him that night. Why would anyone do that to another being?"

Aerén shrugged. "To own him. It's punishment because he refused to cower."

Own him?

Reynner had growled out that furious question at her when he'd found out she'd touched him in his sleep. She didn't want to own him…she'd never do that.

Eve went still when she recalled something else.

That was why he'd ordered her to wash her hands

when she'd first tended to him. Did he think his blood would taint her? And why he didn't want to release himself into her. He thought he'd what? Infect her with evil because that demoness had force-fed him her blood?

Her chest hurt for him. How could he hold himself in such low regard?

She'd only experienced absolute bliss in his arms. She didn't feel any differently, except for that moment when they'd made love and a warm light had flowed through her. There was nothing dark or sinister about it, just undeniable warmth, and a tantalizing masculine essence that was all him.

But talking about Reynner when he'd disappeared so soon after they made love lowered her spirits again. She changed the subject. "Where do we go to locate the Stone?"

He glanced at her. His jaw dropped. Then he grinned. "Eve, your eyes—dammit, they're beautiful."

Eve snorted. He wasn't distracting her that easily. Sleeping with an angel would probably do that. Thankfully, the glowing blue specks had dulled somewhat. "Where, Aerén?"

"New York," he said, crossing to pick up his tee from the bench. "There's nothing for you to fear. We'll be with you every step of the way. We'll keep you safe from any type of danger."

Eve chewed her lip and thought back to when those demoniis had confronted her and Reynner in the alley. She'd been more a liability than a help. Her pepper spray wasn't going to work on immortals.

"Can you teach me to fight? A few techniques that will keep me alive."

His head emerged from the tee. Aerén looked

horrified as if she'd asked him for his royal inheritance. "You don't need to learn to defend yourself. We will do that."

She gave him a level look. "I don't know what the women in your world are like, but where I come from? We prefer to rely on ourselves. However, if you don't want to, fine. I'll go ask Izzeri. He looks quite capable."

A smile tugged at his mouth. "He's an old fae. All he'd want to do is hie off with you. Faes tend to like mortals—keep them as prizes."

Her mouth dropped open. "No way. As in faeries?"

He nodded.

Well, that shot another illusion to dust of faeries being tiny, Tinker Bell-like people. It also explained why he'd stared at her when he'd first seen her. "Jeez, I'm not very safe in this place, am I? That makes it all the more imperative for me to learn."

"Convincing argument," Aerén said, smiling. He ran his gaze over her with an appreciative male look. And nodded his approval at the black sweats and fitted white tee she'd pulled on after her shower. "All right. Come on, then. Let's go teach you to fight, but Reynner's not going to be happy—"

"He's not human," she retorted as they left the gym, then hastily stepped aside as an avalanche headed toward them.

"Hey priest," Aerén called out.

Eve didn't respond. Lucan looked like he'd bathed in a vat of ice. His gaze flickered to her, and he stopped. His narrow-eyed regard made her want to squirm and tell him she hadn't done anything wrong.

Then he nodded and continued down.

God, the man was strange. Eve hurried to catch up

with Aerén.

***

Reynner stepped through the portal and onto the balcony of his home as daylight gave way to dusk.

He stood there, breathing hard through his nose. The pain, instead of easing like it usually did after one of these visits, only hurt more, because he refused to give Inanna the day she demanded. All she wanted was to keep him with her and find ways to change his mind. Get him to submit.

In two thousand years he never had. Why the hell would she think he'd do so now? He pinched the bridge of his nose, like that would help ease him, and scanned for Eve.

Nothing.

Dammit, where was she? The possessive mating streak was already winding him up in knots.

Unable to locate her, he went in search of Izzeri and found him in the kitchen, hands-deep in some white substance. "Have you seen—" Reynner's gaze dropped to the mixing bowl again. "What is that?"

Izzeri's eyes twinkled. "Croissants. The mistress has a fondness for them."

Reynner stared at his manservant. Then shook his head. *He'd* succumbed to Eve's spell so he couldn't blame Izzeri for doing likewise. "Have you seen Eve?"

"The mistress left with the young sire a while ago. They're in the forest."

Possessiveness yanking him hard, Reynner dematerialized. If Aerén touched her, he wouldn't just threaten this time, he'd kill him. But if Eve so much as allowed Aerén within an inch of her, he'd lock her up in his aerie and the prince could damn well find another place to live.

Reynner took form on a flat boulder at the foot of the mountains. His mouth flattened when he thought of the last time he'd seen her with Aerén—he still wanted to break every bone in Aerén's body for kissing Eve.

Whatever reason Aerén had for bringing Eve to the falls, it had damn well better be good.

Despite the roaring water, the tinny sounds of steel clashing caught his attention. Fear raced through him. In preternatural speed, he headed toward the clanging coming from the middle of the forest. And staggered to a halt in shock.

A small sword in her hand, Eve faced Aerén in a crouch then she sprinted, and Aerén came at her in a move so fast, Reynner flew in front of her to prevent the attack. Eve's warm body crashed into him. He hauled her into his arms, swung around in a protective move and waited for Aerén's sword to strike him instead.

"Christ—Reynner, I could have hurt you!" She thumped him hard on his chest, eyes bright with fear. No longer a smoky green, they now sparked with specks of the mating blue. And would for a few more hours before fading.

"He thinks I would have hurt you," Aerén told Eve, amusement quirking his lips.

"Had you done so, you'd already be on your way to Elysium." Reynner cut him a lethal look, unable to get over his scare.

Aerén raised his hands in peace and stepped back.

"No fighting, Eve. Ever. Understand me?" Reynner growled. She, of course, scowled and tried to shake off his hold. "This isn't a damn game." He shook her, hoping some sense would settle in her stubborn head. "You could get hurt."

"Exactly the reason why I want to be able to defend myself," she retorted. "We're going to look for the Stone, and with your enemies lurking about, *I* am a target. I refuse to be helpless."

"And you think I wouldn't be able to protect you?"

"*You* can do anything." She leaned back as far as his arms allowed and glowered. "But I have learned in life to expect the unexpected."

His gut twisted. With Inanna and Darkreans on the loose, Eve would have to be protected twenty-four seven.

"Good thing, I'll be coming along, too," Aerén said, determination hardening his features. A look Reynner knew far too well. "Fine."

With a nod, Aerén dematerialized.

"Doesn't matter," Eve huffed. "I still want to know at least some form of self-defense. I'm not totally useless. I can learn."

"I never thought you were, Eve," Reynner said quietly. "What you did with the scroll is remarkable. The way you understood it…" He shook his head, still unable to comprehend how she knew what to do.

She shrugged. "It was instinct."

"Come, let's go back to the aerie. I'll teach you some defense and maim techniques in the gym."

He may hate the prince anywhere near Eve, but Aerén would be able to keep her safe when he wasn't around for whatever reason.

Yeah right—*whatever reason*. There was only one.
Inanna.

As they walked out from the forest clearing, the wide space Eve put between them sparked his temper. "You got your *moment* from me, so now you keep your distance?"

A shocked sound left her. Color flared across her expressive features as her gaze met his. The evidence of their bonding, staring him in the face, ramped up his virulent mood.

She scowled. "What do you want from me, Reynner?"

Everything! I want every damn thing—to be the very air you breathe.

Except, he could offer her nothing, but danger. And a damaged, ruined mate.

***

"You're not paying attention," Eve heard Reynner growl as he called out instructions. Something about how to evade an attack, but she couldn't get her mind focused on his coaching.

"I thought you wanted to learn to defend yourself?"

She didn't answer. Recalling a move Eric had taught her, she picked up her knee and would have gotten Reynner in the crotch if he hadn't leaped back. She ignored the warning glitter in his dark gaze.

His comment about her using him had stung. She'd only said that because a man like him would not want forever, especially not with a mortal. But the uneasy feeling continued to plague her.

Wherever he'd disappeared to until this afternoon had set off his mood. A familiar scent drifted off him…one she'd smelled before. And then she knew. He'd come back reeking of the same exotic perfume as the night in her apartment not so long ago. Now it clung to his clothes, and it made something inside of her shrivel up.

"What's that smell on you?" she asked in a tight voice, keeping away from him until she had her answer.

"Sweat."

"No." She tried to clamp down on her jealousy and the possessiveness that grew in spades. "It has the aroma of..." In her mind, she ran through all the fragrances she was familiar with.

Distracted, she saw him come at her a second too late. He moved in low and grabbed her by the waist. She tripped, he twisted, took the brunt of the fall, and she landed on him instead.

"That's why you always, *always* pay attention."

Scowling, she pushed up and sat astride his belly, trying not to be aware of his hard, warm body between her legs. His hands settled on her hips. He looked so tempting lying there, his pale hair a sharp contrast against the gray training mat.

"You smell of spice, musk—like Opium perfume. Who is she?"

Being this close, she saw the way his eyes darkened at her question. A nerve pulsed hard on his jaw. Well, she didn't care if she was trespassing in his personal space since he was all but camping in hers.

His grip on her hips loosened. "Why would you think it's a *she*?"

"Don't. It's the same smell I got that night you suddenly left my apartment and came back late."

He shifted her off his stomach and rose to his feet. "We're leaving for New York in a few minutes." He stalked for the door then stopped. A hand on the frame, he glanced back to where she still sat on the floor, said in a voice so low it chilled her to her soul, "She is my penance for my stupidity to trust a woman."

Chapter 19

Eve disappeared into her bedroom soon after they arrived, leaving a curious Aerén to explore her home, while North pit-stopped at her bookshelf.

Reynner stood there in the living room, all tight-lipped and filled with hard-eyed cynicism. Doubtless, he was still mad at her. But his comment about the spicy woman hurt.

Did he think *she* was trying to trap him, too?

Her lips compressing, she yanked on loose white shorts that ended mid-thigh. Then pulled on a light blue, strappy top, before twisting her hair into a loose topknot.

Inhaling deeply and striving for calm, she shoved her feet into flip-flops and made her way to the living room.

The spicy aroma of peppers and soy wafted through the small apartment as Aerén and North sat down for their Chinese takeout dinner.

"Reyn, you joining us?" Aerén asked.

"In a minute—" Reynner turned as she approached. His gaze swept down her and up again to linger on her face.

At that utterly male look, he almost destroyed her composure. But she could do little to stop her cheeks from heating up like a damn furnace. Hastily, she sank into the chair he held out.

"I've finally discovered the food of my soul—Chinese take-out," Aerén said, digging into his *beef chow mein.*

"Anything edible is your soul's food," North grunted.

Aerén snorted. "Eve, your opinion?"

She reached for her water and took a sip. Smiled. "It's my fav, too."

"We have a lot to do," Reynner said, sitting beside her and pulling them back to the job at hand.

A moment later, he set a plate piled with noodles and chicken strips in front of her. He shifted in his seat, and his jean-cladded thigh brushed against her bare one, finally wrecking her calm.

She stared at the food, her hunger deserting her. All she could think off was his big body sliding against hers. She had to steel herself not to reach out and touch him.

As Reynner ate his own food, he spoke to the others about the fight with the Darkreans. He appeared cool, focused, while her stomach tied itself in knots.

He's not interested in more, Eve.

She pushed the noodles around on her plate.

"You're not eating."

She blinked and glanced at Reynner. He moved his empty plate aside and nodded to her still full one.

"I'm not hungry."

Those indigo eyes narrowed. "Try."

Her irritation flared at his order, or maybe it was

because of her unrequited feelings, she snapped, "Don't worry, I won't shrivel up from hunger and faint mid-quest—I'll find your artifact."

His mouth tightened.

With a sigh, Eve stopped baiting him. She picked up her fork, scooped up noodles, and started eating.

"You wounded Sebris. He'll equate then be back," North warned, pulling Reynner's attention away from her. "And he'll have reinforcements around."

"Yeah, he will," Reynner muttered. Leaning back in his chair, and his thigh pressed against hers again.

Her grip tightened on her fork. If she moved away, she'd probably end up on Aerén's lap.

Ugh, it made her realized now just how small the circular dining table was.

Eve kept her focus on North and Aerén, who started to discuss possible locations of the Stone.

"The artifact is eons old," North said, drinking some of his Pepsi. "It could be anywhere, possibly buried in the labyrinth beneath the city."

"We could try cemeteries, bridges, and museums," Aerén suggested, reaching for a spring roll.

"Hell, no. I'm not breaking into a museum again," Eve retorted, setting her glass down with a little thump.

Aerén grinned, took a bite of his roll, chewed. "Hmmm, maybe we should start searching those first?"

"We have little choice but to search *all*," Reynner cut off Aerén's teasing. "Despite the artifact being lost eons ago, it will not be buried, but hidden in plain sight. We are talking about ancient magic, far more powerful than anyone has ever seen. The Stone will want to be found, just not by us. It's why Eve will have to be there."

He leaned his elbows on the table, moved his water

glass to another spot, and looked at her. "Your show's in a few days, right?"

She nodded, and ate another bite of her food.

"What show?" Aerén asked.

"Eve's a sculptor. She debuts her work Saturday night."

"Wonderful. Do I get to see it?"

"Sure, I don't see why not," Eve told Aerén and pushed away from the small dining table, needing coffee more than food.

"No, you can't," Reynner said, sounding a little terse. "I need you here to keep an eye on things. The Darkreans won't give up. We are too close to finding the Stone to make careless mistakes now."

Eve left them to their talks, headed to the galley kitchen, and put on the coffee pot.

"Are we going to dematerialize to these places to begin our search?" North asked.

"No. The distance is too far, and Eve doesn't care for that mode of transport. I'll lease an SUV or something. And no, Aerén, you cannot drive that or the Porsche," Reynner said.

Aerén evidently had already done so.

A chair scraped against the wooden floor, then Aerén said, "Before I leave this realm, it will be my personal quest to do just that."

Eve glanced at them. He winked at her as he crossed to the kitchen. Smiling, she opened the cupboard above her head and reached for the mug when Aerén grasped her by the waist and set her aside.

A low, ferocious growl echoed through the apartment. Startled, Eve dropped the mug. Only Aerén's quick reflexes stopped it from crashing to the floor. She spun around to witness Reynner pinning

Aerén with a lethal glare.

Aerén didn't seem fazed at the warning. He cocked a taunting brow at Reynner, set the mug on the counter, and sauntered over to the fridge. He nabbed an orange soda and headed back for the dining table.

"You're asking for trouble," North muttered to him.

Reynner's gaze stayed on her. Biting her lip at his show of aggression, Eve turned to take out the rest of the mugs, except the other two sat on the higher shelf. Darn, she'd have to hop on the counter.

A powerful forearm reached from behind her for the elusive cups. And a cool, heart-poundingly familiar scent of wild forest surrounded her. Reynner set them down on the counter.

Eve twisted around in the narrow space and was enclosed by his body heat. She had to force the words out. "Thank you."

He nodded.

However, meeting his dark gaze, uneasiness tugged at her. And standing so close, the tension in him vibrated through her like a taut rubber band. She couldn't stop herself from asking, "What's wrong?"

"Nothing."

She wasn't buying it. Something was off with him, had been since they got back from Exilum.

North collected the dishes and leftovers and brought them over. "Do we start scouting this evening?"

"No, not tonight. After Eve's showing."

Reynner's clipped tone pushed her to act. She grabbed his forearm when he would have walked away. He didn't speak, just looked at her.

She took in the light sheen of perspiration on his face, almost like... "You're in pain."

"You're imagining things, Eve. I'm fine."

***

Reynner leaned against the counter a few feet from Eve, and struggled to breathe through the pain garroting him.

He shouldn't have said what he had when she'd asked about Inanna's scent on him. Eve didn't deserve his anger. But seeing her with Aerén, and jealousy, that capricious bastard reared its ugly head that she turned to Aerén, not him for her needs.

But how the hell could he reveal to his mate his unending shame? One moment of weakness that had bound him for eternity to a vicious goddess. Forever at her beck and call.

The strong scent of brewed coffee drifted through the kitchen, obliterating Eve's soft fragrance as she poured the fragrant liquid into mugs and set them on the counter. Her gaze slipped back to him, a frown marring her brow.

He had to quell the urge to pull her close. If he did, he wouldn't let her go, and he had to get out of there. The shit scorching his chest had him reaching his limits of endurance.

Inanna wouldn't win this round.

Biting down on his molars, he didn't dare let Eve see, or sense his discomfort. He'd blocked her from his thoughts and his mind after their bonding because he didn't want her to experience the agony he lived with. And she sure as hell would if he left their telepathic path open.

Unable to linger any longer, Reynner grasped Eve's hand and pulled her away from the kitchen. He stopped at the passage entrance. "I have to go to Exilum for a while."

"But we just got back..." Her worried gaze darted

over his face. "Reynner, you're scaring me. Tell me what's wrong."

He didn't answer her. Couldn't. "I'll be back in the morning. North," he called out, striding to the front door. The warrior turned from where he stood gazing out the window. "Don't leave her alone, not even for a second."

"Reynner, wait." Eve rushed after him.

He shook his head, thankful when North intercepted her, and walked out, only to find Aerén hard on his heels. *Shit.* He didn't need another lecture about why he refused to give in to Inanna.

He'd told Aerén only the bare facts about his foolishness with the goddess.

"Why don't you just go to her?" Aerén demanded. "End this torment. Inanna would get bored soon enough. All goddesses are fickle when something's too easy."

"Once was enough," he said, voice rough. "Do you really think I'll go to her, especially now?"

"Does Eve know?"

"About Inanna? No. And Inanna can never know about Eve."

Aerén shook his head and sighed. "To quote you, *you're so screwed.*"

***

At his aerie, Reynner made his way down the narrow, shadowy flight of stairs to the crude, dug-out archway leading into the dungeon. Unbreakable metal bars ran from floor to ceiling, the gate stood open. Inside, chains with manacles were built into the granite rock face.

Hephaestus, the Greek god, had made them for him eons ago, just for this purpose. He'd used them often, and probably would for the rest of his screwed-up life.

With his mind, he willed the torches on the wall to life. Their flames cast a dim glow in the gloomy place. The small, barred window didn't help since it was night and just a few stars twinkled in the distance.

Reynner pulled off his tee, tossed it aside and rolled his shoulders.

"Go," he ordered Aerén. Inanna had summoned him far too often recently. He refused to play her games any longer. She'd make him pay tonight, of that he had little doubt.

So be it.

"Reyn, ask Lucan, or go back to Empyrea. Allatus will surely know of a way to break this curse," Aerén said from behind the closed gates.

"It's all right. I'm used to this." No need to repeat the story of the lengths he'd gone to remove the shit branded on him. He paced the coarse, dusty floors. Too edgy to do little else, he flexed his fingers. The mark on his chest glowed so brightly—hell, he didn't need the torches—he'd light up the entire damn place soon enough. Just as well he couldn't will the shackles unlocked while in pain. He had to be calm for that to occur.

"Go, but seal the stairway entrance to the dungeon." An order his prince couldn't refuse. For his own protection and that of the people around him, Reynner had to be alone. Sealed in. Or he'd do irrevocable damage.

Eve, being mortal, would never come out of it alive.

One more reason why he could never keep her.

"I'll be back later." His voice gruff with concern, Aerén walked out. And not a minute too soon, as Reynner let go of his rigid control.

His wings snapped open, his power exploded out of him, reverberating off the walls like lightning, nailing him hard. He could do nothing to block it from shocking him. Brought to his knees and held in pain's merciless grip, he burned from the inside out.

Several feathers caught ablaze and floated down to the ground in front of him. The tangy taste of blood flooded his mouth. His mind hazed over, but he crawled to the wall and clicked his restraints in place.

Better...this way...than giving in to Inanna...

***

Eve rubbed her burning eyes after a sleepless night and tried to do some work the following afternoon. But her concentration was shredded to pieces. Reynner hadn't come back.

She had no right to question him about his personal life...or the spicy woman.

But thoughts of the latter grew into a cancerous anger with no outlet. Eventually, she slammed down the sheet of metal, wanting to tear the thing apart with her bare hands. Tears crowded her eyes. Why couldn't he want her? Even a little?

"Are you okay?"

The rare sound of North's voice jerked her out of her self-pity. She nodded.

Eve gave her attention to the sculpture she'd started, but her heart wasn't in it as she melted and molded. All that took form was her rage and hurt in the wild twists and furious turns of pewter and steel.

Warmth stole through her and built up like she had a temperature. The sheet of metal she'd abused in her fit of temper lay distorted on the floor. Running out of steam, desperately unhappy, she dropped to the floor on her knees and stared at her hands. The ugly scars crisscrossing her skin and melting into each other ached, while intense heat radiated through her body. One she didn't understand.

She clenched and unclenched her fingers. What was wrong with her? It felt as if she were on fire. Eve pushed to her feet and staggered to the sink. Holding her hands under the cold water, she struggled to calm down. Filling a glass, she drank some…the heat in her hands and her body slowly subsided.

Movement and low voices distracted her. Lucan stood near the doorway. She hadn't been aware North had let him in. He glanced around the place, seeming intrigued by the tall shelves that held all types of metal. Both purchased and scrapyard finds.

North and Lucan held a conversation in their language. The tensed air between them told her that wherever Lucan had been, things weren't too rosy there. Had he gone to Empyrea?

Thankful she didn't have to talk to him, Eve headed back to her worktable and flipped through several sketches she'd done for her sculpture of Reynner. Selecting the drawing she liked, she began redefining the lines.

"That's good."

Her gaze shot up at the sound of Lucan's voice. She looked around, only to find that North had disappeared, leaving this glacier in his place.

Oh, joy. Alone with the iceberg. But his clipped praise shocked her.

"We need to talk."

Now that wasn't a surprise. "About what?"

His eyes gleamed. Amusement? No, it had to be irritation at her snarly tone.

"In a minute." His gaze dropped to her hands. "How

did you get those scars?"

Her fingers tightened around her pencil, and she stifled the urge to hide her hands. Instead, she started another drawing. "What's it to you?"

"Enlighten me." An order.

He probably never uttered the word, *please*. Scowling, she told him. "Ten years ago, I was involved in a car accident. I tried to drag my dead parents from a burning wreck—hysterical kids tend to do that, with the illusion we can save them and no thoughts to safety."

He didn't respond to her caustic account of the tragedy. His silent scrutiny hauled her out of her anger, making her uneasy. In a sugary-sweet tone full of bite, she asked, "Is that all?"

"What caused the accident?"

Apparently not.

"At fifteen, I was more interested in texting my friends than how my dad drove. They said he swerved to avoid a jaywalker, maybe another car—the damn Easter bunny, I don't remember."

She tore off a sheet, crumpled it in frustration, and tossed it with the pile on her table.

"Where?"

"At Columbus Circle."

Lucan didn't speak for a moment as if considering what she'd revealed. Then he said, "You do understand, Reynner cannot remain on this realm once we find the Stone."

"You're telling me this why?"

Glacial eyes hardened. And she'd always thought turquoise a calming color.

"You know why."

"I'm afraid you're going to have to spell it out. I'm

busy and don't have time for puzzles."

A long stretch of silence followed. His gaze skated over her like winter's kiss, and to think, she'd been sufficiently warm and sticky from the heat until he came.

"When the time comes, will you leave?"

"Where—*why*?" she asked, unable to fathom what he was getting at.

"Empyrea. It's where Reynner will go."

Her heart stopped. Her chest constricted painfully. Reynner had never asked her to go anywhere with him. She had to force out the words from a tightening throat. "Why would I do that?"

"It's good you feel this way. Our realm is ravaged by civil wars. And Darkreans, who fight for rule. You will be a distraction he can ill-afford."

Eve held back a biting retort. She'd sensed Lucan's dislike, but to detest her to such an extent that he would warn her off Reynner? If only he knew the truth. The only thing Reynner thought about was finding the Stone and leaving. She only mattered because they needed her to search for the artifact. And he'd made love to her... *Because I didn't give him much choice*, she realized with painful insight.

She pushed him into doing so. The reality wasn't any easier to swallow two days later.

Even if he had gone off to Exilum last night, it was probably to spare her feelings. Why would he want her when he seemed to hate women, didn't trust them? And who could blame him after what he'd endured in Hell?

"He's been gone too long from Empyrea," Lucan continued, interrupting thoughts that left her raw. Hurting. "Ademéras needs him. When he's gone, the bonding ties will ease—"

Her head snapped up. "The *what*?"

He stared at her for a short, silent moment. "He didn't tell you? I guess I should have given him more credit, despite the temptation your kind presents to us. Mortals were never meant to be mates to our species."

Mate? *Mate*!

"What the hell are you talking about? What mate?" Eve glared at Lucan. And found him studying her. Probably searching for whatever Reynner had seen in her that made him sleep with her.

Then he shook his head. "Impossible to believe…you humans are far too weak. Frail. You would never last the course of being mated to one like us. It's best you make this easy on yourself, tell him you don't want him here."

The superior tone made Eve want to shove him out of her studio. Except the pain inside of her rendered her helpless. She'd spent far too much time with them to not understand what the word *mate* meant. North had lost his wife to the wars in their realm.

Reynner had bonded with her and never said a word. But then he'd never lied about staying with her either. Swallowing her hurt, she pinned Lucan with an unforgiving look. "Relax. I have no plans to taint the purity of your bloodline. Reynner is a free agent. I won't force him to stay, nor will I be your scapegoat. You want him to leave, *you* tell him so."

His piercing turquoise gaze swirled white with power, with knowledge. Tendrils of ice wrapped around her. "You won't win."

"Then you should be glad with me out of the picture. I want him to be happy—can you say the same?"

When she received no answer, she turned away,

growing weary of the conversation. "I thought not. Now, if you don't mind, please leave. I have work to do."

After Lucan left, North sat on the over-turned crate near the door again, staring outside.

Eve leaned her elbows on the work-surface, staring at her faceless sketch of Reynner for several long minutes. And wondered how she'd held herself together as she faced that heartless man.

When he's gone, the bonding ties will ease.

Lucan's words were like a razor peeling off layer after layer of her heart until it bled so profusely, she didn't think she'd ever heal from the shock. The betrayal.

Immortals finding their mates and bonding was cause for celebration. After all, it was the only way they could have children Aerén had said. And yet, Reynner wouldn't acknowledge her.

Tears clogged her throat. Her chest hurt until she could no longer breathe. She dropped her head in her hand, wishing the unbearable pain would ease.

But, no matter how much she hurt, she did want Reynner to be happy, and she'd never force him to stay. Not after what she'd seen—what he'd lived through in Hell.

Chapter 20

Reynner stood outside Eve's studio, feeling like he'd been torn apart and put together again. He watched North head up the darkened alley, not before telling him that Lucan had been by.

Raking a shaky hand through his hair, he retied it. His gait too slow and his body too lax, his strength was that of a babe. Hell, he probably looked as wrung out as he felt. After the period in his dungeon, Aerén had insisted he rest. He didn't agree. With his mind on Eve, desperation clawed at him to return. A night and day had passed since he'd left her.

Reynner scanned the studio and found Eve alone. She had to be busy with her work.

He stepped inside. Amidst the acrid odor of melting metal, the briny scent of tears hit him hard. His stomach in knots, he flashed to her side. "Eve, what's wrong?"

She stiffened at the sound of his voice and dashed at her face with the back of her hand, the movement too fast. His gaze fell on her drawing book, and he saw the soggy patch on her sketch sheet.

"Nothing." She closed the pad, pushed off her chair, and started to clear her table. Frowning, Reynner ran his gaze over the tidy surface. The sketches were placed in their folders, pens in their stands, and even her jellybean jar had received her attention. No longer within her reach, but against the wall. Everything lined up like soldiers.

The place was too damn neat. This wasn't her. One thing he'd learned, Eve liked the chaos on her worktable. He stepped in front of her, blocking her attempts to avoid him. "I know Lucan was here. What the hell did he say?"

She finally looked at him, her eyes filled with pain and betrayal, and red-rimmed from the tears she'd shed. "Only what you didn't."

Like a light had been switched on, his gut tightened, and he knew. The bastard had opened his fucking mouth and spilled. He wanted to kill the mage for interfering in something that was none of his damn business.

"What exactly am I to you?" she asked. Her fingers closed around her pencil, tightening as if she needed the thing to anchor her.

He didn't want to get into this now, not when his head felt like someone had jabbed an ice pick through his skull and mushed his brains. He just wanted to hold her, forget the last tormenting twenty-four hours until Inanna had finally gotten bored and the pain had eased.

"Tell me." A choked demand.

He pinched the bridge of his nose then found her gaze, his mind fuzzy as he answered. "You are who destiny chose for me."

***

Eve stared at him for a long, silent moment. "But not

who *you* would have chosen."

At his baffled look, anger warred with her bitterness. She clamped a lid over it. "Is that why I can sense you—your presence in my mind?"

He nodded. A flare of yearning so powerful crossed his face. It made her insides tremble. But she refused to let hope spring, imagining what she wanted. The fact that he'd kept something this important from her showed her the stark truth.

"Yes, when we were together, we bonded."

When we were together—not *when we made love.* Even his words screamed the truth at her. He wouldn't have touched her had he known. She got that loud and clear.

"I understand." She struggled to raise her protective shields around her emotions. She dropped her pencil on the table and went back to her work in progress. How she managed the simple feat of walking, when it felt like she'd been shattered, every inch of her broken, she had no idea.

"That's it?" he bit out, following her. "No questions about why I didn't tell you?"

She turned dull eyes to him. Why was he so angry? He wasn't the one having to deal with the unbearable pain of being unwanted. "What do you want me to say? You obviously don't want a mate, because if you did, you would have said something. And we both know you only slept with me because I wanted you."

She stuck her earphones on and cranked up her iPod, trying to lose herself in her music and her work. But she had no prayer in hell of that happening when she was aware of him like a tangible force of power behind her. Even his scent taunted her.

He hauled her around, startling her. Her earphones

were ripped off and pocketed, along with her iPod. The metal strip in her hand hit the ground with a thin twang.

He yanked her close, his fingers biting into her upper arms. "We have a problem, you talk to me. Don't shut me out, Eve, or you won't like what I'll do."

"Don't threaten me—" she snapped, pushing away. "You want to talk? Fine. After the Stone's found, what do you plan to do?"

"It matters little what happens after. For now, this is where I'll be. With you."

His decision broke her heart. He would stay with her for now, but the end result remained the same. He *would* leave.

Eve shook her head. Her despairing mind finally registering the lines of pain bracketing his mouth, the paleness of his skin. But she couldn't worry about that—couldn't do this any longer.

"I know it's what I asked for, a moment with you, but this…this *bonding* changes everything. It's not enough anymore."

His expression became stony.

Eve knew what he thought. *You can't trust a woman. Because here she is, changing the stakes again.* But this was her life she was fighting for. "I stay with you a day longer, it will make it that much harder when you leave. I can't live like that—"

"What are you saying?"

"I want a life—a family." *I need them…to forget you…to breathe again.* "I want it all."

"And who's going to give that to you, Eve? You can't touch anyone—"

"You bastard." Pain ripped through her. Eve backed away, felt as if her very foundation had fractured. He'd taken her heart, her feelings, and crushed them into shards with his callousness. Used the very thing that caused her so much hurt against her.

"*Fuck*!" He squeezed his eyes tight. "Eve, I'm—"

"No—" she cut him off. In a voice gone brittle with determination, she said, "I will accept David if he still wants me. Like you pointed out, my choices are limited."

His rigid composure cracked. His eyes snapped open, blazing with savage fire. "That will never happen!"

"God, you're selfish! You don't want me, and no one else can?"

"Don't want you? You have no idea—" His mouth clamped shut. The vein on his neck pulsed so violently she half expected him to shake her. Instead, he stalked off, his fists crashing on the table, making her jump.

Inhaling an agonized breath, Eve turned away, pressed her hand to her chest as if it would ease her shattered heart. She only understood one thing; she had to find a way to move on. If she didn't, she wouldn't survive, not loving him the way she did

***

Chained to the wall for hours, his wrists were rubbed raw and blood dripped down his biceps. His body in a haze of pain from the barbed cat 'o nine tails whip she'd used this time.

Kalinin took pleasure in physical torture, relished in it.

His head hung low, his matted hair fell in dark hunks to block his view of the bitch watching him. She strolled closer. Fingers ran down his chest, digging into the grooves of torn flesh. "Say the words and all this will end—admit I'm your mistress."

Reynner gritted his teeth, so the words wouldn't tumble out. The whip cracked through the air and slashed him again, tearing through flesh. Unmitigated pain surged through him.

A silent scream trapped in his throat.

By all that was merciful, was there no way out of this endless pain?

Urias, end me...let me leave this hellhole.

Oblivion hovered. Elysium, their final resting place was just a heartbeat away.

"Oh, no, my dear Empyrean," she cooed. "I won't let you seek death. You are mine."

She undid his chains, and he fell into the filth, his legs too weak to support him. She scored her wrist with her teeth and pushed the gushing wound to his lips. His stomach gnawed itself in hunger, but he turned his head away. The sludge from the floor coated his face. She grabbed him by his hair and forced the blood into his mouth, ignoring his sputtering.

The coppery taste slid down his parched throat, he gagged, but she held his head down. After a minute, she yanked his head up. "You want water? Say the words."

He didn't speak. He no longer did. Blood dripping down his chin, he pulled his head free from her vicious grip, leaving behind a hunk of his hair. She ran the dull strands against her face, her expression filling with victory.

Despair constricted his chest. He couldn't hold out much longer...she'd win.

No. Can't let her—can't let her—

"Hush, Reynner, I'm here."

The faint fragrance of peaches teased his nose, chasing away the sulfur and coppery stink. He clung to the wispy tendrils like a lifeline and followed it. *There*. He found her. In his soul. A light that burned for him alone. So bright, it led him out of the darkness and into her warmth.

"She can't hurt you." Light fingers smoothed back his hair. "It's over—she's dead. You killed her."

Yes, I killed her...killed her...

"Come back to me, please..." her gentle voice pleaded. Reynner forced his eyelids open and stared into beautiful dark green eyes damp with tears. "She can't hurt you anymore."

Eve sat on the living room floor, stroking his hair. Hers appeared like a dark, tangled halo around her shoulders. The soft sounds of her voice soothed him.

She'd come to him, pulled him out of his nightmares, even when he'd been an utter bastard.

Eve. Her name stuck in his throat. He knew he'd warned her never to touch him when nightmares took him under. He couldn't bear it if he hurt her. A pang of regret settled in his chest that all she did was stroke his hair.

He reached out to touch her face, needing the contact, and stroked her petal-soft skin with his fingers. She leaned into his touch, her eyes squeezing shut. Then she eased away from him, rose to her feet and walked back to her room. Her door closed with a soft click, shutting him out.

Reynner pushed off the couch, agitation knotting his belly. He headed in the direction of her bedroom. But the closed door brought him to an abrupt halt.

His hand rested on the wood, the other rubbing his chest at the pain there. He wasn't even sure what the hell it was any longer. The nightmares that followed him like a shadow, or the star that would soon throb again, reminding him what a crapfest his life was. Or the sheer torture cutting through him to have finally found his mate and that everything was falling apart.

His fist crashed into the wall. Rubble rained down to the floor. Pain exploded as skin split and bones shattered. He stared at his ruined hand. It didn't compare to the agony strangling him.

If he didn't find a way out of this mess, then Eve would do as she threatened, move on and find a life without him…

***

Her numbed emotions were the only thing that got Eve through the day as she dressed the following evening for her art debut. Pulling up the zipper on the side, she turned to the mirror and studied herself, grateful she'd let Kataya pick out her dress several weeks ago.

When she'd protested having to dress so formally, Kataya had insisted. *Just because you're an artist, doesn't mean you have to dress like a hobo.*

The dark blue strapless number with a dull sheen hugged her from her chest to her hips, ending with a swirly flare above her knees. Okay, so the color did look good against her tanned skin. But the hue reminded her too much of Reynner's eyes.

Instantly, she shut off the thought as unhappiness threatened to invade again, but she pushed it all back and concentrated on the evening ahead. Focusing on the show was the key to survival.

"One day at a time," she murmured. "One day at a time, Eve."

Slipping on ice-pick heels that matched her dress, she picked up her black elbow-length gloves and walked out of her bedroom, tugging the bodice up so the inch-long scar on her left breast wouldn't show.

She ignored the gaping hole in the passage wall.

Last night, she'd heard the thud of something hitting the wall and it had shocked her to see the damages this morning. But she didn't ask. She'd seen the light scabs on Reynner's knuckles.

Eve slowed to a standstill near the kitchen counter as Reynner turned from the living room window. No matter how broken she felt, he still took her breath away.

He wore the deep burgundy coat she'd first seen him in. The color offset his golden skin and pale hair. Her reaction to him then, too, had been instantaneous, not realizing just how deeply their paths interconnected.

There was no sign of the destroyed man she'd comforted last night, whose pain had awakened her and drew her to him. But if one looked closely, beneath all that male beauty, one would see the killer held on a tight leash.

Avoiding his gaze, she picked up her cell from the counter and slipped it into her purse.

"Ready?" he asked.

She nodded.

But she felt his eyes skim over her like a physical caress. Blood heated and buzzed in her veins, her stomach dipped. The butterflies in there took flight, making her woozy. She sucked in a deep breath, struggling to steady her nerves.

He was instantly at her side, his warm hand curving around her arm, brow furrowed in concern. "What's wrong?"

She stepped away from him and pulled on her gloves. "Nothing." With her head lowered, she saw his fingers curling into fists at her terse response.

As they walked out of her apartment, a strange sense

of foreboding took hold of her. It made the tiny hairs on her arms stand on end. She rarely prayed because nothing good ever came out of it. But...

Lord, please don't let anything go wrong tonight.

***

The scent of perfume and liquor masked the acrid smell of metal. Soft chatter filled the gallery, the tinkling glasses added to the light dissonance. Eve's head hurt from the harshness of the bright lights and her mouth ached from smiling as the night wore on.

She longed to yank off her gloves from her throbbing palms. The numbness she'd hidden behind the entire day was starting to wear off. She and Reynner hadn't spoken since they left her apartment. Not like she'd given him a chance, but she had to keep him at a distance. How else was she to start living again if she gave in every time he looked at her?

"The shows a brilliant success, Eve," David said, stopping beside her. "I knew it from the moment I saw that first sculpture you sent Eric."

"Yes, I remember." She smiled and took in his appearance. He'd dressed tonight...in a fashion of sorts. Black jeans, neon green shirt teamed with a narrow green and blue tie and a blue coat. And sneakers.

Eve accepted the elegant flute of champagne he held out and took a sip. The bubbly liquid tickled her nose and slid down her throat, easing nerves that had been stretched too taut.

She'd called and apologized to him before she left to Exilum, explaining she had to take a rain check, something urgent had cropped up at the last minute. David, thinking it was work related, had been okay with it.

"You look lovely, Eve." His warm blue eyes drifted over her in pleasure. His hand settled on her lower back.

"Thank you," she murmured and wondered why his touch didn't make her blood soar like Reynner's did.

"Who's that guy you came with?" he asked then, sounding a little disconcerted.

Her heart banged in her chest, her stricken gaze dropping to her glass. She had no idea what to say. *I'm his mate, but he doesn't want me?*

"He's…I er—"

"Eve?" Eric appeared at her side. "Can I see you for a sec? Sorry Dave, business."

David groaned, dropped his hand from her waist. "Darn, just not my night to spend any time with you, is it?"

"Make a date," Eric advised.

David laughed. "Yeah, working on that one." He winked at Eve and strolled off into the crowd.

"You looked like the world collapsed around you for a second there—thought you needed rescuing," Eric said, slipping his arm around her shoulder. She leaned against him, seeking comfort.

"All's well in Reynner-land, hmmn?" He rubbed her arm.

"Yes," she lied. "I'm just tired. It's been a difficult couple of months."

"I know, Eve. It will be over soon. You did exceptional tonight. You can take a few days off and rest, but not too long, you're going to be busy," he said, smiling. "Duke Summers said he hadn't seen anything this compelling in a long time."

Her eyes widened. She wheeled around. "The art critic? Really?"

"Yes."

Pleasure warmed her, coating her bruised heart. Her lips curved into a smile.

"Here comes Reynner. Damn guy will give the rest of us men a complex—does he take time out of his day to look this good?"

She had to force herself not to stare as Reynner wove his way through the crowd towards her.

She knew what everyone was reacting to. That allure Reynner's kind seemed to possess, the untouchable angelic handsomeness all too noticeable. As it was, she had to suffer the baffled looks from more than one woman when they saw Reynner with her. He rarely left her side, unless she was talking to people; only then did he give her space.

Eric drew Reynner into a conversation the moment he stopped beside them.

Brenna cornered her. Her silky black hair skimmed the shoulders of her deep green, sleeveless dress.

"Wow, Evie," she said, draping an arm around Eve's waist, her gaze darting around the packed, buzzing gallery. "So hard to get a moment with you, but great show."

"Yeah, well done," Kataya added, coming to stand beside her. A long, bronze column of a dress hugged her slender body. Her curly hair was piled on her head.

Eve noticed Kataya studying her. "What?"

"Okay. The deed's done. I want deets." She took a sip of her champagne.

Heat flared across Eve's face. She barely stopped herself from groaning.

Brenna's crystal blue eyes darted to her in surprise. She scanned Eve, up and down as if looking for evidence. "How can you tell? She looks the same to me."

Eve cringed. "Jesus—would you guys stop it?"

"Seriously, Bren, you need to get laid more often. If you watch their body language, it's all there. Reynner's not taken his eyes off Eve once. Poor David is on tenterhooks, worrying if he still has a chance."

Eve stole a glance at Reynner and found that Kataya was right. He may have been speaking to Eric, but his gaze remained on her.

"Is that true?" Brenna at least had the decency to whisper because Reynner must have heard Kataya's comments.

"I'm not talking about this." A touch on her elbow, and Eve turned to a man who interrupted them with some queries about her work. She followed him to the sculpture in question.

The moment Eve finished with the guest, she excused herself, only to find David appearing in front of her like an apparition.

"You look like a man on a mission," she teased.

"I sure am." He brushed the hair flopping over his brow, his face flushed from whatever liquor he'd consumed. "That piece you did on nature?"

"Trees in a Storm?" She gave him a curious look. "What about it?"

"I love the wildness depicted. There are two offers on it, but as the artist, you can let me have it, right?" He wiggled his brow at her.

She laughed. "Speak to Eric, I'm sure he can work something out for you—" Eve broke off, aware of the sudden silence around them…the air of expectancy.

Turning, she saw the woman. Tall, dressed in black, her gown hugging every sensuous curve of her body as she sashayed into the gallery. There was only one word to describe her: Exquisite.

Her hair, a shimmering wave of ebony silk, flowed to her waist and was the perfect backdrop for a face of palest honey. A delicate, wide, filigree choker of the purest silver set with a large, deep blue lapis lazuli stone in the center graced her elegant neck.

She moved like some slinky creature searching for prey. Her feline-like topaz eyes sparkled in excitement as she glanced around and settled in on...

Reynner.

Chapter 21

Eve watched the scene unfold like something from her worst nightmare. Her heart pounded and the pressure in her chest mounted.

With a seductive glide of her hips, the woman crossed to Reynner. She said something to him, then she reached up and kissed him right on the mouth.

Eve's brave façade shattered. The glass slipped from her fingers. Kataya swore and grabbed the falling crystal.

"Oh, hun." Brenna slipped her arm around Eve's waist. "I'm sorry..."

But Eve barely heard her.

Reynner stepped back, his expression rigid. The woman laughed, trailing a hand down his chest like she'd done it so many times before. Eve realized then to whom the scent of Opium belonged because the woman looked as sultry and exotic as the fragrance. And very, very beautiful.

Unable to watch, Eve turned away, pain ripping through her. Worse, Reynner didn't even look her way, like she no longer existed. Finally proving to her just how little she mattered. The champagne churning in her stomach rushed up her throat again.

"Aren't you going to do anything?" Kataya growled.

"Why? He made me no promises—he can do whatever he wants. But *I* can leave."

"No, you can't," Brenna protested. "It's your show, Evie."

"It's midnight, and I really don't care—" She swallowed hard, unable to conceal her devastation.

"Oh, hell." Kataya took hold of her arm. Her whiskey-colored eyes darkened with sympathy and ire. "You should have slept with David. At least you'd be spared this. Jesus, Eve, why did you have to fall for him, too?"

"Eve, you okay?" Eric appeared at her side from out of nowhere. Hazel eyes dark with fury, he glared at Reynner.

"Why wouldn't I be?" she asked, keeping her smile bright, even when she felt the cracks spreading through her protective shields. She didn't want their sympathy, or she'd break down in front of everyone. She just wanted to be alone to lick her wounds. But that wasn't going to happen.

Taking a deep breath, Eve weighed her options. Brenna was right. This was her show. She'd invested her life in this, and she had her pride…if she could just find the damn thing. Yep, right there on the floor along with her self-esteem. She dusted it off and hauled it back on.

She'd see this show to its bitter end, even if it killed her.

But when Reynner walked out of the gallery with that woman without a backward glance, the brittle shell she'd erected splintered.

***

Reynner paced the ground floor foyer and all he could see was the devastation in Eve's eyes when Inanna had tried to claim him like some damn possession. And that, he refused to tolerate.

He ground to a halt in front of Inanna. "What the hell are you doing here?"

"Come on, lover, you're so tense. Give over. Come back with me, and I'll show you a pleasurable way to ease all that stress."

Inanna reached for him. Reynner stepped back. He'd spent the entire evening watching other males touch his mate every time they spoke to her, and it had pushed him to the end of his endurance. Then there was that bloody artist, who seemed determined to breathe the same air Eve did. The one she'd threatened to leave him for. He'd tolerated it all because he knew how important this night was to her. And she worked damn hard for it.

"Why are you here?" he reiterated.

A casual shrug. "I enjoy art shows."

"At the very same gallery I happen to be at?"

Her eyes became brown granite. "Who is she? The slut I smell on you? Get rid of her. You won't like what will happen if she gets in the way of me and mine."

At her threat to Eve, Reynner grabbed her by the throat and shoved her against the wall. "You dare threaten me?"

Inanna coughed and tried to tug free of his death-like grip. Despite her hold over him, her physical strength didn't compare to his. Her power flared. The blast hit Reynner hard. He couldn't breathe, the mark on his chest hurt like someone torching his insides. His wings surged against his shielding, it took everything in him to stop them bursting free.

Urias, he was so tired of her shit. He just wanted her to leave him the hell alone.

"It's a promise," she gasped in defiance. "If you don't get rid of her."

"Let's get one thing clear. Come after me like this again, and I won't care if it means my death. I will take you with me from this life." And binding him to her guaranteed that. At least Eve would be safe then.

Reynner shoved away from her.

She hissed her anger, but beneath it a tinge of wariness flickered. The burn inside his chest subsided a little.

"You'll pay dearly for this!"

He didn't care what she did. He just wanted her gone so he could go get Eve, make sure she was all right.

When he said nothing, just stared at her, Inanna screamed and flashed from the foyer.

***

Eve sat in one of the two chairs in the restroom, her head buried in her hands. Kataya and Brenna burst inside. A match flared, and the acrid smell of smoke reached her nostrils.

Her breaths short and jerky, Eve took a tissue from her bag and dried her face. It was useless to pretend in front of her friends.

Kataya took a drag on her cigarette. Brenna leaned against the sink, watching Eve with worried eyes.

"No one is to blame but me," she whispered, swallowing back another bout of tears. "He warned me. I didn't listen."

Kataya exhaled heavily, killed her cigarette, and tossed the remains in the trashcan. She came over and rubbed Eve's shoulder. "Then it's his fucking loss. You don't need him, Eve."

"Kat, let's not be hasty," Brenna said, crossing to Eve.

"Not be hasty? You saw what he did out there?"

"Yes, that woman kissed him." She kneeled in front of Eve, smoothing out the creases in her dress. "Talk to him, hun, there must be a reason for all this."

"God, Brenna, you and your romantic heart! Rein it in fast, or it's going to be the death of you." Kataya glanced at Eve. "You want to leave? It's long gone midnight."

Eve balled the shredded tissue and nodded. She couldn't bear to be near Reynner right now.

"You're talking, Eve, the moment we get home," Kataya warned. "There's something else going on. And I'm betting it has a lot more to do with Reynner than getting rid of the damn V."

They were her best friends, and she so badly wanted to tell them. But what could she say? She was in love with an immortal who didn't want her. That he only needed her to find his artifact. They'd probably think she'd lost her mind.

After she said goodbye to Eric and David, Eve realized her goodbye to David was final, too. No matter what she told Reynner, she could never be with anyone else.

Struggling not to think about him, Eve left the gallery with Kataya and Brenna.

In the elevator, she braced her hand on the metal wall, and as she slipped off her stilettoes, the last time she'd done this flickered through her mind, the night that had changed her life.

Her feet hurt, but she far preferred this pain to the one riding her chest.

Hooking the straps over her gloved finger, she massaged her temples with her other hand.

"You okay, honey?" Brenna stroked her arm.

"It's all right, Bren. I'm fine, really." Or she would be after this weekend. How difficult would it be for immortals to track down the Stone in a city the size of New York?

The elevator pinged and the door rolled open. Reynner stood there, waiting to enter. His gaze zeroed in on her.

A redheaded fury stormed up to him. Kataya snapped, "Stay away from Eve. She's coming home with us."

Shocked, Eve stared. She really hadn't expected Kat to attack him.

Reynner didn't say anything but stepped back. His unwavering gaze held hers, and Eve knew he wouldn't let her leave without him.

"Kat, I'll be okay."

Furious, Kataya swung back to her, her mouth tightened at whatever she saw on Eve's face. Then she stormed out. Brenna gave her a quick hug and hurried after Kataya.

Eve didn't look at Reynner as she followed them, wishing she could leave as easily as her friends had.

Out in the street, she inhaled the oppressive air along with the faint fragrance of exotic spices. It made her heart bleed, knowing that woman had to have been in his arms for him to retain her scent. Eve put more space between them as they headed for his car. The heat from the sidewalk added to the suffocation in her chest.

"You didn't have to come back."

"Don't, Eve." His low, angry tone broke the fragile

hold on her control.

"Don't what, Reynner?" She spun around to face him. The bitter pain she tried to hold back spewed out. "Don't get in your way? Don't make this harder?"

"You think this is any easier for me?" His gaze turned fierce. A nerve pulsed furiously in his jaw.

"I don't see why it's difficult. I'm nothing to you. Just a tool for what you need. So don't pretend otherwise. I made a promise, and I'll get it done. I'll get you your Stone"—she pulled in a trembling breath, stiffened her spine with resolve—"but I don't want you with me any longer. Ask another. North, Aerén—I don't care who, to take your place."

"Don't push me, Eve."

"You think I pushed you to do this?" Outrage flooded her. "I didn't force you into anything, not now, certainly not in the groves of Exilum. I wish *that* never happened. I wish–I wish fate had chosen differently for me."

She turned away and realized she'd stopped beside his car. Her gaze dropped, and she stared dully at her feet. Tears swam in her eyes. Her blue nail polish wavered like dark holes, waiting to suck her into an abyss.

God, please don't let me break down in front of him.

Reynner opened the door for her, and she slid inside. Slamming it shut, he headed to the other side, his expression dark and frustrated. Pulling her gaze away, Eve brushed at her tears and dropped her stilettoes to the floorboard as he got in and shut the door.

The other woman's perfume overrode the smell of the leather seats. Eve closed her eyes. Just as well he didn't want a relationship with her. He would destroy her every time he came back with that scent on him. He may not trust women, but he certainly seemed to want *that* one.

Christ, what was she thinking? She could never hope to compete with someone who looked that beautiful. And had perfect hands.

Eve slid hers under her thighs.

***

The moment Reynner parked the car outside her apartment building, Eve reached for the door, wanting to disappear into the sanctuary of her room. He caught her arm. "Eve, wait—"

She snatched her arm away. "Don't touch me. Not after you've been with her. I had to smell her on you the entire trip trapped in this car—that was her, wasn't it?" God, how much more pathetic could she get? She shook her head. "No, don't answer. It's none of my business."

Before she burst into tears and disgraced herself further, Eve turned blindly for the door. Only she didn't get far.

"Don't touch you?" He grasped her arm again. "I had to watch every fucking male in there touch you."

"So that was your payback? To kiss her in front of the entire gallery?"

"Dammit, I didn't kiss her—it's not what you think."

"I don't care." She yanked free. "We're done."

A furious growl echoed through the interior of the car. He hauled her onto his lap and captured her lips in a mind-shattering kiss. She barely registered her thigh hitting the gears, her elbow banging against the steering wheel, or the pain shooting up her knee and arm.

Eve pushed at his chest, tried to free her mouth, because if she didn't, she'd be begging him to love her.

She didn't want to sink any lower than she already had.

But there was no place for her to move, trapped between Reynner's body and the steering wheel. He ripped off her gloves, tossing them both over his shoulder then shackled her wrists in one hand.

"Why are you doing this?" Her chest heaved from her struggles, her bitterness spilling free.

His anger died, tortured blue eyes met hers. "Because if I don't, Eve, I'm afraid of what I'll do. If you send me away like this…" He inhaled a ragged breath. "I tore down half of Hell and that was just to break free. Without you, I'll do far worse."

She closed her eyes, wanting to believe but too scared to hope. Reynner had so much darkness in his soul. It was clear he felt the physical connection of their bond, why he couldn't keep away, but would he ever let himself feel deeper emotions for her? Ever trust her?

She would accept nothing less than his love, and that brought her right back to her current situation.

His finger brushed her nipple. Her eyes snapped open. His intense gaze sent shivers down her spine. Slowly, he pushed up the hem of her dress and his palm slid along her bare thigh.

"Don't," she pleaded, unable to stop his stroking hand with both of hers trapped. His caressing slowed.

"You don't want me?"

"Every time I allow myself to care, I hurt more later. I've accepted that you don't feel the same way I do—"

"Don't feel the same way?" A tormented sound escaped him. "Without you, I cannot breathe."

"Then why? Why do you always push me away?"

"Because I thought I was protecting you. But I messed up. Badly. I hurt you…" His eyes became an abyss of desperation. "Forgive me, Eve. You are all I've ever wanted. I'll make it right, I promise, just don't leave me."

She swallowed a broken breath, too scared to believe him. "Reynner—"

He shook his head, stopping her. "Everything inside here"—he pressed a fist against his chest—"is so fucking empty, an endless darkness without you. I cannot survive the tomorrows if you're not in it—I just can't…"

He took her mouth in a desperately tender kiss. A tremor darted through her. And the shaky walls she'd erected around her heart splintered.

How could it not, when he was her everything? Eve kissed him back.

His groan of relief had yearning surging through her. Needing to touch him, she freed her hands and pulled the tie from his hair, tangling her fingers in the silky strands. He left her mouth to trail his lips along her jaw in tender little nips and kisses down to her bare shoulder.

He tugged at the tight bodice. "How do you open this thing?"

Breathing hard, Eve reached to the left side of her dress. He took over, unzipped and freed her breasts then lifted her up to straddle him. Her knee hit the door. She forgot the pain the moment his mouth closed on her nipple. Desire like hot molasses pooled between her thighs as he licked and sucked. Darts of pleasure uncurled, streaming through her body.

She pushed at his coat. Letting go of her nipple, he moved his seat back and freed his arms. She unbuttoned his shirt and ran her hands over the warm muscled contours of his torso. She lowered her head and pressed her lips to his chest.

"Gods, Eve—" His hands tightened in her hair. "I need you so damn bad."

***

A visceral hunger tore through him. He had to have her. All of her—had to reclaim her.

This evening had showed him the simple truth. He could never walk away from her. She was the one his heart beat for. Without her, he might as well just hand himself over to Inanna.

Unable to resist her, he took her mouth in another intense kiss. He slipped his hand under her dress and ripped off her panties, too impatient to wait. Then he stroked down her dampness, found her clit and rolled the tiny nub with his thumb. She pulled her mouth away, a breathy moan escaping her. He nipped her jaw as he eased a finger inside. She was too tight—the space too cramped for movement. He shifted and pushed a button on the side to recline his seat.

Eve fell forward and gasped, taking his finger in even deeper. His gaze fixed on her beautiful face, he added another, working her slick passage. Her back arched, her pale breasts and pouty, tan nipples a sensual provocation.

An invitation he couldn't resist. He suckled on the sensitive nub then growled against her flesh, "I want to taste every inch of you, but this damn car makes that impossible."

"Let's go inside, then," she breathed.

"No. Can't wait. Need you."

She reached between them, fiddled with his leathers, and the loud rip of his zipper filled the confined space. She paused, her gaze rushing to his. He knew it was because the last time he hadn't let her touch him.

Now, he simply took her fingers and wrapped them around his rigid sex.

And she damn near unmanned him. Her hand tightened around him, her gaze lowered. She ran her palm up and down his length in wonder.

He almost came in her hand. "No," he rasped. "In you. Now."

She shifted and guided his erection to her wet, heated center and slowly pushed down. Her silky sheath fisted him, bringing an erotic pain. He tightened his grip on her hips as she sank over him. Her eyes closed in pleasure, echoed by the husky moan that left her lips.

"Look at me, Eve." At his gruff demand, her eyes flickered open, settled on him. The familiar blue sparks brightened her gaze again. To know she was joined to him in such an intrinsic way, a primal possessiveness took hold. He cupped her face and covered her mouth in a scorching kiss.

Her palms slid over his shoulders in a rough caress then tangled in his hair. He wanted her touch all over him, wanted it branded in his heart.

She broke free of his mouth, breathing hard. Her nipple so close to his face, he captured it with his lips and sucked on the perky little nub. Another whimper left her, her grip tightened on his hair. She looked down at him.

"Your eyes—glowing," she panted.

"The mating bond—it's what you do to me," he grunted, letting go of her nipple and thrusting harder into her.

"I don't have it anymore."

A rough laugh. "It's there—we're bonded. Can never be broken. It will always glow when we make love, *fiyae.*"

"Feeya?"

Reynner groaned, his body tight, hovering on the brink. "Gods, baby, later—later, I'll tell you all you want to know. Hold—" He took her hands and put them behind her on the steering wheel.

Helpless, she stared at him as he grasped her hips and thrust into her, surging harder, faster now. He slipped his hand to where they were joined. His thumb applied pressure on her clit as he rolled it.

"*Oh!*" she cried out, her body bowing. Her inner muscles squeezing him so tight—fuck! His groin tightened and his release hauled him over. Indescribable pleasure scoring through his body, he spilled himself into her.

Emotions crowded him as the light of their mating bond flared and strengthened. Then he simply held her, his face buried in her neck.

By the heavens, nothing felt this complete. Ever.

After his long, endless life of nightmares and darkness, he'd found his light. His happiness. His peace. Eve.

***

Their heavy breathing filled the car. Eve collapsed against him, her dress in a tangled heap around her waist, his erection still buried deeply within her. The moment too transcendent, she didn't want to move—heck, didn't know if she *could* move. Or if she'd ever want to.

He stirred, his lips gently caressing her cheek. "You think if we slept here, like this, anyone would notice?"

A husky laugh escaped her. "We'd certainly entertain the early risers of New York."

"I love you, Eve."

The words were the softest whisper against her ear. Something inside her shifted, and the last flimsy guard around her heart—one she didn't even know was still there—crumbled. Tears flooded her eyes, spilled down her face and onto his chest.

He went motionless. Then cupped her face in alarm as his gaze searched hers, his eyes back to that sexy night-sky shade, the mating glow no longer visible. "What is it?"

She shook her head, a tremulous smile taking shape. "Nothing. It's just that I never believed this moment would come."

He kissed away her tears. "Is that all?"

"Yes."

He continued to examine her face, then those indigo eyes fixed on hers. His grip tightened. "Eve." A demand.

She knew what he wanted and found it hard to suppress her smile. Brushing his lips in a tender kiss, she whispered, "I love you, too. You know that."

He exhaled roughly as if his heart had settled. "My Eve."

Chapter 22

After several blissful minutes, Reynner pressed his lips to her shoulder. "We need to talk."

Why did those words sound so ominous? Eve shifted on his lap. His sex twitched inside her, his sharp indrawn breath an intoxicating whisper on her senses.

"You move like that, and we'll definitely give your neighbors a show to remember," he rasped.

She didn't care, her body so ready for another bout of lovemaking, even in these cramped quarters. Except her knees were starting to spasm, and the steering wheel dug into her back. With a sigh of reluctance, Eve moved off him. His erection slipped free as she slid back to her seat. Pulling up the top of her dress, she covered her breasts and tugged up her zipper.

Reynner refastened his pants then realigned his seat. Ignoring his open shirt and the coat crushed behind him, he rested his hands on the steering wheel. He seemed to be studying her in the dark. Aware he could probably see her blushing, she hurriedly leaned forward and searched for her torn panties. "What do you want to talk about?"

The silence in the car became heavy. Oppressive.

Anxiety taking hold, Eve turned to him, her underwear forgotten. "Reynner?"

"She was the one who had me trapped in Hell."

Eve knew instantly whom he meant, the woman from the gallery.

"Why," she asked, shocked.

A shoulder lifted in a shrug. "Because I refused to stay and become her long-term play thing."

Jealousy ate at her to know that the woman had been his lover. And just as fast, it fizzled out; anger taking its place that she would do such a horrific thing.

"It meant nothing," he said quietly. "It happened once, eons ago."

"Then why won't she leave you alone?"

"Inanna doesn't like being told no. In a rage, she cursed me to a year in Hell, hoping time there would teach me not to refuse her. In her haste to teach me a lesson, she forgot that a year outside is a damn century in Hell…" he broke off. Then a telling pause. "All that you saw when you touched me…happened. That's when Kalinin got ahold of me."

He turned to stare through the windshield, his jaw hardening. "Without light of any kind, I weaken. It was easy for her to take control with constant attacks from her pets. She wanted the same thing Inanna did, to own one like me. Only with Kalinin, she wanted more, an eternal supply of my blood."

His fingers clenched the steering wheel, knuckles white. But the pain in his voice had Eve's own heart hurting. "My blood gave her the best high she'd ever experienced. She thought feeding me hers would make me dependent. I may have lost my powers in the pits of Hell, but I refused to give in to her. Vengeance was what drove me. At the time, I'd still thought to find and make Inanna pay. It angered Kalinin that I was able to resist..."

Eve laid a hand on his, pulling him back to her when he stopped speaking. His haunted gaze met hers, cutting deep into her soul.

"How did you escape?"

"After another attack from her pets for refusing her, I lay in the filth, torn and bleeding, unable to move. A demon brought water into the cell. He said something, I didn't respond. He probably thought I was unconscious. He opened a vein of fire in the wall—better to see the Empyrean Kalinin had imprisoned for nearly a century." Anger darkened his voice.

Eve longed to wrap her arms around him but didn't interrupt, let him get it all out. She realized this was probably the first time he'd ever spoken about his capture.

"The natural energy of the fire that lit the cell was all I needed. Within seconds, my strength rebuilt. The demon ran when he realized what was happening.

"I couldn't let him get away, alert the others I had escaped. I killed him then found my way to Kalinin's abode of orgies and sin. I grabbed a sword and slaughtered them all. She was in her chambers with her lovers. I skewered her to the bed, massacred her lovers before I decapitated and incinerated her. I brought down the place of depravity to rubble and escaped to this world...

"That's how Michael found me, crazed and killing demoniis like the insane..." He scrubbed a hand down his face. "I'm sorry..."

He was apologizing for what had been done to him?

Because no words could make up for his torture, his

debasement, Eve simply reached across and hugged him. If she got ahold of Inanna, she'd rip her apart for what she'd done to him. "You have nothing to apologize for."

"Eve,"—a heartfelt whisper—"you humble me with that good, kind, and very loving heart."

She eased back. "You endured and lived through a horrific ordeal no being could have survived. Now that I know, you think I don't understand why it took you this long to open up to me? You don't trust easily—no, no, let me finish," she stopped him when he would have interrupted. "You don't trust women. After all that's happened, how can I blame you?"

"No, Eve. You—" His eyes filled with tenderness, with love. "I trust with my life. My heart. You demanded nothing from me." A smile. "Well, except my unconditional love."

"Is it so bad, then?" She pushed his unbound hair from his face so she could see him better in the streetlight. He caught her hand and pressed his lips to the ruined flesh.

"Ah, *me'morae,* never. You see inside me—see who I am. You are all that's right in my life."

"What does that mean? What you called me?"

"*My love.*"

Yes, his. Always. She took a deep breath. Settled.

Then she demanded, "Why do you still allow this woman to see you?"

"I don't. Goddesses are a self-serving lot. She does whatever the hell she pleases."

"You're an immortal. Stop her. Why is it so difficult?" She tried to free her hand from his, but he wouldn't let go. Eve stilled in shock. "She's a *goddess*—not an Empyrean?"

"Inanna is from the Sumerian pantheon. Empyrean females would not dare do what she did."

She recalled what Aerén had told her about Reynner and the women from his world. Despite knowing he loved her, her stomach twisted into a painful knot.

"Eve." He cupped her face and brushed his lips against hers. "That was eons ago. None of them meant anything, until you."

Her throat tightened with suppressed emotions at his words. And deep within her soul she felt his absolute love, like a warm glow.

Eve pulled back, determined to end this goddess's hold on him. "Reynner, tell Inanna no."

"It's not that simple. I gave her my word not to use my powers for that night until I left the next day. But she didn't release me like she'd promised. Instead, she bound me to her while I was in a drugged sleep. No, I have no idea how. Maybe it was through the wine I had, the crap she burns in her place..."

Shaken to her core, Eve whispered, "But you must have mages, oracles who could—"

He shook his head. "I've tried them—tried everything, I even cut the damn brand off my chest, nothing works."

"That star?" she said horrified. "*She* put that on you?"

He nodded.

Now she understood that day in her studio when she'd thought he didn't want her to touch him. It was the star. Eve's fingers balled into fists. She wasn't a violent person, but right then, she wanted the goddess drawn and quartered.

"Eve, there's something else you must understand, must be prepared for. Being with me is dangerous. I don't want you hurt or caught in any crossfire. Inanna is lethal—"

"I don't care."

"She'll use you, hurt you to get me to do what she wants."

At his warning, her heart constricted. "Wh-what are you saying?"

His expression became granite. "Don't worry, I'll handle her."

"Reynner—"

"You are my life, Eve. I will never let anything happen to you." A vow.

Still, unease filled her. She recalled the kiss in the gallery. Ice brushed over her skin in foreboding. In life, nothing was permanent, and that witch could take Reynner away from her.

No. Never. Not if she could help it.

"C'mon, *me'seya*, let's get you inside, you need to rest. We have a long night ahead of us tomorrow. We start scouting for the artifact." He opened the car door, came around to her side, and helped her out.

Before she could ask, he smiled. Said, "Sweetheart."

As they headed into the building, Eve's cell beeped. She retrieved her phone from her bag and read the text message from Kataya. *Are you all right?*

She tried to text but the darn cracked glass made it difficult. Autocorrect was giving her the strangest words. *Damn.* She needed to reassure her friend she was okay.

"May I borrow your cell?" she asked him. "Mine's gone all wonky. It's Kat, she'll think something awful happened if I don't respond." Eve realized then she probably should apologize for her friend's anger at the gallery. "Reynner, I know Kat can be in your face at times, but it's just her way. She saw that woman kissing you, and all her alarms went off."

Reynner stroked her back then handed her his phone. "You don't have to explain anything. Make your call."

***

After Eve had gone to bed, Reynner headed back to the living room. Aerén had taken the bedroom Reynner had used before, but sleep was the last thing on his mind.

Now that he no longer had to hide his feelings from Eve, he slid safely into her mind, needing the contact—the anchor. Heavens, he closed his eyes, reveling in the peace their bond provided him.

A peace he'd never thought possible.

He glanced at the corridor. Longing for her hit him hard. He planted his booted feet to the floor so he wouldn't head back there. She'd had a tiring day, needed the rest, and he needed to think. He had bigger problems now.

He couldn't ignore Inanna's threat from this evening. She rarely made idle ones. He pinched the bridge of his nose.

"Problems?" North asked.

Reynner found the warrior sprawled on the couch, eyeing him instead of the television.

It still shocked him to see the changes in North. A big male, but his skin seemed to have shrunk over his bones. Too lean, almost gaunt now.

How North survived without his mate, Reynner had no idea. Only knew he wouldn't be able to handle it if anything happened to Eve. He realized, too, that no words he uttered in condolence could soften the male's loss.

Still. "I'm sorry about your mate."

North's lips tightened. He nodded and stared at his laced fingers. He didn't say much—hell, he didn't ever speak about his dead mate.

North seemed to collect himself, his lean face set once more in its usual impassive lines. "Anything I can do?"

Reynner shook his head, aware North was referring to his problems. "No. It's my mess to clean up."

He picked up the horse sculpture Eve had given him and ran his fingers over the metal. "Eve... she's all that is pure and good, and she ends up with one like me."

North frowned. "We always thought we couldn't soul-join with mortals. Guess we know differently now."

"Soul-joined or not, I would never let Eve go. But I'm damn grateful to whichever fate brought her to me."

"Our creator—"

"Messed up. There can never be a *perfect* race. It's time the ruling council faced the truth. It can never be how it once was. Urias created us, but to continue to exist, we must do what we can to survive. I think the Stone disappearing...maybe it's a good thing."

Reynner set the sculpture back on the shelf and crossed to the kitchen. "This proves that we can mate with mortals, though I can't see the ruling council agreeing. Can you imagine if I went back to Empyrea with Eve? They would never accept her. Her mortality—her fragility will work against her, and that I will never subject her to."

"Then you're going to remain on this realm with her?"

"Yeah." Reynner helped himself to a soda from the fridge, tore open the tab, and took a deep swallow of the ice cold liquid. "And we'll live in Exilum, too."

Aerén walked into the lounge, wearing only boxers—for which Reynner was eternally grateful.

The prince's silver eyes narrowed. "You're not coming back to Empyrea—to your home?"

"Eve is my home," he said.

Sensing her still awake, he headed for her room.

***

Eve lay in bed, unable to settle, her body far too tense. Everything Reynner had told her about Inanna rattled around in her head like heavy stones.

Throwing aside the cover, she swung her feet to the cool, wooden floors and rubbed the heels of her palms against her burning eyes. God, she had to find a way to help him. No way would she ever accept that evil witch having control over him. Lowering her hands, her gaze fell on Reynner's cell phone on her nightstand.

A thought flashed through her mind. Eve grabbed the phone, grateful it was unlocked, and pressed star one. It was answered instantly. *Oh, God, please let this work.*

"Reynner?" The familiar deep, commanding voice filled her ears. To know she was speaking to *the* archangel sent goosebumps skittering along her skin.

"Er- no, Michael, it's me."

"Eve—is Reynner all right?"

"Yes, he's fine. I...I er- need your help."

"What is it?" He was precise and to the point, like before.

Eve rose and padded to the window. Moving the curtains aside, she peered into the quiet streets. Her voice low, she told the archangel her problem. When she came to an end, he said, "I understand. It is a delicate situation."

"Can you help me?"

"I cannot, but maybe the oracle can. But she's only there for the next day. Don't waste time. Take Reynner and go see her."

Eve winced. "I can't. He er- doesn't want me involved in this."

The archangel deliberated a long, silent moment. "I see... So it's on you then to talk to her." He paused, and for the tiniest moment, Eve thought she'd heard deeper concern in his voice. Worry for her, not Reynner. "I would go with you, Eve. But things are tense right now and I'm needed here."

"I understand. I can do this alone."

"Be careful."

"I will."

Michael recited the address then ended the call. Eve didn't bother to write it down. She knew the place. After all, she'd gone there once, when she'd wanted to get rid of her own curse.

Eve set the cell phone on her dresser, just as the door opened and Reynner walked inside. Guiltily, she rubbed her hands down her shorts.

"Why aren't you asleep?"

"I've tried, I can't." Her gaze widened when he started to unbutton his shirt.

"You didn't think I would share the bed with Aerén now, did you?" He shrugged off the shirt and tossed it onto the armchair.

No, she wasn't thinking at all as joy swept through her.

"This way, we both can rest," he said as he sat on the bed and toed off his boots. They landed with a thud on the floor. His brow rose when she remained rooted near the window.

"You plan to stay there all night?" he asked. Rising

to his feet, he unbuckled his belt, unzipped and got rid of his leathers.

Dressed, Reynner was gorgeous, but naked, he took her breath away faced with all those lickable golden muscles. Her gaze drifted down to his semi-erect sex and her body melted for him. She wanted to touch him—wanted him to touch her again. Then she met his tender gaze and her chest constricted at the absolute love she saw there.

He loved her.

Reynner held out his hand. Eve was so grateful her wobbly knees carried her across to him and that she didn't collapse into a messy puddle of happiness on the floor.

With an inch separating his nakedness from her, he slid his hands up her body. And in a slow, sensual caress, he pulled off her tank top and tossed it aside. "I don't want anything between us."

She couldn't speak, her nerves stretched too taut. Her nipples pebbled at the heated look in his indigo eyes. But he didn't act on his desires, just hooked his fingers in the elastic waist of her sleep shorts and panties, and made quick work of removing them.

Eve slid to the middle of her bed, and he followed, settling her against him. He pulled the covers to their waist. Eve rolled her eyes as she tugged for more coverage.

"Are you cold?"

She glanced at him. His teasing smile was outright sinful. She scrunched her face, her shyness fading. Then she recalled last night, his nightmares. Anxiety took hold. "Will you sleep?"

"With you near me, it's doubtful," he said, his tone wry. "Don't worry about me, Eve, I'll be okay."

No matter. She'd brought him back last night; she'd do so again.

Eve rested her head on his chest and slid her arm over him, just below the cursed star, reminding her of what she had to do. When Reynner pressed his lips to her forehead, she closed her eyes, and for now, savored being in the arms of the man she loved.

***

After a quick shower the following morning, Eve changed and ran a comb through her damp hair. Taking her charm bracelet from the draw, she fastened it around her wrist, her troubled mind on Reynner. It worried her that he hadn't slept at all last night.

As she gathered up their scattered clothes, and his pants that had fallen to the floor, a gleam near it caught her attention. She picked up the tiny, gold half-circle.

Her earring? A quick look on her dresser and she found its twin still there. Frowning, she ran her finger around the almost-prefect loop. She was so sure she'd lost this at the club.

Guess she was mistaken. She hung Reynner's pants back on the armchair. He'd already showered and gone off to the kitchen to get started on coffee. Heat spread across her face when she recalled how he'd awakened her earlier. The man was way too inventive.

Heck, she'd gladly wake up like that every day. A smile curved her mouth. But reality forced her to focus. Before that could happen, she had to find a way to leave without Reynner today and go see the oracle.

She rubbed her earring with her thumb and worried over her dilemma. There was no way he'd allow her to go out on her own. She could ask North to accompany her, but he'd probably tell Reynner where she'd been, and chances were, Reynner would know why and that would ruin everything. The man was far too canny and way too protective.

And Aerén, friendly as he was, he would flat-out refuse.

She paced to the door and looped back to the window, recounting the knots on the wooden floors while she tried to figure out the least suspicious way of leaving.

Crap, this was so damn difficult…unless, she told him she wanted to spend some time with her friends before they headed out to look for the artifact this evening, and that she needed to relax after her showing.

She cringed at the pathetic lie. She really didn't want to leave him.

"Why are you hiding in here?"

Her heart jumped and her head snapped to him.

Reynner leaned against the doorframe, his arms crossed over his chest. The heat in his eyes as he ran his gaze over her just about made her melt. Warmth spread across her cheeks. He was such a predatory male. He liked to take charge when they made love. She should have known when he'd first told her to undress in Exilum.

Smiling, he straightened and strolled over to her, his hands sliding into his jeans pockets. He halted, his brow furrowing as he searched in them. Picking up his leathers from the armchair, he rifled through those, too.

"What's wrong?"

He shook his head as he hunted in his back pockets.

Eve grabbed him, stopping his frantic search. "Reynner, what is it?"

He went still. His gaze dropped to her hand on his arm. He loosened her hold and gently removed the earring she clutched. Then he simply stared at the small piece of metal.

Puzzled, she searched his face. "You want my earring?"

His gaze lifting to hers, he rubbed the back of his neck. For the first time, Eve saw him look uncomfortable. Almost sheepish.

"This was what kept me together," he said softly, his thumb stroking the metal. "When darkness took me under, when I thought I couldn't hold my shit together, this piece of metal was all I had to hold onto. A piece of you that kept me sane."

Eve simply stared at him, his words touching a visceral part of her. He dropped the small hoop back in his pocket and stroked her face with a gentleness she'd never thought possible from such a hard man.

"At the club, when I crashed into you, your earring caught on my shirt. The moment I touched it, I could sense your spirit, your very essence. It drew me and I couldn't let go. Now that I have you, I don't really need it, but I want to keep that piece of you..."

Her heart swelled with tenderness.

"It's my reminder of what I nearly lost with my..." he broke off, searching for a word.

"Pigheadedness?" she teased, trying to get her shaky emotions under control. If she didn't, she'd start blubbering like an idiot.

Amusement lightened his eyes. Lowering his head, he kissed her. "I prefer inflexibility."

He swung her into his arms and crossed to the bed. Then he dropped her. A startled shriek escaped her as she fell. Before she got her breath back, he'd settled between her parted legs and caged her with his big body. She wrapped her arms around his neck.

His eyes warm and tender, he brushed away the stray

strands of hair spilling over her face. "Do you have any idea what you do to me?"

Hiding her grin, she moved her hand down between their bodies to his groin and the delicious bulge there. She stroked him over his jeans. "I think I do."

"*Urias*—"

"So you want me naked, huh?"

"Naked, wet, and all over me—" he broke off, his gaze on her charm bracelet.

Grasping her wrist, he studied the ornaments then fingered the heart.

"It was a present from my friends," she said. "That day we crashed in the club? It was my birthday."

After a moment of silence, he asked, "Who was there?"

"Hmmm, Eric, Bren, Kat and…" *Crap!*

"The artist," he added, his eyes flickering to hers. She bit her lip. His gaze shuttered, his mouth setting in a tight line.

"Reynner, it meant nothing to me."

"Yet you wore it?"

One minute he was touching the heart and the next it was in his palm. The thing melted into a tiny blob.

Not wanting to start their life with a quarrel over a piece of jewelry she didn't want in the first place, Eve didn't comment on what he'd done. She simply grasped his hair, wound it around her hand, pulled him close and kissed him.

It took a moment and a little persuasion. Yep, her man possessed that inflexible will.

Meeting his cool blue gaze thankfully still edged with lust, she bit him. With a low growl, he tossed the piece of gold aside and kissed her deeply. Possessively. "You're mine, Eve. Mine."

He deftly freed the buttons of her blouse. His head dipping lower, he suckled her nipple through her bra. Her breath caught. Desire spread like wildfire. She unfastened and slid her hand into his jeans—grasped his erection when reality knocked her sideways.

If she gave in now, then she would never be able to find a way to free Reynner. Today was all she had. Michael had said the oracle would be away for a while. No, she couldn't risk waiting. If the horrid goddess came back and found out the truth about their relationship, there was no telling what she'd do to Reynner.

It got her moving. "Let me up." She pushed at him, despite her body rebelling at being denied his.

"No." He sucked on her other nipple.

She grabbed his head to stop his sensual torment before she became lost in him. "Reynner, please."

Instantly, he stilled. Lifting his head, his gaze dark with need, he searched her face. "What's wrong?"

"I can't, not right now. I promised my friends I'd spend the morning with them." Even to her ears it sounded like the flimsy excuse it was. "Kat's not in a good place with Jake away. I said I'd stop by..."

For a long moment, he stared at her. Without a word, he rolled off her to lie on his back and stare at the ceiling.

"I'm sorry." She sat up. "More than anything I want to be here with you."

"There's no need to apologize, Eve. I'm your mate, not your jailor." Cool words.

Guilt gnawed at her. She lowered her gaze to her unfastened top, saw the wet patch on her bra where he'd sucked her. Slowly, Eve redid her buttons. She hated that she'd hurt him, but if she stayed, then Inanna would win.

"Reynner, it's just for a few hours."

He sat up and zipped himself. Arms braced on his thighs, he turned to her. "Eve, I don't like you being on your own."

"I won't be alone. I'll be with Kataya. And Brenna's staying the weekend with her. Besides, you said immortals cannot enter human homes if not invited."

"I know what I said." He cut her a terse look. Then he exhaled heavily. "All right. I'll take you there. But under no circumstances do you leave her apartment. Understand?"

Eve nodded and fiddled with a button on her shirt, unable to look at him.

How could she? She was going to break her word the moment she got to Kat's place.

Chapter 23

At Greenwich Village, Eve restlessly paced the floor of her friend's spacious living room. She hated keeping the truth from Reynner, but if he had an inkling of what she'd planned, he'd stop her. She couldn't have that. She loved him and would use her last breath to find a way to free him.

He'd kept her earring.

She couldn't get over that. Smiling, she stopped at the window and glanced at the busy street below, trying to figure out how to borrow Kat's Fiat.

Cars idled at the red traffic lights as a few early-morning health fanatics jogged past them. The flower seller adjacent to Kataya's building, wearing a large straw hat to keep the morning heat off him, rearranged the colorful blooms in his stall.

At the draggy slaps of bare feet on the hardwood, Eve turned as Brenna staggered into the lounge half asleep and flopped onto the dark green armchair, her eyes still shut.

"How do you not knock into walls and such?" Eve asked in amusement.

"It takes loads of practice and many learning bruises. Besides, it's not the first time I've spent the night here. Oh, and never rearranging the furniture helps a lot—mornin', Eve, you're early."

Kataya snorted, walking into the room, a soda in her hand. "It's eleven A.M. All of New York is up."

"It's Sunday," Brenna grumbled.

"Then they should be up." Kataya handed Eve her orange drink. "It's all I have loaded with sugar. So what happened last night? When you called, you said all was okay?"

"It is, it is…" Eve looked at both of her friends. "He loves me," she burst out even, unable to contain her joy, even if there was a big fat black cloud hanging over her happiness.

Brenna's eyes popped open. Then a huge grin spread across her face. "Oh, Evie, to finally see you happy—" She jumped up from the armchair, did a little dance-wiggle, and hugged her. "I'm so thrilled for you. And darn, Reynner is scrumptious—I can still say that, right?" she asked quickly.

Eve laughed. "You can say anything, Bren."

"Oh, good." She dropped down on the armchair again.

"I can see by the blush on your face how pleased you are." Kataya said, studying her with a small smile on her lips. "I'm happy for you. But what about that woman from last night?"

Her happiness dimmed a little. "He explained everything about her. She's an ex-lover who doesn't want to let him go even though he wants nothing to do with her."

"And?" Kataya picked up her coffee from the counter that separated the kitchen from the living room and sat down on the green and navy striped futon.

"Later. I promise I'll tell you all then." Eve jerked to her feet and rubbed her damp palms down her jeans. "First, I need to borrow your car for an hour."

"Why? What happened to yours?"

"I couldn't use it because Reynner dropped me off. But I really need to make a quick trip somewhere and be back before he comes for me."

Kataya eyed her for a silent, suspicious second. "Why?"

Darn. Eve heaved a sigh. Now wasn't the time to spill the truth about Reynner. It would take too long to make a skeptic like Kataya believe her. At least Brenna was a little more open-minded. "Please, Kat, lend me your car, it's really important."

Her friend studied her for another moment, then nodded. "All right. With all the agitation flying off you, it must be. I'll take you, as soon as Bren moves her butt off that couch."

"I'm moving, I'm moving," Brenna objected, lurching to her feet.

Eve really didn't want to drag her friends into this. But if she said no, they'd both dig their toes in. They could be so stubborn. "Fine."

***

Ten minutes later, they climbed into the Fiat and buckled in. Kataya raised the air-conditioning to cool the stifling heat trapped inside the car. "All right, where to?" she asked.

Eve hesitated, then said, "Lila Smith."

"The oracle?" her friends blurted out in unison, turning stunned faces to her.

Eve grimaced. "Yes."

"Why are we going to see the oracle? Are you trying

to get rid of that curse on your hands again?" Kataya demanded as she merged into the traffic.

"No. This isn't about me."

"Then who?"

"It's about…" She sucked in a breath. "Reynner."

Brenna leaned forward from the backseat. "You mean, he's cursed with something similar"—she gestured to Eve's hands—"like *that*?"

"Not exactly." Dammit, how did she even begin to explain?

At a red light, Kataya halted and both her friends fixed her with curious looks. Eve cleared her throat and said, "We all know that supernatural things happen, right? I mean, we know that since…" She wiggled her scarred fingers in response.

"Yeah. So?" Kataya stepped on the gas when the lights turned green. Though she kept her attention on the road, her sharp gaze cut to Eve once every few seconds.

"So, what if I told you there was more?"

"More?" Brenna asked, coiling a length of Eve's hair.

"Much more." Eve sighed. Then she told them what had happened. "The night when Reynner came to David's show and offered to drive me home, I got sucked into a world I still can't completely wrap my mind around. But it all comes down to demons existing and Reynner being…an angel."

Kataya slammed on the brakes. Tires screeched on the tarmac, and the Fiat came to a grinding halt almost rear-ending the car that had stopped in front of them for a red light. Eve grabbed the dashboard.

She burst out laughing. "Yeah, right."

A little annoyed, Eve sat back and deliberately

waved her damaged hand in front of Kataya to remind her of just how different she was.

"Shit," she muttered, then shut her mouth. At the sounds of irate honking behind them, she ground the gears and took off again.

"Oh my God." Brenna grabbed Eve's shoulder, fingers digging through her top and into her flesh. "An angel?"

She bore her friend's painful grip. "Yes, but not like the celestial ones from Heaven. Reynner's kind are called Empyreans..." Then Eve told them everything that happened from the night of her birthday until two hours ago.

Both stared at her in utter silence. At least there was no more laughter. Hopefully they were starting to believe her.

"So this angelic realm you speak of is fading and they need your help? Those big, strong angels need you, *a human*, to help save them?" Brenna asked, her expression still a little puzzled.

Eve frowned. "Well, I suppose so, since I seem to be the only one who can call to this artifact."

Kataya, paler than usual, frowned as she parked her Fiat in front of Lila's brownstone. "And now we're here to rid him of a bitch goddess who wants to own him?"

"Yes, that's what I hope Lila can help me with." Eve glanced at the house. The place hadn't changed since she'd been here ten years ago. Except for the overgrown pots of vines trailing over the doorway like swaying sentinels.

"But how can she, a human psychic, who couldn't help you, help an immortal?" Kataya demanded. "Surely he must have tried to break this curse?"

Eve turned back to her friends. "He's tried, with their oracles and mages, but nothing has worked. And who's to say Lila can't know something? I have to try." Besides, Michael had sent her here. And the archangel wouldn't do anything just for shits and grins.

"Because you want him to stay?" Kataya asked as they all got out.

"No, because I love him. And I want him to have a choice in his life."

"Aww, that's so romantic," Brenna said in a dreamy voice as she shut her door.

Kataya's head whipped around. "Oh, no, you don't, Bren. You find a decent *human* man. That's an order! You see what kind of trouble comes falling at our doorstep when you hang out with"—she cut an incredulous glance to the sky, then shook her head—"angels."

"Yes, mother." A quick grin flashed on Brenna's attractive face. "C'mon, then. Let's go find out how to get rid of a goddess."

***

Lila Smith opened the door before Eve even knocked. She looked exactly as Eve remembered with her smooth cocoa skin and friendly dark eyes. And like the last time, she wore a long, flowing dress, but in blue. Her salt and pepper hair she'd pulled back in a single braid.

She smiled in welcome, creating little lines around her eyes.

"Eve. It's good to see you. I did wonder when you would call again. You are well?"

"Yes, Lila, I am." It surprised Eve that Lila still remembered her name after all this time. Heck, she'd been fifteen then. "You remember my friends?"

"I do. Come." She stepped aside and ushered them in, her dark gaze studying Kataya. "Your fate will soon be tested, child. Be strong."

Before Kataya spewed her irritation on Lila, Brenna stepped in front of her. "I do love those vines outside," she told Lila. "The flowers are striking."

"My little hobbies sometimes turn out surprising results." Lila smiled. "I never expected those flowers to be purple since they only come in white."

She led them into the living room and turned to Eve. "What can I do for you, my dear?"

"I need your help. No, it's not about me," she said quickly when Lila glanced at her scarred hands. Before she could explain about Inanna binding Reynner, Lila grasped her fingers.

Eve sank into an abyss as she stared into those obsidian eyes.

A swirling sensation swamped her at the touch, but she didn't pick up any thoughts from Lila—a sudden, mind-numbing pain took her hard, stealing her breath. Gasping, Eve snatched her hands and stumbled back, felt as though her entire being were splitting apart. She wrapped her arms around her waist and fought to hold herself together, fought not to curl up on the floor in a ball of pain.

Kataya and Brenna hurried to her, but she held them off. Gasped, "I'm fine—I'm fine. I just need a m-moment..."

"You have chosen a difficult path," Lila said, softly. "What you seek will come at a price. It is only the beginning."

Eve struggled to get air into her lungs. "So much pain," she whispered. "Whose is it?"

Sympathy clouded Lila's expression. And then the

truth hit Eve like a punch in the belly. "Why?"

"You know why. It's the price he pays for resisting."

Oh, God—oh dear lord! She ran out the door and vomited into the vines Brenna admired.

Reynner suffered because of Inanna's binding? Tears filled her eyes.

Gentle hands stroked her back. A glass of water appeared in front of her. Eve took it. The cool liquid splashed on her trembling fingers. She drank deeply. Brenna took the glass from her.

Lila led her back indoors. "For every curse, every spell ever chanted, there is a counter one. But yours will not be easy."

Eve faced her. "It doesn't matter what I have to do. I won't let him suffer because of some selfish goddess."

Brenna appeared at her side and touched her elbow. "Evie, maybe you should sit."

"No, I can't sit—" She needed to walk, to work off her anger. Eve brought her determined gaze back to Lila. "Tell me. What must I do?"

"When the time comes, you need to follow your instincts. Your abilities will aid you. But remember, once you start to break the binding, it must be completed or what you fear most will come to pass."

A shiver of unease slithered over her skin at the oracle's prediction.

Lila patted Eve's scarred hand. "Do not fear, child, it's the strength of the heart that matters."

As Eve climbed into the car and shut the door, she was unable to rid herself of the weight in her chest. If she failed, she would tie Reynner to Inanna for eternity. She knew it without a doubt because that was her greatest fear.

Jesus, she was only human, how the hell could she

take on a goddess and win?

***

Kataya parked her car near the flower stall. Someone had taken her parking spot, much to her annoyance. They crossed the busy road back to the apartment.

Eve searched for the new cell Reynner had given her that morning, but it wasn't in her bag or her pockets, she stopped. "Darn. I think I dropped my phone in the car. Kat, give me your keys. I won't be long."

"Hang on a sec, hun, I'm coming. You're not supposed to go anywhere alone—remember?" Brenna reminded her.

Eve huffed in exasperation. "It's just across the street. Kat, you sure you don't want to come along, too?"

"I'm good, I'll wait here." Kataya tossed her the keys.

Brenna tucked her arm through Eve's and they cut through the cars halted at the red traffic lights. "After all you told us, Evie, it's better you're careful rather than sorry, right?"

Eve sighed. Her friend was too softhearted for her own good. But…"You're right, Bren. Let's just get the phone and leave."

"Oh, those violets are so pretty. I must order some for my store," Brenna said, eyeing the flower stall as Eve unlocked the car door. She found her cell on the floorboard.

"You don't really think you'll win, do you?" a taunting female voice purred.

Eve's head jerked up. Her gaze widened at the woman clad in a fitted red dress, standing beside her. Perfect, wavy ebony hair framed a stunning face she'd seen once before. One she'd never forget. After all, like a lust seeking missile, the witch had found Reynner.

"Don't look so surprised that I know which tart he's now sleeping with," Inanna snapped. "Over the centuries, he's strayed. It's what males do. But always, he comes back to me."

"I'm surprised you hunted me down to warn me," Eve shot back, pushing her cell into her jeans pocket. She cut a quick look at Brenna who was still studying the floral display.

"Your friends can't help you—they cannot see me," Inanna said, looking down her nose at Eve as if she were a pesky insect. "You mortals, so full of yourselves. A flick of my fingers and you'd be no more."

Eve heard the threat and had to plant her feet on the sidewalk not to take a cautious step back, refusing to show this vindictive goddess any fear. "What do you want?"

"Merely letting you know he belongs to me. For two thousand years he has."

"And he bedded you just once in all that time?"

Topaz eyes blazed like the pits of Hell. A flick of her hand, and Eve went flying into the flower stall behind her. Pain splintered in her head and crashed through her body in huge waves.

Someone screamed her name. Cars honked. Brakes screeched. People yelled…hurrying footsteps.

Then hands were on her. She resisted. Shoved at them, tried to evade the helpers and made skin contact in the process. Thoughts, feelings, and images flooded her mind.

Unable to cope with the overload of their emotions, darkness stole her consciousness, just as a tall man with impossibly cold eyes picked her up.

Chapter 24

Reynner glanced at the digital clock on the DVD player as he prowled the living room. Even trapped in Hell, time hadn't moved this bloody slow.

Sounds erupted from the flatscreen. Rocks scattering. A horse braying in protest, then a loud splash as it hit the water.

"Damnation!" Aerén snarled from the couch while he fought with his latest passion, *"Skyrim,"* a PlayStation game that had captured his attention. "To think, in reality, I can do this blindfolded in Empyrea's cliffs with the rebels and Darkreans about—but not in this cursed game."

The apartment door flew open and banged against the wall as Lucan strode inside. A wave of his hand and he shut the door.

Reynner glared. He hadn't forgotten what the bastard had put Eve through. "The door's there for a reason," he muttered. "Pity it can't keep you out."

Lucan cocked a brow at him before he turned to Aerén. "Where's North?"

"Grounding at Exilum."

"Damn. A power spike has occurred and it doesn't feel right. Go check it out."

Reynner didn't care about the spike of power. He wanted to go get Eve. Another hour and he was outta here.

The moment Aerén had left, Reynner staked Lucan with a flat-out warning, "Don't ever speak to Eve about our relationship again."

"You're complaining because?"

"You have no damn clue what your 'little talk' did to her, do you?" Reynner shoved his hands in his pants pockets so he wouldn't punch Lucan in the face and vent the frustration prowling through him.

Lucan strolled over to the window and glanced outside. "You are with her, are you not?"

"Should I thank you for crushing her? For making her think I didn't care?"

Lucan turned, asked coolly, "Did you?"

"Piss off, Luc," he growled because the mage was right. He was the one who'd hurt Eve, pushed her away, not Lucan.

"Shouldn't you be with your mate?"

Lucan, it seemed, wanted that punch. Even if Reynner didn't agree with the smug bastard's method of bringing them together, his words held a damn lot of merit. But he didn't want Eve to ever feel trapped. He knew how that could destroy a person. Yet, it didn't stop him from wanting to go over to her friend's and haul her back to him where she'd be safe. Being parted from her was steadily eroding his sanity.

He stiffened. Pain speared through him, filling his mind, his chest. Reynner gritted back a curse. What the hell? This was nothing like the shit Inanna tortured him with. His soul hurt as if—*Eve!*

"Something's wrong!" He opened his mind-link to her. *Eve, what's wrong?*

As he asked the question, he dematerialized to her friend's apartment, taking form in a quiet backstreet. With inhuman speed, he tore to the front, only to be faced with the commotion across the street near the flower stall. He raced over, dodging cars and a crowd of shocked onlookers. Scanned the ruckus of people and found Eve's redheaded friend. "Where's Eve?"

The shocked expression on Kataya's pale face had dread fisting his heart.

"Eve—" she babbled. "There was an accident."

"Where is she?" Lucan demanded, having followed him.

"I don't know—I don't know." Kataya pushed back her tangled hair with shaky hands. "She and Brenna crossed to the flower seller, then everything happened so fast. There was a flare—a wave of light. It slammed into us. And Eve, she—she just disappeared." She glanced wildly about her. "Oh, God—oh, God—*Brenna*!" She darted forward, shoving the crowd apart with her hands.

Then Reynner saw the other female lying on the sidewalk, bleeding from a head wound. Flowers and metal containers were spilled all over the place. The noise escalated as more people gathered.

"I'll take care of this," Lucan said.

Reynner scanned the streets. *Eve?* he called through their telepathic link... Nothing.

Dammit, he'd never explained to her how to keep connected to him because he'd been keeping her safe from his pain. He tried again, but only silence answered him.

"She's not responding." Reynner tried to keep calm.

"I can't sense her. Luc, that power spike you felt—Darkreans?"

"No. It's different." Lucan's irises swirled with flames of blue and green. He was keeping his powers contained in front of the humans who persisted in lingering at the site of the fracas. "What I feel here…the essence of the power has the same signature strains as the one that comes off you."

"What the hell are you talking about?"

Fuck. Reynner cursed viciously, his anger exploding. *Inanna.*

***

Reynner stormed into Inanna's temple, his temper on a thin leash.

She lay on a chaise lounger. Two handmaidens attended her, putting her hair up in an intricate style.

"Reynner!" A wide smile curved her mouth when she saw him. An impatient wave of her hand and she dismissed the females. They scurried past him, but not before sending him a seductive look from beneath their lashes.

"What the hell did you do?" he snapped. "You dare harm a mortal?" He knew better than to tell her what Eve was to him because then she'd tell him squat.

He shoved his fists in his pants pockets and encountered Eve's earring. His chest tightened, unable to breathe past the pain, knowing his mate was in danger and he had to beg this accursed female to tell him where she was.

Eve, answer me. Nothing. Just unending silence.

Inanna sat up on the low divan. The strap of her gossamer blue gown slipped off one shoulder. She patted the spot next to her, completely disregarding his question. "Come sit, lover."

He ignored that. His fingers fisting around the small hoop, he struggled to keep his fury checked. "I asked you a damn question."

She scowled. "I warned you."

Pushed beyond endurance as his fear for Eve grew, he hauled her off the divan and thrust her against the wall then snatched a scimitar displayed above her head and pressed the lethal blade to her throat. A thin trickle of blood seeped from the gash. Her laughter echoed in the chamber. "Yes, lover, harder."

He should have known nothing scared her. Taking a couple of deep breaths, he flung the dagger aside. "Pray to whoever the fuck you do, Eve is not harmed. We've waited eons to find her to aid our realm. Anything happens to her—you can be sure the Sumerian pantheon will no longer exist after we're done."

Wariness entered her eyes at his promise of Empyrea's reckoning.

"Don't fret, lover." She waved a hand over her neck, healing the wound. "I just made it known to that foolish mortal she stood no chance with you. I didn't take her," she grumbled. "Some male—one of your kind did."

Darkreans.

His gut knotting, Reynner flashed out from the chamber. If the Darkreans touched a hair on her head, Heavens help them, he would make Sebris and his band of assholes pay before he destroyed them.

***

Eve blinked bleary eyes as she came to. And felt like someone had hammered steel spikes into her skull. Gingerly, she touched the painful spot on her forehead and winced. She swiped the blood trailing down her face. Rubbing her hand on her jeans, she glanced around the unfamiliar, musty smelling place. Stringy cobwebs decorated the corners.

A little light coming in from the ceiling-high windows revealed it was still day. The soothing sounds of water drew her attention. Exilum? No, the aerie was pretty—this was dusty, grimy. Vague memories flittered through her mind...she'd been searching for her cell phone in Kataya's car...a woman warning her...

Inanna.

Eve cursed and inhaled a sharp breath, the spikes in her head digging deeper.

That malicious witch had tried to warn her away from Reynner and then slammed her with a blast of power. A man had picked her up...

Eve looked around again...*oh, no, no, no!* Her chest constricted with fear. She was in a basement and lying on a thin mattress on the cold, cement floor.

Oh, God, Reynner, he'd be frantic by now—her friends! She pulled her cell from her pocket—

The door to the basement creaked open.

Her heart racing to her throat, Eve pushed to her feet, biting back pain from limbs that seemed to have contracted rigor mortis. Light flooded the now gloomy place, making her blink. Three striking goth-like men with tatts and piercings entered. The one in black jeans and a tunic style shirt stepped forward.

His hair, like polished sheets of nickel bronze, fell from a distinct widow's peak in careless disorder to brush his shoulders. His angular features appearing carved from the same ice reflected in his onyx eyes. But beneath the cool exterior, Eve sensed the cold calculation as he studied her.

She shrank against the wall.

"That won't help you"—he nodded to the cell she clutched—"this place is protected with a spell. If you're concerned, we won't hurt you." His low tone sent wariness trickling through her. "It seems we have been lacking in manners. When I said keep her under lock—I didn't mean the cellar."

"My apologies." The man with the white-tipped brown mohawk spoke in an even tone—again, devoid of emotions. A hint of black streaked through his amber-blue irises. Wide leather cuffs with strange writings embedded in them circled his wrists. Some kind of tattoos scrolled up his arms to his neck.

So, he was the one who'd tossed her hide in here, then. Eve rubbed her damp palms on her jeans.

"We do not mistreat our guests. Come," onyx-eyes said.

Despite her wariness, Eve had to know. "Did she ask you to kidnap me?"

His expressionless gaze came back to her. "Who?"

"Inanna."

"Now why would a goddess want to do that? Did you take something of hers?" A smile curled his lips, one that didn't reach his detached eyes. "Ah, yes, the Empyrean."

Eve's breath caught in her throat. If that crazy witch wasn't behind this abduction, then that meant only one thing.

Oh, crap. Talk about a double whammy. Straight from her confrontation with that vindictive cow, she'd fallen right into the Darkreans' waiting arms.

"She happened to mention she knew where you were, and without your protector. I saw no reason not to act. We merely waited until you showed up."

Her stomach knotted. She'd walked right into the spider's trap, manipulated by the awful goddess. Reynner was going to be so angry. Not only had she broken her word and went off elsewhere, but she'd been outside and in a place where *both* his enemies had accosted her.

Swallowing her trepidation, Eve followed him and took comfort in the fact that once out of this dank basement, she'd be able to make a break for it.

Pushing her cell in her pocket, she eyed the blond man on her right. Tall and lean with ink-work on his biceps, he appeared equally remote. Mohawk on her left had the same inaccessible expression.

Strangely, she sensed nothing from them, not hatred or curiosity. Absolute nothing. Their very presence made the temperature in the cellar drop several degrees.

Uneasy, she limped up the few stairs and had to bite back a whimper at the pain shooting up her hips. Once they entered the main part of the house, Eve was dumbstruck. Had to be from watching too many movies where the bad guys always had a dilapidated, rundown shanty. And locked in a cobweb-infested cellar, she had no reason to think otherwise.

This place was a freakin' mansion. Cream walls meandered in front of her with some serious cachet of paintings. The decor boasted classy, period furniture, fancy light fixtures...nothing at all like the granite splendor of raw mountainous beauty where Reynner had excavated his home.

A pang of misery overrode her bravado. She missed him, had no idea how much time had passed. It felt like years.

The leader opened the door and led her into a very

masculine room—a study with dark, paneled walls. An enormous desk occupied one corner. Deep brown couches and chairs were placed around a low coffee table.

How come this place doesn't look like evil beings reside here? she wondered.

"I am Sebris," onyx eyes paused. Eve said nothing. "From your lack of surprise, I see you are aware of us. Good. Explanations can be so tedious. You'll be given a room during your stay with us."

That's what he thought. She was fleeing the first chance she got, even if she had no idea where the heck she was. That could be learned later, she figured, after she'd escaped.

"I wouldn't advise running. My warriors guard the perimeter of this property. We are not human, little mortal. I will know if you attempt to leave."

"What do you want?" Christ, had she lost her mind at her foolish demand? Of course, she knew what they wanted.

"There's a seat. You appear in need of it."

Her woozy head and sore hips took the choice from her. She eased into the armchair behind her but kept her gaze fixed on him. Their lack of emotions terrified her. He'd showed no remorse at her discomfort and pain. They were just words carried off with the right expressions, because nothing ever touched his eyes.

Reynner made no mention of just how cold and emotionless these men were. They'd probably end her life and think nothing of it. Warily, Eve glanced around the silent room. The others had disappeared. And she was alone with this robot.

"What are you called?" Sebris asked. He strolled closer, looking like he had all the time in the world for this conversation.

"Eve."

"Eve," he repeated softly as he strolled around her chair. "We can make this easy or hard, all depends on your answer." He stopped in front of her, his hands slipped in his jeans pocket. "What did the Empyrean find out about the artifact? Enlighten me. If I like your answers, you may get your wish to leave."

Was he reading her? Eve tried to erect a wall around her thoughts. This kidnapping fiend would demand answers when Reynner had worked so hard, spent centuries trying to find the artifact.

"Even if I knew where the Stone was, I wouldn't tell you. Why aren't *you* looking for the artifact if it's that important?" she demanded, despite her quaking insides. "You seem to want it bad enough. Is it so *you* can rule Empyrea? The Stone's magic should benefit all of Empyrea—not just one person."

Instantly, his eyes took on the appearance of black diamonds. Eve shivered. Crap, had she just said that? What's to stop him from killing her?

Calm down, calm down. He needs you *to find the Stone.*

"Little mortal, it would bode well for your future if you refrain from making comments about a world you know little of. You make us out to be the villains—perhaps we are." Another cold smile crossed his face. "Become difficult, and my courtesy will be rescinded. Your stay in the cellar will appear like paradise. Now we wait."

"Wait for what?"

"Until the Empyrean arrives."

Eve stiffened. "You think to use me to trap Reynner—to bargain for the Stone?" Her fear fled, she glared at him. "It will never happen."

"Don't waste your time with him, little mortal," he drawled. "Immortals don't consort with mortal females on a permanent basis."

Jesus, why her? She'd left one prejudice-minded mage to land with their equally opinionated enemy. She said in a stony voice, "I'm glad we were put here for your amusement."

"You are angry. Emotions are overrated, you'll find." He indicated the sideboard set against a window, laid out with a coffee pot and a covered plate. "Eat."

"I'd rather eat with the devil."

"Your wish is granted."

Eve scowled. She clamped her lips shut and made her decision. She had to touch the fiend, find out what he planned to do, and prayed she wouldn't black out in the process. No way would she allow Reynner to walk into a trap.

***

Sebris bit back on the pain mowing through his bones like acid. Taking a deep breath, he studied the seated female. He found it interesting the angry red flush streaking her face at his promise of trapping the Empyrean.

"Enlighten me," he said, his gaze traveling down her body and back up again. There was something different about her. He couldn't quite decipher what it was. "You've been with the Empyrean a while now. What does he do?"

In response, she got up and headed for the sideboard only to stumble. She let out a strangled gasp, her body shuddering as she fell against him. Sebris caught her.

What was wrong with this female? Was she defective?

Humans. So damn frail.

His gaze lit on the wound near her hairline. A wet scab had formed over it. Yes. Her blood would tell him the truth.

"Sorry," she mumbled.

He dumped her back on the chair and willed the gash to start bleeding. Swiped a finger over the blood trailing down her forehead.

She gasped and jerked away. "What are you doing?"

He licked the trace of red on his finger. Said coolly, "Tasting your blood."

Color drained from her face. "Why?"

"Because I can." A coppery taste coated his palate and a slight hum rose in him only to dissipate. This wasn't what he picked up when he nabbed her from that street. She was mortal, yes, but no hint of the power that roiled so furiously through him and made his body tighten.

He stilled, his heightened senses picking up on the disturbances outside.

He headed for the sideboard, poured a shot of vodka in a squat glass and sucked back the liquor, enjoying the blistering trail burning his throat. It blurred the pain for a brief second, but it crawled right back into his bones again. He'd come back far too soon, didn't equate long enough.

And for what?

This human had too little of the magic in her. Which meant he'd taken the wrong female from the chaos. And yet the Empyrean guarded her like a rabid wolf.

Turning, he leaned against the sideboard and studied her. She shifted warily in her seat. He recalled the blood scent, that strain of magic hitting him square in the chest. No, it wasn't from this female. Another was on the street, hurt—the only thing that made sense.

Sebris retrieved his cell phone and made a call. Keeping the conversation in his language, he told Paxyn what he required then slipped the device back into his pocket.

Time to end this and face his enemy.

He glanced at the female he'd wasted valuable days trying to capture because the Empyrean got her first. "Let's go."

Chapter 25

Upstate, near the Hudson, Reynner eyed the two-story building opposite him as he waited for the others. The rich scent of soil and trees filled his lungs as he drew in another harsh breath.

His fists clenched. Pain tore through him. He wasn't in the least bit surprised at Inanna's retaliation after his attack on her. Usually, he didn't give a fuck what she did, except the damn agony prevented him from completely opening his mind to Eve.

He concentrated on the house and found several Darkreans scattered throughout the building. North was right, the Darkreans had called in reinforcements, and Eve was in there. Thank the heavens he'd soul-joined with her, or he'd never have been able to track her.

He cast an impatient glance at the moon, which seemed determined to pinpoint to his enemy exactly where he was, bathing the area in silvery light. He summoned a bank of thick rain clouds that sailed across the velvet night sky and shielded the eerie brightness. Darkness cloaked the forest and its surroundings once more. The cacophony of night insects quietened as if sensing danger. Even the gentle whispers of the foliage stilled.

Reynner detected North and Aerén not far behind him.

Needing the contact, he opened his mind again to Eve and hoped she didn't experience his penance. But she seemed to have thrown a wall over her thoughts. Frustration and worry prowled through him.

He, an immortal who'd endured a century in Hell then destroyed the shithole and killed the demoness who'd tortured him, and he couldn't even keep his mate safe.

North appeared beside him like a shadow. "The place is guarded tighter than a fortress."

"Matters little, I'm going in through that balcony." He nodded to the small one with rambling vines on the railings.

"You can't. It's surrounded by magic," Lucan informed him, stepping out from the trees.

"You think I can't feel it? How the fuck can they do that? They have a mage in there with them?"

"With their limitation of power once off Dregarus, they will always be prepared," Lucan said, his attention fixed on the house. "I need to find a weakness in the incantation." He raised his hands as he worked.

Reynner prowled to the edges of the trees then came back again. "What's taking you so bloody long?"

"Give me a damn minute," Lucan muttered, his hand weaving in a series of complicated movements. "Unraveling this spell is not child's play."

"I don't have time for this shit." Reynner headed in the direction of the house. North blocked him.

"Get outta my way," he snarled, power rolling through him. The winds picked up. More clouds gathered.

"Dammit, Reyn." Aerén strode out of the darkness, back from his recon. "Keep the weather constant. Those degenerates will disappear with her if they know we're here. They could very well take her back to Dregarus."

That stopped him cold. In that barren ice land, Eve wouldn't survive.

She was probably terrified out of her mind, trapped with those emotionless fuckers.

"We have to get her out. I have to get her—I can't—" he broke off, unable to think past his terror of her being hurt.

North remained silent. Aerén glared at the house.

"I sense her," Lucan said then he cursed. "They know we're here."

Darkreans swarmed the grounds like bees escaping a hive.

Hell, yeah, perfect. Finally able to vent the fear and fury raging within him, Reynner summoned his sword and dematerialized.

***

Go where? Eve wondered irritably. She wiped the blood trailing down her forehead with the back of her hand and stumbled after the Darkrean leader as he headed outside.

He'd been so intent on getting answers, and then, suddenly, he'd changed his mind? She had no idea why.

And her ruse at falling so she could touch him? What a waste of time. She'd picked up wisps of thoughts, a bad snowstorm someplace, but most baffling of all, no emotions.

Uneasy now, she rubbed her arms. It was as if she'd

been sucked into a void and spat out again. How could a person feel nothing?

She followed Sebris onto a softly lit portico. Ignoring the pain shooting up her hips, she limped down the stairs leading onto the lawn. Cool night air surrounded her, rich with the mossy-green smell of wood.

Garden lights highlighted the riotously growing wild roses. Weeds appeared to have won the fight and taken over the grass. Tall looming trees surrounded the boundaries of the two-story mansion, making her feel cut off from the rest of the world. More dark clouds rolled across the sky, obscuring what was left of the moonlight.

She trampled through the ankle-length grass when sounds of clanging reached her ears.

She remembered them from before; when Reynner had fought the demoniis in the alley. Her heart pitched to her throat as they rounded to the front of the house and confronted the fracas on the lawn. Swords flashed, grunts and growls of the fighting figures filled the air. And in the horde of fighting men, she saw a flash of pale hair.

Reynner.

She darted forward, but Sebris grabbed her by the arm and hauled her back.

"Let me go, damn you!" She fought to free herself, then elbowed him in the belly. He merely tightened his grip, making her wince.

Unable to free herself, Eve pressed a hand to her heaving stomach. Oh, God. So many men! Where had they come from? Wild-eyed with fear, she watched.

Reynner fought with a blond man. As if sensing her, he turned, their eyes locked.

Then someone killed all the garden lights.

A brick wall rammed into her. She hit the ground hard, landing on her side, unable to breathe as pain fired through her hurt limbs once again.

"*Eve!*"

Amidst the chaos, she heard Reynner's terrified yell. Enormous boots leaped over her as swords swung, clashing over her head. Trapped in a sea of lethal, fighting men, Eve pushed into a crouch and looked for a way out.

A sword winged toward her, the tinny sound of the blade's whisper stopping her heart. Eve squeezed her eyes shut. She didn't want to see the blow that would end her life—a hand yanked her against a hard body, knocking out what little breath she had.

A vortex of colors surrounded her in the space of a heartbeat, and then she was dumped on the outskirts of the battle.

Lucan gave her an annoyed look and flashed back into the fray, his sword swinging.

The man was as vicious in a fight as he was with his words. He nailed several Darkreans with the precision of a paid killer.

Her gaze darted around and she spotted Aerén fighting Sebris. Aerén's sword swung in a deadly arc to decapitate. Sebris leaped back and vanished...only to reappear behind her.

He yanked her to him, just as Reynner materialized in front of them, his chest heaving. Blood dripped from a gash on his arm. His eyes glowed with intense rage. "Let. Her. Go."

Eve tugged at her arm, but Sebris merely readjusted his grip like he was holding a pesky fly. Then he caressed her neck with a rough finger. Eve jerked her head back.

Reynner snarled. Power rolled off him, lightning streaked across the sky, and a bolt diverted, hitting the mansion with a violent display of sizzling sparks.

"Careful, Empyrean, you wouldn't want to strike her now, would you?" Sebris murmured. The next second, the winds died down and the black clouds disappeared. "I could so easily end her life, but why bother? Mortals and their firefly lifespan," he mused, his voice filled with pity before it hardened. "Call them off."

"North," Reynner yelled. North and Aerén flashed to flank him, their faces grim, swords braced for another attack. Aerén eyed Sebris with utter hatred. She remembered that he blamed the Darkreans for his parents' disappearance. But the power coming off Aerén hurt her, like pinpricks of electrical surges. She swayed, and Sebris tightened his hold.

"So frail," he murmured. "She won't be able to withstand your *anger* much longer before something in her gives out. Her heart perhaps? It does beat quite fast. Unnaturally so."

"Dammit, Aerén, shield!" Reynner snapped. The next instant, the power surrounding her switched off like a light bulb.

"Thanks for the er- training," Sebris drawled like this vicious fight mattered little to him. He let her go.

***

Bruised and battered, her face streaked with blood, Eve stumbled across the overgrown grass. Reynner flashed to her side and gathered her close, pressing his lips to her head. A sob escaped her, her arms tightened around his waist.

But her pain cut through him as if it were his own. He had to stomp down the urge to destroy the bastard in front of him, he had to get Eve to safety. Sweeping her into his arms, he nailed Sebris with a deadly look. "I will find you again, Darkrean, make no mistake."

"I'm sure you will. Be thankful I saved the female," Sebris said, glancing at his shirt where a dark, wet stain was spreading.

"Saved her? You fucking abducted her!"

"Make no mistake, Empyrean, when it comes to the Stone, I will do—and risk—anything." His gaze settled on Eve again, his meaning clear. The asshole had made his point. Then Sebris added, "She has a powerful enemy in the goddess."

At the Darkrean's words, Reynner's gut churned. How the hell did he know about Inanna?

"She told them," Eve whispered.

Her trembling body wrenched his mind back, and he regained control over his need for retribution.

About to dematerialize, he cursed. The dissolving of their molecules would hurt her more. He tore off his tee. In a swish, his wings flared out. He swept Eve back into his arms and took to the skies. He held her close and out of the rush of wind created by his extremities. With his mind, he cast a haze around them to keep them undetected from human eyes. But he sensed North and Aerén following him.

"I'm all right," she whispered.

"No, you're not," he growled, knowing she'd said that to ease him.

She sighed and rested her face against his chest. Her fingers stroked his nape along the line of tension that remained coiled in him.

"These injuries aren't from them—the Darkreans. When that horrible goddess struck me, I landed in a flower stall. Then people tried to help..."

And she'd passed out from all the emotions flooding her, making it easy for the emotionless fucks to take her. The fact that Inanna had dared to attack Eve had his blood buzzing in rage. But deep down, Reynner knew the goddess would have done far worse than the Darkreans if she'd taken Eve.

***

Reynner scowled at the closed bathroom door. Eve had shut him out—shut him out because he'd wanted to heal her first.

Reining in his frustration, he willed the door open and a cloud of steam enclosed him. The noisy splattering of water filled the small space. Eve turned, and her wide green eyes met his through the misty shower glass.

Did she really think she'd keep him out? Arms crossed over his chest, he leaned against the basin and watched her soap her injured body. Felt every wince as she ran the sponge over herself.

Finally, she shut off the water. As she stepped out from the shower, he held the towel open and gently wrapped it around her. Then he took another and dried her hair. The swelling on her forehead had darkened to an ugly purple. Several bruises marred her shoulder. His lips tight, he tossed the towel aside.

"Reynner—" She pushed the tangled damp strands from her face. "I'm sorry, but I needed a bath first." She stroked his chest, like that would pacify him. "I'm fine, really," she murmured and limped from the bathroom to her room.

"Fine?" He followed, temper flaring. He shut the door quietly behind them, resisting the urge to slam the thing. "Then why are you limping?"

A red flush streaked across her cheeks. Casting him

a wary look, she shuffled to her closet, opened a drawer, and took out underwear. Pulling on pink panties, she stiffened. Her loose, damp hair hid her expression, but her indrawn breath told him how bad it was.

Jaw rigid, he stripped the towel from her, ignoring her gasp of indignation. Faced with the ugly contusions on her hips, the little insect bites on her arms and legs, his anger morphed into fear again. "Gods, Eve, look at you. You're hurt so bad."

"I didn't want to worry you," she whispered, eyes mossy green with pain. "But I needed a bath more. Reynner, I slept on a flea-infested mattress." A tremor of distaste crossed her face as if that justified waiting to be healed. "A few more minutes wouldn't make my injuries life-threatening."

A low snarl rumbled from him. His mate had a way of pushing his buttons.

"Please," she said, coming closer. "It's just a few bruises. You can heal me now."

She stood in front of him, so fragile and small. And frighteningly brave. Still, it was damn difficult to let go of his terror of what could have happened. He took the bra she held and tossed it on the bed.

"What were you doing out on the street?" he asked while he examined the bruises.

She eyed him warily, lifted a shoulder in a half-shrug. "We, er, went to buy flowers."

He'd almost lost her because she'd gone to buy goddamn flowers.

Mouth clamped, he laid his hand on the swollen, dark flesh surrounding the split skin on her forehead, aware of her worried gaze on him. He summoned his healing abilities, but the weak flow of light drew his anger closer to the surface. He could heal a torn earlobe, but not a more severe injury. A mere trickle of it seeped into her body. This lame shit wasn't going to cut it.

"Lucan!" Taking the towel he'd tossed on her bed, he wrapped it around her again.

"No, no. Don't call him," she protested. "It's okay, I'll heal on my own, or see a doctor."

"Lucan—dammit!"

The door opened and North stood at the entrance. "He's not here yet. Can I be of help?"

Reynner found it hard to talk through a jaw gone rigid. "Heal her."

Eve sat on the bed and eyed North uneasily, her hands gripping the edges of her towel. North crossed to her and lowered to his haunches, his leathers squeaking as he studied her injuries with a clinical expression. He laid his hand inches away from her head wound. A glow seeped out, sweeping over Eve's entire body...

Reynner watched, a sense of unworthiness crawling through him. He couldn't do this simple feat for his mate, forced to rely on another. A curse he'd had to live with since his imprisonment in Hell. The blood Kalinin had force-fed him had messed with the purity of his healing gifts.

After North had left, Reynner sat on the bed and pulled Eve onto his lap. He crushed her to him and buried his face in the warm hollow of her neck.

She stroked his hair. "Are you all right?"

Always it was about him, never her.

"Yeah." He captured her mouth in a desperate kiss, needing to accept that she was safe.

She shifted and straddled him. The towel fell away. Warm, luscious breasts pressed against his bare chest, his groin hardened. A breathy moan escaped her, her center pressing against his painfully rigid cock when she gasped, broke free, and scrambled off him.

"Oh, God. Brenna—Kat." Horror filled her face. "I must call them. They'll be so worried."

Reynner swallowed his groan. He rose, trying to ignore his throbbing dick. Damn, he hated this part, but she had to be told.

"Eve…" He took her hands. Saying "don't get upset" was guaranteed to do just that. So he just said it. "Brenna got hurt in the crossfire and is in the hospital."

Her eyes widened. The blood drained from her face. "How—how bad is she?"

"She hurt her head. She's in—"

"A coma? Oh, no." She pivoted away from him. "I have to go to her. She's hurt because of me."

"Eve. It's two A.M. You need to eat and rest. We'll go in the morning."

"Kataya. I must speak to her. Tell her I'm all right." She grabbed her cell off the dresser then tossed it aside. "Dammit! Not charged."

"Eve, calm down. Here, use mine." He handed her his phone. He cupped her chin and tilted her face to his. It pierced him in the heart, the fear and guilt clouding her eyes. "You can't fall apart now. It won't help Brenna. Make your call while I go get you something to eat. And Eve, if you're to leave this room, put on some clothes first."

Reynner walked out of the room and rubbed a hand down his face. *He* was responsible for this mess, for his mate's terror, her pain, and the hurt she'd endured because he'd failed to protect her from his enemies.

Well, no more. She was never leaving his sight again.

***

The rich aroma of scrambled eggs filled the kitchen as Reynner scooped up his attempt at cooking and piled them onto two slices of toast, and poured a glass of OJ.

Then he leaned against the kitchen counter, picked up his coffee, and took a sip.

Aerén, an unrestrained force of agitation, wore a path on wooden the floors, looping around the furniture. A faded bruise remained on his left cheek and his knuckles sported scabs.

North slouched on a barstool and reached for the jellybean jar, helping himself to a colorful handful.

"Why did the Darkreans let Eve go? They're after the artifact, too," he said, popping some of the candy into his mouth. "Could they not feel the magic in her?"

"Right now, I care little as to why, just that Sebris let her go." Reynner set his empty mug on the counter.

Aerén stalked over, rested his fists on the granite top. "Lucan spoke of a spike, I found nothing. What was that about?"

Reynner's expression darkened. "Inanna. She attacked Eve. It's what caused the power hike."

"Where's Lucan?" North ate a yellow candy. "It's not like him to disappear in the middle of the search for the artifact."

"Probably in Exilum," Reynner said, glancing back at the corridor for Eve. "He must have gone there to Ground."

"No, I don't think so, he was still at the Darkreans' place when we left." North headed for the door. "I'll go find him."

Aerén made to follow, but Reynner stopped him with a hard stare. He remembered the pain on Eve's face. Aerén's power had hurt her. "Lucan can look after himself. You need to get that power Grounded. I can't have you around Eve riding the edge."

While the mating bond leveled his own power, Aerén's was too unstable. The white quartzite found in the Exilum mountains helped siphon off powers from Empyreans with excess. It's why Reynner preferred to live there.

Aerén scowled. "I can manage. We're close to finding the artifact."

"I'm not taking Eve out so soon after her ordeal. A day or two will be good enough to start. Go."

"Go where?" Eve asked, joining them, still a little too pale for his liking. Reynner drew her to his side.

"Your mate just kicked me out." Aerén shot him an annoyed glare. "I must go to Exilum and Ground before I hurt you, or I can forget being part of your protection team."

Eve glanced at him.

"He goes," Reynner said before she opened her mouth, his tone allowing no argument. "And you need to eat and rest."

Chapter 26

The midday sun warmed Eve's skin as she made her way to the studio. It did little to ease the ice settling inside of her after her visit to Brenna earlier that day. Her vibrant friend just lay there—so still.

For the first time in ten years, she'd finally touched her friend and felt nothing, just blurriness. Eve found it hard to swallow past the lump lodged in her throat.

Reynner drew her close to his side and stroked her arm in a soothing gesture. He remained silent, his presence offering her the steadiness she needed.

Work would help, since he refused to continue the search for the Stone, insisting she take it easy after her ordeal. She suspected it was more for his peace of mind, but she didn't say so, glad for the quiet time.

Once she'd disengaged the alarm to her studio, Eve wandered around the empty place. The acrid smell of soldered metal filled her nostrils. It was a soothing comfort to be in her zone of serenity. She'd have to stock up on more of her raw supplies. The shelves were low on metal sheets and copper wire.

Her cell beeped, distracting her. She retrieved it from

her pocket and scanned the text from Echo.

Would love for you and Reynner to come to the castle. 3PM?

Let me know.

Eve cast a quick look at Reynner. He'd stopped at her worktable, occupied with studying the series of drawings she'd done of him for her latest project. Without the face sketched in, it would be impossible to tell who the person was.

Smiling, she left him with his puzzle and texted Echo with her acceptance. And got an instant response with directions.

Satisfied everything was arranged for the afternoon, Eve tried to come up with the best way to tell him about her plans for later that day. And hoped he didn't freak out.

Pulling down metal strips from the shelf, she hauled them over to her workstation and set them on the small bench nearby. She studied the sculpture she'd started. It was a right ol' mess. Remnants of that awful afternoon when Lucan had told her to let Reynner go crept into her thoughts.

Ugh, she really didn't want to think of that horrible time.

Deciding to start over again, she pushed the ruined piece aside to dismantle later. Back at the table, she flipped through the drawings Reynner held.

"I need this one. Thanks." Ignoring his narrow-eyed look, she took the sketch she wanted and turned to leave. His finger hooked in the waist of her jeans and he hauled her back.

"Is this why we're here?"

She blinked up at him. "What?"

He nodded at the sketches, shifted his hold from her

jeans, and grasped her waist. "Are you waiting for him?"

Reynner it seemed was obsessed with her latest project. Just who did he think it was? She arched her brow. "I *can* work from memory. I'm an artist, remember? Besides, I know him quite well."

"Eve." A warning.

Yep, he wasn't pleased. Still...

"I can't forget the shape of him—" The possessive bonding glow flared in his narrowed eyes. Eve's heart fluttered, but she pushed on. "The feel of his muscles, the width of his torso, the color of his eyes, and especially the curve of his lips..." Unable to contain her smile, she let her gaze drift over him. "You'd make a good model. A difficult one for sure, since you're never still for very long, but an excellent subject with that sexy body."

Tossing that last bit in, she yanked free and beat a fast track from him, except she didn't get far when he swept her off her feet. Startled laughter escaped her. He dumped her ass on the table.

"You think to taunt me?" He braced his hands on either side of her hips, caging her, and pushed that gorgeous face in front of hers.

"No. I would never do that." She stroked his jawline, her expression tender. "I couldn't tell you how much of an impact you'd made in my life. Or that I was falling in love with you, so, I started this."

"Eve." Reverence in that single word. He closed his eyes and leaned his forehead against hers. "You undo me. Only you."

One more evil to get rid of, she thought grimly. She would find a way to free him from Inanna.

"Would you do something for me?" she asked,

stroking his sensual bottom lip. Then her gaze locked on the puckered skin of her finger against his perfect mouth. Grimacing, she dropped her hand. He simply brought it back and kissed her finger. "Don't do that, Eve, I'm crazy about you—every bit of you. What is it that you want?"

"Echo invited us to the castle."

He went dead still. Those night-sky eyes slitted dangerously. "I told you to leave it alone."

She lifted her chin. "So you did. Reynner, you can't live with the guilt that eats at you forever. Either we go together, or I'll just drive there on my own since she invited us and I'm not turning her down last minute."

His expression hardened as her meaning became clear. "You think to blackmail me?"

"Blackmail? Me?" She blinked innocently then added, "No, I would never do that to you. I love you, you stubborn man. It's why I do this." She kissed him, hopped off the table, and headed back to her work. "We leave at two."

***

The long drive to the island just off Manhasset Bay was undertaken in thick silence. If she wanted to touch him, she'd probably have to wade through it first, Eve thought in wry amusement.

The dark shades Reynner wore shielded his eyes. He appeared unapproachable, his hair tied in a smooth, stubby ponytail revealing the stark line of his gorgeous face. But she saw more. She saw past the facade of his beauty. Saw the unyielding set to his jaw, the clenched hands and white knuckles. And the fact that he had yet to crack a smile or look at her.

As they crossed the bridge over the Sounds to the island, she looked through her window at the deep blue sea beneath them. Her hands felt too stiff. She curled and uncurled her fingers, trying to ease the tautness in her hands.

"Does it hurt?"

She turned. He'd lost that closed-off expression. A relieved smile curved her mouth. "It's all right. I'm used to it."

A warm hand covered hers on her lap and squeezed. She laced her fingers with his.

Moments later, they left the bridge behind. The first sight of the enormous island with its lush vegetation and sheer cliffs on the north side captivated her. Reynner slowed down, and as they approached the huge wrought-iron gates, they swung open.

A winding driveway snaked between the tall trees. Rays of sunlight poured through the canopy of leaves. After several more minutes, suddenly, brilliant light exploded around them as they left the trees behind. Eve shaded her eyes with her hand.

A rolling vista of manicured gardens surrounded them, and the castle came into view. Golden sunlight caressed its somber gray walls, heavy with creeping ivy, and highlighted the turrets.

Eve sighed in appreciation. "Isn't that the most beautiful building?"

"I thought you liked my aerie." Droll words.

"I *fell off* your aerie," she snorted.

"Never again. I had railings installed."

"Don't forget to put in stairs, I want to be able to visit the falls."

"In a mountain? Why not an elevator?"

"Super idea. Now why didn't I think of that?" She hid her smile, aware of the responding one tugging his mouth as he let go of her hand and brought the Porsche to a halt.

The enormous front door opened. Echo and Aethan walked out.

She turned to Reynner, but his expression remained unreadable, his attention on the couple. "Are you still upset with me for insisting you come here?" she asked quietly.

"No. You are right, this has to be faced."

Reassured, Eve focused on the man with Echo. She still couldn't get over Aethan being Aerén's brother. They had similar features, the same lean face and stunning looks. And that hair. Except Aerén's reminded her of a faded summer sky, blue with hints of white, and this man had more black in his, like a summer's night.

"Don't stare at him, *me'morae*. Or I'll be jealous."

She laughed. "Their resemblance is uncanny, except for the hair. Are you going to tell him about Aerén?"

"I don't know, Eve." After a moment, he pulled off his shades and tossed them on the dash then got out and came around to open her door, pinning her with a reprimanding stare that she'd already done so. Eve patted his arm as she stepped out. "I'm sure I'm safe here."

Reynner shut the door as Echo hurried over to them, a smile lighting her angular features. Her bi-colored amber and gray eyes glowed brightly, a striking contrast to her tanned skin.

"Reynner, it's wonderful to finally meet one of Aethan's friends," she said.

Reynner gave Echo a half bow in greeting.

Her gaze shifted to Eve. "I'm really glad you came."

So used to being with Reynner and her friends who didn't touch her bare hands, Eve reacted a second too late when Echo grasped hers. A gasp tore out of her. Pain punched her in the chest. Images crashed into her mind—*a little girl, a dark basement. Terror. Slaps, kicks.* Mind-numbing agony.

Eve broke free, swayed as blackness edged her vision. Reynner grabbed her.

"It's okay—I have you, Eve, *me'seya*. Breathe. Slow, deep."

She struggled to hold on and tried not to let the shadows take her under... From a distance, she heard Echo's frantic apology. "What is it? Did I do something?"

"No. Just don't touch her, at least not her hands," Reynner said, holding her against him and stroking her back.

Breathe Eve, breathe, sweetheart. I'm here, hang onto me, he whispered in her mind.

His warmth seeped through her, easing away the darkness and pain. In the deepest heart of her, his presence glowed like sunlight, and she knew then, it was through their joined souls that he had calmed and aided her.

Reynner had anchored her. *He'll never let the darkness win.*

"Eve cannot touch another without the person's memories and thoughts hurting her," she heard him explain.

"Oh, Eve, I'm so sorry." Regret and dismay colored Echo's voice.

As the darkness receded, Eve let go of Reynner and offered him a reassuring smile at his look of concern. "I'm fine—I'm fine, really. Thank you."

She turned to Echo and Aethan, heat flaring across her cheeks. "I'm sorry about that. It's not your fault. I should have put on gloves. It's just that being with Reynner, I forget to wear them."

"No, don't apologize," Echo said, still looking a little concerned. "Let's go inside."

Eve followed her up the stairs to the portico. But the memories she'd picked up from Echo left a raw pit in her stomach.

"Echo," Eve began hesitantly as the younger woman pushed open the front door. "I'm sorry for what happened."

"You saw it...*all*?"

"No, flashes only—a basement, a little girl..."

Echo paused in the foyer. She didn't say anything for a second as if caught in another moment. Another place. Then she nodded. "My foster parents when I was young. Not a good time—thank God that's all in the past." A smile lit her face, her mismatched eyes glowed. "Come. Hedori's made the most delicious carrot cake for tea."

***

The moment Eve disappeared into the castle, Reynner met his friend's even stare. There was no recrimination there, just acceptance.

The anguish he'd seen in Aethan's gaze when his sister lay dying on the ground had vanished. He looked content. Being mated would do that to a male. Reynner ought to know. Eve had brought light back into his life.

"Let's walk a while."

Reynner nodded and followed Aethan around the castle and through the trellised walkway covered with brightly colored flowers. A light breeze blew across the island, bringing with it the salty tang of sea. Squirrels darted across the grounds, scattering the fallen leaves.

"This place is peaceful." Now wasn't that a real ice

breaker? Truth was, Reynner had no idea what to say. Where to start.

Aethan nodded. "Yeah. It's served us well for centuries." Then he asked, "You've seen Vallex?"

At the name of their friend, who'd been in the arena on that tragic day, Reynner frowned. He hadn't paid much attention then, too filled with guilt. "Once. Briefly. Then I left. I haven't seen him since."

Truth was, Reynner found it strange that Vallex hadn't shown up in the search for the missing artifact.

Aethan nodded, stopping near a stream with silver flashes of tiny fishes darting about.

Reynner glanced at his friend. "You seem happy."

"I am. It took me a while to get here." A smile touched Aethan's mouth as if he remembered something pleasurable. Then he nailed Reynner with a determined look. "I have never blamed you for Ariana's death. It was an accident. If any, I blamed myself for a long, long time. Echo was the one who made me see how shit can happen."

Reynner nodded. He understood now. Eve made him see. Hell, she'd practically whacked him upside the head, hauled him out of his self-loathing, and put his ass right back on track. "I always thought if I hadn't taunted you into a fight, Ariana would still be alive."

"There is something you should know about that day, what happened. Ariana…she was meant to die."

"What?" Reynner snapped. Had Aethan lost his bloody mind? "What the hell are you talking about?"

"I can understand your anger. I was in that place too. For three millennia. Until several months ago," Aethan said quietly. "A helluva thing to learn that death was my sister's destiny. It's all about prophecies. Hell, I never would have believed it if I hadn't lived through it."

"Prophecies?"

"Yeah. I was tied into one, as was my mate. *I* had to leave Empyrea," Aethan said. "Though it didn't seem like it at the time when all I felt was rage. And just when I thought fate had kicked me in the teeth once too often, I ended up finding salvation. My mate."

"What about Ariana," Reynner pushed, needing closure.

"She took my mother's place in the Celestial Realm."

And all this time—all this time they'd both lived with the guilt and self-recrimination.

"So, Ariana's one of *those* angels?"

"Ironic, isn't it?" Aethan said with a wry smile. "We were created like them, and yet *we* are so unworthy."

"Don't let Michael hear you. He'd never let us live that down."

Aethan laughed. They ambled back toward the castle. Reynner glanced around, absorbing the tranquility of the park-like gardens. As they cleared the trellis walkway and headed for the front, he asked, "Will you ever go back to Empyrea?"

"No. My obligations are to this world, and Echo likes her realm. Besides, I'm a Guardian. My allegiance is to Gaia."

They stopped near the stairs leading up to the huge front door. The sun gleamed off the paintwork on his Porsche. Reynner noticed the slight dent where the demonii had crashed onto the hood. He should get that seen to.

"What have you been up to—well, since I last saw you in Empyrea?" Aethan asked him.

Uneasy, Reynner hooked his thumbs in his pockets.

Tell Aethan he'd left their realm to search for him? Or about all the shit that had happened to him since? Yeah, he'd rather be thrown back in Hell.

"Things changed after you left..." Reynner told Aethan about the Stone of Light's disappearance, about finding Eve and her abilities to help find the artifact. "Once the Stone is found, should be in a matter of days now, Lucan will take the artifact back. After that, we'll make our home here and at Exilum. Like your mate, Eve prefers this place."

A pleased smile touched Aethan's mouth. "That is good to hear."

Reynner didn't care for this part, to wipe away his friend's happiness. Nor could he keep something this important to himself. With no other way to do this, he just said it, "There's something else you should know. It's about your parents...they're missing."

Shock killed all expression on Aethan's face. Then his head lowered, he stared at the ground.

Hell, wasn't he the bringer of cheerful tidings? "One more thing, Aerén now lives with me."

Aethan's gaze snapped back to him. "He's here? On this realm?"

For a second, there was such yearning in his friend's expression, Reynner almost called Aerén to get his ass here, only to recall he'd ordered him to Ground.

"Yeah. He took on the rebels to find your parents. Daén wants him safe. In Empyrea, he wouldn't be. Nor could I keep him caged in Exilum. Far better he's part of the detail in Eve's protection, it gives him something to do."

Aethan nodded, but didn't say anything. Reynner waited for his decision. Which came after a long time.

"Don't—" he broke off, then took a deep breath "—

don't let Aerén know I'm here. He must go back to Empyrea." Another pause. "If it's not too much trouble, keep me posted on my parents?"

Reynner nodded.

"I'm glad you told me and that you're back," Aethan said. And that easy smile he'd sported in another life reappeared, brought back sharp memories of an old friendship torn apart but never forgotten. Reynner simply reached out and hugged Aethan as three thousand years of separation and guilt dropped away.

***

Eve stared anxiously out the French doors. Reynner had been gone for so long. She hoped he'd worked things out with his friend.

Easing her tight hold on her mug, she set it on the counter.

Soft voices drew her attention back to the massive kitchen, separated from the casual dining section by an island counter. Echo spoke with Hedori, who worked in the prep area.

Hedori looked nothing like Eve's idea of a butler. Older than the other Empyreans she'd met, with his erect bearing, he appeared more like a bodyguard. His long hair hung down his back in a plaited steel-colored rope.

The door swung open. Aethan walk in, followed by Reynner. The easy camaraderie between them loosened the knot in her stomach. They'd worked things out.

Midnight blue eyes found hers.

Eve hurried over. "Are you okay?"

He cupped her face with gentle, callused palms and kissed her in answer.

She smiled. "I'm glad."

He slipped his arm around her waist and introduced

her. "Eve, this is Aethan. My old friend."

"I'm so pleased to meet you," Eve said.

Aethan smiled as he gave her that half bow. "And I, his mate."

"Sire?"

Reynner pivoted, his shock soon replaced by a grin as the butler approached.

"Hedori, it has been far too long. I'm glad to see you're damage free." He slapped the other man on his back, showing Eve glimpses of who Reynner had been in another life.

Aethan snorted and helped himself to coffee. Echo stopped at his side and spoke softly. He bent his head, listened to whatever she said. Then he brushed the shallow dimple on her chin and nodded. She left the kitchen.

Reynner drew Eve back to him and explained about the disasters Aethan had caused when he came into his unexpected abilities during his teens. "He couldn't lose his temper without casualties. Hedori, as his bodyguard, often ended up with no hair and his clothes singed to ash until Aethan learned control."

Hedori chuckled. "Damages like that are now non-existent, have been for centuries. Aethan's finally settled down, like you have, as my lady Echo informs me."

Reynner nodded, his fingers caressing Eve slowly up her sides. "Yes, that I have."

"I'm happy for you, and congratulations. Coffee, or something stronger?"

"No. I'm good."

Relief rushed through Eve to see him happy. Tomorrow, they'd be back to searching for the Stone. She still had to find that witch goddess and eliminate her from their lives. How, she had no idea. And just like that her moment of happiness dimmed, despair seeping into her.

Reynner stroked her back. "Don't think of tomorrow," he said softly. "It will be here soon enough. Just enjoy this free time we have."

She exhaled a shaky breath. He was right.

"Reyn?" Aethan's voice from the other end of the kitchen broke them apart. "There's someone you should meet."

Reynner looked up. Eve turned as the kitchen door opened. Echo walked in, her mismatched eyes sparkling, followed by the most breathtaking woman Eve had ever seen. And she'd thought the goddess exquisite. This woman far surpassed that.

She appeared far younger. Tall. Lean. Her white-blond hair fastened in a high, braided ponytail brushed her lower back. Low-riding black jeans hugged her long legs, and she'd teamed it with a gray tank top.

It was then she became aware of Reynner motionless beside her.

"Aethan, you wanted to see me?" the vision said. "I've a training session scheduled with Týr in a few minutes."

Aethan smiled and nodded to them.

She glanced at them. Eyes the color of new pennies widened. Her creamy skin rapidly lost its color, Eve thought she'd faint.

And Reynner, he looked like someone had sucker-punched him. Shock, disbelief, and pain filled his gorgeous face as he stared at the woman. Unease took hold of Eve. "Reynner?"

But she doubted he heard her. He put her aside and strode across the vast kitchen, straight to the blonde, who rushed to him. The next moment they were in each other's arms. The woman cried, deep, gut-wrenching sobs as she clung to him, her face buried in his neck. Reynner's eyes closed in anguish.

Eve's chest tightened. Before she could settle on the emotions crawling through her, at another woman in Reynner's arms, one he obviously had deep feelings for, Echo appeared beside her. "That's his sister," she said softly.

The thread of uneasiness gave way to disbelief. Eve's head snapped to Echo. "His *what?*"

He'd never spoken of his family, she realized. Then she saw the similarities. They had the same color hair, pale as moonbeams, and the same breathtaking features.

"Sister," Echo said from beside her. "She left Empyrea unable to stay there any longer. She wanted her own life, she came here. What we didn't know then until recently was that she'd been searching for Reynner—"

"Eve?" Reynner approached with his sister in tow. Despite the red-rimmed eyes and face blotchy from tears, up close she was even more stunning. Damp eyes gleaming like polished bronze studied Eve in curiosity. Then her gaze shifted back to her brother. "Is she...?"

Reynner drew Eve to him and nodded. "My mate, yes. Ely, this is Eve. Eve, my sister, Elytani, who, apparently, is now a Guardian—I'm gonna kick Michael's ass for dragging you into this life."

Elytani brushed away her tears. A watery smile lit her face. "Still trying to protect me, huh?"

"That will never change. *Urias*—" He shook his head again. "I can't get used to the changes in you—you being here."

"You disappeared, and it was never the same again. I left to look for you and ended up here. I like this life I have now." Elytani turned to Eve, her eyes bright with gratitude. "You have no idea how grateful I am my brother found his mate."

Then she grabbed Eve.

"Ely *don't*!"

But Reynner's words came too late. Elytani hugged her so tightly, Eve wondered if she'd suffered rib damage as she stepped back. It made her aware, too, of just how puny her strength truly was.

"She is like you," Eve hurriedly reassured him. "I can't read anything off her. I'm fine, Reynner."

A low growl left him. "My heart isn't."

"What—what?" Elytani's gaze flashed to Reynner in alarm.

Reynner explained to his sister why Eve couldn't touch anyone. "It hurts Eve to absorbs another's thoughts, and at times, she loses consciousness."

Elytani turned to Eve, eyes bright with compassion. "I'm so sorry. But don't worry, you'll be safe around us. We immortals are a tough lot, have thick skins."

Smiling, Eve picked up her coffee and took a sip of the lukewarm beverage. The door opened again. The archangel himself walked into the kitchen. Hard eyes, rigid features, a stern mouth. But he was as equally stunning as they all were.

Eve took a deep breath. She stood a few feet from a being mortals thought a myth.

Michael's eerie blues rested on her. "You are well?"

Eve understood he wanted to know if she'd seen the oracle. "Yes. Thank you."

With a nod, Michael shifted his attention to Reynner.

"I feel like I'm about to be judged and sentenced,"

Reynner muttered.

"Be wary, I'd say. Very wary," Aethan added with a smirk. "I've never known Michael to attend any social gathering unless he's after something."

Oh, yes, something was up, Eve would bet her life on it. And from Reynner's expression, he knew what it was.

A gasp left Elytani.

So, she knew, as well. Heck, they all knew except her, Eve realized.

Amusement lurked in Michael's eyes but didn't touch his mouth, his attention back on Reynner. "I will reissue the invitation I made centuries ago. Will you now accept?"

Chapter 27

As they left her apartment the next evening, Eve checked her cell for messages. Nothing important. She pushed her phone in her jeans pocket, her mind on Brenna.

Earlier that day, she'd been to visit her friend in the hospital, and still no change. Guilt continued to gnaw at her. No matter how much Reynner and Kataya tried to convince her otherwise, this was her fault. If she hadn't gone looking for her cell, Brenna would have been safe.

A warm hand stroked her nape. Somehow, Reynner always seemed to know her state of mind. She drew his hand down and laced their fingers. They took the stairwell to the ground level. As the indistinct sounds of traffic and people yelling out on the streets drifted to her, her mind buzzed around one thought only.

"You're thinking too much again," he murmured.

She looked up and found him watching her, a smile lurking in his indigo eyes.

"Are you going to accept Michael's offer?"

"I don't know, Eve." His brow furrowed. "There are

other things to consider, and the Stone is first priority...but I've been doing the same thing, killing demoniis for millennia with Michael on my ass even then. Shouldn't be too difficult a leap to become a Guardian."

"And your sister lives here now," Eve pointed out. They exited the stairwell into the well-lit, foyer. She squinted at the harsh glare.

"There is that. But, this is your world, *me'morae*. And you are far more important to me than anything else. I wouldn't take you away from it."

Eve stopped, overwhelmed at his words. "You'd do that for me?"

He smiled, his gaze tender. "For you, I'd do anything."

Grabbing a handful of his shirt, she tugged him down and pressed her lips to his. "Concrete walls don't make a home, Reynner. Mine is wherever you are."

"As is mine, Eve." He stroked her cheek. "As is mine."

He dropped his arm around her shoulders and they walked out of the building into the moist, heat-filled night. North and Aerén waited for them on the street, dressed in their inevitable black leathers and t-shirts.

"Does Aethan know Aerén is here, too?" she lowered her voice to ask.

Reynner nodded. "Yeah. He thinks it's better Aerén doesn't know. Says he has to go back to Empyrea."

She had a bad feeling Aerén wouldn't appreciate being kept in the dark. "I think it's a mistake not telling him. There's always the chance their paths could cross."

"It's Aethan's call. Things could change."

"If it was me, I'd want to know—" She broke off,

spying the gleaming black GMC parked on the street.

"I got that this morning." He nodded at the SUV. "Figured we'd need one while hunting for the artifact."

Of course, it was stupid to think he'd use the Porsche with four of them. And these men were no lightweights.

Aerén smirked at Reynner. "So, I get to drive?"

"Not if you want to see tomorrow." Reynner opened the front passenger door for her, saw her inside then circled to the driver's side.

Snorting, Aerén joined North in the back.

"I found something odd," North said, soon after they'd taken off. Reynner glanced at him through the rearview mirror. "What?"

Eve peered at North in the dark, the streetlights occasionally lighting his stern expression and the grim set of his mouth.

"I went back to the Darkrean's hideout, searching for Lucan. The house is shut down, they've left." He ran a hand through his hair, in a seldom seen gesture. "Why leave now when the Stone's not yet found?"

"Don't care. At least they won't be breathing down our necks," Aerén muttered from behind her.

"I don't like it," North added. "And Lucan, there's no sign of him."

"He'll turn up. He's been known to lurk if he's after something's—he can be damn tenacious at times," Reynner said, stopping for a red light.

Eve bit back a laugh. Amazing. These men took stubbornness to a new level, and they thought Lucan obstinate.

Reynner shot her a questioning look at her amusement.

"Nothing," she murmured.

A stare.

How did he do that? Just a look, and desire flared like a flame. She squirmed in her seat because she knew exactly what he'd do to get her to talk.

The lights changed. Reynner pulled his attention back to the busy street, apparently satisfied he'd gotten his message across. "Whatever Luc's up to, he'll let us know when he returns. Now, let's go find the Stone."

***

They'd scoured nearly half the city for the Stone. It wasn't that difficult, not when she just had to play tourist and walk past everything.

First, they stopped at the arch at Grand Plaza. The missing Stone should light up like the sun when she got close, Reynner had said. So far, nothing.

It had to be close to midnight. They'd ended in Central Park at the bronze and granite Alice in Wonderland monument. Eve forced her tired feet to circle the massive sculpture. It failed to fill her with the joy it normally did. She sensed nothing here. Not even a stupid hum. Only aware of the muggy heat and sweat rolling down her back.

She glanced around her, hoping for a buzz of magic to touch her like the scroll did. Nothing. Just trees, shrubs, and the dissonance of insects surrounding them. Moonlight brightened the paved pathway edged with trees as they headed toward the street.

Sudden pain snatched her breath, rolling like a wave through her. Inhaling harshly, she glanced over her shoulder at Reynner, who walked with North behind her. His brow rose in question, but she shook her head and turned back to Aerén, the pain fading.

Eve wiped her damp palms down her capri jeans, regretting she hadn't worn shorts instead. Heck, how did all of these men stay cool in their leathers?

"How do you do it?" she asked Aerén. "You're wearing animal hide, surely you must feel like a sauna in those pants."

"Animal hide?" He grinned. "Ah, but we have a secret weapon." He leaned closer and whispered in her ear, "We can lower or raise our body temperature."

Her mouth dropped open. "You're kidding? Right?"

He smirked.

She rolled her eyes. "Of course. Why not? You have everything else, immortality, good looks, why not that, too?"

"Jealous?"

"Absolutely. But only of your ability to not get all sweaty like me," she grumbled.

"But Eve..." His grin widened. Eyebrows wiggled. "You look very sexy, all damp and wet."

She laughed. Aerén was an undeniable flirt.

Reynner's low growl rippled over her. Aerén quickly put distance between them and gave Reynner the peace sign over his shoulder.

She ignored Reynner's territorial manner and snorted. "You're no different from human men. Your mind moves in one direction only..." She paused, uneasiness sliding through her again. Something wasn't right. Once more, she glanced over her shoulder to Reynner, her anxiety growing.

He stepped beside her. Rubbed her back as they exited the park and stopped at the curb. Cars swished past. The traffic lights changed. He took her hand and crossed the street in the direction of the enormous monument there.

"What's wrong?" he asked quietly.

Unable to explain her worry, she showed him her

empty Aquafina bottle. "Thirsty."

His gaze skimmed over her face. "And you're tired. Why didn't you say something?"

"This is important to you."

"No, Eve, you are more important. Wait here. I'll get you some water then we can leave for the apartment."

She watched him go. His gait appeared a little too stiff, not his usual easy stride as he crossed the busy street. Ignoring the irate honking of cars, he headed for the little all-night café down Broadway crowded with people.

Frowning, Eve tossed her bottle into a trash receptacle and rubbed her chest as more pain seeped into her…then it hit her. She felt his pain. Reynner had left out that little detail when he'd explained about his binding to Inanna. But she'd known from the moment in the oracle's house when gut-wrenching agony had swept through her body what it was. This had the same feel, a burn so intense it felt like she was incinerating from the inside.

That damn bitch goddess was at it again, hurting Reynner because he refused to give into her.

Her teeth clenched in anger. She'd find a way to end the hold the evil witch had on Reynner.

Inhaling a shaky breath, Eve glanced around and stopped, her belly cramping when she realized exactly where she was. *No, not here!*

Despair crushing her, she sank on the step bordering the Columbus Circle monument and dropped her head in her hands. This was where she'd lost her parents a decade ago. Usually, she avoided this spot if she could.

"Eve?" Aerén sat beside her. "Are you all right?"

She didn't answer. Closing her eyes, she tried to lock away her sorrow, but all the images came rushing back.

The loud explosion. Glass splintering, the tinny sound of metal crunching, fire licking her skin, and pain as she tried to pull her parents out...

A humming sensation slithered beneath her skin.

Her head shot up, her gaze flying to where North stood, a few feet away from her, waiting for Reynner.

Had he brought the scroll with him? Why would he do that? She rubbed her arms, the humming vibrated beneath her skin like a tuning fork on steroids, heating her blood. *Dammit!* She thrust to her aching feet and paced around the statue, needing to be in motion.

Aerén followed, dodging her heels. "Eve, you can't go wandering off."

She shot him an irate look over her shoulder. Growled. "Back off."

Surprised, he widened his eyes. He raised his hands in surrender. "Whoa, take it easy there."

Reynner returned with the bottles of water and tossed them to Aerén. She shot him a dark scowl and continued her impatient march-a-thon, rubbing at her too tight skin. Frustration and helplessness twisting her tummy.

Christ. So many failures. Stuck here in the place where she'd failed to help her parents. Now, she couldn't find the Stone. Reynner was in pain, which he'd zipped up about. And the damn scroll was playing havoc with her again.

"Eve?"

Just her name. A soft command. One she couldn't ignore.

"Why did North have to bring that thing along?" She rounded on him. "I thought you needed *me* to find the Stone, not the scroll. Tell him to take it away."

She pivoted for her walk-a-thon again. He grabbed

her arms, holding her still. "We didn't bring the scroll. It's at Exilum."

"Well, you brought something. One of you did."

The iridescent spray of water falling into the fountain beckoned her. Eve pushed away from him and walked straight into the man-made rain. Cool and soothing, it flowed over her heated body to wash away the sweat and sloshed into her sneakers, drenching her sore feet. She sighed in pleasure.

But the humming grew louder. She stared up at the statue of Christopher Columbus then walked around it and stopped in front of the angel on the lower base. A sudden buzz whined through her, coalescing. The circle of water she stood in started to spin—or was that her?

"Eve!" Reynner's yell came from a great distance. A sudden burst of power—a light erupted from somewhere deep inside her and sent her flying backward into the shallow water.

A loud noise. Something shattered. Debris rained over her as she fell, her head hitting the mosaic tiles in the fountain. Dark spots danced in front of her vision. Pain rippled in her skull as the water and darkness cascaded over her…

***

With inhuman speed, Reynner appeared at Eve's side, the water from the burst pipe drenching him. What the hell happened? One minute he'd been watching her, and the next, she was flying backwards as a powerful light exploded from her.

He kneeled beside her and scanned for injuries. North and Aerén appeared beside him as he examined the back of her head with his hands. But there was no bump or any other damages.

Dripping wet, Reynner carried her out of the

fountain, circled the smattering of curious onlookers, and sat on the low wall, cradling her on his lap. He inhaled a sharp breath at the scorching pain inside his chest. And tightened his psychic shields so it had no chance of seeping through their mating bond and hurting Eve.

North and Aerén flanked him, their clothes equally soaked. They scanned the place, keeping inquisitive humans away and clearing their minds of Eve glowing like a lightbulb. And maintained vigilant guard while the crowds gathered to stare at the ruined fountain.

"I haven't found any reason for this," North murmured, eyes narrowing.

"No," Aerén agreed, looking equally concerned. "Or any unexplained Others here."

Reynner carefully touched Eve's mind with his. Now that her shields weren't up, he saw images...mostly of him, but he saw the past, too. A different time...her parents in a vehicle, a white, oval rock hurtling toward them. A burst of light. Splintering glass as the windshield shattered...

Dread grabbed him in a chokehold. *Fuck, no!*

The *Stone* had caused the accident?

Oh, shit, this was so fucking bad.

More worrying, the artifact was no longer whole, but in fragments. And Eve, he realized in shock, was part of that equation.

Feeling like he'd been run over by a tanker, he rasped, "There is no Stone—Eve is the source."

"What in Urias's name are you talking about?" Aerén snapped in irritation. "We've been hunting for that relic for centuries, and now you say there's nothing."

"What do you mean she's the source?" North asked,

his attention sliding back to Eve.

His attention fixed on his mate who lay so still in his arms; Reynner brushed her damp hair away from her face. "Eve is the one. I should have known, suspected, since she possesses magic in her blood."

"Reyn, for Urias's sake, just spit it out," Aerén barked.

In a daze, he explained, "After Eve made contact with the scroll, she had to come back to this precise place where the crash occurred for the Stone's power to resurrect." Then he told them about what he'd seen in her memories, about the accident that had killed Eve's parents, the Stone crashing into their vehicle—the reason for the tragedy. "It seems residue of the magic attached itself to the monument, which would explain why Eve reacted the way she did. The power recognized her and probably linked to her."

"Hell's shit," Aerén muttered. "Once Eve knows, we're so screwed."

Reynner pressed a troubled kiss to her brow. "Not a word to her," he warned. "I have to be the one to tell her—to explain."

How did he inform his mate his world was responsible for the pain she'd suffered, for the loss of her parents?

A hand stroking his face brought him back. He found her watching him with those beautiful dark green eyes. Relief flowed through him and he pushed his worries aside for now. Smiled. "Eve."

"Why are you all wet?" She brushed the water dripping from his hair onto his face.

"I decided to join you in the fountain. It's far too humid tonight."

She glanced around at the noisy crowd. "What

happened?"

"A burst water pipe," he evaded. "Can you stand?"

She nodded. He set her on her feet and rose, but kept an arm around her waist. A frown marred her brow. "Wait, I remember. I felt dizzy, a bright light or whatever that was disorientated me for a moment and... I fell?"

"Yeah. You knocked your head on the fountain floor." He scanned her again, found no bumps, which surprised him. She seemed to be checking herself as well, then she snorted. "I'm fine, I'm not that fragile."

"I'm just glad you weren't hurt."

The noise level around them escalated. Reynner eyed the growing crowd. "Why don't you sit down while we handle this confusion? Then we'll leave."

Making sure she was seated where he could keep an eye on her, Reynner glanced at North. "Let's do this, before anything else goes wrong."

"Reynner?"

He pivoted to find her behind him, raking back a tangle of wet hair. "Eve, I told you—"

She stopped him, a hand on his chest. "Did you find the Stone? I felt a humming, the Stone should be here, right?"

He shook his head. This wasn't the place to talk about something this monumental, or for Eve to find out the truth about her parents' deaths.

"Later." He brushed a quick kiss on her lips and left to go deal with the cleanup and memory wipes.

***

Eve watched Reynner as he walked slowly through the noisy crowd. He nodded at whatever North said. With no idea how a mind sweep worked, she went back to the steps and surveyed the chaos around her.

Naturally, everyone would think the underground water pipe feeding the fountain had burst. But deep down, Eve knew she'd caused that. Something had happened when that light—power, whatever it was, exploded from her.

A sudden wave of pain swept through her. *Oh, Christ,* she gasped, unable to breathe. *Doesn't that bitch ever take a break?*

Panting to ease the torturous onslaught, she searched for Reynner, her anxiety increasing. She found him alone, moving unhurriedly through the gaping crowd. He appeared calm, focused, but her heart knew differently.

That Inanna would punish him like this for spurning her clawed at Eve's gut. She had to find a way to stop this, if that malicious witch ever found out the truth about their relationship, she'd hurt him more. Or worse, have him back in her bed.

Eve knew, to keep her safe, Reynner would do anything.

Inhaling another harsh breath, unable to bear that thought, she hurried to him and grasped his arm.

"Eve," he began then his expression tensed. "What's wrong?"

Jesus, how could he be this brave, this strong, for so many centuries?

"Nothing." She smiled. Tried to be strong for him. "I-I didn't want to be alone."

He drew her close and studied her face in the lights surrounding the fountain. Eve ducked her head, hiding in his chest. She didn't want him to see her pain. "Please, let's go home."

***

Reynner bit down on his molars as another wave of

pure agony rode him. Eve gasped, a hand flying to her left breast, ending in a clenched fist, and then he knew. "You're in pain."

She shook her head. "I'm fine—I'm fine. It will pass."

The fuck it would. He knew just how long this shit could ride, days before Inanna got bored and found something else to occupy her. And now every time she wanted to hurt him, Eve would suffer because of their strengthening bond.

He had to leave before that damn demented female took it into her head to come after him.

"Aerén," he growled, the lines of pain bracketing Eve's mouth eating at him. While he could stand this torture, he couldn't bear for her to suffer.

His prince jogged over. "What's up?"

"Take Eve back to the apartment."

"No—no!" She clutched his shirt in panic. "Reynner, wait—"

"Take her." He didn't want Eve witnessing what he'd been reduced to do.

***

"No." Eve fisted his damp tee. "Where are you going?"

He didn't respond, his lips drawn tight. She saw the answer in his eyes.

"No, Reynner. Please, don't," she cried. "I can endure this—I can."

"I won't have you suffer a burden that was never yours."

"No, you can't let her win—oh, God, please don't go." She shook him hard. "I won't let you go."

"It's the only way. I'm sorry, Eve. I won't have you hurt." The cold determination in his expression spoke volumes.

Shaken, she stared at him, her entire being fracturing. "You-you're leaving me, to save me?"

His eyes gone impossibly cold, he peeled her fingers from his shirt and turned to Aerén. In a voice she'd never heard before, like he'd shut down every facet of emotion, he said, "Keep her safe."

Then he strode off, crossed the busy street, and headed into the park, the darkness swallowing him.

Eve couldn't breathe. The pain spilling through her gave way to a new one as her heart fractured.

"Eve?" Aerén took her arm. She shrugged him off, prayed with everything in her soul that Reynner would come back.

He didn't.

She swayed, didn't protest the hands that swept her off her feet. Utter desolation stole through her. She had to live with the despair, the agony, knowing *she* had driven Reynner into Inanna's arms. She'd ruined their lives, their momentary happiness because she'd been unable to block those flashes of pain.

Chapter 28

The scent of disinfectant and illness was an unpleasant smell to his heightened senses, but a small price to pay, Sebris decided, striding into the hospital.

One of the females in white hurried over to them as they stalked down the quiet corridor, past the nurses' station. With Paxyn left to deal with the nurse, knowing the warrior would do a good job with mind control, Sebris and Xever headed for the ward.

Sebris had waited two days, paying heed to the fact that she had to remain there to heal. They could do little about that on this realm, and they needed her up and about as soon as possible. They had shut down the house and taken up residence in a nearby hotel so they could keep an eye on the female. He was well aware the Empyrean and Eve visited every day.

If he could, he'd take the female and disappear. But while on this realm, and weakened, he refused to have the Empyreans coming after them until he had the Stone. Plans had to be put into action, false memories inserted and info added to the records humans kept.

He wavered on his feet. Damn, he could barely stay

upright much longer with agony eating through his bones. He ignored the looks Xever sent him and entered the ward. Stopping at the foot of the bed, Sebris studied the female lying there.

Her caramel skin appeared ashy. A large bruise covered her left cheek. Black hair lay limp and lifeless like seaweed on the pillow. The vibration that hummed through him was muted now. It had to be because she was unconscious. But the essence of it remained exactly like what he'd experienced on the street.

He frowned at the underlying floral scent taunting his senses. The fragrance a lot like the flowers that grew wildly at the house on the Hudson—damn thing hiked his problem. Pain spiked through his skull, his molars mowed together.

A soft moan came from the bed. Confused, dulled, crystalline blue eyes flickered open and stared blankly at him.

"You should go Equate, I'll keep an eye on her," Xever said quietly from beside him.

Sebris ignored him.

Digging deep into his psyche, he summoned the last bit of his waning power and sent her back to sleep. Unsheathing his dagger hidden beneath his tunic, he headed for her. He picked up her slender hand and sliced across the pad of her thumb. A ruby red line appeared.

He licked the blood. A coppery taste flooded his mouth, and like a fist to his belly the air was knocked out of him. His body heated, his groin stirred. His heart rate sped up. Struggling to breathe, he dropped her hand.

Yes, *she* was the foretold one.

"Take her."

***

Eve stood by the window, unable to move. So sure her fractured heart would collapse if she did. Aerén had tried to convince her that Reynner had gone to Exilum, where he'd lock himself in the dungeon until the agony passed.

But Eve knew the truth. He was with Inanna. She felt none of his pain in her now.

Blurry-eyed, she stared at the stars wavering in the dark skies and blinked away her tears. Hours had past, she had no idea how many, since they'd gotten back to the apartment. Her clothes were damp and her skin itched.

"Eve, you should eat." Aerén stopped next to her, tone roughened in concern.

"Not hungry."

"He'll be back," he consoled.

Yes, he would. The Stone had to be found, but *they* would never be the same again. She shuddered on a broken breath. *Dammit, no*—she refused to let that bitch win. She turned to Aerén. "Take me to Exilum."

"Eve, don't. He wouldn't want you to see him this way."

"Don't you see? For two thousand years he resisted her, and now, because of me—" Her breath hitched. Tears crowded her eyes. "Please, just take me."

Whatever Aerén saw in her face, the desperation, the pain, or the tears that wouldn't stop, he exhaled roughly and nodded.

***

Eve stepped through the portal into Exilum and Reynner's mountain home. The brilliant afternoon sunlight had her shading her eyes. She breathed in the fresh, moisture-laden air while the portal closed with a soft hiss. The roaring waterfall, the stark beauty of the meandering mountains gave her no comfort. All it did was remind her of Reynner.

"Is he here?" she asked Aerén. He pushed back swathes of hair escaping its tie, his brow furrowed as he scanned the place. "No. I don't sense him... I thought he'd be here."

She bit her lip and wondered if her heart could break anymore. "The Sumerian pantheon. He has to be there. Let's go—"

"Eve, no, you can't," he said horrified. "You're mortal. Inanna would sense you the moment you step foot there. She will break you. She'll use you to get Reynner back."

And I am his weakness.

She sucked in a ragged breath, hating her mortality. "I have to help him. Please, would you go?"

A pained expression crossed his face. "I can't leave you alone. If anything happened here, there would be no way for you to leave, and Reynner would kick my ass. He still hasn't forgiven me for kissing you."

It seemed so long ago when Reynner had turned on Aerén for touching her, and now she had to live with the thought of him with Inanna, probably touching her, kissing her...

No—no! She wrapped her arms around her waist. He may not want to, but he'd do it to keep her safe.

"Ah, hell." Aerén rubbed his neck with a helpless look. "Very well. I'll try to be back as fast as I can." He opened a portal, stepped through it, and vanished from sight.

Slowly, Eve walked indoors.

"Mistress?" An agitated Izzeri confronted her as she entered the foyer. "Why are you here?"

Usually, Reynner's houseman appeared happy to see her. Now he looked harassed. Upset. "Izzeri, what's wrong?"

And just as quick his expression cleared. "Nothing." A quick smile. "You took me by surprise, mistress. Where is sire Aerén?"

"He had something to do. He'll be back soon." Truth was, she had no idea how long it would take for Aerén to go to the Sumerian pantheon and be back again. "Don't worry, I won't get in your way."

"No, mistress. It's always a pleasure when you are here. I shall prepare you a meal."

Eve nodded. She didn't have the heart to tell him she wasn't hungry. Izzeri disappeared into the kitchen. She wandered to the living room and came to an abrupt halt.

There through the windows, she saw the granite balustrades edging the balcony. Her breath caught in her throat. Reynner had finally put in railings to keep her safe. Unable to look at them, she rushed from the room, stopping only when she found herself on the lower level, a few feet from the gym entrance with nowhere else to go.

God, she rubbed her burning eyes. How could she stay here, utterly helpless and unable to do anything?

A cool breeze blew over her heated skin. Eve glanced around, searching for the source. Stepping closer to the granite wall on her left, she examined the rough surface. Not even a crack there. Where did the draft come from?

Frowning, she ran her hand over the coarse surface and realized why she hadn't noticed the passageway.

Slabs of granite overlapped, giving the illusion of a continuous wall. She stepped behind it into a narrow, gloomy passage and found herself on the top stair. It led down a crudely cut stairwell in the rock face disappearing into darkness.

Her stomach in a knot, Eve stepped into its gaping mouth. She wanted to see this dungeon Reynner'd used for so long to thwart Inanna.

A hand on the wall, she slowly made her way down. Stale air and the smell of mildew clogged her nose. Flickering lights below caught her attention. Eve carefully picked her way down the stuffy stairway to the firelight. She reached up and pulled the old-fashioned, broom-like torch off the wall. And continued down the stairs.

Deep inside the mountain, the air grew chilly. It seeped into her damp tank and capri jeans. She shivered, goosebumps scattering over her bare arms. But determination propelled her forward until she hit the last step.

A muffled sound carried to her.

Reynner?

Her heart drumming against her ribs, Eve tossed the torch to the floor. The flame died and pulled the gloom over her once more. A faint glow coming from the distance guided her. Hope, like a bright shiny light exploded in her heart and she sprinted toward the flickering light.

Aerén was right. He didn't go to that malicious heifer—he'd come here. She'd wait with him while he rode this out, she would never leave him to suffer alone—and came to a grinding halt.

Oh, Christ, no! Her hand rushed to her mouth, holding back a pained sob.

Manacled to the wall, Reynner hung by his wrists. His head bowed, his hair swung in damp swathes, concealing his face. His body contorted, muscles bunching as he suffered in silence. His beautiful wings dragged on the ground. Power bounced off the rough granite walls like streaks of lightning. And there, in the center of the power storm, Inanna stood several feet from him like some evil entity in a long black gown, safe from harm. So engrossed in Reynner, she didn't notice Eve.

Why didn't she feel his pain?

Her chest hurt at the truth. He still shielded her despite his immense agony.

"Why do you persist in suffering, lover?" Inanna snapped in irritation. "You know it can be good between us again. Say yes and this will all be over."

Eve remembered similar words. The demoness had said the same thing when she'd trapped him.

"I'll even allow you your little human plaything," Inanna coaxed.

A low, animal-like snarl left him.

"You only have yourself to blame!" She weaved her hand and the glow in him upped. The eight-point star blazed, his body glowed like a flame engulfing him from within, the muscles in his chest and arms bunched in suffering. Several singed feathers floated to the ground.

Nooo! Eve rushed into the dungeon—she would kill her for hurting him.

At the sound of her footsteps echoing on the stone floor, Reynner raised his head. She veered at last second and rushed over to him, instead, and touched his face, tears blurring her vision.

"Oh, Reynner," she whispered. And there, in his agonized night-sky eyes, she saw it, a flicker of awareness. And then fear.

A feral hiss erupted behind her. Inanna grabbed a hunk of Eve's hair and hauled her away from him, flinging her aside. Eve hit the bars, pain flooding her scalp and spine.

Inanna's smile widened with pure malevolence. "How quaint, your little pet came to rescue you. She'll pay."

"No!" A hoarse snarl left Reynner. His shields dropped, and he lost control.

Eve stumbled, a wave of unadulterated agony spreading through her as if her insides were on fire. She fell to her knees, unable to breathe, finally experiencing what he truly suffered.

But the desperation to save the man she loved, pushed her to her feet, gave her the strength she needed. Her outraged cry rang out through the dungeon. "Leave him alone!"

"He is not yours, filthy human—"

"Eve—no, don't!" Reynner rasped, his voice guttural and thick with pain.

"He's *my* mate!" Too angry to stop, Eve charged and rammed Inanna hard with both hands and sent her back several feet. Inanna lashed out, delivered a vicious blow to Eve's face. Pain exploded in her jaw, stars zipping across her vision as she landed on the ground.

Reynner lurched toward her. Only then did she realize that he wasn't chained, but holding onto the fetters.

Inanna waved her hand, her temper congealing the air. Whatever she did next, she had Reynner writhing on the floor. "I still own you, lover, never forget that. And for mating this tramp, you'll pay dearly. It won't be a year this time."

Eve lost all rational cognizance at the threat to

Reynner, the promise to trap him back in Hell where he'd been so cruelly tortured and violated. Adrenaline jetting into her veins, she pushed off the ground, lunged for Inanna and wrapped her hands around the goddess's throat.

Eve gasped at the onslaught, thoughts flooding her mind. Inanna's utter delight at knowing she'd win. Eve saw her own death and she didn't care. She struggled to hold on despite the darkness seeping into her consciousness. More images bled into her...*Inanna leaning over Reynner, a dagger in her hand, blood seeping from the wound on his chest—into a blue stone...a dark figure in the cavern...echoes of an eerie chant*, and the truth crashed through Eve.

The vicious black-hearted heifer!

Inanna laughed. "You puny little mortal, I'll squash you like the bug you are!" She shoved Eve off her.

Eve's hold slipped. Her fingers caught in the choker fastened around Inanna's neck. The filigree design sunk into her palms and it took on life, each lattice piece cut through her soft flesh like being slashed with razors. She cried out in agony.

"Eve..."

At the rough whisper, her head whipped around. Reynner struggled to his feet. The star on his chest pulsed brightly as if he were seconds away from incinerating. Inanna growled, flung out a hand, holding him back while she tried to pry Eve off her with the other.

Blood seeped down Eve's wrists, drenching her hands as strips of the filigree hit bone. Pain seared her brain and burned her palms. At the excruciating torture, she loosened her grip and Lila's words flashed through her mind.

No matter how unbearable it is, you have to see it through, or that which you most fear will come to pass.

No! Inanna will never have him, even if it meant losing her own life.

Eve summoned all of her waning strength. Working only on adrenaline, she tugged on the necklace.

Inanna's laugh grew wild. "No one touches my amulet and lives. Goodbye, mortal."

Oh, Lord, pleeeease!

Eve yanked hard at the evil necklet mangling her hands. And from deep within her soul, the warmth that helped shape her metals streamed out. No glow, just an incredible heat flowing out of her palms. The necklace melted, separated in two. The deep blue lapis lazuli stone cracked. Dark red liquid seeped out, thick and sticky, it ran over Eve's hand. An obscure shadow filled with icy malevolence slithered over her.

"My amulet!" Inanna screeched. She scrambled to retrieve the broken lapis pieces. Failing. Her face twisted in fury. "You slut!" Power streamed out of her. With a wave of her hand, she picked Eve up like a rag doll and slammed her hard on the granite ground.

Unbelievable agony consumed Eve. She lay immobile on the cold floor, struggling to breathe through lungs that felt like a thousand daggers had punctured them.

She'd seen this moment…seen her death.

I'm broken.

A sudden shriek of anger bounced off the walls.

Through hazy eyes, she saw Inanna fly backward and be pinned by an invisible force to the craggy rock face. She screeched. A blast flared out from her hands in the direction where Eve lay.

"Don't you fucking dare," Reynner snarled, his

wings slashing the air. A flick of his hand and he trapped Inanna's wrists to the wall. Her power diverted, it hit the granite surface, and rubble rained to the ground in a dust storm. Then it faded and died.

Unable to hold on, Eve closed her eyes and let oblivion claim her.

***

Released from the pain that held him in its grip for millennia, disoriented, Reynner shook his head, and tried to shake off the strange stillness stealing through him. No burn in his chest, just an unnatural quiet. Then those thoughts flew right out of his mind as he stumbled to where Eve lay so still on the ground.

"*Noooo*," Inanna screamed.

With a thought, he cut off her vocals.

"Eve, what did you do?" He dropped to his knees, his words raw, anguished. He pressed two fingers to her neck and found a heartbeat. Then he took her bloody, mangled hands in his, gently eased open her fingers, and saw pieces of metal and broken lapis embedded in her torn flesh.

"Oh, Eve." His gaze misted. It was one thing for him to endure pain, but not her. He eased the pieces out of her palms that had suffered so brutally, first at trying to save her parents and now him. Her blood flowed faster, coating his fingers.

He did a psychic scan of her injuries and his stomach constricted. Three fractured ribs, one broken. Her right shoulder dislocated. The blow from Inanna's fist had split her lip. Blood trailed down her chin.

At her injuries, he couldn't breathe, felt like a huge vise tightening around his chest. No! He refused to lose her.

The words flew out of him, knowing how much she

hated being ordered, "Don't you dare leave me, Eve. I won't let you go. *You* fought with me, for me. Now you bloody well make sure you're here to keep me in line—"

He maneuvered her shoulder. A pop sounded as it slipped back into its socket. Then he called on the healing powers he'd been born with, instead of the useless trickle he'd lived with for so long. Pushed harder. "Come on, damn you…"

Long forgotten warmth coursed through him. A powerful force of pale blue light gushed out from his hand and coalesced over her. Soon, his healing light cloaked her like a shroud.

Her fractured ribs healed, the broken one merged and mended, the bruising around her shoulder faded, along with the swelling on her lip. Finally, the few buried pieces of the lapis popped free from her palm and the skin knitted. He ran his fingers over her sealed flesh and scanned again, needing to reassure himself that she was truly healed.

"Reynner?"

At the faint whisper, his gaze flew to hers. And through his blurred vision he found those beautiful green eyes on him. Unable to speak past the lump in his throat, he pulled her into a fierce hold.

"Can't breathe—can't breathe." She squirmed in protest, forcing him to ease back.

"Don't you ever do that again," he said, sounding like he'd swallowed gravel. "I thought I'd lost you."

She reached out and touched his jaw. "I couldn't let her destroy you, and she was."

Urias, he'd always thought her fragile, but his mate completely undid him. He turned his face and kissed her bloody palm. Licking the coppery wetness off his lips, he swept her into his arms and rose.

"Reynner, wait, put me down."

"No."

"Please, Reynner. I want to see that you're okay."

Unable to deny her anything, he let her slide down his body, reveling in the sensation of her living, breathing one. All he wanted was to spend the next few hours, hell the next few years alone with her, far away from any crap this world batted at them, but he had things to take care of first. One of which was still pinned to his dungeon wall, her face mottled red, her screeches stifled.

Eve braced her hands on his chest and eased back, her gaze darting all over him, as if searching for signs of injury. He left her to her investigation and stroked her cheeks, her jaw, then wiped away the blood there. She ran her fingers over his left pec. Confusion wrinkled her smooth brow.

"It's gone." Awe filled her voice. "Reynner, it's gone."

"What is?"

"That star on your chest." She smoothed her hand over his left pectoral again.

He glanced down and froze. No cursed scar was branded there. The constant pain, the burn he'd lived with for centuries had disappeared. Just peace remained, and the gentle presence of Eve. She'd taken away his darkness and filled him with her love. She'd done this for him. She'd saved him, and had almost died in the process.

"I saw what she did," Eve said, shooting Inanna a killing look. "She took your blood after she drugged you, added it to hers, and with the spell of a demon she bound you to her. She wore it in that amulet." Eve nodded to the broken pieces scattered on the dusty floor, looking ready to tear into Inanna again.

Reynner didn't even glance at Inanna. He hauled Eve into his arms, unable to get the words past his throat gone tight with emotion. All that came out was a hoarsely whispered, "I love you."

A muffled screech came from the wall at his declaration.

Eve hugged him and rubbed her cheek against his chest. "I know. It gave me the strength to end this. You held on through the centuries against all odds, I could do no less."

"I'm bigger, stronger, *me'morae,* it's expected—but you humble me." He leaned down and kissed her. Eve slid her arms up his torso to clasp around his neck as he deepened the kiss.

***

Happiness overwhelming her, Eve simply held him. It was over. She'd freed him.

Easing back, her gaze lit on his wings. She remembered the burning feathers. In awe, she reached up and stroked the healed ones, ran her fingers inside the arch. God, but she loved the silky feel of his wings. His erection jerked against her.

He growled, his eyes flaring with desire. With love.

She smiled, and when he didn't retract his wings, her heart soared.

"You." He nipped her bottom lip. "Have no idea—" A lick and a firmer nibble, his hands slid up her arms to grasp her hands. "What you mean to me."

She looked up, and that sexy, barely there smile distracted her as he walked her backward. "And that is why—" he diverted her with another mindless kiss. She squirmed when he raised her hand above her head "—

I'm forced to do this."

A mental clang echoed in the stuffy air of the gloomy dungeon.

"Reynner?" Her brow puckered in puzzlement. Tugging her right hand, she found herself chained to the wall with one of the dull metal cuffs he'd been hanging onto earlier fastened on her wrist.

Her gaze snapped to him. "Reynner?"

He stood in front of her, arms crossed over his chest. "Here's what is. You are my life, Eve, and when you put yourself in danger, I won't tolerate it. Now that I know you'll be safe, I will deal with Inanna. Then I'll be back."

Her mouth dropped open. She pulled at her cuffed wrist, rattling the chain. "You're leaving me here? Chained?"

"Not for long, a few minutes." A wave of his hand and all the torches in the gloomy, dusty place came alight. "Don't bruise your lovely skin, Eve, or I'll be very angry."

"Dammit, Reynner, let me go. Or I swear I'll–I'll never speak to you again."

He didn't react to her threats but caressed her cheek with the back of his knuckles. In a shimmer, his retracted wings vanished. He turned as his houseman somehow materialized out of the shadows.

"Izzeri, stay with my mate until I get back." With that curt order, he strode across to the red-faced, muffled-cursing witch. A touch of his hand on Inanna's arm and they both disappeared.

"Mistress, please don't tug the chain, you'll hurt yourself," Izzeri pleaded.

Eve narrowed her eyes at him. "You didn't tell me Reynner was here."

"My apologies, mistress." He dipped his head in regret. "I acted on the sire's instruction in case you turned up."

Yes, Reynner knew she'd try to find him. And threatening Izzeri wouldn't work. She attempted a sweet smile. "Please, Izzeri, release me."

"I cannot, mistress. Only the sire can."

Oh, the black-hearted fiend!

She grew more frustrated when her heating ability that aided her so often in her work didn't help. Not even a flicker of warmth. Furious, she yanked at the chain again and again.

Izzeri winced. After yelling at the several ways she intended to get even with Reynner, Eve slumped against the wall and was surprised when the chain loosened, enabling her to sit down on the dusty floor.

A bunched-up bundle of black fabric lay nearby in the dirt. Reaching for it, she discovered it was his shirt and pressed it to her face, inhaling his clean male scent with a hint of leather. Her chest cramped, a pang hit her at how close she'd come to losing him.

Then she scowled. He'd chained her in this dreadful place. Crushing the shirt in a ball, she sat on it and wrapped her arm around her knees. And waited.

***

The furious roar of the waterfalls at his back, Reynner leaned against the balustrades, his attention on Inanna restrained to the walls of his aerie. Her once attractive face blotchy with rage, topaz eyes burning with fury.

And he felt nothing.

Not even anger at her for throwing him into Hell for a century, or for being at her mercy for millennia.

Straightening, he strolled over and stopped in front of her. With his last oath to Inanna null and void since

Eve had broken the binding, Reynner made a new one. "Listen to me well, you foolish female. I will say this only once. You ever come near my mate or me again, I will end you, and that is a promise."

Her eyes widened when he finally let her see the truth of exactly whom she was dealing with. Not the bound male she'd tormented, but a powerful Empyrean, one who could crush not only her, but her pantheon, too.

A muffled sound was her answer.

"Good. We understand each other well."

A tremor in the air distracted him. Reynner frowned at the male who came around the bend of the balcony. Aerén followed behind.

So, his prince was responsible for this latest guest and for bringing Eve here.

Not that he needed any help. Inanna wouldn't try her shit now that he was released from her.

Aerén grinned, gave him the thumbs-up sign, and vanished.

Reynner studied the male approaching. Swarthy skinned, dark-haired, the male's narrow face was set in rigid lines. Dumuzi, the God of Fertility and the Underworld was not a happy man.

With a terse nod at Reynner, he stopped in front of his wayward consort. Inanna's restrained movements became frantic. Of all her liaisons, her consort was the only one whom she had a thread of fear for, it seemed.

"What's going on?" Dumuzi asked him.

Reynner wasn't surprised the male had no idea what she was up to since he spent most of his time in the underworld.

"It will bode well for the future of the Sumerian pantheon if you keep her leashed." At his warning,

Dumuzi pinched the bridge of his nose then dropped his hand, his gaze hardening.

Reynner released her, and she stumbled forward. Dark fire burned in her eyes. She glared at him. "*You dare trap me?*"

Dumuzi grabbed her arm. "Enough. I put up with a lot, Inanna. But this goes too far. You would put our pantheon at war with the Empyreans when it barely thrives?"

She shoved at her mate. Dumuzi didn't let go. Anger rolling off him, he escorted his wayward consort back to their pantheon.

The gods were a scandalous lot, but Dumuzi had to be admired for putting up with Inanna's shit. The idiot must be blind with love to have agreed to spend half his life in Hell for her.

Inanna, however, was no longer his problem.

Reynner smiled when he thought of Eve waiting…no, not waiting, more likely ready to tear into him. Her safety was all that mattered, though. When he thought of her going against a crazy bitch like Inanna, he broke out in a cold sweat all over again. Yeah, best she was out of the way while he dealt with this problem.

Now, time to go release his mate, and face her ire.

Chapter 29

Reynner took the stairwell to the dungeon. The air carried the slight smell of mold. A cool breeze drifted over his bare chest and he remembered that Eve still wore her damp clothes from her fall into the fountain. He jogged down the steps.

It would be a while, hell, a damn long time before he got rid of the sheer terror seizing him every time he thought about her lying broken on the floor.

He rubbed a hand over his face. Eve had to understand that she couldn't place herself in danger like that again. Fighting Inanna to save him... He frowned. How had she known what to do? For millennia, he'd tried everything to get rid of the curse.

He walked into the dungeon and nodded at his servant. Izzeri rose from the ground and flashed out.

Eve sat on the dusty floor, her face hidden in her knees, her arms wrapped around them.

His leathers creaking, he crouched in front of her.

"Go away, you fiend." The words were muffled. Ah, so she was aware he'd come back. He slipped into her mind, surrounded her with his love and kissed her bent head.

I love you, Eve, he said through their mind-link.

She lifted her head and scowled. "You chained me, left me in this horrible place."

He caressed her cheek, but lingered in her mind, felt her annoyance, but more, he reeled at her love for him. Like a brilliant light, it poured through him. About to release her, an image blindsided him. Left him dumbstruck.

And wary.

Then a smile tugged his mouth. It may have been a dream, but one he could make come true. He wasn't one to deny her anything.

"Just so you know, I'm going back home—*my* home. Alone." She hurled another threat at him.

Like he'd let that happen. So she was pissed at him. It didn't matter for what he had in mind. He drew her to her feet as he rose. Then he grabbed the end of the chains and looped the extra length around a metal handle attached to the wall and raised her arm up.

Glowering at him, she pressed her lips in a tight line when he shackled her other wrist above her head. He stepped back and summoned his dagger. The moment his weapon materialized in his hand, she eyed him warily.

He stroked the sharp edge against his thumb. "Afraid of me, are you, Eve?"

"Oh, yes. Over that puny blade, I'm heaps afraid," she shot back.

He didn't let his smile show. Merely caught the front of her tank and sliced it neatly down the center. Her top fell apart. Her mouth dropped open. She wore no bra, which was good. Her nipples tightened in the cool air.

He circled the stiff nub with his fingertip. "Very

nice."

A gasp left her. "What are you doing?"

"Giving you what you want."

She frowned as he unbuttoned and unzipped her jeans. Crouching, he pulled off her damp sneakers. Leaving her panties on, he tugged the denim down and tapped her thigh with the flat side of his blade. "Lift."

When she didn't move, but instead glared at him, he simply lifted her foot and removed her jeans.

***

Eve's heart thumped hard in wariness as Reynner rose to his feet, his expression cool, focused. But the look in his indigo eyes held her spellbound. Love and desire edged with anger. Yep, he was still furious at her for taking on Inanna.

He took a step back, his gaze skimming over her. Apparently, satisfied he had her restrained the way he wanted, he came closer, the blade gleaming in his hand.

"Look, if you're angry about what happened with the goddess—darn it, Reynner, I had to do something. I couldn't let her continue to hurt you. And I would do it again," she added for good measure.

His expression didn't change. "How did you know what to do, hmmn?"

His off-handed tone worried her. "I didn't. I saw Lila. She's an oracle who lives in the Village."

His eyes narrowed as understanding dawned. Eve bit her lip, a flare of guilt enflaming her cheeks. She had gone against his wishes and put herself in danger, and as a result, both Inanna and the Darkreans had easy access to her.

"So you broke your promise *and* lied to me when I asked why you'd been on the street."

"I had to..." she mumbled, cautious now at the sudden flash of fury that turned his dark eyes to molten blue.

"What did she say?" Cool. Controlled once more.

"The oracle?"

A stare.

Crap. "That I would know what to do when the time came, but I had to confront the goddess."

"Why didn't you tell me all this?" The cold steel trailed slowly over the curve of her left breast. A shudder rippled through her body.

"Because I knew you'd never agree," she said, her gaze following the blade gliding down her belly.

"And why is that, Eve?"

She didn't answer. Her fingers tightened around the chains. She tried again to summon her abilities to melt the chain. Darn. Still nothing—not even a chink in the stupid links. Almost like she no longer possessed that skill.

"I didn't die, okay?"

"You could have."

Oh, hell. That chill in his voice didn't bode well for her. She tugged uneasily on the restraints holding her prisoner. His attention shifted to the rattling fetters, reminding her of a predator toying with prey.

He stopped his torture with the blade and stepped back. "Those chains were made by the god Hephaestus," he said softly. "They won't be affected by your capabilities. Now answer me. Why did I not want you anywhere near Inanna?"

"I had to see it to the end," she evaded. "Or you'd be tied to her for eternity. And that, I refused to let happen."

At his unrelenting stare, she finally caved. "Because

I'm mortal, and I can die—you don't want anything to happen to me—oh, yeah, and I'm your mate." She threw the last one in quickly, hoping to pacify him.

He didn't say a word. His eyes still retained that icy edge. Damn. He closed the space between them. Then the gleaming tip of the blade glided lightly down her chest, over the curve of her breast to circle her nipple. She trembled. He bent his head, and his warm tongue followed the path of his weapon.

A hiss of desire escaped her. The chain rattled when she tried to hold him, and she remembered that she was still anchored to the wall. But she lost her train of thought when he trailed his lips to her other breast. He licked her nipple once, twice, only to bite down. Hard. Her moan turned to a sharp yelp.

"Owww!" She glowered at him. "You bit me."

"So you'd know never to put your life in danger like that again."

Was he freaking kidding her? She'd do it all over again. Only this time, she would keep her mouth shut.

"Don't even consider it, Eve," he murmured as if he'd read her mind. "Or I'll keep you at Exilum for as long as we both live." He lowered his head and his warm mouth suckled her abused nipple. A moan broke free. "Reynner, please, release me."

A moment, then two passed before he pulled his mouth away from her breast. He didn't respond to her plea, but traced the dagger down her abdomen, past her navel, stopping at the edges of her panties. Then his lips followed the path made by his dagger.

Déjà vu hit her hard. Her dream from what seemed like a lifetime ago took hold of her.

On his haunches in front of her, he looked up—his eyes glowing an intense blue. The rasp in his voice set her senses alight. "What do you want, Eve?"

"You, just you." The words tangled in her throat.

His gaze holding hers, he stroked a fingertip between her legs over the barrier of her silky panties. A moan tore out of her. Desire like red-hot lava rose, spiking her arousal.

A quick slash of the blade and her panties fell from her. He tossed his weapon and her ruined underwear aside then slid his fingers through her wet, feminine flesh. She jolted, her mind in a haze. The chains rattled.

"Reynner, please. Take off the cuffs." She yanked at the chain again.

"Not yet."

"Yes, now," she growled.

***

Reynner bit back his smile as he rose. He was so bloody hard, he wanted nothing more than to end this torment. But his mate had to learn she couldn't put her life at risk.

He trailed soft kisses over the curve of her breast and suckled the perky nub, a shade darker than her gorgeous skin. A husky whimper filled his ears. Parting her legs with his knee, he skimmed his hand down the length of her body and then finally between her legs. Lightly, he stroked her slick flesh, avoiding the spot where she needed his touch the most.

She squirmed against his hand, her body undulating against him. The seductive, musky scent of her arousal clouded his mind, fisting his cock into painful rigidity. Too bad for his mate, he'd learned control trapped in the deepest, darkest pit of Hell.

He eased back, ignoring her low whimper of frustration. "You will never endanger yourself again, understand?"

She tried to find his mouth with hers, but he held her off. She whined. He ran his finger down her center, avoiding her clit. She shuddered. He circled her point of pleasure and drifted away. She cursed.

"I'm waiting."

"Fine. All right—damn you!"

"It's not nice to curse your mate, *me'morae*, but I'll overlook it this time."

He cupped her face and took her sulky mouth in a deep, heated kiss to leave her panting, and him past the point of no return. He broke away and lowered to a crouch, pushing her one leg over his shoulder.

Reynner stroked her cleft, before parting her. Dying for a taste of his mate, he licked her around her clit then fastened his mouth on the neglected little nub and sucked. A moan tore out of her. He teased his finger into her taut body. The chains clanged. He tightened his grip on her hips as he lashed her clit with his tongue, before licking and sucking her again. Feeling her close to the edge, he bit down on the sensitive flesh—a high-pitched moan ripped from her throat, her muscles spasming around his fingers as she came.

Unable to hold out any longer, he rose, undid his zipper, and freed himself. Stroking his aching length, he pulled her legs around his waist. With one thrust, he buried himself deep inside her.

Reynner groaned, her tight, slick body squeezing him like a sweet, fucking fist, and struggled to hold on. He rested a hand against the wall behind her head, panting harshly.

Damn, he'd hurt her if he pushed her up against the abrasive surface.

"Reynner, please—"

With his mind, he released the chains restraining her,

and they fell with a clatter against the walls.

Her hands dropped to his shoulder. Her legs wrapped tighter around him, she sank onto his cock, took him deeper as he carried her across to the metal bars running from the ceiling to the ground.

"Hold onto that," he grunted, pushing her arms behind her. She grabbed the bars above her head. Tightening his hold on her, Reynner pulled out, and drove back into her.

"Oh, god," she moaned, her eyes shutting.

"No, Eve," he growled. "Look at me. I want to see you break all over me."

***

At his raspy order, Eve pulled in a strangled breath and forced her eyelids open. The emotion in Reynner's dark blue gaze trapped her.

In that single moment, she knew, he'd fulfilled her desires while creating new memories for himself to replace those of his awful time imprisoned in that hellish place.

Now he was all wild hunger and raw passion, and all hers.

"*Urias*, Eve. You're so damn amazing. Perfect. Mine," he rasped. His grunts grew harsher, his movements faster, as he slammed into her. "Say it."

"Yes. Perfect—mine—I mean yours—whatever you say," she moaned, all her focus on what he was doing to her body, the pressure inside her unbearable.

Another growl of satisfaction.

"Reynner," she whimpered, needing that push.

"I have you, baby." He angled his hips and thrust back into her, his cock rubbing against her swollen clit. Lightning hot pleasure shot up and exploded through her. With a strangled cry, Eve let go of the bars and wrapped her arms around his neck as she fell apart.

Seconds later, she felt Reynner's body tense. His grip tightened on her then he came with a harsh groan...

***

When Eve opened her eyes again, she had no idea how she'd ended up in bed. Reynner's warm and very naked body tangled with hers. He kissed her neck, his hand caressing her hips, making her sigh in contentment.

Turning, she reached for him and froze.

She jerked upright, dislodging his stroking hand. "*You* bought it?" Her accusing gaze flew to him. "Why?"

"*Why?*" An eyebrow shot up. "You didn't think I would let anyone else see you like that, did you? As if you'd just been made love to? The artist should count his blessings he still breathes for daring to imagine you so."

She rolled her eyes. "Jesus, Reynner. David *is* an artist. And there's nothing sexy about the truth. I was sick that day. Too many pills, add alcohol to the mix, and that," she pointed to the painting, "is what you get."

In a rapid move, he had her flat on her back. Ignoring her startled protest, he leaned over her, his pale hair cascading around her like a beam of moonlight. "The only one who looks at you that way—" he growled, "is me."

"Bossy much?" she teased, looping her arms around his neck.

No, Eve, me'morae, *it's because you are mine,* his whisper coasted through her mind.

Eyes wide, she met his amused gaze. "You spoke to me like that before, too."

He brushed her hair back with a tender hand. "I did. Try it."

Where Eve felt the warmth of his presence in her soul, she mind-linked with him then complained. *Why are you telling me this now?*

His pleasure dimmed. "I couldn't before. I didn't want you to experience the pain Inanna inflicted on me, yet somehow you did anyway."

Not wanting to remember that awful time in Columbus Circle when he'd left her, she pulled his head down and slid her lips against his in a seductive glide.

He kissed her tenderly then murmured against her mouth, "Much as I want to remain in bed and make up for lost time, we can't. They are all here, waiting for us."

"*They?*" She pulled back. "I thought only Aerén would be here."

"I can hear them." He gave her a quick kiss and rolled off her, pushing aside the dark gray sheets tangled around their limbs. "They think they should just come up here and have the meeting."

"What?" Eve grabbed the sheet to her chest then groaned, heat surging into her face. "God, this is so embarrassing. They know why we're not there yet."

"Eve, I don't care if they know. I'm their target because I want to kick them all out but can't." Reynner tugged the sheets away, swept her into his arms, and strode to the bathroom. "A shower first. Then we go get this settled and get rid of them."

Chapter 30

After their shower, Reynner changed into jeans and a t-shirt while Eve, wrapped in a towel, took her spare clothes from the closet. That reminded him that he had to make sure she had more clothes here, too.

He grasped her waist and ran his lips down the damp skin of her nape. Her laughter turned into a moan before she pushed him away. "Nah-uh, I'm not standing here naked with threats of your friends about to walk in on us."

Sighing, Reynner picked up a suede strip from the drawer and tied his hair. He had to tell her the truth about the accident before they met with the others, and could just imagine how well that would go down. Hell, she still mourned the loss of her parents.

After pulling on her navy yoga pants, she turned to him, her green tee still in her hand, not yet obstructing his view of her breasts and those tempting nipples.

Get your shit together and tell her, or else you can forget getting anywhere near her.

He scrubbed a hand over his face.

"Now, there's a look I haven't seen in... oh, the last

two hours," she teased him.

Urias, but she made him smile. Then he sobered. "We need to talk."

"What is it?" She pulled on her top and covered her lithe body, hiding his view.

"It's about the Stone."

"I'm sorry I didn't find it. Maybe we could try elsewhere?" She glanced around, found his brush on the shelf and tidied the sexy mess of her coffee-colored hair.

"There is no need. The Stone is no longer in its original form."

She spun to him in surprise. "What? You mean it's changed appearance now?"

"In a manner of speaking. Eve, the Stone's magic resides in your blood."

Slowly, she set the brush down. "I know my blood has some kind of magic that responded to the scroll."

"That's not what I mean. It is part of you. It's why the scroll reacts to you. Our high mage is here, since Lucan's still a no show—"

"Now you sound like Lucan, trying to scare the hell out of me," she said, cutting him off.

He didn't want to frighten her. But gods, he couldn't bear her walking away, leaving him once she learned the truth. "Eve—"

She shook her head. "It's okay. Let's go down and see what he has to say." She took his hand and urged him through the door. "He's a high mage, I'm sure he'll have some kind of explanation for all this, you'll see."

Reynner followed her, unable to stop the queasiness churning his gut.

***

Eve stopped at the entrance to the living room, her gaze on the stranger who stood near the picturesque windows talking to Aerén and North. A gentle tug on her hand and Reynner pulled her inside.

The mage turned, and eyes like an endless night surveyed them. The length of his braided white hair remained hidden beneath his navy robes.

"Eve, this is Allatus, high mage of Empyrea," Reynner introduced her. "Allatus, my mate, Eve."

"Hello." She rubbed her hands down her pants.

"We have waited a long time for you," Allatus said by way of welcome.

She smiled, and not knowing what else to say, she blurted out, "Reynner says the Stone's magic is in me?"

"Yes," Allatus said, studying her. "Its essence is in your blood. When it's time, *you* would have to go to Empyrea."

Go to another world? Eve swallowed. Panicked. "Why can't you summon the magic from me? I thought your realm needs it urgently?"

Allatus nodded. "Yes, we do. But we've waited centuries—a few more weeks won't change much," he told her. "It's not just you, Eve, even though you do possess more of the magic. We have to wait until the rest of the pieces are located. Then the journey to Empyrea will be made."

Reynner leaned his shoulder against the doorjamb, his brow creased in a frown. "What pieces?"

"When the Stone plummeted to Earth, it shattered," Allatus explained. "A part of it, Eve absorbed."

"How do we find the rest of it?" Aerén asked. "It could be lying anywhere."

"No." Allatus shook his head. "When the Stone

fragmented, it would have selected the humans to keep it safe. Now, we search for the mortals who were wounded on the day of the accident. If they have magic in their blood, the scroll would respond to them. Once all are found, then we will take them to Empyrea."

"That should go down well," North muttered.

"Where do we start looking—yeah, I know, New York," Aerén said. "But from what I've seen, humans move around. A lot."

"With Eve's blood, we'll be able to scry for their locations using the scroll." Allatus smiled at her, as if not to scare her.

Too late.

The hollow in Eve's belly grew. She should have stayed in their room and let Reynner explain all this to her.

Reynner pulled her to him and brushed his lips over her hair. She took a deep, anxious breath and tried to calm down. Go to Empyrea—a place unknown, a place somewhere in the solar system she couldn't even imagine. Heck, she hadn't even left the state of New York. She tensed up again.

"I will be there with you, Eve," Reynner reassured her. "And it's not forever. I won't take you away from your world. But we have to make the trip once all the humans are found to trigger the Stones of Light back to full power."

"What happens when the Stone's power fades again?" she asked him.

"Then those females not mated will reside in the tower of the mage," Lucan answered, sauntering into the sitting room. Looking far too healthy for a missing man. "And you will visit when needed. Before you ask, the magic in the Stone would have found a way to keep them single, until the time's right."

Like it had with her. Eve had to bite back her irritation. "How do you know it's only women? Men—"

Lucan shook his head. "This particular artifact is feminine in its power. It will choose likewise. Proven by the very fact that you were the first we located."

Her mouth tightened, he had an answer for everything. "What makes you think they will come?"

"Why not? You did."

She scowled. A pity he was a mage and would remain celibate. It would have been something to see him knocked off his imperious pedestal by some woman.

Soft laughter garnered her attention. Eve found Allatus watching her, his dark eyes twinkling. Crap. She hoped he hadn't read her bitchy thoughts. Annoyance still prowling through her, she shot Lucan a glare. "You forget one tiny little detail. I'm mortal," she reminded him. "I have just a few decades. Then what?"

Reynner stiffened at the mention of her mortality, his grip tightening on her waist. She didn't want to hurt him at the reminder, but Lucan made her so mad.

Amusement flickered in Lucan's eyes, cracking a little of his typically cold façade, like he knew something monumental. He glanced at Reynner then back at her.

"When your souls joined and became one, you took on the lifespan of your mate. It's why when one dies, the other has the option to follow. And why I had to give you both a shove in the right direction. Or *you*—" He pinned Eve with those lethal, swirling turquoise eyes. "Would have lived alone for centuries if Reynner left."

"Then you need to work on your people skills," Eve snipped at him, remembering that horrible day in her studio when his words had sunk in—knocked her for a loop. Her mouth dropped open.

"Yes, you will have a long life, but you can still die as mortals do," Allatus cautioned her.

Her heart in her throat, wide-eyed, she spun to Reynner. He smiled and drew her into his arms. "Eternity with you is a gift, one I never expected. I would have gladly followed you into the afterlife if it wasn't so."

Eve swallowed at his absolute love for her when she remembered something else he'd said. "You mentioned the accident. How exactly did the artifact become a part of me?"

He brushed the scar on her left breast and a chill swept through her.

"The Stone shattered on impact when it hit the car you were travelling in several years ago. It seems a shard of it became embedded in your chest and dissolved into your blood."

At his explanation, ice seeped through her veins. Slowly, she pushed away from him. "You're telling me I lost my parents because a rock from your world hit our car—killing them?"

Silence. It swept in and wiped away every sound at her question.

Reynner straightened.

The tightness in her chest made it hard to breathe. Pain pushed to the surface.

"Eve," he began.

"No." She backed away, tears clouding her eyes. Pivoting, she rushed outside, unable to bear being the focus of all their attention.

Indistinct voices followed her.

"Get the fuck off me!" Reynner snarled like he was held back.

Eve stopped at the balustrade. The spray of water from the waterfalls dampened her skin, but nothing took away her sense of despair. Sorrow swept through her. Logically, she understood Reynner wasn't to blame. It was an accident, but when old loss filled her, she couldn't think clearly...

She squeezed her eyes tight and rubbed her chest to ease the pain spreading through her. But the ache grew, sharper than before, piercing in its intensity.

She rubbed her chest again...no, not her.

Reynner.

Being connected to him, she'd feel every nuance of his emotions as he did hers.

She wheeled around. She had to put things right and saw Allatus ambling toward her. The breeze blew his cloak open, revealing his black tunic and trews.

"If you had a choice to go back in time, would you use it to save your parents or remain with the male you love?"

Eve stared at him, her heart literally stopping. Leave Reynner behind—tied to that horrible witch?

"I thought not." Allatus smiled. "Come, he's like a caged beast, he won't hold out much longer."

She followed Allatus back into the lounge. Flanked by North and Aerén, Reynner watched her with shielded eyes. How could she have been so stupid to hurt him?

Eve rushed over to where he stood near the door and flung her arms around his waist, she didn't care that the others were watching her. "I'm sorry—I'm sorry," she whispered. "The shock of hearing about the accident—I didn't handle it well. I didn't mean to hurt you."

A deep sigh left him, and his arms came around her. "It was my fear of what you'd do when you heard about the accident."

"Leave you? I could never." She hugged him tightly.

Allatus headed for the coffee table. He picked up a pitcher of pale lemony-colored liquid and poured a glass.

"My dear," Allatus said, taking a sip of his drink, and Eve glanced at the mage. "Nothing in life is black or white. It was their destiny to die in that accident, and yours. But fate decreed otherwise for you. Instead, the sliver embedded in you, saved your life. You were never meant to be alone. Just to wait for the right person. I sent Reynner to this place because his destiny ties in with yours."

He drank more of his juice. "This nectar's really good." He set the glass aside. "Reynner had to find you. He would not have done so of his own accord had he known the true reason. Lucan informs me it's like getting the white cliffs of Empyrea to move when it comes to this male."

"You were playing with my life—Eve's?" Reynner growled, his arms tensing around her.

Allatus merely said, "Love soothes hurts, but hatred and violence deepens them. Had you gone on in that manner, you would have ended up in the last place you wanted. Be thankful you took that step and healed old wounds."

Eve glanced at Reynner, worried at how he'd react to the high mage's words. Her heart settled when she saw him scowl. He wasn't angry.

"There's something else," Lucan said. "The

Darkreans let Eve go because they believe she isn't the foretold one—just an Empyrean's mate."

Reynner went motionless behind her. "They knew?"

"Their leader tasted her blood, but we have more pressing problems in light of what I've just heard about the Stone shattering. It seems they have found another of the females who possess the Stone's magic."

"We have to go get her. Where is she?" North asked.

"It's not that simple," Lucan said. "It was a cell phone call Sebris took. I stayed behind after we rescued Eve and tried to track them, but they shut down the house and disappeared. However, I saw one of them in the city."

"And the woman?" Aerén asked.

"No idea." Lucan features became cast in ice once more. "We must find her first. They cannot have her."

Allatus nodded at Lucan. "Now that the quest is back in your hands, it's time I returned to Empyrea. But first, I will avail myself of Izzeri's mouthwatering feast." He headed for the door.

Eve pulled away from Reynner. She had to speak with Allatus before he left. But Reynner grabbed her hand and frowned. "Where are you going?"

"I won't be long." She offered him a quick smile, patted his chest, and hurried after the departing mage. "Allatus?"

The high mage turned, his cloak sweeping around him in a gentle swish. "Yes, my dear?"

Eve opened her mouth to speak and asked him something totally different from what she'd intended. "If I'd chosen to go back, would you've really been able to send me?"

Those unending black eyes studied her. "You were tempted?"

She thought it over and shook her head. "No. I loved my parents and always will, but Reynner is my heart. I just wanted to say thank you for sending him to me."

Lines crinkled the corner of his eyes. He dipped his head in acknowledgment. "It's my great pleasure."

Arms stole around her waist and a muscled wall pressed up against her back. He smelled so good, all warm male and cool green forest. She wasn't surprised he'd followed her.

"I'm glad to hear that," Reynner murmured in her ear.

A smile tugged her mouth and filled her heart. His silky hair brushed her cheek as he kissed her nape. A blaze of heat spiraled low in her belly. Her breath hitched when she felt his semi-erect sex pressing into her. Unable to resist, discreetly, she moved her bottom against his groin.

He stilled. His grip tightened on her waist. *You play a dangerous game,* me'morae.

Eve bit her lip, smiled innocently at his telepathic words.

"Now that this is settled," Allatus said, distracting her. "I have another headache brewing, and one far more stubborn than you," he informed Reynner.

Reynner snorted.

"I know you'll keep him in line," Allatus told her and disappeared into the kitchen.

Eve turned to him and smiled. "Keep you in line? I like that idea." Then she rubbed the spot on his chest where she'd felt his hurt at her earlier words. "I didn't mean to hurt you."

"Ah, *me'morae,* you were grieving so you lashed out. It won't be the first disagreement we'll have. Unfortunately. With your tendency to question my orders, these things are bound to happen," he said with that heart-stopping smile. Her scowl vanished. "And you have a lot of making up to do, especially with your little stunt just now."

She slid her hands up his chest. "Then I'd better get started—"

"Eve?" Aerén called, exiting the lounge and interrupting them.

A low growl rumbled out of Reynner. "Not now."

Aerén grinned then his expression sobered. "Eve, about your friend, Brenna? Her family's taken her home to Scotland to recover."

Disappointment, but also heartfelt relief settled in Eve. It could only be Brenna's sister that had taken her back. At least she'd be cared for. As soon as she got back to her apartment, she'd call them.

"Now that you conveyed your news, get lost," Reynner ordered.

"I'm going, I'm going. I can tell when I'm not wanted." Laughing, Aerén headed back for the living room.

"Where's Reynner?" Lucan's voice drifted to them. "We have to get started."

"You're not going to get him back here, Luc," Aerén said, then raised his voice. "Unless you go get him."

His brow lowering in irritation, Reynner grabbed her hand and headed for the balcony.

"Where are we going?" Eve asked, hurrying to keep up. "I think Lucan wants you."

"Too bad." He stopped on the balcony, lowered his voice in a seductive whisper. "Do you want to dance?"

She glanced around her. "Here? On the balcony? There's no music."

A grin slipped over his lips. "Let me show you."

He pulled off his shirt and tossed it aside. His beautiful wings shimmered into view and spread open. She reached out and stroked a gleaming bronze feather.

His eyes blazed with heat. "Do that again, and I'll have you stripped and up against that wall in a heartbeat." A blush heated her cheeks. He stared at her then shook his head. "No, not here. There's something else I want to do with you first."

"Yes, dance." She teased him, eyeing his rippling body and his smooth, unmarred pecs.

He swept her into his arms. His wings spread out and he cut through the air currents in a leap and flew high up. She laughed, holding onto him. His bare skin and warmth surrounded her. "Where are we going?"

Amused midnight blue eyes met hers. "Nowhere."

She raised a skeptical brow. "We're just going to hover in the air..." She glanced down, shuddered, and grabbed him tighter. Everything below appeared like small smudges of color, even the mountains looked like a snaking gray line. "We're like a million miles above ground. I can fall and—"

"I'll be there to catch you, Eve," he whispered. "I'll never let you fall." He kissed the corner of her mouth. Then his wings shimmered and disappeared, and they dropped down with deadly speed.

"*Reynnerrrrrr...*" Her voice lost to the winds, her heart hammered in her ears. But at the sheer pleasure on his handsome face, Eve tried to let go of her fear. Failing, she shut her eyes.

"Can't dance with wings," he said as the winds flowed around them and they fell to earth. Meters from the ground, a rustle of feathers and the death-like velocity slowed. He landed them on the sun-warmed bedrocks, near the place where they'd first made love.

"Oh, God!" She clutched his biceps to steady herself. And hoped the world stopped spinning soon. He brushed at her wind-tangled hair. "Are you okay?"

Her lids snapped open and met his concerned gaze. "When I find my head and my heart beats like a normal person's, ask me then."

His gaze drifted over her face, his smile faded.

"What is it?" she asked softly. "Are you okay?"

"Yeah. Yeah, I'm fine." Then he simply shook his head. "I never believed in miracles—"

"Yet here you are."

His eyes lit with amusement, with love. "My line."

Her heart close to exploding with all the emotions surging within her, she whispered, "I love you."

She didn't care how sappy she sounded. Reynner of Ademéras was her very own miracle.

Acknowledgements

To these amazing people: Anna, Celia, Nancy and Joceline, thank you for your wonderful feedback and comments in making this story come alive and shine.
Anna, for always having my back through my crisis.
Sara, all your little messages made me laugh when things got too stressed while working on this manuscript and trying to make the deadline.
Annette and Carolyn, for your excellent catches.

Montana Jade: Darling girl, thank you for setting me on this path again. YES, for even locking me in the study that afternoon five years ago and demanding I write, or else I know I'll still be playing online games or have my nose buried in books. And especially for all the "either or" and for letting me nit-pick your brain—nope, that will never stop.

As for your absolutely gorgeous cover, no, I'm no longer drooling, okay, maybe a little. You know *my* mind, and my heroes so well. I miss you; wish you weren't thousands of miles away.

Most of all to my wonderful family, you gave me the time to write. There are no words to reflect my thanks and love. Tyke, love you for just being.

Also by Georgia Lyn Hunter

FALLEN GUARDIANS
Absolute Surrender #1
Echo, Mine #1.5
Breaking Fate #2
Tangled Sin (Standalone)
Guardian Unraveled #3
For You, I Will #3.5
Heart's Inferno #4

WARLORDS OF EMPYREA
Darkness Undone #1

CONTEMPORARY: PLAYERS TO MEN
Breathless

About the Author

Georgia Lyn Hunter loves to create characters who'll take you to the far and beyond to unforgettable adventures, steamy encounters and heart-stopping love stories...

She grew up in the sultry climate of South Africa and currently lives in the Middle East with her family. An avid reader from a young age, she devoured every book she got her hands on. When she's not writing or plotting her next novel, she loves trolling flea markets and buying things she'd never use (because they're so pretty,) traveling, painting, and being with her wonderfully supportive family.

And there you have it, all the boring stuff.

Want more? Then subscribe to her new release:
Newsletter: http://eepurl.com/bpHvET
Website: www.georgialynhunter.com
FB: https://www.facebook.com/GeorgiaLynHunter
Twitter: https://twitter.com/GeorgialynH

Made in United States
Troutdale, OR
04/08/2025

30439897R00246